The Collected
Strange & Science Fiction
of
H. G. Wells
Volume 1

The Collected Strange & Science Fiction of H. G. Wells Volume 1

The Time Machine

The Wonderful Visit

and

The Island of Doctor Moreau

H. G. Wells

LEONAUR

The Collected
Strange & Science Fiction
of
H. G. Wells
Volume 1
The Time Machine
The Wonderful Visit
and
The Island of Doctor Moreau
By H. G. Wells

FIRST EDITION

First published under the titles
The Time Machine
The Wonderful Visit
and
The Island of Doctor Moreau

Leonaur is an imprint of Oakpast Ltd

Copyright in this form © 2019 Oakpast Ltd

ISBN: 978-1-78282-852-5 (hardcover)
ISBN: 978-1-78282-853-2 (softcover)

http://www.leonaur.com

Publisher's Notes

Contents

The Time Machine

Contents

CHAPTER 1

The Introduction

The Time Traveller (for so it will be convenient to speak of him) was expounding a recondite matter to us. His pale grey eyes shone and twinkled, and his usually pale face was flushed and animated. The fire burnt brightly, and the soft radiance of the incandescent lights in the lilies of silver caught the bubbles that flashed and passed in our glasses. Our chairs, being his patents, embraced and caressed us rather than submitted to be sat upon, and there was that luxurious after-dinner atmosphere, when thought runs gracefully free of the trammels of precision. And he put it to us in this way—marking the points with a lean forefinger—as we sat and lazily admired his earnestness over this new paradox (as we thought it) and his fecundity.

"You must follow me carefully. I shall have to controvert one or two ideas that are almost universally accepted. The geometry, for instance, they taught you at school is founded on a misconception."

"Is not that rather a large thing to expect us to begin upon?" said Filby, an argumentative person with red hair.

"I do not mean to ask you to accept anything without reasonable ground for it. You will soon admit as much as I need from you. You know of course that a mathematical line, a line of thickness *nil*, has no real existence. They taught you that? Neither has a mathematical plane. These things are mere abstractions."

"That is all right," said the Psychologist.

"Nor, having only length, breadth, and thickness, can a cube have a real existence."

"There I object," said Filby. "Of course, a solid body may exist. All real things—"

"So, most people think. But wait a moment. Can an *instantaneous* cube exist?"

"Don't follow you," said Filby.

"Can a cube that does not last for any time at all, have a real existence?"

Filby became pensive. "Clearly," the Time Traveller proceeded, "any real body must have extension in *four* directions: it must have Length, Breadth, Thickness, and—Duration. But through a natural infirmity of the flesh, which I will explain to you in a moment, we incline to overlook this fact. There are really four dimensions, three which we call the three planes of Space, and a fourth, Time. There is, however, a tendency to draw an unreal distinction between the former three dimensions and the latter, because it happens that our consciousness moves intermittently in one direction along the latter from the beginning to the end of our lives."

"That," said a very young man, making spasmodic efforts to relight his cigar over the lamp; "that . . . very clear indeed."

"Now, it is very remarkable that this is so extensively overlooked," continued the Time Traveller, with a slight accession of cheerfulness. "Really this is what is meant by the Fourth Dimension, though some people who talk about the Fourth Dimension do not know they mean it. It is only another way of looking at Time. *There is no difference between Time and any of the three dimensions of Space except that our consciousness moves along it.* But some foolish people have got hold of the wrong side of that idea. You have all heard what they have to say about this Fourth Dimension?"

"*I* have not," said the Provincial Mayor.

"It is simply this. That Space, as our mathematicians have it, is spoken of as having three dimensions, which one may call Length, Breadth, and Thickness, and is always definable by reference to three planes, each at right angles to the others. But some philosophical people have been asking why *three* dimensions particularly—why not another direction at right angles to the other three?—and have even tried to construct a Four-Dimensional geometry. Professor Simon Newcomb was expounding this to the New York Mathematical Society only a month or so ago. You know how on a flat surface, which has only two dimensions, we can represent a figure of a three-dimensional solid, and similarly they think that by models of three dimensions they could represent one of four—if they could master the perspective of the thing. See?"

"I think so," murmured the Provincial Mayor; and, knitting his brows, he lapsed into an introspective state, his lips moving as one who repeats mystic words. "Yes, I think I see it now," he said after some time, brightening in a quite transitory manner.

"Well, I do not mind telling you I have been at work upon this

geometry of Four Dimensions for some time. Some of my results are curious. For instance, here is a portrait of a man at eight years old, another at fifteen, another at seventeen, another at twenty-three, and so on. All these are evidently sections, as it were, Three-Dimensional representations of his Four-Dimensioned being, which is a fixed and unalterable thing.

"Scientific people," proceeded the Time Traveller, after the pause required for the proper assimilation of this, "know very well that Time is only a kind of Space. Here is a popular scientific diagram, a weather record. This line I trace with my finger shows the movement of the barometer. Yesterday it was so high, yesterday night it fell, then this morning it rose again, and so gently upward to here. Surely the mercury did not trace this line in any of the dimensions of Space generally recognised? But certainly, it traced such a line, and that line, therefore, we must conclude, was along the Time-Dimension."

"But," said the Medical Man, staring hard at a coal in the fire, "if Time is really only a fourth dimension of Space, why is it, and why has it always been, regarded as something different? And why cannot we move in Time as we move about in the other dimensions of Space?"

The Time Traveller smiled. "Are you so sure we can move freely in Space? Right and left we can go, backward and forward freely enough, and men always have done so. I admit we move freely in two dimensions. But how about up and down? Gravitation limits us there."

"Not exactly," said the Medical Man. "There are balloons."

"But before the balloons, save for spasmodic jumping and the inequalities of the surface, man had no freedom of vertical movement."

"Still they could move a little up and down," said the Medical Man.

"Easier, far easier down than up."

"And you cannot move at all in Time, you cannot get away from the present moment."

"My dear sir, that is just where you are wrong. That is just where the whole world has gone wrong. We are always getting away from the present moment. Our mental existences, which are immaterial and have no dimensions, are passing along the Time-Dimension with a uniform velocity from the cradle to the grave. Just as we should travel *down* if we began our existence fifty miles above the earth's surface."

"But the great difficulty is this," interrupted the Psychologist. "You *can* move about in all directions of Space, but you cannot move about in Time."

"That is the germ of my great discovery. But you are wrong to say

that we cannot move about in Time. For instance, if I am recalling an incident very vividly, I go back to the instant of its occurrence: I become absent-minded, as you say. I jump back for a moment. Of course, we have no means of staying back for any length of Time, any more than a savage or an animal has of staying six feet above the ground. But a civilised man is better off than the savage in this respect. He can go up against gravitation in a balloon, and why should he not hope that ultimately he may be able to stop or accelerate his drift along the Time-Dimension, or even turn about and travel the other way?"

"Oh, *this*," began Filby, "is all—"

"Why not?" said the Time Traveller.

"It's against reason," said Filby.

"What reason?" said the Time Traveller.

"You can show black is white by argument," said Filby, "but you will never convince me."

"Possibly not," said the Time Traveller. "But now you begin to see the object of my investigations into the geometry of Four Dimensions. Long ago I had a vague inkling of a machine—"

"To travel through Time!" exclaimed the Very Young Man.

"That shall travel indifferently in any direction of Space and Time, as the driver determines."

Filby contented himself with laughter.

"But I have experimental verification," said the Time Traveller.

"It would be remarkably convenient for the historian," the Psychologist suggested. "One might travel back and verify the accepted account of the Battle of Hastings, for instance!"

"Don't you think you would attract attention?" said the Medical Man. "Our ancestors had no great tolerance for anachronisms."

"One might get one's Greek from the very lips of Homer and Plato," the Very Young Man thought.

"In which case they would certainly plough you for the Little-go. The German scholars have improved Greek so much."

"Then there is the future," said the Very Young Man. "Just think! One might invest all one's money, leave it to accumulate at interest, and hurry on ahead!"

"To discover a society," said I, "erected on a strictly communistic basis."

"Of all the wild extravagant theories!" began the Psychologist.

"Yes, so it seemed to me, and so I never talked of it until—"

"Experimental verification!" cried I. "You are going to verify *that*?"

14

"The experiment!" cried Filby, who was getting brain-weary.

"Let's see your experiment anyhow," said the Psychologist, "though it's all humbug, you know."

The Time Traveller smiled round at us. Then, still smiling faintly, and with his hands deep in his trousers pockets, he walked slowly out of the room, and we heard his slippers shuffling down the long passage to his laboratory.

The Psychologist looked at us. "I wonder what he's got?"

"Some sleight-of-hand trick or other," said the Medical Man, and Filby tried to tell us about a conjuror he had seen at Burslem, but before he had finished his preface the Time Traveller came back, and Filby's anecdote collapsed.

CHAPTER 2

The Machine

The thing the Time Traveller held in his hand was a glittering metallic framework, scarcely larger than a small clock, and very delicately made. There was ivory in it, and some transparent crystalline substance. And now I must be explicit, for this that follows—unless his explanation is to be accepted—is an absolutely unaccountable thing. He took one of the small octagonal tables that were scattered about the room, and set it in front of the fire, with two legs on the hearthrug. On this table he placed the mechanism. Then he drew up a chair, and sat down. The only other object on the table was a small shaded lamp, the bright light of which fell upon the model. There were also perhaps a dozen candles about, two in brass candlesticks upon the mantel and several in sconces, so that the room was brilliantly illuminated. I sat in a low armchair nearest the fire, and I drew this forward so as to be almost between the Time Traveller and the fireplace. Filby sat behind him, looking over his shoulder. The Medical Man and the Provincial Mayor watched him in profile from the right, the Psychologist from the left. The Very Young Man stood behind the Psychologist. We were all on the alert. It appears incredible to me that any kind of trick, however subtly conceived and however adroitly done, could have been played upon us under these conditions.

The Time Traveller looked at us, and then at the mechanism.

"Well?" said the Psychologist.

"This little affair," said the Time Traveller, resting his elbows upon the table and pressing his hands together above the apparatus, "is only a model. It is my plan for a machine to travel through time. You will

notice that it looks singularly askew, and that there is an odd twinkling appearance about this bar, as though it was in some way unreal." He pointed to the part with his finger. "Also, here is one little white lever, and here is another."

The Medical Man got up out of his chair and peered into the thing. "It's beautifully made," he said.

"It took two years to make," retorted the Time Traveller. Then, when we had all imitated the action of the Medical Man, he said: "Now I want you clearly to understand that this lever, being pressed over, sends the machine gliding into the future, and this other reverses the motion. This saddle represents the seat of a time traveller. Presently I am going to press the lever, and off the machine will go. It will vanish, pass into future Time, and disappear. Have a good look at the thing. Look at the table too, and satisfy yourselves there is no trickery. I don't want to waste this model, and then be told I'm a quack."

There was a minute's pause perhaps. The Psychologist seemed about to speak to me, but changed his mind. Then the Time Traveller put forth his finger towards the lever. "No," he said suddenly. "Lend me your hand." And turning to the Psychologist, he took that individual's hand in his own and told him to put out his forefinger. So that it was the Psychologist himself who sent forth the model Time Machine on its interminable voyage. We all saw the lever turn. I am absolutely certain there was no trickery. There was a breath of wind, and the lamp flame jumped. One of the candles on the mantel was blown out, and the little machine suddenly swung round, became indistinct, was seen as a ghost for a second perhaps, as an eddy of faintly glittering brass and ivory; and it was gone—vanished! Save for the lamp the table was bare.

Everyone was silent for a minute. Then Filby said he was damned.

The Psychologist recovered from his stupor, and suddenly looked under the table. At that the Time Traveller laughed cheerfully. "Well?" he said, with a reminiscence of the Psychologist. Then, getting up, he went to the tobacco jar on the mantel, and with his back to us began to fill his pipe.

We stared at each other. "Look here," said the Medical Man, "are you in earnest about this? Do you seriously believe that that machine has travelled into time?"

"Certainly," said the Time Traveller, stooping to light a spill at the fire. Then he turned, lighting his pipe, to look at the Psychologist's face. (The Psychologist, to show that he was not unhinged, helped

himself to a cigar and tried to light it uncut.) "What is more, I have a big machine nearly finished in there"—he indicated the laboratory—"and when that is put together I mean to have a journey on my own account."

"You mean to say that that machine has travelled into the future?" said Filby.

"Into the future or the past—I don't, for certain, know which."

After an interval the Psychologist had an inspiration. "It must have gone into the past if it has gone anywhere," he said.

"Why?" said the Time Traveller.

"Because I presume that it has not moved in space, and if it travelled into the future it would still be here all this time, since it must have travelled through this time."

"But," said I, "If it travelled into the past it would have been visible when we came first into this room; and last Thursday when we were here; and the Thursday before that; and so forth!"

"Serious objections," remarked the Provincial Mayor, with an air of impartiality, turning towards the Time Traveller.

"Not a bit," said the Time Traveller, and, to the Psychologist: "You think. *You* can explain that. It's presentation below the threshold, you know, diluted presentation."

"Of course," said the Psychologist, and reassured us. "That's a simple point of psychology. I should have thought of it. It's plain enough, and helps the paradox delightfully. We cannot see it, nor can we appreciate this machine, any more than we can the spoke of a wheel spinning, or a bullet flying through the air. If it is travelling through time fifty times or a hundred times faster than we are, if it gets through a minute while we get through a second, the impression it creates will of course be only one-fiftieth or one-hundredth of what it would make if it were not travelling in time. That's plain enough." He passed his hand through the space in which the machine had been. "You see?" he said, laughing.

We sat and stared at the vacant table for a minute or so. Then the Time Traveller asked us what we thought of it all.

"It sounds plausible enough tonight," said the Medical Man; "but wait until tomorrow. Wait for the common sense of the morning."

"Would you like to see the Time Machine itself?" asked the Time Traveller. And therewith, taking the lamp in his hand, he led the way down the long, draughty corridor to his laboratory. I remember vividly the flickering light, his queer, broad head in silhouette, the dance

17

of the shadows, how we all followed him, puzzled but incredulous, and how there in the laboratory we beheld a larger edition of the little mechanism which we had seen vanish from before our eyes. Parts were of nickel, parts of ivory, parts had certainly been filed or sawn out of rock crystal. The thing was generally complete, but the twisted crystalline bars lay unfinished upon the bench beside some sheets of drawings, and I took one up for a better look at it. Quartz it seemed to be.

"Look here," said the Medical Man, "are you perfectly serious? Or is this a trick—like that ghost you showed us last Christmas?"

"Upon that machine," said the Time Traveller, holding the lamp aloft, "I intend to explore time. Is that plain? I was never more serious in my life."

None of us quite knew how to take it.

I caught Filby's eye over the shoulder of the Medical Man, and he winked at me solemnly.

CHAPTER 3
The Time Traveller Returns

I think that at that time none of us quite believed in the Time Machine. The fact is, the Time Traveller was one of those men who are too clever to be believed: you never felt that you saw all round him; you always suspected some subtle reserve, some ingenuity in ambush, behind his lucid frankness. Had Filby shown the model and explained the matter in the Time Traveller's words, we should have shown *him* far less scepticism. For we should have perceived his motives: a pork-butcher could understand Filby. But the Time Traveller had more than a touch of whim among his elements, and we distrusted him. Things that would have made the fame of a less clever man seemed tricks in his hands. It is a mistake to do things too easily. The serious people who took him seriously never felt quite sure of his deportment; they were somehow aware that trusting their reputations for judgment with him was like furnishing a nursery with eggshell china.

So, I don't think any of us said very much about time travelling in the interval between that Thursday and the next, though its odd potentialities ran, no doubt, in most of our minds: its plausibility, that is, its practical incredibleness, the curious possibilities of anachronism and of utter confusion it suggested. For my own part, I was particularly preoccupied with the trick of the model. That I remember discussing with the Medical Man, whom I met on Friday at the Linnæan.

He said he had seen a similar thing at Tübingen, and laid considerable stress on the blowing-out of the candle. But how the trick was done he could not explain.

The next Thursday I went again to Richmond—I suppose I was one of the Time Traveller's most constant guests—and, arriving late, found four or five men already assembled in his drawing-room. The Medical Man was standing before the fire with a sheet of paper in one hand and his watch in the other. I looked round for the Time Traveller, and—"It's half-past seven now," said the Medical Man. "I suppose we'd better have dinner?"

"Where's——?" said I, naming our host.

"You've just come? It's rather odd. He's unavoidably detained. He asks me in this note to lead off with dinner at seven if he's not back. Says he'll explain when he comes."

"It seems a pity to let the dinner spoil," said the Editor of a well-known daily paper; and thereupon the Doctor rang the bell.

The Psychologist was the only person besides the Doctor and myself who had attended the previous dinner. The other men were Blank, the Editor aforementioned, a certain journalist, and another—a quiet, shy man with a beard—whom I didn't know, and who, as far as my observation went, never opened his mouth all the evening. There was some speculation at the dinner-table about the Time Traveller's absence, and I suggested time travelling, in a half-jocular spirit. The Editor wanted that explained to him, and the Psychologist volunteered a wooden account of the "ingenious paradox and trick" we had witnessed that day week. He was in the midst of his exposition when the door from the corridor opened slowly and without noise. I was facing the door, and saw it first.

"Hallo!" I said. "At last!"

And the door opened wider, and the Time Traveller stood before us. I gave a cry of surprise.

"Good heavens! man, what's the matter?" cried the Medical Man, who saw him next. And the whole tableful turned towards the door.

He was in an amazing plight. His coat was dusty and dirty, and smeared with green down the sleeves; his hair disordered, and as it seemed to me greyer—either with dust and dirt or because its colour had actually faded. His face was ghastly pale; his chin had a brown cut on it—a cut half-healed; his expression was haggard and drawn, as by intense suffering. For a moment he hesitated in the doorway, as if he had been dazzled by the light. Then he came into the room. He

walked with just such a limp as I have seen in footsore tramps. We stared at him in silence, expecting him to speak.

He said not a word, but came painfully to the table, and made a motion towards the wine. The Editor filled a glass of champagne, and pushed it towards him. He drained it, and it seemed to do him good: for he looked round the table, and the ghost of his old smile flickered across his face. "What on earth have you been up to, man?" said the Doctor.

The Time Traveller did not seem to hear. "Don't let me disturb you," he said, with a certain faltering articulation. "I'm all right." He stopped, held out his glass for more, and took it off at a draught. "That's good," he said. His eyes grew brighter, and a faint colour came into his cheeks. His glance flickered over our faces with a certain dull approval, and then went round the warm and comfortable room. Then he spoke again, still as it were feeling his way among his words. "I'm going to wash and dress, and then I'll come down and explain thing. . Save me some of that mutton. I'm starving for a bit of meat."

He looked across at the Editor, who was a rare visitor, and hoped he was all right. The Editor began a question. "Tell you presently," said the Time Traveller. "I'm—funny! Be all right in a minute."

He put down his glass, and walked towards the staircase door. Again, I remarked his lameness and the soft padding sound of his footfall, and standing up in my place, I saw his feet as he went out. He had nothing on them but a pair of tattered, bloodstained socks. Then the door closed upon him. I had half a mind to follow, till I remembered how he detested any fuss about himself. For a minute, perhaps, my mind was wool-gathering. Then, "Remarkable Behaviour of an Eminent Scientist," I heard the Editor say, thinking (after his wont) in headlines. And this brought my attention back to the bright dinner-table.

"What's the game?" said the Journalist. "Has he been doing the Amateur Cadger? I don't follow." I met the eye of the Psychologist, and read my own interpretation in his face. I thought of the Time Traveller limping painfully upstairs. I don't think anyone else had noticed his lameness.

The first to recover completely from this surprise was the Medical Man, who rang the bell—the Time Traveller hated to have servants waiting at dinner—for a hot plate. At that the Editor turned to his knife and fork with a grunt, and the Silent Man followed suit. The dinner was resumed. Conversation was exclamatory for a little while with gaps of wonderment; and then the Editor got fervent in his cu-

riosity. "Does our friend eke out his modest income with a crossing? or has he his Nebuchadnezzar phases?" he inquired.

"I feel assured it's this business of the Time Machine," I said, and took up the Psychologist's account of our previous meeting.

The new guests were frankly incredulous. The Editor raised objections. "What *was* this time travelling? A man couldn't cover himself with dust by rolling in a paradox, could he?" And then, as the idea came home to him, he resorted to caricature. Hadn't they any clothes-brushes in the Future?

The Journalist too, would not believe at any price, and joined the Editor in the easy work of heaping ridicule on the whole thing. They were both the new kind of journalist—very joyous, irreverent young men. "Our Special Correspondent in the Day after Tomorrow reports," the Journalist was saying—or rather shouting—when the Time Traveller came back. He was dressed in ordinary evening clothes, and nothing save his haggard look remained of the change that had startled me.

"I say," said the Editor hilariously, "these chaps here say you have been travelling into the middle of next week! Tell us all about little Rosebery, will you? What will you take for the lot?"

The Time Traveller came to the place reserved for him without a word. He smiled quietly, in his old way. "Where's my mutton?" he said. "What a treat it is to stick a fork into meat again!"

"Story!" cried the Editor.

"Story be damned!" said the Time Traveller. "I want something to eat. I won't say a word until I get some peptone into my arteries. Thanks. And the salt."

"One word," said I. "Have you been time travelling?"

"Yes," said the Time Traveller, with his mouth full, nodding his head.

"I'd give a shilling a line for a verbatim note," said the Editor.

The Time Traveller pushed his glass towards the Silent Man and rang it with his fingernail; at which the Silent Man, who had been staring at his face, started convulsively, and poured him wine. The rest of the dinner was uncomfortable. For my own part, sudden questions kept on rising to my lips, and I dare say it was the same with the others. The Journalist tried to relieve the tension by telling anecdotes of Hettie Potter. The Time Traveller devoted his attention to his dinner, and displayed the appetite of a tramp. The Medical Man smoked a cigarette, and watched the Time Traveller through his eyelashes. The

Silent Man seemed even more clumsy than usual, and drank champagne with regularity and determination out of sheer nervousness.

At last the Time Traveller pushed his plate away, and looked round us. "I suppose I must apologise," he said. "I was simply starving. I've had a most amazing time." He reached out his hand for a cigar, and cut the end. "But come into the smoking-room. It's too long a story to tell over greasy plates." And ringing the bell in passing, he led the way into the adjoining room.

"You have told Blank, and Dash, and Chose about the machine?" he said to me, leaning back in his easy-chair and naming the three new guests.

"But the thing's a mere paradox," said the Editor.

"I can't argue tonight. I don't mind telling you the story, but I can't argue. I will," he went on, "tell you the story of what has happened to me, if you like, but you must refrain from interruptions. I want to tell it. Badly. Most of it will sound like lying. So be it! It's true—every word of it, all the same. I was in my laboratory at four o'clock, and since then. . . .I've lived eight days. . . .such days as no human being ever lived before! I'm nearly worn out, but I shan't sleep till I've told this thing over to you. Then I shall go to bed. But no interruptions! Is it agreed?"

"Agreed," said the Editor, and the rest of us echoed "Agreed."

And with that the Time Traveller began his story as I have set it forth. He sat back in his chair at first, and spoke like a weary man. Afterwards he got more animated. In writing it down I feel with only too much keenness the inadequacy of pen and ink—and, above all, my own inadequacy—to express its quality. You read, I will suppose, attentively enough; but you cannot see the speaker's white, sincere face in the bright circle of the little lamp, nor hear the intonation of his voice. You cannot know how his expression followed the turns of his story! Most of us hearers were in shadow, for the candles in the smoking-room had not been lighted, and only the face of the Journalist and the legs of the Silent Man from the knees downward were illuminated. At first, we glanced now and again at each other. After a time, we ceased to do that, and looked only at the Time Traveller's face.

Chapter 4
Time Travelling

"I told some of you last Thursday of the principles of the Time Machine, and showed you the actual thing itself, incomplete in the

workshop. There it is now, a little travel-worn, truly; and one of the ivory bars is cracked, and a brass rail bent; but the rest of it's sound enough. I expected to finish it on Friday; but on Friday, when the putting together was nearly done, I found that one of the nickel bars was exactly one inch too short, and this I had to get remade; so that the thing was not complete until this morning. It was at ten o'clock today that the first of all Time Machines began its career. I gave it a last tap, tried all the screws again, put one more drop of oil on the quartz rod, and sat myself in the saddle. I suppose a suicide who holds a pistol to his skull feels much the same wonder at what will come next as I felt then. I took the starting lever in one hand and the stopping one in the other, pressed the first, and almost immediately the second. I seemed to reel; I felt a nightmare sensation of falling; and, looking round, I saw the laboratory exactly as before. Had anything happened? For a moment I suspected that my intellect had tricked me. Then I noted the clock. A moment before, as it seemed, it had stood at a minute or so past ten; now it was nearly half-past three!

"I drew a breath, set my teeth, gripped the starting lever with both hands, and went off with a thud. The laboratory got hazy and went dark. Mrs. Watchett came in and walked, apparently without seeing me, towards the garden door. I suppose it took her a minute or so to traverse the place, but to me she seemed to shoot across the room like a rocket. I pressed the lever over to its extreme position. The night came like the turning out of a lamp, and in another moment came tomorrow. The laboratory grew faint and hazy, then fainter and ever fainter. Tomorrow night came black, then day again, night again, day again, faster and faster still. An eddying murmur filled my ears, and a strange, dumb confusedness descended on my mind.

"I am afraid I cannot convey the peculiar sensations of time travelling. They are excessively unpleasant. There is a feeling exactly like that one has upon a switchback—of a helpless headlong motion! I felt the same horrible anticipation, too, of an imminent smash. As I put on pace, night followed day like the flapping of a black wing. The dim suggestion of the laboratory seemed presently to fall away from me, and I saw the sun hopping swiftly across the sky, leaping it every minute, and every minute marking a day. I supposed the laboratory had been destroyed and I had come into the open air. I had a dim impression of scaffolding, but I was already going too fast to be conscious of any moving things. The slowest snail that ever crawled dashed by too fast for me. The twinkling succession of darkness and light was

excessively painful to the eye. Then, in the intermittent darknesses, I saw the moon spinning swiftly through her quarters from new to full, and had a faint glimpse of the circling stars. Presently, as I went on, still gaining velocity, the palpitation of night and day merged into one continuous greyness; the sky took on a wonderful deepness of blue, a splendid luminous colour like that of early twilight; the jerking sun became a streak of fire, a brilliant arch, in space; the moon a fainter fluctuating band; and I could see nothing of the stars, save now and then a brighter circle flickering in the blue.

"The landscape was misty and vague. I was still on the hillside upon which this house now stands, and the shoulder rose above me grey and dim. I saw trees growing and changing like puffs of vapour, now brown, now green; they grew, spread, shivered, and passed away. I saw huge buildings rise up faint and fair, and pass like dreams. The whole surface of the earth seemed changed—melting and flowing under my eyes. The little hands upon the dials that registered my speed raced round faster and faster. Presently I noted that the sun belt swayed up and down, from solstice to solstice, in a minute or less, and that consequently my pace was over a year a minute; and minute by minute the white snow flashed across the world, and vanished, and was followed by the bright, brief green of spring.

"The unpleasant sensations of the start were less poignant now. They merged at last into a kind of hysterical exhilaration. I remarked, indeed, a clumsy swaying of the machine, for which I was unable to account. But my mind was too confused to attend to it, so with a kind of madness growing upon me, I flung myself into futurity. At first, I scarce thought of stopping, scarce thought of anything but these new sensations. But presently a fresh series of impressions grew up in my mind—a certain curiosity and therewith a certain dread—until at last they took complete possession of me.

"What strange developments of humanity, what wonderful advances upon our rudimentary civilisation, I thought, might not appear when I came to look nearly into the dim elusive world that raced and fluctuated before my eyes! I saw great and splendid architecture rising about me, more massive than any buildings of our own time, and yet, as it seemed, built of glimmer and mist. I saw a richer green flow up the hillside, and remain there, without any wintry intermission. Even through the veil of my confusion the earth seemed very fair. And so, my mind came round to the business of stopping.

"The peculiar risk lay in the possibility of my finding some sub-

stance in the space which I, or the machine, occupied. So long as I travelled at a high velocity through time, this scarcely mattered: I was, so to speak, attenuated—was slipping like a vapour through the interstices of intervening substances! But to come to a stop involved the jamming of myself, molecule by molecule, into whatever lay in my way; meant bringing my atoms into such intimate contact with those of the obstacle that a profound chemical reaction—possibly a far-reaching explosion—would result, and blow myself and my apparatus out of all possible dimensions—into the Unknown.

"This possibility had occurred to me again and again while I was making the machine; but then I had cheerfully accepted it as an unavoidable risk—one of the risks a man has got to take! Now the risk was inevitable, I no longer saw it in the same cheerful light. The fact is that, insensibly, the absolute strangeness of everything, the sickly jarring and swaying of the machine, above all, the feeling of prolonged falling, had absolutely upset my nerves. I told myself that I could never stop, and with a gust of petulance I resolved to stop forthwith. Like an impatient fool, I lugged over the lever, and incontinently the thing went reeling over, and I was flung headlong through the air.

"There was the sound of a clap of thunder in my ears. I may have been stunned for a moment. A pitiless hail was hissing round me, and I was sitting on soft turf in front of the overset machine. Everything still seemed grey, but presently I remarked that the confusion in my ears was gone. I looked round me. I was on what seemed to be a little lawn in a garden, surrounded by rhododendron bushes, and I noticed that their mauve and purple blossoms were dropping in a shower under the beating of the hailstones. The rebounding, dancing hail hung in a little cloud over the machine, and drove along the ground like smoke. In a moment I was wet to the skin. 'Fine hospitality,' said I, 'to a man who has travelled innumerable years to see you.'

"Presently I thought what a fool I was to get wet. I stood up and looked round me. A colossal figure, carved apparently in some white stone, loomed indistinctly beyond the rhododendrons through the hazy downpour. But all else of the world was invisible.

"My sensations would be hard to describe. As the columns of hail grew thinner, I saw the white figure more distinctly. It was very large, for a silver birch-tree touched its shoulder. It was of white marble, in shape something like a winged sphinx, but the wings, instead of being carried vertically at the sides, were spread so that it seemed to hover. The pedestal, it appeared to me, was of bronze, and was thick with

verdigris. It chanced that the face was towards me; the sightless eyes seemed to watch me; there was the faint shadow of a smile on the lips. It was greatly weather-worn, and that imparted an unpleasant suggestion of disease. I stood looking at it for a little space—half a minute, perhaps, or half an hour. It seemed to advance and to recede as the hail drove before it denser or thinner. At last I tore my eyes from it for a moment, and saw that the hail curtain had worn threadbare, and that the sky was lightening with the promise of the sun.

"I looked up again at the crouching white shape, and the full temerity of my voyage came suddenly upon me. What might appear when that hazy curtain was altogether withdrawn? What might not have happened to men? What if cruelty had grown into a common passion? What if in this interval the race had lost its manliness, and had developed into something inhuman, unsympathetic, and overwhelmingly powerful? I might seem some old-world savage animal, only the more dreadful and disgusting for our common likeness—a foul creature to be incontinently slain.

"Already I saw other vast shapes—huge buildings with intricate parapets and tall columns, with a wooded hillside dimly creeping in upon me through the lessening storm. I was seized with a panic fear. I turned frantically to the Time Machine, and strove hard to readjust it. As I did so the shafts of the sun smote through the thunderstorm. The grey downpour was swept aside and vanished like the trailing garments of a ghost. Above me, in the intense blue of the summer sky, some faint brown shreds of cloud whirled into nothingness. The great buildings about me stood out clear and distinct, shining with the wet of the thunderstorm, and picked out in white by the unmelted hail-stones piled along their courses. I felt naked in a strange world. I felt as perhaps a bird may feel in the clear air, knowing the hawk wings above and will swoop. My fear grew to frenzy. I took a breathing space, set my teeth, and again grappled fiercely, wrist and knee, with the machine. It gave under my desperate onset and turned over. It struck my chin violently. One hand on the saddle, the other on the lever, I stood panting heavily in attitude to mount again.

"But with this recovery of a prompt retreat my courage recovered. I looked more curiously and less fearfully at this world of the remote future. In a circular opening, high up in the wall of the nearer house, I saw a group of figures clad in rich soft robes. They had seen me, and their faces were directed towards me.

"Then I heard voices approaching me. Coming through the bush-

es by the White Sphinx were the heads and shoulders of men running. One of these emerged in a pathway leading straight to the little lawn upon which I stood with my machine. He was a slight creature—perhaps four feet high—clad in a purple tunic, girdled at the waist with a leather belt. Sandals or buskins—I could not clearly distinguish which—were on his feet; his legs were bare to the knees, and his head was bare. Noticing that, I noticed for the first time how warm the air was.

"He struck me as being a very beautiful and graceful creature, but indescribably frail. His flushed face reminded me of the more beautiful kind of consumptive—that hectic beauty of which we used to hear so much. At the sight of him I suddenly regained confidence. I took my hands from the machine.

CHAPTER 5
In the Golden Age

"In another moment we were standing face to face, I and this fragile thing out of futurity. He came straight up to me and laughed into my eyes. The absence from his bearing of any sign of fear struck me at once. Then he turned to the two others who were following him and spoke to them in a strange and very sweet and liquid tongue.

"There were others coming, and presently a little group of perhaps eight or ten of these exquisite creatures were about me. One of them addressed me. It came into my head, oddly enough, that my voice was too harsh and deep for them. So, I shook my head, and, pointing to my ears, shook it again. He came a step forward, hesitated, and then touched my hand. Then I felt other soft little tentacles upon my back and shoulders. They wanted to make sure I was real. There was nothing in this at all alarming. Indeed, there was something in these pretty little people that inspired confidence—a graceful gentleness, a certain childlike ease. And besides, they looked so frail that I could fancy myself flinging the whole dozen of them about like ninepins. But I made a sudden motion to warn them when I saw their little pink hands feeling at the Time Machine. Happily, then, when it was not too late, I thought of a danger I had hitherto forgotten, and reaching over the bars of the machine I unscrewed the little levers that would set it in motion, and put these in my pocket. Then I turned again to see what I could do in the way of communication.

"And then, looking more nearly into their features, I saw some further peculiarities in their Dresden china type of prettiness. Their

hair, which was uniformly curly, came to a sharp end at the neck and cheek; there was not the faintest suggestion of it on the face, and their ears were singularly minute. The mouths were small, with bright red, rather thin lips, and the little chins ran to a point. The eyes were large and mild; and—this may seem egotism on my part—I fancied even that there was a certain lack of the interest I might have expected in them.

"As they made no effort to communicate with me, but simply stood round me smiling and speaking in soft cooing notes to each other, I began the conversation. I pointed to the Time Machine and to myself. Then, hesitating for a moment how to express Time, I pointed to the sun. At once a quaintly pretty little figure in chequered purple and white followed my gesture, and then astonished me by imitating the sound of thunder.

"For a moment I was staggered, though the import of his gesture was plain enough. The question had come into my mind abruptly: were these creatures fools? You may hardly understand how it took me. You see, I had always anticipated that the people of the year Eight Hundred and Two Thousand odd would be incredibly in front of us in knowledge, art, everything. Then one of them suddenly asked me a question that showed him to be on the intellectual level of one of our five-year-old children—asked me, in fact, if I had come from the sun in a thunderstorm! It let loose the judgment I had suspended upon their clothes, their frail light limbs, and fragile features. A flow of disappointment rushed across my mind. For a moment I felt that I had built the Time Machine in vain.

"I nodded, pointed to the sun, and gave them such a vivid rendering of a thunderclap as startled them. They all withdrew a pace or so and bowed. Then came one laughing towards me, carrying a chain of beautiful flowers altogether new to me, and put it about my neck. The idea was received with melodious applause; and presently they were all running to and fro for flowers, and laughingly flinging them upon me until I was almost smothered with blossom. You who have never seen the like can scarcely imagine what delicate and wonderful flowers countless years of culture had created. Then someone suggested that their plaything should be exhibited in the nearest building, and so I was led past the sphinx of white marble, which had seemed to watch me all the while with a smile at my astonishment, towards a vast grey edifice of fretted stone. As I went with them the memory of my confident anticipations of a profoundly grave and intellectual poster-

ity came, with irresistible merriment, to my mind.

"The building had a huge entry, and was altogether of colossal dimensions. I was naturally most occupied with the growing crowd of little people, and with the big open portals that yawned before me shadowy and mysterious. My general impression of the world I saw over their heads was a tangled waste of beautiful bushes and flowers, a long neglected and yet weedless garden. I saw a number of tall spikes of strange white flowers, measuring a foot perhaps across the spread of the waxen petals. They grew scattered, as if wild, among the variegated shrubs, but, as I say, I did not examine them closely at this time. The Time Machine was left deserted on the turf among the rhododendrons.

"The arch of the doorway was richly carved, but naturally I did not observe the carving very narrowly, though I fancied I saw suggestions of old Phoenician decorations as I passed through, and it struck me that they were very badly broken and weather-worn. Several more brightly clad people met me in the doorway, and so we entered, I, dressed in dingy nineteenth-century garments, looking grotesque enough, garlanded with flowers, and surrounded by an eddying mass of bright, soft-coloured robes and shining white limbs, in a melodious whirl of laughter and laughing speech.

"The big doorway opened into a proportionately great hall hung with brown. The roof was in shadow, and the windows, partially glazed with coloured glass and partially unglazed, admitted a tempered light. The floor was made up of huge blocks of some very hard white metal, not plates nor slabs—blocks, and it was so much worn, as I judged by the going to and fro of past generations, as to be deeply channelled along the more frequented ways. Transverse to the length were innumerable tables made of slabs of polished stone, raised, perhaps, a foot from the floor, and upon these were heaps of fruits. Some I recognised as a kind of hypertrophied raspberry and orange, but for the most part they were strange.

"Between the tables was scattered a great number of cushions. Upon these my conductors seated themselves, signing for me to do likewise. With a pretty absence of ceremony, they began to eat the fruit with their hands, flinging peel and stalks, and so forth, into the round openings in the sides of the tables. I was not loath to follow their example, for I felt thirsty and hungry. As I did so I surveyed the hall at my leisure.

"And perhaps the thing that struck me most was its dilapidated

look. The stained-glass windows, which displayed only a geometrical pattern, were broken in many places, and the curtains that hung across the lower end were thick with dust. And it caught my eye that the corner of the marble table near me was fractured. Nevertheless, the general effect was extremely rich and picturesque. There were, perhaps, a couple of hundred people dining in the hall, and most of them, seated as near to me as they could come, were watching me with interest, their little eyes shining over the fruit they were eating. All were clad in the same soft, and yet strong, silky material.

"Fruit, by the bye, was all their diet. These people of the remote future were strict vegetarians, and while I was with them, in spite of some carnal cravings, I had to be frugivorous also. Indeed, I found afterwards that horses, cattle, sheep, dogs, had followed the Ichthyosaurus into extinction. But the fruits were very delightful; one, in particular, that seemed to be in season all the time I was there—a floury thing in a three-sided husk—was especially good, and I made it my staple. At first, I was puzzled by all these strange fruits, and by the strange flowers I saw, but later I began to perceive their import.

"However, I am telling you of my fruit dinner in the distant future now. So soon as my appetite was a little checked, I determined to make a resolute attempt to learn the speech of these new men of mine. Clearly that was the next thing to do. The fruits seemed a convenient thing to begin upon, and holding one of these up I began a series of interrogative sounds and gestures. I had some considerable difficulty in conveying my meaning.

"At first my efforts met with a stare of surprise or inextinguishable laughter, but presently a fair-haired little creature seemed to grasp my intention and repeated a name. They had to chatter and explain the business at great length to each other, and my first attempts to make the exquisite little sounds of their language caused an immense amount of genuine, if uncivil, amusement. However, I felt like a schoolmaster amidst children, and persisted, and presently I had a score of noun substantives at least at my command; and then I got to demonstrative pronouns, and even the verb 'to eat.' But it was slow work, and the little people soon tired and wanted to get away from my interrogations, so I determined, rather of necessity, to let them give their lessons in little doses when they felt inclined. And very little doses I found they were before long, for I never met people more indolent or more easily fatigued.

The Sunset of Mankind

"A queer thing I soon discovered about my little hosts, and that was their lack of interest. They would come to me with eager cries of astonishment, like children, but, like children they would soon stop examining me, and wander away after some other toy. The dinner and my conversational beginnings ended, I noted for the first time that almost all those who had surrounded me at first were gone. It is odd, too, how speedily I came to disregard these little people. I went out through the portal into the sunlit world again as soon as my hunger was satisfied. I was continually meeting more of these men of the future, who would follow me a little distance, chatter and laugh about me, and, having smiled and gesticulated in a friendly way, leave me again to my own devices.

"The calm of evening was upon the world as I emerged from the great hall, and the scene was lit by the warm glow of the setting sun. At first things were very confusing. Everything was so entirely different from the world I had known—even the flowers. The big building, I had left, was situated on the slope of a broad river valley, but the Thames had shifted, perhaps, a mile from its present position. I resolved to mount to the summit of a crest, perhaps a mile and a half away, from which I could get a wider view of this our planet in the year Eight Hundred and Two Thousand Seven Hundred and One, A.D. For that, I should explain, was the date the little dials of my machine recorded.

"As I walked, I was watching for every impression that could possibly help to explain the condition of ruinous splendour in which I found the world—for ruinous it was. A little way up the hill, for instance, was a great heap of granite, bound together by masses of aluminium, a vast labyrinth of precipitous walls and crumpled heaps, amidst which were thick heaps of very beautiful pagoda-like plants—nettles possibly—but wonderfully tinted with brown about the leaves, and incapable of stinging. It was evidently the derelict remains of some vast structure, to what end built I could not determine. It was here that I was destined, at a later date, to have a very strange experience—the first intimation of a still stranger discovery—but of that I will speak in its proper place.

"Looking round, with a sudden thought, from a terrace on which I rested for a while, I realised that there were no small houses to be seen.

Apparently, the single house, and possibly even the household, had vanished. Here and there among the greenery were palace-like buildings, but the house and the cottage, which form such characteristic features of our own English landscape, had disappeared.

"'Communism,' said I to myself.

"And on the heels of that came another thought. I looked at the half-dozen little figures that were following me. Then, in a flash, I perceived that all had the same form of costume, the same soft hairless visage, and the same girlish rotundity of limb. It may seem strange, perhaps, that I had not noticed this before. But everything was so strange. Now, I saw the fact plainly enough. In costume, and in all the differences of texture and bearing that now mark off the sexes from each other, these people of the future were alike. And the children seemed to my eyes to be but the miniatures of their parents. I judged then that the children of that time were extremely precocious, physically at least, and I found afterwards abundant verification of my opinion.

"Seeing the ease and security in which these people were living, I felt that this close resemblance of the sexes was after all what one would expect; for the strength of a man and the softness of a woman, the institution of the family, and the differentiation of occupations are mere militant necessities of an age of physical force. Where population is balanced and abundant, much childbearing becomes an evil rather than a blessing to the State; where violence comes but rarely and offspring are secure, there is less necessity—indeed there is no necessity—for an efficient family, and the specialisation of the sexes with reference to their children's needs disappears. We see some beginnings of this even in our own time, and in this future age it was complete. This, I must remind you, was my speculation at the time. Later, I was to appreciate how far it fell short of the reality.

"While I was musing upon these things, my attention was attracted by a pretty little structure, like a well under a cupola. I thought in a transitory way of the oddness of wells still existing, and then resumed the thread of my speculations. There were no large buildings towards the top of the hill, and as my walking powers were evidently miraculous, I was presently left alone for the first time. With a strange sense of freedom and adventure I pushed on up to the crest.

"There I found a seat of some yellow metal that I did not recognise, corroded in places with a kind of pinkish rust and half smothered in soft moss, the arm-rests cast and filed into the resemblance of

32

griffins' heads. I sat down on it, and I surveyed the broad view of our old world under the sunset of that long day. It was as sweet and fair a view as I have ever seen. The sun had already gone below the horizon and the west was flaming gold, touched with some horizontal bars of purple and crimson. Below was the valley of the Thames, in which the river lay like a band of burnished steel. I have already spoken of the great palaces dotted about among the variegated greenery, some in ruins and some still occupied. Here and there rose a white or silvery figure in the waste garden of the earth, here and there came the sharp vertical line of some cupola or obelisk. There were no hedges, no signs of proprietary rights, no evidences of agriculture; the whole earth had become a garden.

"So, watching, I began to put my interpretation upon the things I had seen, and as it shaped itself to me that evening, my interpretation was something in this way. (Afterwards I found I had got only a half-truth—or only a glimpse of one facet of the truth.)

"It seemed to me that I had happened upon humanity upon the wane. The ruddy sunset set me thinking of the sunset of mankind. For the first time I began to realise an odd consequence of the social effort in which we are at present engaged. And yet, come to think, it is a logical consequence enough. Strength is the outcome of need; security sets a premium on feebleness. The work of ameliorating the conditions of life—the true civilising process that makes life more and more secure—had gone steadily on to a climax. One triumph of a united humanity over Nature had followed another. Things that are now mere dreams had become projects deliberately put in hand and carried forward. And the harvest was what I saw!

"After all, the sanitation and the agriculture of today are still in the rudimentary stage. The science of our time has attacked but a little department of the field of human disease, but, even so, it spreads its operations very steadily and persistently. Our agriculture and horticulture destroy a weed just here and there and cultivate perhaps a score or so of wholesome plants, leaving the greater number to fight out a balance as they can. We improve our favourite plants and animals—and how few they are—gradually by selective breeding; now a new and better peach, now a seedless grape, now a sweeter and larger flower, now a more convenient breed of cattle. We improve them gradually, because our ideals are vague and tentative, and our knowledge is very limited; because Nature, too, is shy and slow in our clumsy hands. Someday all this will be better organised, and still better.

That is the drift of the current in spite of the eddies. The whole world will be intelligent, educated, and co-operating; things will move faster and faster towards the subjugation of Nature. In the end, wisely and carefully we shall readjust the balance of animal and vegetable life to suit our human needs.

"This adjustment, I say, must have been done, and done well; done indeed for all Time, in the space of Time across which my machine had leapt. The air was free from gnats, the earth from weeds or fungi; everywhere were fruits and sweet and delightful flowers; brilliant butterflies flew hither and thither. The ideal of preventive medicine was attained. Diseases had been stamped out. I saw no evidence of any contagious diseases during all my stay. And I shall have to tell you later that even the processes of putrefaction and decay had been profoundly affected by these changes.

"Social triumphs, too, had been effected. I saw mankind housed in splendid shelters, gloriously clothed, and as yet I had found them engaged in no toil. There were no signs of struggle, neither social nor economical struggle. The shop, the advertisement, traffic, all that commerce which constitutes the body of our world, was gone. It was natural on that golden evening that I should jump at the idea of a social paradise. The difficulty of increasing population had been met, I guessed, and population had ceased to increase.

"But with this change in condition comes inevitably adaptations to the change. What, unless biological science is a mass of errors, is the cause of human intelligence and vigour? Hardship and freedom: conditions under which the active, strong, and subtle survive and the weaker go to the wall; conditions that put a premium upon the loyal alliance of capable men, upon self-restraint, patience, and decision. And the institution of the family, and the emotions that arise therein, the fierce jealousy, the tenderness for offspring, parental self-devotion, all found their justification and support in the imminent dangers of the young. *Now*, where are these imminent dangers? There is a sentiment arising, and it will grow, against connubial jealousy, against fierce maternity, against passion of all sorts; unnecessary things now, and things that make us uncomfortable, savage survivals, discords in a refined and pleasant life.

"I thought of the physical slightness of the people, their lack of intelligence, and those big abundant ruins, and it strengthened my belief in a perfect conquest of Nature. For after the battle comes Quiet. Humanity had been strong, energetic, and intelligent, and had used all

its abundant vitality to alter the conditions under which it lived. And now came the reaction of the altered conditions.

"Under the new conditions of perfect comfort and security, that restless energy, that with us is strength, would become weakness. Even in our own time certain tendencies and desires, once necessary to survival, are a constant source of failure. Physical courage and the love of battle, for instance, are no great help—may even be hindrances—to a civilised man. And in a state of physical balance and security, power, intellectual as well as physical, would be out of place. For countless years I judged there had been no danger of war or solitary violence, no danger from wild beasts, no wasting disease to require strength of constitution, no need of toil. For such a life, what we should call the weak are as well-equipped as the strong, are indeed no longer weak. Better equipped indeed they are, for the strong would be fretted by an energy for which there was no outlet. No doubt the exquisite beauty of the buildings I saw was the outcome of the last surgings of the now purposeless energy of mankind before it settled down into perfect harmony with the conditions under which it lived—the flourish of that triumph which began the last great peace. This has ever been the fate of energy in security; it takes to art and to eroticism, and then come languor and decay.

"Even this artistic impetus would at last die away—had almost died in the Time I saw. To adorn themselves with flowers, to dance, to sing in the sunlight: so much was left of the artistic spirit, and no more. Even that would fade in the end into a contented inactivity. We are kept keen on the grindstone of pain and necessity, and it seemed to me that here was that hateful grindstone broken at last!

"As I stood there in the gathering dark, I thought that in this simple explanation I had mastered the problem of the world—mastered the whole secret of these delicious people. Possibly the checks they had devised for the increase of population had succeeded too well, and their numbers had rather diminished than kept stationary. That would account for the abandoned ruins. Very simple was my explanation, and plausible enough—as most wrong theories are!

Chapter 7
A Sudden Shock

"As I stood there musing over this too perfect triumph of man, the full moon, yellow and gibbous, came up out of an overflow of silver light in the north-east. The bright little figures ceased to move about

below, a noiseless owl flitted by, and I shivered with the chill of the night. I determined to descend and find where I could sleep.

"I looked for the building I knew. Then my eye travelled along to the figure of the White Sphinx upon the pedestal of bronze, growing distinct as the light of the rising moon grew brighter. I could see the silver birch against it. There was the tangle of rhododendron bushes, black in the pale light, and there was the little lawn. I looked at the lawn again. A queer doubt chilled my complacency. 'No,' said I stoutly to myself, 'that was not the lawn.'

"But it *was* the lawn. For the white leprous face of the sphinx was towards it. Can you imagine what I felt as this conviction came home to me? But you cannot. The Time Machine was gone!

"At once, like a lash across the face, came the possibility of losing my own age, of being left helpless in this strange new world. The bare thought of it was an actual physical sensation. I could feel it grip me at the throat and stop my breathing. In another moment I was in a passion of fear and running with great leaping strides down the slope. Once I fell headlong and cut my face; I lost no time in stanching the blood, but jumped up and ran on, with a warm trickle down my cheek and chin. All the time I ran I was saying to myself: 'They have moved it a little, pushed it under the bushes out of the way.' Nevertheless, I ran with all my might. All the time, with the certainty that sometimes comes with excessive dread, I knew that such assurance was folly, knew instinctively that the machine was removed out of my reach. My breath came with pain. I suppose I covered the whole distance from the hill crest to the little lawn, two miles perhaps, in ten minutes. And I am not a young man. I cursed aloud, as I ran, at my confident folly in leaving the machine, wasting good breath thereby. I cried aloud, and none answered. Not a creature seemed to be stirring in that moonlit world.

"When I reached the lawn, my worst fears were realised. Not a trace of the thing was to be seen. I felt faint and cold when I faced the empty space among the black tangle of bushes. I ran round it furiously, as if the thing might be hidden in a corner, and then stopped abruptly, with my hands clutching my hair. Above me towered the sphinx, upon the bronze pedestal, white, shining, leprous, in the light of the rising moon. It seemed to smile in mockery of my dismay.

"I might have consoled myself by imagining the little people had put the mechanism in some shelter for me, had I not felt assured of their physical and intellectual inadequacy. That is what dismayed me:

the sense of some hitherto unsuspected power, through whose intervention my invention had vanished. Yet, for one thing I felt assured: unless some other age had produced its exact duplicate, the machine could not have moved in time. The attachment of the levers—I will show you the method later—prevented anyone from tampering with it in that way when they were removed. It had moved, and was hid, only in space. But then, where could it be?

"I think I must have had a kind of frenzy. I remember running violently in and out among the moonlit bushes all round the sphinx, and startling some white animal that, in the dim light, I took for a small deer. I remember, too, late that night, beating the bushes with my clenched fist until my knuckles were gashed and bleeding from the broken twigs. Then, sobbing and raving in my anguish of mind, I went down to the great building of stone. The big hall was dark, silent, and deserted. I slipped on the uneven floor, and fell over one of the malachite tables, almost breaking my shin. I lit a match and went on past the dusty curtains, of which I have told you.

"There I found a second great hall covered with cushions, upon which, perhaps, a score or so of the little people were sleeping. I have no doubt they found my second appearance strange enough, coming suddenly out of the quiet darkness with inarticulate noises and the splutter and flare of a match. For they had forgotten about matches. 'Where is my Time Machine?' I began, bawling like an angry child, laying hands upon them and shaking them up together. It must have been very queer to them. Some laughed, most of them looked sorely frightened. When I saw them standing round me, it came into my head that I was doing as foolish a thing as it was possible for me to do under the circumstances, in trying to revive the sensation of fear. For, reasoning from their daylight behaviour, I thought that fear must be forgotten.

"Abruptly, I dashed down the match, and knocking one of the people over in my course, went blundering across the big dining-hall again, out under the moonlight. I heard cries of terror and their little feet running and stumbling this way and that. I do not remember all I did as the moon crept up the sky. I suppose it was the unexpected nature of my loss that maddened me. I felt hopelessly cut off from my own kind—a strange animal in an unknown world. I must have raved to and fro, screaming and crying upon God and Fate. I have a memory of horrible fatigue, as the long night of despair wore away; of looking in this impossible place and that; of groping among moonlit ruins

37

and touching strange creatures in the black shadows; at last, of lying on the ground near the sphinx and weeping with absolute wretchedness, even anger at the folly of leaving the machine having leaked away with my strength. I had nothing left but misery. Then I slept, and when I woke again it was full day, and a couple of sparrows were hopping round me on the turf within reach of my arm.

"I sat up in the freshness of the morning, trying to remember how I had got there, and why I had such a profound sense of desertion and despair. Then things came clear in my mind. With the plain, reasonable daylight, I could look my circumstances fairly in the face. I saw the wild folly of my frenzy overnight, and I could reason with myself. 'Suppose the worst?' I said. 'Suppose the machine altogether lost—perhaps destroyed? It behoves me to be calm and patient, to learn the way of the people, to get a clear idea of the method of my loss, and the means of getting materials and tools; so that in the end, perhaps, I may make another.' That would be my only hope, a poor hope, perhaps, but better than despair. And, after all, it was a beautiful and curious world.

"But probably the machine had only been taken away. Still, I must be calm and patient, find its hiding-place, and recover it by force or cunning. And with that I scrambled to my feet and looked about me, wondering where I could bathe. I felt weary, stiff, and travel-soiled. The freshness of the morning made me desire an equal freshness. I had exhausted my emotion. Indeed, as I went about my business, I found myself wondering at my intense excitement overnight. I made a careful examination of the ground about the little lawn. I wasted some time in futile questionings, conveyed, as well as I was able, to such of the little people as came by. They all failed to understand my gestures; some were simply stolid, some thought it was a jest and laughed at me. I had the hardest task in the world to keep my hands off their pretty laughing faces. It was a foolish impulse, but the devil begotten of fear and blind anger was ill curbed and still eager to take advantage of my perplexity.

"The turf gave better counsel. I found a groove ripped in it, about midway between the pedestal of the sphinx and the marks of my feet where, on arrival, I had struggled with the overturned machine. There were other signs of removal about, with queer narrow footprints like those I could imagine made by a sloth. This directed my closer attention to the pedestal. It was, as I think I have said, of bronze. It was not a mere block, but highly decorated with deep framed panels on either side. I went and rapped at these. The pedestal was hollow. Examining

the panels with care I found them discontinuous with the frames. There were no handles or keyholes, but possibly the panels, if they were doors, as I supposed, opened from within. One thing was clear enough to my mind. It took no very great mental effort to infer that my Time Machine was inside that pedestal. But how it got there was a different problem.

"I saw the heads of two orange-clad people coming through the bushes and under some blossom-covered apple-trees towards me. I turned smiling to them, and beckoned them to me. They came, and then, pointing to the bronze pedestal, I tried to intimate my wish to open it. But at my first gesture towards this they behaved very oddly. I don't know how to convey their expression to you. Suppose you were to use a grossly improper gesture to a delicate-minded woman—it is how she would look. They went off as if they had received the last possible insult. I tried a sweet-looking little chap in white next, with exactly the same result. Somehow, his manner made me feel ashamed of myself. But, as you know, I wanted the Time Machine, and I tried him once more. As he turned off, like the others, my temper got the better of me. In three strides I was after him, had him by the loose part of his robe round the neck, and began dragging him towards the sphinx. Then I saw the horror and repugnance of his face, and all of a sudden, I let him go.

"But I was not beaten yet. I banged with my fist at the bronze panels. I thought I heard something stir inside—to be explicit, I thought I heard a sound like a chuckle—but I must have been mistaken. Then I got a big pebble from the river, and came and hammered till I had flattened a coil in the decorations, and the verdigris came off in powdery flakes. The delicate little people must have heard me hammering in gusty outbreaks a mile away on either hand, but nothing came of it. I saw a crowd of them upon the slopes, looking furtively at me. At last, hot and tired, I sat down to watch the place. But I was too restless to watch long; I am too Occidental for a long vigil. I could work at a problem for years, but to wait inactive for twenty-four hours—that is another matter.

"I got up after a time, and began walking aimlessly through the bushes towards the hill again. 'Patience,' said I to myself. 'If you want your machine again you must leave that sphinx alone. If they mean to take your machine away, it's little good your wrecking their bronze panels, and if they don't, you will get it back as soon as you can ask for it. To sit among all those unknown things before a puzzle like that

is hopeless. That way lies monomania. Face this world. Learn its ways, watch it, be careful of too hasty guesses at its meaning. In the end you will find clues to it all.' Then suddenly the humour of the situation came into my mind: the thought of the years I had spent in study and toil to get into the future age, and now my passion of anxiety to get out of it. I had made myself the most complicated and the most hopeless trap that ever a man devised. Although it was at my own expense, I could not help myself. I laughed aloud.

"Going through the big palace, it seemed to me that the little people avoided me. It may have been my fancy, or it may have had something to do with my hammering at the gates of bronze. Yet I felt tolerably sure of the avoidance. I was careful, however, to show no concern and to abstain from any pursuit of them, and in the course of a day or two things got back to the old footing. I made what progress I could in the language, and in addition I pushed my explorations here and there. Either I missed some subtle point or their language was excessively simple—almost exclusively composed of concrete substantives and verbs.

"There seemed to be few, if any, abstract terms, or little use of figurative language. Their sentences were usually simple and of two words, and I failed to convey or understand any but the simplest propositions. I determined to put the thought of my Time Machine and the mystery of the bronze doors under the sphinx, as much as possible in a corner of memory, until my growing knowledge would lead me back to them in a natural way. Yet a certain feeling, you may understand, tethered me in a circle of a few miles round the point of my arrival.

CHAPTER 8

Explanation

"So far as I could see, all the world displayed the same exuberant richness as the Thames valley. From every hill I climbed I saw the same abundance of splendid buildings, endlessly varied in material and style, the same clustering thickets of evergreens, the same blossom-laden trees and tree ferns. Here and there water shone like silver, and beyond, the land rose into blue undulating hills, and so faded into the serenity of the sky. A peculiar feature, which presently attracted my attention, was the presence of certain circular wells, several, as it seemed to me, of a very great depth. One lay by the path up the hill which I had followed during my first walk. Like the others, it was rimmed with bronze, curiously wrought, and protected by a little cupola from

the rain. Sitting by the side of these wells, and peering down into the shafted darkness, I could see no gleam of water, nor could I start any reflection with a lighted match. But in all of them I heard a certain sound: a thud—thud—thud, like the beating of some big engine; and I discovered, from the flaring of my matches, that a steady current of air set down the shafts. Further, I threw a scrap of paper into the throat of one, and, instead of fluttering slowly down, it was at once sucked swiftly out of sight.

"After a time, too, I came to connect these wells with tall towers standing here and there upon the slopes; for above them there was often just such a flicker in the air as one sees on a hot day above a sun-scorched beach. Putting things together, I reached a strong suggestion of an extensive system of subterranean ventilation, whose true import it was difficult to imagine. I was at first inclined to associate it with the sanitary apparatus of these people. It was an obvious conclusion, but it was absolutely wrong.

"And here I must admit that I learnt very little of drains and bells and modes of conveyance, and the like conveniences, during my time in this real future. In some of these visions of Utopias and coming times which I have read, there is a vast amount of detail about building, and social arrangements, and so forth. But while such details are easy enough to obtain when the whole world is contained in one's imagination, they are altogether inaccessible to a real traveller amid such realities as I found here. Conceive the tale of London which a negro, fresh from Central Africa, would take back to his tribe! What would he know of railway companies, of social movements, of telephone and telegraph wires, of the Parcels Delivery Company, and postal orders and the like?

"Yet we, at least, should be willing enough to explain these things to him! And even of what he knew, how much could he make his untravelled friend either apprehend or believe? Then, think how narrow the gap between a negro and a white man of our own times, and how wide the interval between myself and these of the Golden Age! I was sensible of much which was unseen, and which contributed to my comfort; but save for a general impression of automatic organisation, I fear I can convey very little of the difference to your mind.

"In the matter of sepulture, for instance, I could see no signs of crematoria nor anything suggestive of tombs. But it occurred to me that, possibly, there might be cemeteries (or crematoria) somewhere beyond the range of my explorings. This, again, was a question I de-

liberately put to myself, and my curiosity was at first entirely defeated upon the point. The thing puzzled me, and I was led to make a further remark, which puzzled me still more: that aged and infirm among this people there were none.

"I must confess that my satisfaction with my first theories of an automatic civilisation and a decadent humanity did not long endure. Yet I could think of no other. Let me put my difficulties. The several big palaces I had explored were mere living places, great dining-halls and sleeping apartments. I could find no machinery, no appliances of any kind. Yet these people were clothed in pleasant fabrics that must at times need renewal, and their sandals, though undecorated, were fairly complex specimens of metalwork. Somehow such things must be made. And the little people displayed no vestige of a creative tendency. There were no shops, no workshops, no sign of importations among them. They spent all their time in playing gently, in bathing in the river, in making love in a half-playful fashion, in eating fruit and sleeping. I could not see how things were kept going.

"Then, again, about the Time Machine: something, I knew not what, had taken it into the hollow pedestal of the White Sphinx. *Why?* For the life of me I could not imagine. Those waterless wells, too, those flickering pillars. I felt I lacked a clue. I felt—how shall I put it? Suppose you found an inscription, with sentences here and there in excellent plain English, and interpolated therewith, others made up of words, of letters even, absolutely unknown to you? Well, on the third day of my visit, that was how the world of Eight Hundred and Two Thousand Seven Hundred and One presented itself to me!

"That day, too, I made a friend—of a sort. It happened that, as I was watching some of the little people bathing in a shallow, one of them was seized with cramp and began drifting downstream. The main current ran rather swiftly, but not too strongly for even a moderate swimmer. It will give you an idea, therefore, of the strange deficiency in these creatures, when I tell you that none made the slightest attempt to rescue the weakly crying little thing which was drowning before their eyes. When I realised this, I hurriedly slipped off my clothes, and, wading in at a point lower down, I caught the poor mite and drew her safe to land. A little rubbing of the limbs soon brought her round, and I had the satisfaction of seeing she was all right before I left her. I had got to such a low estimate of her kind that I did not expect any gratitude from her. In that, however, I was wrong.

"This happened in the morning. In the afternoon I met my little

woman, as I believe it was, as I was returning towards my centre from an exploration, and she received me with cries of delight and presented me with a big garland of flowers—evidently made for me and me alone. The thing took my imagination. Very possibly I had been feeling desolate. At any rate I did my best to display my appreciation of the gift. We were soon seated together in a little stone arbour, engaged in conversation, chiefly of smiles. The creature's friendliness affected me exactly as a child's might have done. We passed each other flowers, and she kissed my hands. I did the same to hers. Then I tried talk, and found that her name was Weena, which, though I don't know what it meant, somehow seemed appropriate enough. That was the beginning of a queer friendship which lasted a week, and ended—as I will tell you!

"She was exactly like a child. She wanted to be with me always. She tried to follow me everywhere, and on my next journey out and about it went to my heart to tire her down, and leave her at last, exhausted and calling after me rather plaintively. But the problems of the world had to be mastered. I had not, I said to myself, come into the future to carry on a miniature flirtation. Yet her distress when I left her was very great, her expostulations at the parting were sometimes frantic, and I think, altogether, I had as much trouble as comfort from her devotion. Nevertheless, she was, somehow, a very great comfort. I thought it was mere childish affection that made her cling to me. Until it was too late, I did not clearly know what I had inflicted upon her when I left her. Nor until it was too late did I clearly understand what she was to me. For, by merely seeming fond of me, and showing in her weak, futile way that she cared for me, the little doll of a creature presently gave my return to the neighbourhood of the White Sphinx almost the feeling of coming home; and I would watch for her tiny figure of white and gold so soon as I came over the hill.

"It was from her, too, that I learnt that fear had not yet left the world. She was fearless enough in the daylight, and she had the oddest confidence in me; for once, in a foolish moment, I made threatening grimaces at her, and she simply laughed at them. But she dreaded the dark, dreaded shadows, dreaded black things. Darkness to her was the one thing dreadful. It was a singularly passionate emotion, and it set me thinking and observing. I discovered then, among other things, that these little people gathered into the great houses after dark, and slept in droves. To enter upon them without a light was to put them into a tumult of apprehension. I never found one out of doors, or one

sleeping alone within doors, after dark. Yet I was still such a blockhead that I missed the lesson of that fear, and in spite of Weena's distress, I insisted upon sleeping away from these slumbering multitudes.

"It troubled her greatly, but in the end her odd affection for me triumphed, and for five of the nights of our acquaintance, including the last night of all, she slept with her head pillowed on my arm. But my story slips away from me as I speak of her. It must have been the night before her rescue that I was awakened about dawn. I had been restless, dreaming most disagreeably that I was drowned, and that sea anemones were feeling over my face with their soft palps. I woke with a start, and with an odd fancy that some greyish animal had just rushed out of the chamber. I tried to get to sleep again, but I felt restless and uncomfortable. It was that dim grey hour when things are just creeping out of darkness, when everything is colourless and clear cut, and yet unreal. I got up, and went down into the great hall, and so out upon the flagstones in front of the palace. I thought I would make a virtue of necessity, and see the sunrise.

"The moon was setting, and the dying moonlight and the first pallor of dawn were mingled in a ghastly half-light. The bushes were inky black, the ground a sombre grey, the sky colourless and cheerless. And up the hill I thought I could see ghosts. Three several times, as I scanned the slope, I saw white figures. Twice I fancied I saw a solitary white, ape-like creature running rather quickly up the hill, and once near the ruins I saw a leash of them carrying some dark body. They moved hastily. I did not see what became of them. It seemed that they vanished among the bushes. The dawn was still indistinct, you must understand. I was feeling that chill, uncertain, early-morning feeling you may have known. I doubted my eyes.

"As the eastern sky grew brighter, and the light of the day came on and its vivid colouring returned upon the world once more, I scanned the view keenly. But I saw no vestige of my white figures. They were mere creatures of the half-light. 'They must have been ghosts,' I said; 'I wonder whence they dated.' For a queer notion of Grant Allen's came into my head, and amused me. If each generation die and leave ghosts, he argued, the world at last will get overcrowded with them. On that theory they would have grown innumerable some Eight Hundred Thousand Years hence, and it was no great wonder to see four at once. But the jest was unsatisfying, and I was thinking of these figures all the morning, until Weena's rescue drove them out of my head. I associated them in some indefinite way with the white animal I had startled

44

in my first passionate search for the Time Machine. But Weena was a pleasant substitute. Yet all the same, they were soon destined to take far deadlier possession of my mind.

"I think I have said how much hotter than our own was the weather of this Golden Age. I cannot account for it. It may be that the sun was hotter, or the earth nearer the sun. It is usual to assume that the sun will go on cooling steadily in the future. But people, unfamiliar with such speculations as those of the younger Darwin, forget that the planets must ultimately fall back one by one into the parent body. As these catastrophes occur, the sun will blaze with renewed energy; and it may be that some inner planet had suffered this fate. Whatever the reason, the fact remains that the sun was very much hotter than we know it.

"Well, one very hot morning—my fourth, I think—as I was seeking shelter from the heat and glare in a colossal ruin near the great house where I slept and fed, there happened this strange thing. Clambering among these heaps of masonry, I found a narrow gallery, whose end and side windows were blocked by fallen masses of stone. By contrast with the brilliancy outside, it seemed at first impenetrably dark to me. I entered it groping, for the change from light to blackness made spots of colour swim before me. Suddenly I halted spellbound. A pair of eyes, luminous by reflection against the daylight without, was watching me out of the darkness.

"The old instinctive dread of wild beasts came upon me. I clenched my hands and steadfastly looked into the glaring eyeballs. I was afraid to turn. Then the thought of the absolute security in which humanity appeared to be living came to my mind. And then I remembered that strange terror of the dark. Overcoming my fear to some extent, I advanced a step and spoke. I will admit that my voice was harsh and ill-controlled. I put out my hand and touched something soft. At once the eyes darted sideways, and something white ran past me. I turned with my heart in my mouth, and saw a queer little ape-like figure, its head held down in a peculiar manner, running across the sunlit space behind me. It blundered against a block of granite, staggered aside, and in a moment was hidden in a black shadow beneath another pile of ruined masonry.

"My impression of it is, of course, imperfect; but I know it was a dull white, and had strange large greyish-red eyes; also, that there was flaxen hair on its head and down its back. But, as I say, it went too fast for me to see distinctly. I cannot even say whether it ran on all fours, or

only with its forearms held very low. After an instant's pause I followed it into the second heap of ruins. I could not find it at first; but, after a time in the profound obscurity, I came upon one of those round well-like openings of which I have told you, half closed by a fallen pillar. A sudden thought came to me. Could this Thing have vanished down the shaft? I lit a match, and, looking down, I saw a small, white, moving creature, with large bright eyes which regarded me steadfastly as it retreated. It made me shudder. It was so like a human spider! It was clambering down the wall, and now I saw for the first time a number of metal foot and hand rests forming a kind of ladder down the shaft. Then the light burned my fingers and fell out of my hand, going out as it dropped, and when I had lit another the little monster had disappeared.

"I do not know how long I sat peering down that well. It was not for some time that I could succeed in persuading myself that the thing I had seen was human. But, gradually, the truth dawned on me: that Man had not remained one species, but had differentiated into two distinct animals: that my graceful children of the Upper World were not the sole descendants of our generation, but that this bleached, obscene, nocturnal Thing, which had flashed before me, was also heir to all the ages.

"I thought of the flickering pillars and of my theory of an under-ground ventilation. I began to suspect their true import. And what, I wondered, was this Lemur doing in my scheme of a perfectly bal-anced organisation? How was it related to the indolent serenity of the beautiful Overworlders? And what was hidden down there, at the foot of that shaft? I sat upon the edge of the well telling myself that, at any rate, there was nothing to fear, and that there I must descend for the solution of my difficulties. And withal I was absolutely afraid to go! As I hesitated, two of the beautiful upperworld people came running in their amorous sport across the daylight in the shadow. The male pursued the female, flinging flowers at her as he ran.

"They seemed distressed to find me, my arm against the over-turned pillar, peering down the well. Apparently, it was considered bad form to remark these apertures; for when I pointed to this one, and tried to frame a question about it in their tongue, they were still more visibly distressed and turned away. But they were interested by my matches, and I struck some to amuse them. I tried them again about the well, and again I failed. So presently I left them, meaning to go back to Weena, and see what I could get from her. But my mind was

already in revolution; my guesses and impressions were slipping and sliding to a new adjustment. I had now a clue to the import of these wells, to the ventilating towers, to the mystery of the ghosts; to say nothing of a hint at the meaning of the bronze gates and the fate of the Time Machine! And very vaguely there came a suggestion towards the solution of the economic problem that had puzzled me.

"Here was the new view. Plainly, this second species of Man was subterranean. There were three circumstances in particular which made me think that its rare emergence above ground was the outcome of a long-continued underground habit. In the first place, there was the bleached look common in most animals that live largely in the dark—the white fish of the Kentucky caves, for instance. Then, those large eyes, with that capacity for reflecting light, are common features of nocturnal things—witness the owl and the cat. And last of all, that evident confusion in the sunshine, that hasty yet fumbling awkward flight towards dark shadow, and that peculiar carriage of the head while in the light—all reinforced the theory of an extreme sensitiveness of the retina.

"Beneath my feet, then, the earth must be tunnelled enormously, and these tunnellings were the habitat of the New Race. The presence of ventilating shafts and wells along the hill slopes—everywhere, in fact, except along the river valley—showed how universal were its ramifications. What so natural, then, as to assume that it was in this artificial Underworld that such work as was necessary to the comfort of the daylight race was done? The notion was so plausible that I at once accepted it, and went on to assume the *how* of this splitting of the human species. I dare say you will anticipate the shape of my theory; though, for myself, I very soon felt that it fell far short of the truth.

"At first, proceeding from the problems of our own age, it seemed clear as daylight to me that the gradual widening of the present merely temporary and social difference between the Capitalist and the Labourer was the key to the whole position. No doubt it will seem grotesque enough to you—and wildly incredible!—and yet even now there are existing circumstances to point that way. There is a tendency to utilise underground space for the less ornamental purposes of civilisation; there is the Metropolitan Railway in London, for instance, there are new electric railways, there are subways, there are underground workrooms and restaurants, and they increase and multiply. Evidently, I thought, this tendency had increased till Industry had gradually lost its birthright in the sky. I mean that it had gone deeper

and deeper into larger and ever larger underground factories, spending a still-increasing amount of its time therein, till, in the end—! Even now, does not an East-end worker live in such artificial conditions as practically to be cut off from the natural surface of the earth?

"Again, the exclusive tendency of richer people—due, no doubt, to the increasing refinement of their education, and the widening gulf between them and the rude violence of the poor—is already leading to the closing, in their interest, of considerable portions of the surface of the land. About London, for instance, perhaps half the prettier country is shut in against intrusion. And this same widening gulf—which is due to the length and expense of the higher educational process and the increased facilities for and temptations towards refined habits on the part of the rich—will make that exchange between class and class, that promotion by intermarriage which at present retards the splitting of our species along lines of social stratification, less and less frequent.

"So, in the end, above ground you must have the Haves, pursuing pleasure and comfort and beauty, and below ground the Have-nots, the Workers getting continually adapted to the conditions of their labour. Once they were there, they would no doubt have to pay rent, and not a little of it, for the ventilation of their caverns; and if they refused, they would starve or be suffocated for arrears. Such of them as were so constituted as to be miserable and rebellious would die; and, in the end, the balance being permanent, the survivors would become as well adapted to the conditions of underground life, and as happy in their way, as the Overworld people were to theirs. As it seemed to me, the refined beauty and the etiolated pallor followed naturally enough.

"The great triumph of Humanity I had dreamed of took a different shape in my mind. It had been no such triumph of moral education and general co-operation as I had imagined. Instead, I saw a real aristocracy, armed with a perfected science and working to a logical conclusion the industrial system of today. Its triumph had not been simply a triumph over Nature, but a triumph over Nature and the fellow-man. This, I must warn you, was my theory at the time. I had no convenient cicerone in the pattern of the Utopian books. My explanation may be absolutely wrong. I still think it is the most plausible one. But even on this supposition the balanced civilisation that was at last attained must have long since passed its zenith, and was now far fallen into decay. The too-perfect security of the Overworlders had led them to a slow movement of degeneration, to a general dwindling in size, strength, and intelligence. That I could see clearly enough al-

ready. What had happened to the Undergrounders I did not yet suspect; but, from what I had seen of the Morlocks—that, by the bye, was the name by which these creatures were called—I could imagine that the modification of the human type was even far more profound than among the 'Eloi,' the beautiful race that I already knew.

"Then came troublesome doubts. Why had the Morlocks taken my Time Machine? For I felt sure it was they who had taken it. Why, too, if the Eloi were masters, could they not restore the machine to me? And why were they so terribly afraid of the dark? I proceeded, as I have said, to question Weena about this Underworld, but here again I was disappointed. At first, she would not understand my questions, and presently she refused to answer them. She shivered as though the topic was unendurable. And when I pressed her, perhaps a little harshly, she burst into tears. They were the only tears, except my own, I ever saw in that Golden Age. When I saw them, I ceased abruptly to trouble about the Morlocks, and was only concerned in banishing these signs of her human inheritance from Weena's eyes. And very soon she was smiling and clapping her hands, while I solemnly burnt a match.

CHAPTER 9

The Morlocks

"It may seem odd to you, but it was two days before I could follow up the new-found clue in what was manifestly the proper way. I felt a peculiar shrinking from those pallid bodies. They were just the half-bleached colour of the worms and things one sees preserved in spirit in a zoological museum. And they were filthily cold to the touch. Probably my shrinking was largely due to the sympathetic influence of the Eloi, whose disgust of the Morlocks I now began to appreciate.

"The next night I did not sleep well. Probably my health was a little disordered. I was oppressed with perplexity and doubt. Once or twice I had a feeling of intense fear for which I could perceive no definite reason. I remember creeping noiselessly into the great hall where the little people were sleeping in the moonlight—that night Weena was among them—and feeling reassured by their presence. It occurred to me even then, that in the course of a few days the moon must pass through its last quarter, and the nights grow dark, when the appearances of these unpleasant creatures from below, these whitened Lemurs, this new vermin that had replaced the old, might be more abundant.

"And on both these days I had the restless feeling of one who shirks

an inevitable duty. I felt assured that the Time Machine was only to be recovered by boldly penetrating these mysteries of underground. Yet I could not face the mystery. If only I had had a companion it would have been different. But I was so horribly alone, and even to clamber down into the darkness of the well appalled me. I don't know if you will understand my feeling, but I never felt quite safe at my back.

"It was this restlessness, this insecurity, perhaps, that drove me farther and farther afield in my exploring expeditions. Going to the south-westward towards the rising country that is now called Combe Wood, I observed far-off, in the direction of nineteenth-century Banstead, a vast green structure, different in character from any I had hitherto seen. It was larger than the largest of the palaces or ruins I knew, and the *façade* had an Oriental look: the face of it having the lustre, as well as the pale-green tint, a kind of bluish-green, of a certain type of Chinese porcelain. This difference in aspect suggested a difference in use, and I was minded to push on and explore.

"But the day was growing late, and I had come upon the sight of the place after a long and tiring circuit; so, I resolved to hold over the adventure for the following day, and I returned to the welcome and the caresses of little Weena. But next morning I perceived clearly enough that my curiosity regarding the Palace of Green Porcelain was a piece of self-deception, to enable me to shirk, by another day, an experience I dreaded. I resolved I would make the descent without further waste of time, and started out in the early morning towards a well near the ruins of granite and aluminium.

"Little Weena ran with me. She danced beside me to the well, but when she saw me lean over the mouth and look downward, she seemed strangely disconcerted. 'Goodbye, little Weena,' I said, kissing her; and then putting her down, I began to feel over the parapet for the climbing hooks. Rather hastily, I may as well confess, for I feared my courage might leak away! At first, she watched me in amazement. Then she gave a most piteous cry, and running to me, she began to pull at me with her little hands. I think her opposition nerved me rather to proceed. I shook her off, perhaps a little roughly, and in another moment, I was in the throat of the well. I saw her agonised face over the parapet, and smiled to reassure her. Then I had to look down at the unstable hooks to which I clung.

"I had to clamber down a shaft of perhaps two hundred yards. The descent was effected by means of metallic bars projecting from the sides of the well, and these being adapted to the needs of a creature

much smaller and lighter than myself, I was speedily cramped and fatigued by the descent. And not simply fatigued! One of the bars bent suddenly under my weight, and almost swung me off into the blackness beneath. For a moment I hung by one hand, and after that experience I did not dare to rest again. Though my arms and back were presently acutely painful, I went on clambering down the sheer descent with as quick a motion as possible. Glancing upward, I saw the aperture, a small blue disc, in which a star was visible, while little Weena's head showed as a round black projection. The thudding sound of a machine below grew louder and more oppressive. Everything save that little disc above was profoundly dark, and when I looked up again Weena had disappeared.

"I was in an agony of discomfort. I had some thought of trying to go up the shaft again, and leave the Underworld alone. But even while I turned this over in my mind I continued to descend. At last, with intense relief, I saw dimly coming up, a foot to the right of me, a slender loophole in the wall. Swinging myself in, I found it was the aperture of a narrow horizontal tunnel in which I could lie down and rest. It was not too soon. My arms ached, my back was cramped, and I was trembling with the prolonged terror of a fall. Besides this, the unbroken darkness had had a distressing effect upon my eyes. The air was full of the throb and hum of machinery pumping air down the shaft.

"I do not know how long I lay. I was aroused by a soft hand touching my face. Starting up in the darkness I snatched at my matches and, hastily striking one, I saw three stooping white creatures similar to the one I had seen above ground in the ruin, hastily retreating before the light. Living, as they did, in what appeared to me impenetrable darkness, their eyes were abnormally large and sensitive, just as are the pupils of the abysmal fishes, and they reflected the light in the same way. I have no doubt they could see me in that rayless obscurity, and they did not seem to have any fear of me apart from the light. But, so soon as I struck a match in order to see them, they fled incontinently, vanishing into dark gutters and tunnels, from which their eyes glared at me in the strangest fashion.

"I tried to call to them, but the language they had was apparently different from that of the Overworld people; so that I was needs left to my own unaided efforts, and the thought of flight before exploration was even then in my mind. But I said to myself, 'You are in for it now,' and, feeling my way along the tunnel, I found the noise of machinery grow louder. Presently the walls fell away from me, and I came to a

large open space, and striking another match, saw that I had entered a vast arched cavern, which stretched into utter darkness beyond the range of my light. The view I had of it was as much as one could see in the burning of a match.

"Necessarily my memory is vague. Great shapes like big machines rose out of the dimness, and cast grotesque black shadows, in which dim spectral Morlocks sheltered from the glare. The place, by the bye, was very stuffy and oppressive, and the faint halitus of freshly-shed blood was in the air. Some way down the central vista was a little table of white metal, laid with what seemed a meal. The Morlocks at any rate were carnivorous! Even at the time, I remember wondering what large animal could have survived to furnish the red joint I saw. It was all very indistinct: the heavy smell, the big unmeaning shapes, the obscene figures lurking in the shadows, and only waiting for the darkness to come at me again! Then the match burnt down, and stung my fingers, and fell, a wriggling red spot in the blackness.

"I have thought since how particularly ill-equipped I was for such an experience. When I had started with the Time Machine, I had started with the absurd assumption that the men of the Future would certainly be infinitely ahead of ourselves in all their appliances. I had come without arms, without medicine, without anything to smoke— at times I missed tobacco frightfully!—even without enough matches. If only I had thought of a Kodak! I could have flashed that glimpse of the Underworld in a second, and examined it at leisure. But, as it was, I stood there with only the weapons and the powers that Nature had endowed me with—hands, feet, and teeth; these, and four safety-matches that still remained to me.

"I was afraid to push my way in among all this machinery in the dark, and it was only with my last glimpse of light I discovered that my store of matches had run low. It had never occurred to me until that moment that there was any need to economise them, and I had wasted almost half the box in astonishing the Overworlders, to whom fire was a novelty. Now, as I say, I had four left, and while I stood in the dark, a hand touched mine, lank fingers came feeling over my face, and I was sensible of a peculiar unpleasant odour. I fancied I heard the breathing of a crowd of those dreadful little beings about me. I felt the box of matches in my hand being gently disengaged, and other hands behind me plucking at my clothing. The sense of these unseen creatures ex-amining me was indescribably unpleasant. The sudden realisation of my ignorance of their ways of thinking and doing came home to me

very vividly in the darkness. I shouted at them as loudly as I could. They started away, and then I could feel them approaching me again.

"They clutched at me more boldly, whispering odd sounds to each other. I shivered violently, and shouted again—rather discordantly. This time they were not so seriously alarmed, and they made a queer laughing noise as they came back at me. I will confess I was horribly frightened. I determined to strike another match and escape under the protection of its glare. I did so, and eking out the flicker with a scrap of paper from my pocket, I made good my retreat to the narrow tunnel. But I had scarce entered this when my light was blown out and, in the blackness, I could hear the Morlocks rustling like wind among leaves, and pattering like the rain, as they hurried after me.

"In a moment I was clutched by several hands, and there was no mistaking that they were trying to haul me back. I struck another light, and waved it in their dazzled faces. You can scarce imagine how nauseatingly inhuman they looked—those pale, chinless faces and great, lidless, pinkish-grey eyes!—as they stared in their blindness and bewilderment. But I did not stay to look, I promise you: I retreated again, and when my second match had ended, I struck my third. It had almost burnt through when I reached the opening into the shaft. I lay down on the edge, for the throb of the great pump below made me giddy.

"Then I felt sideways for the projecting hooks, and, as I did so, my feet were grasped from behind, and I was violently tugged backward. I lit my last match. . . .and it incontinently went out. But I had my hand on the climbing bars now, and, kicking violently, I disengaged myself from the clutches of the Morlocks, and was speedily clambering up the shaft, while they stayed peering and blinking up at me: all but one little wretch who followed me for some way, and well-nigh secured my boot as a trophy.

"That climb seemed interminable to me. With the last twenty or thirty feet of it a deadly nausea came upon me. I had the greatest difficulty in keeping my hold. The last few yards was a frightful struggle against this faintness. Several times my head swam, and I felt all the sensations of falling. At last, however, I got over the well-mouth somehow, and staggered out of the ruin into the blinding sunlight. I fell upon my face. Even the soil smelt sweet and clean. Then I remember Weena kissing my hands and ears, and the voices of others among the Eloi. Then, for a time, I was insensible.

When the Night Came

"Now, indeed, I seemed in a worse case than before. Hitherto, except during my night's anguish at the loss of the Time Machine, I had felt a sustaining hope of ultimate escape, but that hope was staggered by these new discoveries. Hitherto I had merely thought myself impeded by the childish simplicity of the little people, and by some unknown forces which I had only to understand to overcome; but there was an altogether new element in the sickening quality of the Morlocks—a something inhuman and malign. Instinctively I loathed them. Before, I had felt as a man might feel who had fallen into a pit: my concern was with the pit and how to get out of it. Now I felt like a beast in a trap, whose enemy would come upon him soon.

"The enemy I dreaded may surprise you. It was the darkness of the new moon. Weena had put this into my head by some at first incomprehensible remarks about the Dark Nights. It was not now such a very difficult problem to guess what the coming Dark Nights might mean. The moon was on the wane: each night there was a longer interval of darkness. And I now understood to some slight degree at least the reason of the fear of the little Upperworld people for the dark. I wondered vaguely what foul villainy it might be that the Morlocks did under the new moon.

"I felt pretty sure now that my second hypothesis was all wrong. The Upperworld people might once have been the favoured aristocracy, and the Morlocks their mechanical servants: but that had long since passed away. The two species that had resulted from the evolution of man were sliding down towards, or had already arrived at, an altogether new relationship. The Eloi, like the Carlovignan kings, had decayed to a mere beautiful futility. They still possessed the earth on sufferance: since the Morlocks, subterranean for innumerable generations, had come at last to find the daylit surface intolerable.

"And the Morlocks made their garments, I inferred, and maintained them in their habitual needs, perhaps through the survival of an old habit of service. They did it as a standing horse paws with his foot, or as a man enjoys killing animals in sport: because ancient and departed necessities had impressed it on the organism. But, clearly, the old order was already in part reversed. The Nemesis of the delicate ones was creeping on apace. Ages ago, thousands of generations ago, man had thrust his brother man out of the ease and the sunshine. And

now that brother was coming back—changed! Already the Eloi had begun to learn one old lesson anew. They were becoming reacquainted with Fear. And suddenly there came into my head the memory of the meat I had seen in the Underworld. It seemed odd how it floated into my mind: not stirred up as it were by the current of my meditations, but coming in almost like a question from outside. I tried to recall the form of it. I had a vague sense of something familiar, but I could not tell what it was at the time.

"Still, however helpless the little people in the presence of their mysterious Fear, I was differently constituted. I came out of this age of ours, this ripe prime of the human race, when Fear does not paralyse and mystery has lost its terrors. I at least would defend myself. Without further delay I determined to make myself arms and a fastness where I might sleep. With that refuge as a base, I could face this strange world with some of that confidence I had lost in realising to what creatures night by night I lay exposed. I felt I could never sleep again until my bed was secure from them. I shuddered with horror to think how they must already have examined me.

"I wandered during the afternoon along the valley of the Thames, but found nothing that commended itself to my mind as inaccessible. All the buildings and trees seemed easily practicable to such dexterous climbers as the Morlocks, to judge by their wells, must be. Then the tall pinnacles of the Palace of Green Porcelain and the polished gleam of its walls came back to my memory; and in the evening, taking Weena like a child upon my shoulder, I went up the hills towards the south-west. The distance, I had reckoned, was seven or eight miles, but it must have been nearer eighteen. I had first seen the place on a moist afternoon when distances are deceptively diminished. In addition, the heel of one of my shoes was loose, and a nail was working through the sole—they were comfortable old shoes I wore about indoors—so that I was lame. And it was already long past sunset when I came in sight of the palace, silhouetted black against the pale yellow of the sky.

"Weena had been hugely delighted when I began to carry her, but after a while she desired me to let her down, and ran along by the side of me, occasionally darting off on either hand to pick flowers to stick in my pockets. My pockets had always puzzled Weena, but at the last she had concluded that they were an eccentric kind of vases for floral decoration. At least she utilised them for that purpose. And that reminds me! In changing my jacket, I found . . ."

The Time Traveller paused, put his hand into his pocket, and silently placed

two withered flowers, not unlike very large white mallows, upon the little table. Then he resumed his narrative.

"As the hush of evening crept over the world and we proceeded over the hill crest towards Wimbledon, Weena grew tired and wanted to return to the house of grey stone. But I pointed out the distant pinnacles of the Palace of Green Porcelain to her, and contrived to make her understand that we were seeking a refuge there from her Fear. You know that great pause that comes upon things before the dusk? Even the breeze stops in the trees. To me there is always an air of expectation about that evening stillness. The sky was clear, remote, and empty save for a few horizontal bars far down in the sunset. Well, that night the expectation took the colour of my fears. In that darkling calm my senses seemed preternaturally sharpened. I fancied I could even feel the hollowness of the ground beneath my feet: could, indeed, almost see through it the Morlocks on their ant-hill going hither and thither and waiting for the dark. In my excitement I fancied that they would receive my invasion of their burrows as a declaration of war. And why had they taken my Time Machine?

"So, we went on in the quiet, and the twilight deepened into night. The clear blue of the distance faded, and one star after another came out. The ground grew dim and the trees black. Weena's fears and her fatigue grew upon her. I took her in my arms and talked to her and caressed her. Then, as the darkness grew deeper, she put her arms round my neck, and, closing her eyes, tightly pressed her face against my shoulder. So, we went down a long slope into a valley, and there in the dimness I almost walked into a little river. This I waded, and went up the opposite side of the valley, past a number of sleeping houses, and by a statue—a Faun, or some such figure, *minus* the head. Here too were acacias. So far, I had seen nothing of the Morlocks, but it was yet early in the night, and the darker hours before the old moon rose were still to come.

"From the brow of the next hill I saw a thick wood spreading wide and black before me. I hesitated at this. I could see no end to it, either to the right or the left. Feeling tired—my feet, in particular, were very sore—I carefully lowered Weena from my shoulder as I halted, and sat down upon the turf. I could no longer see the Palace of Green Porcelain, and I was in doubt of my direction. I looked into the thickness of the wood and thought of what it might hide. Under that dense tangle of branches, one would be out of sight of the stars. Even were there no other lurking danger—a danger I did not care to let my imagination

loose upon—there would still be all the roots to stumble over and the tree-boles to strike against. I was very tired, too, after the excitements of the day; so, I decided that I would not face it, but would pass the night upon the open hill.

"Weena, I was glad to find, was fast asleep. I carefully wrapped her in my jacket, and sat down beside her to wait for the moonrise. The hillside was quiet and deserted, but from the black of the wood there came now and then a stir of living things. Above me shone the stars, for the night was very clear. I felt a certain sense of friendly comfort in their twinkling. All the old constellations had gone from the sky, however: that slow movement which is imperceptible in a hundred human lifetimes, had long since rearranged them in unfamiliar groupings. But the Milky Way, it seemed to me, was still the same tattered streamer of star-dust as of yore. Southward (as I judged it) was a very bright red star that was new to me; it was even more splendid than our own green Sirius. And amid all these scintillating points of light one bright planet shone kindly and steadily like the face of an old friend.

"Looking at these stars suddenly dwarfed my own troubles and all the gravities of terrestrial life. I thought of their unfathomable distance, and the slow inevitable drift of their movements out of the unknown past into the unknown future. I thought of the great precessional cycle that the pole of the earth describes. Only forty times had that silent revolution occurred during all the years that I had traversed. And during these few revolutions all the activity, all the traditions, the complex organisations, the nations, languages, literatures, aspirations, even the mere memory of Man as I knew him, had been swept out of existence. Instead were these frail creatures who had forgotten their high ancestry, and the white Things of which I went in terror.

"Then I thought of the Great Fear that was between the two species, and for the first time, with a sudden shiver, came the clear knowledge of what the meat I had seen might be. Yet it was too horrible! I looked at little Weena sleeping beside me, her face white and starlike under the stars, and forthwith dismissed the thought.

"Through that long night I held my mind off the Morlocks as well as I could, and whiled away the time by trying to fancy I could find signs of the old constellations in the new confusion. The sky kept very clear, except for a hazy cloud or so. No doubt I dozed at times. Then, as my vigil wore on, came a faintness in the eastward sky, like the reflection of some colourless fire, and the old moon rose, thin and peaked and white. And close behind, and overtaking it, and overflow-

ing it, the dawn came, pale at first, and then growing pink and warm. No Morlocks had approached us. Indeed, I had seen none upon the hill that night. And in the confidence of renewed day it almost seemed to me that my fear had been unreasonable. I stood up and found my foot with the loose heel swollen at the ankle and painful under the heel; so, I sat down again, took off my shoes, and flung them away.

"I awakened Weena, and we went down into the wood, now green and pleasant instead of black and forbidding. We found some fruit wherewith to break our fast. We soon met others of the dainty ones, laughing and dancing in the sunlight as though there was no such thing in nature as the night. And then I thought once more of the meat that I had seen. I felt assured now of what it was, and from the bottom of my heart I pitied this last feeble rill from the great flood of humanity. Clearly, at some time in the Long-Ago of human decay the Morlocks' food had run short. Possibly they had lived on rats and such-like vermin.

"Even now man is far less discriminating and exclusive in his food than he was—far less than any monkey. His prejudice against human flesh is no deep-seated instinct. And so, these inhuman sons of men——! I tried to look at the thing in a scientific spirit. After all, they were less human and more remote than our cannibal ancestors of three or four thousand years ago. And the intelligence that would have made this state of things a torment had gone. Why should I trouble myself? These Eloi were mere fatted cattle, which the ant-like Morlocks preserved and preyed upon—probably saw to the breeding of. And there was Weena dancing at my side!

"Then I tried to preserve myself from the horror that was coming upon me, by regarding it as a rigorous punishment of human selfishness. Man had been content to live in ease and delight upon the labours of his fellow-man, had taken Necessity as his watchword and excuse, and in the fullness of time Necessity had come home to him. I even tried a Carlyle-like scorn of this wretched aristocracy in decay. But this attitude of mind was impossible. However great their intellectual degradation, the Eloi had kept too much of the human form not to claim my sympathy, and to make me perforce a sharer in their degradation and their Fear.

"I had at that time very vague ideas as to the course I should pursue. My first was to secure some safe place of refuge, and to make myself such arms of metal or stone as I could contrive. That necessity was immediate. In the next place, I hoped to procure some means of

fire, so that I should have the weapon of a torch at hand, for nothing, I knew, would be more efficient against these Morlocks. Then I wanted to arrange some contrivance to break open the doors of bronze under the White Sphinx. I had in mind a battering ram. I had a persuasion that if I could enter those doors and carry a blaze of light before me, I should discover the Time Machine and escape. I could not imagine the Morlocks were strong enough to move it far away. Weena I had resolved to bring with me to our own time. And turning such schemes over in my mind I pursued our way towards the building which my fancy had chosen as our dwelling.

CHAPTER 11

The Palace of Green Porcelain

"I found the Palace of Green Porcelain, when we approached it about noon, deserted and falling into ruin. Only ragged vestiges of glass remained in its windows, and great sheets of the green facing had fallen away from the corroded metallic framework. It lay very high upon a turfy down, and looking north-eastward before I entered it, I was surprised to see a large estuary, or even creek, where I judged Wandsworth and Battersea must once have been. I thought then— though I never followed up the thought—of what might have happened, or might be happening, to the living things in the sea.

"The material of the Palace proved on examination to be indeed porcelain, and along the face of it I saw an inscription in some unknown character. I thought, rather foolishly, that Weena might help me to interpret this, but I only learnt that the bare idea of writing had never entered her head. She always seemed to me, I fancy, more human than she was, perhaps because her affection was so human.

"Within the big valves of the door—which were open and broken—we found, instead of the customary hall, a long gallery lit by many side windows. At the first glance I was reminded of a museum. The tiled floor was thick with dust, and a remarkable array of miscellaneous objects was shrouded in the same grey covering. Then I perceived, standing strange and gaunt in the centre of the hall, what was clearly the lower part of a huge skeleton. I recognised by the oblique feet that it was some extinct creature after the fashion of the Megatherium. The skull and the upper bones lay beside it in the thick dust, and in one place, where rain-water had dropped through a leak in the roof, the thing itself had been worn away. Further in the gallery was the huge skeleton barrel of a Brontosaurus. My museum hypothesis

was confirmed. Going towards the side I found what appeared to be sloping shelves, and clearing away the thick dust, I found the old familiar glass cases of our own time. But they must have been air-tight to judge from the fair preservation of some of their contents.

"Clearly we stood among the ruins of some latter-day South Kensington! Here, apparently, was the Palaeontological Section, and a very splendid array of fossils it must have been, though the inevitable process of decay that had been staved off for a time, and had, through the extinction of bacteria and fungi, lost ninety-nine hundredths of its force, was nevertheless, with extreme sureness if with extreme slowness at work again upon all its treasures. Here and there I found traces of the little people in the shape of rare fossils broken to pieces or threaded in strings upon reeds. And the cases had in some instances been bodily removed—by the Morlocks, as I judged. The place was very silent. The thick dust deadened our footsteps. Weena, who had been rolling a sea urchin down the sloping glass of a case, presently came, as I stared about me, and very quietly took my hand and stood beside me.

"And at first I was so much surprised by this ancient monument of an intellectual age that I gave no thought to the possibilities it presented. Even my preoccupation about the Time Machine receded a little from my mind.

"To judge from the size of the place, this Palace of Green Porcelain had a great deal more in it than a Gallery of Palaeontology; possibly historical galleries; it might be, even a library! To me, at least in my present circumstances, these would be vastly more interesting than this spectacle of old-time geology in decay. Exploring, I found another short gallery running transversely to the first. This appeared to be devoted to minerals, and the sight of a block of sulphur set my mind running on gunpowder. But I could find no saltpetre; indeed, no nitrates of any kind. Doubtless they had deliquesced ages ago. Yet the sulphur hung in my mind, and set up a train of thinking. As for the rest of the contents of that gallery, though on the whole they were the best preserved of all I saw, I had little interest.

"I am no specialist in mineralogy, and I went on down a very ruinous aisle running parallel to the first hall I had entered. Apparently, this section had been devoted to natural history, but everything had long since passed out of recognition. A few shrivelled and blackened vestiges of what had once been stuffed animals, desiccated mummies in jars that had once held spirit, a brown dust of departed plants: that

was all! I was sorry for that, because I should have been glad to trace the patient readjustments by which the conquest of animated nature had been attained. Then we came to a gallery of simply colossal proportions, but singularly ill-lit, the floor of it running downward at a slight angle from the end at which I entered.

"At intervals white globes hung from the ceiling—many of them cracked and smashed—which suggested that originally the place had been artificially lit. Here I was more in my element, for rising on either side of me were the huge bulks of big machines, all greatly corroded and many broken down, but some still fairly complete. You know I have a certain weakness for mechanism, and I was inclined to linger among these; the more so as for the most part they had the interest of puzzles, and I could make only the vaguest guesses at what they were for. I fancied that if I could solve their puzzles, I should find myself in possession of powers that might be of use against the Morlocks.

"Suddenly Weena came very close to my side. So suddenly that she startled me. Had it not been for her I do not think I should have noticed that the floor of the gallery sloped at all. (It may be, of course, that the floor did not slope, but that the museum was built into the side of a hill.) The end I had come in at was quite above ground, and was lit by rare slit-like windows. As you went down the length, the ground came up against these windows, until at last there was a pit like the 'area' of a London house before each, and only a narrow line of daylight at the top. I went slowly along, puzzling about the machines, and had been too intent upon them to notice the gradual diminution of the light, until Weena's increasing apprehensions drew my attention.

"Then I saw that the gallery ran down at last into a thick darkness. I hesitated, and then, as I looked round me, I saw that the dust was less abundant and its surface less even. Further away towards the dimness, it appeared to be broken by a number of small narrow footprints. My sense of the immediate presence of the Morlocks revived at that. I felt that I was wasting my time in the academic examination of machinery. I called to mind that it was already far advanced in the afternoon, and that I had still no weapon, no refuge, and no means of making a fire. And then down in the remote blackness of the gallery I heard a peculiar pattering, and the same odd noises I had heard down the well.

"I took Weena's hand. Then, struck with a sudden idea, I left her and turned to a machine from which projected a lever not unlike those in a signal-box. Clambering upon the stand, and grasping this lever in my hands, I put all my weight upon it sideways. Suddenly

Weena, deserted in the central aisle, began to whimper. I had judged the strength of the lever pretty correctly, for it snapped after a minute's strain, and I rejoined her with a mace in my hand more than sufficient, I judged, for any Morlock skull I might encounter. And I longed very much to kill a Morlock or so. Very inhuman, you may think, to want to go killing one's own descendants! But it was impossible, somehow, to feel any humanity in the things. Only my disinclination to leave Weena, and a persuasion that if I began to slake my thirst for murder my Time Machine might suffer, restrained me from going straight down the gallery and killing the brutes I heard.

"Well, mace in one hand and Weena in the other, I went out of that gallery and into another and still larger one, which at the first glance reminded me of a military chapel hung with tattered flags. The brown and charred rags that hung from the sides of it, I presently recognised as the decaying vestiges of books. They had long since dropped to pieces, and every semblance of print had left them. But here and there were warped boards and cracked metallic clasps that told the tale well enough. Had I been a literary man I might, perhaps, have moralised upon the futility of all ambition. But as it was, the thing that struck me with keenest force was the enormous waste of labour to which this sombre wilderness of rotting paper testified. At the time I will confess that I thought chiefly of the *Philosophical Transactions* and my own seventeen papers upon physical optics.

"Then, going up a broad staircase, we came to what may once have been a gallery of technical chemistry. And here I had not a little hope of useful discoveries. Except at one end where the roof had collapsed, this gallery was well preserved. I went eagerly to every unbroken case. And at last, in one of the really air-tight cases, I found a box of matches. Very eagerly I tried them. They were perfectly good. They were not even damp. I turned to Weena. 'Dance,' I cried to her in her own tongue. For now, I had a weapon indeed against the horrible creatures we feared. And so, in that derelict museum, upon the thick soft carpeting of dust, to Weena's huge delight, I solemnly performed a kind of composite dance, whistling *The Land of the Leal* as cheerfully as I could. In part it was a modest *cancan*, in part a step dance, in part a skirt dance (so far as my tail-coat permitted), and in part original. For I am naturally inventive, as you know.

"Now, I still think that for this box of matches to have escaped the wear of time for immemorial years was a most strange, as for me it was a most fortunate, thing. Yet, oddly enough, I found a far unlikelier sub-

stance, and that was camphor. I found it in a sealed jar, that by chance, I suppose, had been really hermetically sealed. I fancied at first that it was paraffin wax, and smashed the glass accordingly. But the odour of camphor was unmistakable. In the universal decay this volatile substance had chanced to survive, perhaps through many thousands of centuries. It reminded me of a sepia painting I had once seen done from the ink of a fossil Belemnite that must have perished and become fossilised millions of years ago. I was about to throw it away, but I remembered that it was inflammable and burnt with a good bright flame—was, in fact, an excellent candle—and I put it in my pocket. I found no explosives, however, nor any means of breaking down the bronze doors. As yet my iron crowbar was the most helpful thing I had chanced upon. Nevertheless, I left that gallery greatly elated.

"I cannot tell you all the story of that long afternoon. It would require a great effort of memory to recall my explorations in at all the proper order. I remember a long gallery of rusting stands of arms, and how I hesitated between my crowbar and a hatchet or a sword. I could not carry both, however, and my bar of iron promised best against the bronze gates. There were numbers of guns, pistols, and rifles. The most were masses of rust, but many were of some new metal, and still fairly sound. But any cartridges or powder there may once have been had rotted into dust. One corner I saw was charred and shattered; perhaps, I thought, by an explosion among the specimens. In another place was a vast array of idols—Polynesian, Mexican, Grecian, Phoenician, every country on earth, I should think. And here, yielding to an irresistible impulse, I wrote my name upon the nose of a steatite monster from South America that particularly took my fancy.

"As the evening drew on, my interest waned. I went through gallery after gallery, dusty, silent, often ruinous, the exhibits sometimes mere heaps of rust and lignite, sometimes fresher. In one place I suddenly found myself near the model of a tin mine, and then by the merest accident I discovered, in an air-tight case, two dynamite cartridges! I shouted 'Eureka!' and smashed the case with joy. Then came a doubt. I hesitated. Then, selecting a little side gallery, I made my essay. I never felt such a disappointment as I did in waiting five, ten, fifteen minutes for an explosion that never came. Of course, the things were dummies, as I might have guessed from their presence. I really believe that had they not been so, I should have rushed off incontinently and blown Sphinx, bronze doors, and (as it proved) my chances of finding the Time Machine, all together into non-existence.

"It was after that, I think, that we came to a little open court within the palace. It was turfed, and had three fruit-trees. So, we rested and refreshed ourselves. Towards sunset I began to consider our position. Night was creeping upon us, and my inaccessible hiding-place had still to be found. But that troubled me very little now. I had in my possession a thing that was, perhaps, the best of all defences against the Morlocks—I had matches! I had the camphor in my pocket, too, if a blaze were needed. It seemed to me that the best thing we could do would be to pass the night in the open, protected by a fire. In the morning there was the getting of the Time Machine. Towards that, as yet, I had only my iron mace. But now, with my growing knowledge, I felt very differently towards those bronze doors. Up to this, I had refrained from forcing them, largely because of the mystery on the other side. They had never impressed me as being very strong, and I hoped to find my bar of iron not altogether inadequate for the work.

Chapter 12
In the Darkness

"We emerged from the Palace while the sun was still in part above the horizon. I was determined to reach the White Sphinx early the next morning, and ere the dusk I purposed pushing through the woods that had stopped me on the previous journey. My plan was to go as far as possible that night, and then, building a fire, to sleep in the protection of its glare. Accordingly, as we went along, I gathered any sticks or dried grass I saw, and presently had my arms full of such litter. Thus loaded, our progress was slower than I had anticipated, and besides Weena was tired. And I, also, began to suffer from sleepiness too; so that it was full night before we reached the wood. Upon the shrubby hill of its edge Weena would have stopped, fearing the darkness before us; but a singular sense of impending calamity, that should indeed have served me as a warning, drove me onward. I had been without sleep for a night and two days, and I was feverish and irritable. I felt sleep coming upon me, and the Morlocks with it.

"While we hesitated, among the black bushes behind us, and dim against their blackness, I saw three crouching figures. There was scrub and long grass all about us, and I did not feel safe from their insidious approach. The forest, I calculated, was rather less than a mile across. If we could get through it to the bare hillside, there, as it seemed to me, was an altogether safer resting-place; I thought that with my matches and my camphor I could contrive to keep my path illuminated

through the woods. Yet it was evident that if I was to flourish matches with my hands, I should have to abandon my firewood; so, rather reluctantly, I put it down. And then it came into my head that I would amaze our friends behind by lighting it. I was to discover the atrocious folly of this proceeding, but it came to my mind as an ingenious move for covering our retreat.

"I don't know if you have ever thought what a rare thing flame must be in the absence of man and in a temperate climate. The sun's heat is rarely strong enough to burn, even when it is focused by dewdrops, as is sometimes the case in more tropical districts. Lightning may blast and blacken, but it rarely gives rise to widespread fire. Decaying vegetation may occasionally smoulder with the heat of its fermentation, but this rarely results in flame. In this decadence, too, the art of fire-making had been forgotten on the earth. The red tongues that went licking up my heap of wood were an altogether new and strange thing to Weena.

"She wanted to run to it and play with it. I believe she would have cast herself into it had I not restrained her. But I caught her up, and in spite of her struggles, plunged boldly before me into the wood. For a little way the glare of my fire lit the path. Looking back presently, I could see, through the crowded stems, that from my heap of sticks the blaze had spread to some bushes adjacent, and a curved line of fire was creeping up the grass of the hill. I laughed at that, and turned again to the dark trees before me. It was very black, and Weena clung to me convulsively, but there was still, as my eyes grew accustomed to the darkness, sufficient light for me to avoid the stems. Overhead it was simply black, except where a gap of remote blue sky shone down upon us here and there. I lit none of my matches because I had no hand free. Upon my left arm I carried my little one, in my right hand I had my iron bar.

"For some way I heard nothing but the crackling twigs under my feet, the faint rustle of the breeze above, and my own breathing and the throb of the blood-vessels in my ears. Then I seemed to know of a pattering behind me. I pushed on grimly. The pattering grew more distinct, and then I caught the same queer sound and voices I had heard in the Underworld. There were evidently several of the Morlocks, and they were closing in upon me. Indeed, in another minute I felt a tug at my coat, then something at my arm. And Weena shivered violently, and became quite still.

"It was time for a match. But to get one I must put her down.

I did so, and, as I fumbled with my pocket, a struggle began in the darkness about my knees, perfectly silent on her part and with the same peculiar cooing sounds from the Morlocks. Soft little hands, too, were creeping over my coat and back, touching even my neck. Then the match scratched and fizzed. I held it flaring, and saw the white backs of the Morlocks in flight amid the trees. I hastily took a lump of camphor from my pocket, and prepared to light it as soon as the match should wane. Then I looked at Weena. She was lying clutching my feet and quite motionless, with her face to the ground. With a sudden fright I stooped to her. She seemed scarcely to breathe. I lit the block of camphor and flung it to the ground, and as it split and flared up and drove back the Morlocks and the shadows, I knelt down and lifted her. The wood behind seemed full of the stir and murmur of a great company!

"She seemed to have fainted. I put her carefully upon my shoulder and rose to push on, and then there came a horrible realisation. In manoeuvring with my matches and Weena, I had turned myself about several times, and now I had not the faintest idea in what direction lay my path. For all I knew, I might be facing back towards the Palace of Green Porcelain. I found myself in a cold sweat. I had to think rapidly what to do. I determined to build a fire and encamp where we were. I put Weena, still motionless, down upon a turfy bole, and very hastily, as my first lump of camphor waned, I began collecting sticks and leaves. Here and there out of the darkness round me the Morlocks' eyes shone like carbuncles.

"The camphor flickered and went out. I lit a match, and as I did so, two white forms that had been approaching Weena dashed hastily away. One was so blinded by the light that he came straight for me, and I felt his bones grind under the blow of my fist. He gave a whoop of dismay, staggered a little way, and fell down. I lit another piece of camphor, and went on gathering my bonfire. Presently I noticed how dry was some of the foliage above me, for since my arrival on the Time Machine, a matter of a week, no rain had fallen. So, instead of casting about among the trees for fallen twigs, I began leaping up and dragging down branches. Very soon I had a choking smoky fire of green wood and dry sticks, and could economise my camphor. Then I turned to where Weena lay beside my iron mace. I tried what I could to revive her, but she lay like one dead. I could not even satisfy myself whether or not she breathed.

"Now, the smoke of the fire beat over towards me, and it must have

made me heavy of a sudden. Moreover, the vapour of camphor was in the air. My fire would not need replenishing for an hour or so. I felt very weary after my exertion, and sat down. The wood, too, was full of a slumberous murmur that I did not understand. I seemed just to nod and open my eyes. But all was dark, and the Morlocks had their hands upon me. Flinging off their clinging fingers I hastily felt in my pocket for the matchbox, and—it had gone! Then they gripped and closed with me again.

"In a moment I knew what had happened. I had slept, and my fire had gone out, and the bitterness of death came over my soul. The forest seemed full of the smell of burning wood. I was caught by the neck, by the hair, by the arms, and pulled down. It was indescribably horrible in the darkness to feel all these soft creatures heaped upon me. I felt as if I was in a monstrous spider's web. I was overpowered, and went down. I felt little teeth nipping at my neck. I rolled over, and as I did so my hand came against my iron lever. It gave me strength. I struggled up, shaking the human rats from me, and, holding the bar short, I thrust where I judged their faces might be. I could feel the succulent giving of flesh and bone under my blows, and for a moment I was free.

"The strange exultation that so often seems to accompany hard fighting came upon me. I knew that both I and Weena were lost, but I determined to make the Morlocks pay for their meat. I stood with my back to a tree, swinging the iron bar before me. The whole wood was full of the stir and cries of them. A minute passed. Their voices seemed to rise to a higher pitch of excitement, and their movements grew faster. Yet none came within reach. I stood glaring at the blackness. Then suddenly came hope. What if the Morlocks were afraid? And close on the heels of that came a strange thing. The darkness seemed to grow luminous.

"Very dimly I began to see the Morlocks about me—three battered at my feet—and then I recognised, with incredulous surprise, that the others were running, in an incessant stream, as it seemed, from behind me, and away through the wood in front. And their backs seemed no longer white, but reddish. As I stood agape, I saw a little red spark go drifting across a gap of starlight between the branches, and vanish. And at that I understood the smell of burning wood, the slumberous murmur that was growing now into a gusty roar, the red glow, and the Morlocks' flight.

"Stepping out from behind my tree and looking back, I saw,

through the black pillars of the nearer trees, the flames of the burning forest. It was my first fire coming after me. With that I looked for Weena, but she was gone. The hissing and crackling behind me, the explosive thud as each fresh tree burst into flame, left little time for reflection. My iron bar still gripped, I followed in the Morlocks' path. It was a close race. Once the flames crept forward so swiftly on my right as I ran that I was outflanked and had to strike off to the left. But at last I emerged upon a small open space, and as I did so, a Morlock came blundering towards me, and past me, and went on straight into the fire!

"And now I was to see the most weird and horrible thing, I think, of all that I beheld in that future age. This whole space was as bright as day with the reflection of the fire. In the centre was a hillock or tumulus, surmounted by a scorched hawthorn. Beyond this was another arm of the burning forest, with yellow tongues already writhing from it, completely encircling the space with a fence of fire. Upon the hillside were some thirty or forty Morlocks, dazzled by the light and heat, and blundering hither and thither against each other in their bewilderment. At first, I did not realise their blindness, and struck furiously at them with my bar, in a frenzy of fear, as they approached me, killing one and crippling several more. But when I had watched the gestures of one of them groping under the hawthorn against the red sky, and heard their moans, I was assured of their absolute helplessness and misery in the glare, and I struck no more of them.

"Yet every now and then one would come straight towards me, setting loose a quivering horror that made me quick to elude him. At one time the flames died down somewhat, and I feared the foul creatures would presently be able to see me. I was thinking of beginning the fight by killing some of them before this should happen; but the fire burst out again brightly, and I stayed my hand. I walked about the hill among them and avoided them, looking for some trace of Weena. But Weena was gone.

"At last I sat down on the summit of the hillock, and watched this strange incredible company of blind things groping to and fro, and making uncanny noises to each other, as the glare of the fire beat on them. The coiling uprush of smoke streamed across the sky, and through the rare tatters of that red canopy, remote as though they belonged to another universe, shone the little stars. Two or three Morlocks came blundering into me, and I drove them off with blows of my fists, trembling as I did so.

"For the most part of that night I was persuaded it was a nightmare. I bit myself and screamed in a passionate desire to awake. I beat the ground with my hands, and got up and sat down again, and wandered here and there, and again sat down. Then I would fall to rubbing my eyes and calling upon God to let me awake. Thrice I saw Morlocks put their heads down in a kind of agony and rush into the flames. But, at last, above the subsiding red of the fire, above the streaming masses of black smoke and the whitening and blackening tree stumps, and the diminishing numbers of these dim creatures, came the white light of the day.

"I searched again for traces of Weena, but there were none. It was plain that they had left her poor little body in the forest. I cannot describe how it relieved me to think that it had escaped the awful fate to which it seemed destined. As I thought of that, I was almost moved to begin a massacre of the helpless abominations about me, but I contained myself. The hillock, as I have said, was a kind of island in the forest. From its summit I could now make out through a haze of smoke the Palace of Green Porcelain, and from that I could get my bearings for the White Sphinx.

"And so, leaving the remnant of these damned souls still going hither and thither and moaning, as the day grew clearer, I tied some grass about my feet and limped on across smoking ashes and among black stems that still pulsated internally with fire, towards the hiding-place of the Time Machine. I walked slowly, for I was almost exhausted, as well as lame, and I felt the intensest wretchedness for the horrible death of little Weena. It seemed an overwhelming calamity. Now, in this old familiar room, it is more like the sorrow of a dream than an actual loss. But that morning it left me absolutely lonely again—terribly alone. I began to think of this house of mine, of this fireside, of some of you, and with such thoughts came a longing that was pain.

"But, as I walked over the smoking ashes under the bright morning sky, I made a discovery. In my trouser pocket were still some loose matches. The box must have leaked before it was lost.

Chapter 13
The Trap of the White Sphinx

"About eight or nine in the morning I came to the same seat of yellow metal from which I had viewed the world upon the evening of my arrival. I thought of my hasty conclusions upon that evening and could not refrain from laughing bitterly at my confidence. Here was

the same beautiful scene, the same abundant foliage, the same splendid palaces and magnificent ruins, the same silver river running between its fertile banks. The gay robes of the beautiful people moved hither and thither among the trees. Some were bathing in exactly the place where I had saved Weena, and that suddenly gave me a keen stab of pain. And like blots upon the landscape rose the cupolas above the ways to the Underworld. I understood now what all the beauty of the Overworld people covered. Very pleasant was their day, as pleasant as the day of the cattle in the field. Like the cattle, they knew of no enemies and provided against no needs. And their end was the same.

"I grieved to think how brief the dream of the human intellect had been. It had committed suicide. It had set itself steadfastly towards comfort and ease, a balanced society with security and permanency as its watchword, it had attained its hopes—to come to this at last. Once, life and property must have reached almost absolute safety. The rich had been assured of his wealth and comfort, the toiler assured of his life and work. No doubt in that perfect world there had been no unemployed problem, no social question left unsolved. And a great quiet had followed.

"It is a law of nature we overlook, that intellectual versatility is the compensation for change, danger, and trouble. An animal perfectly in harmony with its environment is a perfect mechanism. Nature never appeals to intelligence until habit and instinct are useless. There is no intelligence where there is no change and no need of change. Only those animals partake of intelligence that have to meet a huge variety of needs and dangers.

"So, as I see it, the Upperworld man had drifted towards his feeble prettiness, and the Underworld to mere mechanical industry. But that perfect state had lacked one thing even for mechanical perfection—absolute permanency. Apparently as time went on, the feeding of an Underworld, however it was effected, had become disjointed. Mother Necessity, who had been staved off for a few thousand years, came back again, and she began below. The Underworld being in contact with machinery, which, however perfect, still needs some little thought outside habit, had probably retained perforce rather more initiative, if less of every other human character, than the Upper. And when other meat failed them, they turned to what old habit had hitherto forbidden. So, I say I saw it in my last view of the world of Eight Hundred and Two Thousand Seven Hundred and One. It may be as wrong an explanation as mortal wit could invent. It is how the thing

shaped itself to me, and as that I give it to you.

"After the fatigues, excitements, and terrors of the past days, and in spite of my grief, this seat and the tranquil view and the warm sunlight were very pleasant. I was very tired and sleepy, and soon my theorising passed into dozing. Catching myself at that, I took my own hint, and spreading myself out upon the turf I had a long and refreshing sleep.

"I awoke a little before sunsetting. I now felt safe against being caught napping by the Morlocks, and, stretching myself, I came on down the hill towards the White Sphinx. I had my crowbar in one hand, and the other hand played with the matches in my pocket.

"And now came a most unexpected thing. As I approached the pedestal of the sphinx, I found the bronze valves were open. They had slid down into grooves.

"At that I stopped short before them, hesitating to enter.

"Within was a small apartment, and on a raised place in the corner of this was the Time Machine. I had the small levers in my pocket. So here, after all my elaborate preparations for the siege of the White Sphinx, was a meek surrender. I threw my iron bar away, almost sorry not to use it.

"A sudden thought came into my head as I stooped towards the portal. For once, at least, I grasped the mental operations of the Morlocks. Suppressing a strong inclination to laugh, I stepped through the bronze frame and up to the Time Machine. I was surprised to find it had been carefully oiled and cleaned. I have suspected since that the Morlocks had even partially taken it to pieces while trying in their dim way to grasp its purpose.

"Now as I stood and examined it, finding a pleasure in the mere touch of the contrivance, the thing I had expected happened. The bronze panels suddenly slid up and struck the frame with a clang. I was in the dark—trapped. So, the Morlocks thought. At that I chuckled gleefully.

"I could already hear their murmuring laughter as they came towards me. Very calmly I tried to strike the match. I had only to fix on the levers and depart then like a ghost. But I had overlooked one little thing. The matches were of that abominable kind that light only on the box.

"You may imagine how all my calm vanished. The little brutes were close upon me. One touched me. I made a sweeping blow in the dark at them with the levers, and began to scramble into the saddle of the machine. Then came one hand upon me and then another. Then

I had simply to fight against their persistent fingers for my levers, and at the same time feel for the studs over which these fitted. One, indeed, they almost got away from me. As it slipped from my hand, I had to butt in the dark with my head—I could hear the Morlock's skull ring—to recover it. It was a nearer thing than the fight in the forest, I think, this last scramble.

"But at last the lever was fixed and pulled over. The clinging hands slipped from me. The darkness presently fell from my eyes. I found myself in the same grey light and tumult I have already described.

CHAPTER 14

The Further Vision

"I have already told you of the sickness and confusion that comes with time travelling. And this time I was not seated properly in the saddle, but sideways and in an unstable fashion. For an indefinite time, I clung to the machine as it swayed and vibrated, quite unheeding how I went, and when I brought myself to look at the dials again, I was amazed to find where I had arrived. One dial records days, and another thousands of days, another millions of days, and another thousands of millions. Now, instead of reversing the levers, I had pulled them over so as to go forward with them, and when I came to look at these indicators, I found that the thousands hand was sweeping round as fast as the seconds hand of a watch—into futurity.

"As I drove on, a peculiar change crept over the appearance of things. The palpitating greyness grew darker; then—though I was still travelling with prodigious velocity—the blinking succession of day and night, which was usually indicative of a slower pace, returned, and grew more and more marked. This puzzled me very much at first. The alternations of night and day grew slower and slower, and so did the passage of the sun across the sky, until they seemed to stretch through centuries. At last a steady twilight brooded over the earth, a twilight only broken now and then when a comet glared across the darkling sky. The band of light that had indicated the sun had long since disappeared; for the sun had ceased to set—it simply rose and fell in the west, and grew ever broader and more red. All trace of the moon had vanished. The circling of the stars, growing slower and slower, had given place to creeping points of light.

"At last, some time before I stopped, the sun, red and very large, halted motionless upon the horizon, a vast dome glowing with a dull heat, and now and then suffering a momentary extinction. At one time

it had for a little while glowed more brilliantly again, but it speedily reverted to its sullen red heat. I perceived by this slowing down of its rising and setting that the work of the tidal drag was done. The earth had come to rest with one face to the sun, even as in our own time the moon faces the earth. Very cautiously, for I remembered my former headlong fall, I began to reverse my motion. Slower and slower went the circling hands until the thousands one seemed motionless and the daily one was no longer a mere mist upon its scale. Still slower, until the dim outlines of a desolate beach grew visible.

"I stopped very gently and sat upon the Time Machine, looking round. The sky was no longer blue. North-eastward it was inky black, and out of the blackness shone brightly and steadily the pale white stars. Overhead it was a deep Indian red and starless, and south-east-ward it grew brighter to a glowing scarlet where, cut by the horizon, lay the huge hull of the sun, red and motionless. The rocks about me were of a harsh reddish colour, and all the trace of life that I could see at first was the intensely green vegetation that covered every project-ing point on their south-eastern face. It was the same rich green that one sees on forest moss or on the lichen in caves: plants which like these grow in a perpetual twilight.

"The machine was standing on a sloping beach. The sea stretched away to the south-west, to rise into a sharp bright horizon against the wan sky. There were no breakers and no waves, for not a breath of wind was stirring. Only a slight oily swell rose and fell like a gentle breathing, and showed that the eternal sea was still moving and living. And along the margin where the water sometimes broke was a thick incrustation of salt—pink under the lurid sky. There was a sense of oppression in my head, and I noticed that I was breathing very fast. The sensation reminded me of my only experience of mountaineer-ing, and from that I judged the air to be more rarefied than it is now.

"Far away up the desolate slope I heard a harsh scream, and saw a thing like a huge white butterfly go slanting and fluttering up into the sky and, circling, disappear over some low hillocks beyond. The sound of its voice was so dismal that I shivered and seated myself more firmly upon the machine. Looking round me again, I saw that, quite near, what I had taken to be a reddish mass of rock was moving slowly towards me. Then I saw the thing was really a monstrous crab-like creature. Can you imagine a crab as large as yonder table, with its many legs moving slowly and uncertainly, its big claws swaying, its long antennae, like carters' whips, waving and feeling, and its stalked

eyes gleaming at you on either side of its metallic front? Its back was corrugated and ornamented with ungainly bosses, and a greenish incrustation blotched it here and there. I could see the many palps of its complicated mouth flickering and feeling as it moved.

"As I stared at this sinister apparition crawling towards me, I felt a tickling on my cheek as though a fly had lighted there. I tried to brush it away with my hand, but in a moment, it returned, and almost immediately came another by my ear. I struck at this, and caught something threadlike. It was drawn swiftly out of my hand. With a frightful qualm, I turned, and I saw that I had grasped the antenna of another monster crab that stood just behind me. Its evil eyes were wriggling on their stalks, its mouth was all alive with appetite, and its vast ungainly claws, smeared with an algal slime, were descending upon me. In a moment my hand was on the lever, and I had placed a month between myself and these monsters. But I was still on the same beach, and I saw them distinctly now as soon as I stopped. Dozens of them seemed to be crawling here and there, in the sombre light, among the foliated sheets of intense green.

"I cannot convey the sense of abominable desolation that hung over the world. The red eastern sky, the northward blackness, the salt Dead Sea, the stony beach crawling with these foul, slow-stirring monsters, the uniform poisonous-looking green of the lichenous plants, the thin air that hurts one's lungs: all contributed to an appalling effect. I moved on a hundred years, and there was the same red sun—a little larger, a little duller—the same dying sea, the same chill air, and the same crowd of earthy crustacea creeping in and out among the green weed and the red rocks. And in the westward sky, I saw a curved pale line like a vast new moon.

"So, I travelled, stopping ever and again, in great strides of a thousand years or more, drawn on by the mystery of the earth's fate, watching with a strange fascination the sun grow larger and duller in the westward sky, and the life of the old earth ebb away. At last, more than thirty million years hence, the huge red-hot dome of the sun had come to obscure nearly a tenth part of the darkling heavens. Then I stopped once more, for the crawling multitude of crabs had disappeared, and the red beach, save for its livid green liverworts and lichens, seemed lifeless. And now it was flecked with white. A bitter cold assailed me. Rare white flakes ever and again came eddying down. To the north-eastward, the glare of snow lay under the starlight of the sable sky, and I could see an undulating crest of hillocks pinkish

white. There were fringes of ice along the sea margin, with drifting masses farther out; but the main expanse of that salt ocean, all bloody under the eternal sunset, was still unfrozen.

"I looked about me to see if any traces of animal life remained. A certain indefinable apprehension still kept me in the saddle of the machine. But I saw nothing moving, in earth or sky or sea. The green slime on the rocks alone testified that life was not extinct. A shallow sandbank had appeared in the sea and the water had receded from the beach. I fancied I saw some black object flopping about upon this bank, but it became motionless as I looked at it, and I judged that my eye had been deceived, and that the black object was merely a rock. The stars in the sky were intensely bright and seemed to me to twinkle very little.

"Suddenly I noticed that the circular westward outline of the sun had changed; that a concavity, a bay, had appeared in the curve. I saw this grow larger. For a minute perhaps I stared aghast at this blackness that was creeping over the day, and then I realised that an eclipse was beginning. Either the moon or the planet Mercury was passing across the sun's disk. Naturally, at first I took it to be the moon, but there is much to incline me to believe that what I really saw was the transit of an inner planet passing very near to the earth.

"The darkness grew apace; a cold wind began to blow in freshening gusts from the east, and the showering white flakes in the air increased in number. From the edge of the sea came a ripple and whisper. Beyond these lifeless sounds the world was silent. Silent? It would be hard to convey the stillness of it. All the sounds of man, the bleating of sheep, the cries of birds, the hum of insects, the stir that makes the background of our lives—all that was over. As the darkness thickened, the eddying flakes grew more abundant, dancing before my eyes; and the cold of the air more intense. At last, one by one, swiftly, one after the other, the white peaks of the distant hills vanished into blackness. The breeze rose to a moaning wind. I saw the black central shadow of the eclipse sweeping towards me. In another moment the pale stars alone were visible. All else was rayless obscurity. The sky was absolutely black.

"A horror of this great darkness came on me. The cold, that smote to my marrow, and the pain I felt in breathing, overcame me. I shivered, and a deadly nausea seized me. Then like a red-hot bow in the sky appeared the edge of the sun. I got off the machine to recover myself. I felt giddy and incapable of facing the return journey. As

I stood sick and confused, I saw again the moving thing upon the shoal—there was no mistake now that it was a moving thing—against the red water of the sea. It was a round thing, the size of a football perhaps, or, it may be, bigger, and tentacles trailed down from it; it seemed black against the weltering blood-red water, and it was hopping fitfully about. Then I felt I was fainting. But a terrible dread of lying helpless in that remote and awful twilight sustained me while I clambered upon the saddle.

CHAPTER 15

The Time Traveller's Return

"So, I came back. For a long time, I must have been insensible upon the machine. The blinking succession of the days and nights was resumed, the sun got golden again, the sky blue. I breathed with greater freedom. The fluctuating contours of the land ebbed and flowed. The hands spun backward upon the dials. At last I saw again the dim shadows of houses, the evidences of decadent humanity. These, too, changed and passed, and others came. Presently, when the million dial was at zero, I slackened speed. I began to recognise our own pretty and familiar architecture, the thousands hand ran back to the starting-point, the night and day flapped slower and slower. Then the old walls of the laboratory came round me. Very gently, now, I slowed the mechanism down.

"I saw one little thing that seemed odd to me. I think I have told you that when I set out, before my velocity became very high, Mrs. Watchett had walked across the room, travelling, as it seemed to me, like a rocket. As I returned, I passed again across that minute when she traversed the laboratory. But now her every motion appeared to be the exact inversion of her previous ones. The door at the lower end opened, and she glided quietly up the laboratory, back foremost, and disappeared behind the door by which she had previously entered. Just before that I seemed to see Hillyer for a moment; but he passed like a flash.

"Then I stopped the machine, and saw about me again the old familiar laboratory, my tools, my appliances just as I had left them. I got off the thing very shakily, and sat down upon my bench. For several minutes I trembled violently. Then I became calmer. Around me was my old workshop again, exactly as it had been. I might have slept there, and the whole thing have been a dream.

"And yet, not exactly! The thing had started from the south-east

corner of the laboratory. It had come to rest again in the north-west, against the wall where you saw it. That gives you the exact distance from my little lawn to the pedestal of the White Sphinx, into which the Morlocks had carried my machine.

"For a time, my brain went stagnant. Presently I got up and came through the passage here, limping, because my heel was still painful, and feeling sorely begrimed. I saw the *Pall Mall Gazette* on the table by the door. I found the date was indeed today, and looking at the timepiece, saw the hour was almost eight o'clock. I heard your voices and the clatter of plates. I hesitated—I felt so sick and weak. Then I sniffed good wholesome meat, and opened the door on you. You know the rest. I washed, and dined, and now I am telling you the story.

CHAPTER 16
After the Story

"I know," he said, after a pause, "that all this will be absolutely incredible to you, but to me the one incredible thing is that I am here tonight in this old familiar room looking into your friendly faces and telling you these strange adventures." He looked at the Medical Man. "No. I cannot expect you to believe it. Take it as a lie—or a prophecy. Say I dreamed it in the workshop. Consider I have been speculating upon the destinies of our race, until I have hatched this fiction. Treat my assertion of its truth as a mere stroke of art to enhance its interest. And taking it as a story, what do you think of it?"

He took up his pipe, and began, in his old accustomed manner, to tap with it nervously upon the bars of the grate. There was a momentary stillness. Then chairs began to creak and shoes to scrape upon the carpet. I took my eyes off the Time Traveller's face, and looked round at his audience. They were in the dark, and little spots of colour swam before them. The Medical Man seemed absorbed in the contemplation of our host. The Editor was looking hard at the end of his cigar—the sixth. The Journalist fumbled for his watch. The others, as far as I remember, were motionless.

The Editor stood up with a sigh. "What a pity it is you're not a writer of stories!" he said, putting his hand on the Time Traveller's shoulder.

"You don't believe it?"

"Well——"

"I thought not."

The Time Traveller turned to us. "Where are the matches?" he said.

He lit one and spoke over his pipe, puffing. "To tell you the truth. . . . I hardly believe it myself. And yet. . ."

His eye fell with a mute inquiry upon the withered white flowers upon the little table. Then he turned over the hand holding his pipe, and I saw he was looking at some half-healed scars on his knuckles.

The Medical Man rose, came to the lamp, and examined the flowers. "The *gynaeceum's* odd," he said. The Psychologist leant forward to see, holding out his hand for a specimen.

"I'm hanged if it isn't a quarter to one," said the Journalist. "How shall we get home?"

"Plenty of cabs at the station," said the Psychologist.

"It's a curious thing," said the Medical Man; "but I certainly don't know the natural order of these flowers. May I have them?"

The Time Traveller hesitated. Then suddenly: "Certainly not."

"Where did you really get them?" said the Medical Man.

The Time Traveller put his hand to his head. He spoke like one who was trying to keep hold of an idea that eluded him. "They were put into my pocket by Weena, when I travelled into Time." He stared round the room. "I'm damned if it isn't all going. This room and you and the atmosphere of every day is too much for my memory. Did I ever make a Time Machine, or a model of a Time Machine? Or is it all only a dream? They say life is a dream, a precious poor dream at times—but I can't stand another that won't fit. It's madness. And where did the dream come from? . . . I must look at that machine. If there is one!"

He caught up the lamp swiftly, and carried it, flaring red, through the door into the corridor. We followed him. There in the flickering light of the lamp was the machine sure enough, squat, ugly, and askew, a thing of brass, ebony, ivory, and translucent glimmering quartz. Solid to the touch—for I put out my hand and felt the rail of it—and with brown spots and smears upon the ivory, and bits of grass and moss upon the lower parts, and one rail bent awry.

The Time Traveller put the lamp down on the bench, and ran his hand along the damaged rail. "It's all right now," he said. "The story I told you was true. I'm sorry to have brought you out here in the cold." He took up the lamp, and, in an absolute silence, we returned to the smoking-room.

He came into the hall with us and helped the Editor on with his coat. The Medical Man looked into his face and, with a certain hesitation, told him he was suffering from overwork, at which he laughed

hugely. I remember him standing in the open doorway, bawling good-night.

I shared a cab with the Editor. He thought the tale a "gaudy lie." For my own part I was unable to come to a conclusion. The story was so fantastic and incredible, the telling so credible and sober. I lay awake most of the night thinking about it. I determined to go next day and see the Time Traveller again. I was told he was in the laboratory, and being on easy terms in the house, I went up to him. The laboratory, however, was empty. I stared for a minute at the Time Machine and put out my hand and touched the lever. At that the squat substantial-looking mass swayed like a bough shaken by the wind. Its instability startled me extremely, and I had a queer reminiscence of the childish days when I used to be forbidden to meddle. I came back through the corridor. The Time Traveller met me in the smoking-room. He was coming from the house. He had a small camera under one arm and a knapsack under the other. He laughed when he saw me, and gave me an elbow to shake. "I'm frightfully busy," said he, "with that thing in there."

"But is it not some hoax?" I said. "Do you really travel through time?"

"Really and truly I do." And he looked frankly into my eyes. He hesitated. His eye wandered about the room. "I only want half an hour," he said. "I know why you came, and it's awfully good of you. There's some magazines here. If you'll stop to lunch, I'll prove you this time travelling up to the hilt, specimens and all. If you'll forgive my leaving you now?"

I consented, hardly comprehending then the full import of his words, and he nodded and went on down the corridor. I heard the door of the laboratory slam, seated myself in a chair, and took up a daily paper. What was he going to do before lunch-time? Then suddenly I was reminded by an advertisement that I had promised to meet Richardson, the publisher, at two. I looked at my watch, and saw that I could barely save that engagement. I got up and went down the passage to tell the Time Traveller.

As I took hold of the handle of the door, I heard an exclamation, oddly truncated at the end, and a click and a thud. A gust of air whirled round me as I opened the door, and from within came the sound of broken glass falling on the floor. The Time Traveller was not there. I seemed to see a ghostly, indistinct figure sitting in a whirling mass of black and brass for a moment—a figure so transparent that the

bench behind with its sheets of drawings was absolutely distinct; but this phantasm vanished as I rubbed my eyes. The Time Machine had gone. Save for a subsiding stir of dust, the further end of the laboratory was empty. A pane of the skylight had, apparently, just been blown in.

I felt an unreasonable amazement. I knew that something strange had happened, and for the moment could not distinguish what the strange thing might be. As I stood staring, the door into the garden opened, and the man-servant appeared.

We looked at each other. Then ideas began to come. "Has Mr. —— gone out that way?" said I.

"No, sir. No one has come out this way. I was expecting to find him here."

At that I understood. At the risk of disappointing Richardson, I stayed on, waiting for the Time Traveller; waiting for the second, perhaps still stranger story, and the specimens and photographs he would bring with him. But I am beginning now to fear that I must wait a lifetime. The Time Traveller vanished three years ago. And, as everybody knows now, he has never returned.

The Epilogue

One cannot choose but wonder. Will he ever return? It may be that he swept back into the past, and fell among the blood-drinking, hairy savages of the Age of Unpolished Stone; into the abysses of the Cretaceous Sea; or among the grotesque saurians, the huge reptilian brutes of the Jurassic times. He may even now—if I may use the phrase—be wandering on some plesiosaurus-haunted Oolitic coral reef, or beside the lonely saline seas of the Triassic Age. Or did he go forward, into one of the nearer ages, in which men are still men, but with the riddles of our own time answered and its wearisome problems solved? Into the manhood of the race: for I, for my own part, cannot think that these latter days of weak experiment, fragmentary theory, and mutual discord are indeed man's culminating time!

I say, for my own part. He, I know—for the question had been discussed among us long before the Time Machine was made—thought but cheerlessly of the Advancement of Mankind, and saw in the growing pile of civilisation only a foolish heaping that must inevitably fall back upon and destroy its makers in the end. If that is so, it remains for us to live as though it were not so. But to me the future is still black and blank—is a vast ignorance, lit at a few casual places by the memory of his story. And I have by me, for my comfort, two strange

white flowers—shrivelled now, and brown and flat and brittle—to witness that even when mind and strength had gone, gratitude and a mutual tenderness still lived on in the heart of man.

The Wonderful Visit

Contents

CHAPTER 1
The Night of the Strange Bird

On the Night of the Strange Bird, many people at Sidderton (and some nearer) saw a Glare on the Sidderford moor. But no one in Sidderford saw it, for most of Sidderford was abed.

All day the wind had been rising, so that the larks on the moor chirruped fitfully near the ground, or rose only to be driven like leaves before the wind. The sun set in a bloody welter of clouds, and the moon was hidden. The glare, they say, was golden like a beam shining out of the sky, not a uniform blaze, but broken all over by curving flashes like the waving of swords. It lasted but a moment and left the night dark and obscure. There were letters about it in *Nature*, and a rough drawing that no one thought very like. (You may see it for yourself—the drawing that was unlike the glare—on page 42 of Vol. cclx. of that publication.)

None in Sidderford saw the light, but Annie, Hooker Durgan's wife, was lying awake, and she saw the reflection of it—a flickering tongue of gold—dancing on the wall.

She, too, was one of those who heard the sound. The others who heard the sound were Lumpy Durgan, the half-wit, and Amory's mother. They said it was a sound like children singing and a throbbing of harp strings, carried on a rush of notes like that which sometimes comes from an organ.

It began and ended like the opening and shutting of a door, and before and after they heard nothing but the night wind howling over the moor and the noise of the caves under Sidderford cliff. Amory's mother said she wanted to cry when she heard it, but Lumpy was only sorry he could hear no more.

That is as much as anyone can tell you of the glare upon Sidderford Moor and the alleged music therewith. And whether these had any real connexion with the Strange Bird whose history follows, is more than I can say. But I set it down here for reasons that will be more apparent as the story proceeds.

The Coming of the Strange Bird

Sandy Bright was coming down the road from Spinner's carrying a side of bacon he had taken in exchange for a clock. He saw nothing of the light but he heard and saw the Strange Bird. He suddenly heard a flapping and a voice like a woman wailing, and being a nervous man and all alone, he was alarmed forthwith, and turning (all a-tremble) saw something large and black against the dim darkness of the cedars up the hill. It seemed to be coming right down upon him, and incontinently he dropped his bacon and set off running, only to fall headlong.

He tried in vain—such was his state of mind—to remember the beginning of the Lord's Prayer. The strange bird flapped over him, something larger than himself, with a vast spread of wings, and, as he thought, black. He screamed and gave himself up for lost. Then it went past him, sailing down the hill, and, soaring over the vicarage, vanished into the hazy valley towards Sidderford.

And Sandy Bright lay upon his stomach there, for ever so long, staring into the darkness after the strange bird. At last he got upon his knees and began to thank Heaven for his merciful deliverance, with his eyes downhill. He went on down into the village, talking aloud and confessing his sins as he went, lest the strange bird should come back. All who heard him thought him drunk. But from that night he was a changed man, and had done with drunkenness and defrauding the revenue by selling silver ornaments without a licence. And the side of bacon lay upon the hillside until the tallyman from Portburdock found it in the morning.

The next who saw the Strange Bird was a solicitor's clerk at Iping Hanger, who was climbing the hill before breakfast, to see the sunrise. Save for a few dissolving wisps of cloud the sky had been blown clear in the night. At first, he thought it was an eagle he saw. It was near the zenith, and incredibly remote, a mere bright speck above the pink cirri, and it seemed as if it fluttered and beat itself against the sky, as an imprisoned swallow might do against a window pane. Then down it came into the shadow of the earth, sweeping in a great curve towards Portburdock and round over the Hanger, and so vanishing behind the woods of Siddermorton Park. It seemed larger than a man. Just before it was hidden, the light of the rising sun smote over the edge of the downs and touched its wings, and they flashed with the brightness of

flames and the colour of precious stones, and so passed, leaving the witness agape.

A ploughman going to his work, along under the stone wall of Siddermorton Park, saw the Strange Bird flash over him for a moment and vanish among the hazy interstices of the beech trees. But he saw little of the colour of the wings, witnessing only that its legs, which were long, seemed pink and bare like naked flesh, and its body mottled white. It smote like an arrow through the air and was gone.

These were the first three eye-witnesses of the Strange Bird.

Now in these days one does not cower before the devil and one's own sinfulness, or see strange iridescent wings in the light of dawn, and say nothing of it afterwards. The young solicitor's clerk told his mother and sisters at breakfast, and, afterwards, on his way to the office at Portburdock, spoke of it to the blacksmith of Hammerpond, and spent the morning with his fellow clerks marvelling instead of copying deeds. And Sandy Bright went to talk the matter over with Mr Jekyll, the "Primitive" minister, and the ploughman told old Hugh and afterwards the vicar of Siddermorton.

"They are not an imaginative race about here," said the Vicar of Siddermorton, "I wonder how much of that was true. Barring that he thinks the wings were brown it sounds uncommonly like a Flamingo."

CHAPTER 3

The Hunting of the Strange Bird

The Vicar of Siddermorton (which is nine miles inland from Siddermouth as the crow flies) was an ornithologist. Some such pursuit, botany, antiquity, folk-lore, is almost inevitable for a single man in his position. He was given to geometry also, propounding occasionally impossible problems in the *Educational Times*, but ornithology was his *forte*. He had already added two visitors to the list of occasional British birds. His name was well-known in the columns of the *Zoologist* (I am afraid it may be forgotten by now, for the world moves apace). And on the day after the coming of the Strange Bird, came first one and then another to confirm the ploughman's story and tell him, not that it had any connection, of the Glare upon Sidderford moor.

Now, the Vicar of Siddermorton had two rivals in his scientific pursuits; Gully of Sidderton, who had actually seen the glare, and who it was sent the drawing to *Nature*, and Borland the natural history dealer, who kept the marine laboratory at Portburdock. Borland, the Vicar thought, should have stuck to his copepods, but instead he kept

a taxidermist, and took advantage of his littoral position to pick up rare sea birds. It was evident to anyone who knew anything of collecting that both these men would be scouring the country after the strange visitant, before twenty-four hours were out.

The Vicar's eye rested on the back of Saunders' British Birds, for he was in his study at the time. Already in two places there was entered: "the only known British specimen was secured by the Rev. K. Hilyer, Vicar of Siddermorton." A third such entry. He doubted if any other collector had that.

He looked at his watch—*two*. He had just lunched, and usually he "rested" in the afternoon. He knew it would make him feel very disagreeable if he went out into the hot sunshine—both on the top of his head and generally Yet Gully perhaps was out, prowling observant. Suppose it was something very good and Gully got it!

His gun stood in the corner. (The thing had iridescent wings and pink legs! The chromatic conflict was certainly exceedingly stimulating). He took his gun.

He would have gone out by the glass doors and verandah, and down the garden into the hill road, in order to avoid his housekeeper's eye. He knew his gun expeditions were not approved of. But advancing towards him up the garden, he saw the curate's wife and her two daughters, carrying tennis rackets. His curate's wife was a young woman of immense will, who used to play tennis on his lawn, and cut his roses, differ from him on doctrinal points, and criticise his personal behaviour all over the parish. He went in abject fear of her, was always trying to propitiate her. But so far, he had clung to his ornithology.

However, he went out by the front door.

★★★★★★

If it were not for collectors England would be full, so to speak, of rare birds and wonderful butterflies, strange flowers and a thousand interesting things. But happily, the collector prevents all that, either killing with his own hands or, by buying extravagantly, procuring people of the lower classes to kill such eccentricities as appear. It makes work for people, even though Acts of Parliament interfere. In this way, for instance, he is killing off the chough in Cornwall, the Bath white butterfly, the Queen of Spain Fritillary; and can plume himself upon the extermination of the Great Auk, and a hundred other rare birds and plants and insects.

All that is the work of the collector and his glory alone. In the name of Science. And this is right and as it should be; eccentricity, in

fact, is immorality—think over it again if you do not think so now—just as eccentricity in one's way of thinking is madness (I defy you to find another definition that will fit all the cases of either); and if a species is rare it follows that it is not Fitted to Survive.

The collector is after all merely like the foot soldier in the days of heavy armour—he leaves the combatants alone and cuts the throats of those who are overthrown. So, one may go through England from end to end in the summer time and see only eight or ten commonplace wild flowers, and the commoner butterflies, and a dozen or so common birds, and never be offended by any breach of the monotony, any splash of strange blossom or flutter of unknown wing.

All the rest have been "collected" years ago. For which cause we should all love Collectors, and bear in mind what we owe them when their little collections are displayed. These camphorated little drawers of theirs, their glass cases and blotting-paper books, are the graves of the Rare and the Beautiful, the symbols of the Triumph of Leisure (morally spent) over the Delights of Life. (All of which, as you very properly remark, has nothing whatever to do with the Strange Bird.)

<center>★★★★★★</center>

There is a place on the moor where the black water shines among the succulent moss, and the hairy sundew, eater of careless insects, spreads its red-stained hungry hands to the God who gives his creatures—one to feed another. On a ridge thereby grow birches with a silvery bark, and the soft green of the larch mingles with the dark green fir. Thither through the honey humming heather came the Vicar, in the heat of the day, carrying a gun under his arm, a gun loaded with swan-shot for the Strange Bird. And over his disengaged hand he carried a pocket handkerchief wherewith, ever and again, he wiped his beady face.

He went by and on past the big pond and the pool full of brown leaves where the Sidder arises, and so by the road (which is at first sandy and then chalky) to the little gate that goes into the park. There are seven steps up to the gate and on the further side six down again—lest the deer escape—so that when the Vicar stood in the gateway his head was ten feet or more above the ground. And looking where a tumult of bracken fronds filled the hollow between two groups of beech, his eye caught something parti-coloured that wavered and went. Suddenly his face gleamed and his muscles grew tense; he ducked his head, clutched his gun with both hands, and stood still. Then watching keenly, he came on down the steps into the park, and

<center>91</center>

still holding his gun in both hands, crept rather than walked towards the jungle of bracken.

Nothing stirred, and he almost feared that his eyes had played him false, until he reached the ferns and had gone rustling breast high into them. Then suddenly rose something full of wavering colours, twenty yards or less in front of his face, and beating the air. In another moment it had fluttered above the bracken and spread its pinions wide. He saw what it was, his heart was in his mouth, and he fired out of pure surprise and habit.

There was a scream of superhuman agony, the wings beat the air twice, and the victim came slanting swiftly downward and struck the ground—a struggling heap of writhing body, broken wing and flying bloodstained plumes—upon the turfy slope behind.

The Vicar stood aghast, with his smoking gun in his hand. It was no bird at all, but a youth with an extremely beautiful face, clad in a robe of saffron and with iridescent wings, across whose pinions great waves of colour, flushes of purple and crimson, golden green and intense blue, pursued one another as he writhed in his agony. Never had the Vicar seen such gorgeous floods of colour, not stained-glass windows, not the wings of butterflies, not even the glories of crystals seen between prisms, no colours on earth could compare with them. Twice the Angel raised himself, only to fall over sideways again. Then the beating of the wings diminished, the terrified face grew pale, the floods of colour abated, and suddenly with a sob he lay prone, and the changing hues of the broken wings faded swiftly into one uniform dull grey hue.

"Oh! *What* has happened to me?" cried the Angel (for such it was), shuddering violently, hands outstretched and clutching the ground, and then lying still.

"Dear me!" said the Vicar. "I had no idea." He came forward cautiously. "Excuse me," he said, "I am afraid I have shot you."

It was the obvious remark.

The Angel seemed to become aware of his presence for the first time. He raised himself by one hand, his brown eyes stared into the Vicar's. Then, with a gasp, and biting his nether lip, he struggled into a sitting position and surveyed the Vicar from top to toe.

"A man!" said the Angel, clasping his forehead; "a man in the maddest black clothes and without a feather upon him. Then I was not deceived. I am indeed in the Land of Dreams!"

CHAPTER 4
The Vicar and the Angel

Now there are some things frankly impossible. The weakest intellect will admit this situation is impossible. The *Athenaeum* will probably say as much should it venture to review this. Sun-bespattered ferns, spreading beech trees, the Vicar and the gun are acceptable enough. But this Angel is a different matter. Plain sensible people will scarcely go on with such an extravagant book. And the Vicar fully appreciated this impossibility. But he lacked decision. Consequently, he went on with it, as you shall immediately hear. He was hot, it was after dinner, he was in no mood for mental subtleties. The Angel had him at a disadvantage, and further distracted him from the main issue by irrelevant iridescence and a violent fluttering.

For the moment it never occurred to the Vicar to ask whether the Angel was possible or not. He accepted him in the confusion of the moment, and the mischief was done. Put yourself in his place, my dear *Athenaeum*. You go out shooting. You hit something. That alone would disconcert you. You find you have hit an Angel, and he writhes about for a minute and then sits up and addresses you. He makes no apology for his own impossibility. Indeed, he carries the charge clean into your camp. "A man!" he says, pointing. "A man in the maddest black clothes and without a feather upon him. Then I was not deceived. I am indeed in the Land of Dreams!" You *must* answer him. Unless you take to your heels. Or blow his brains out with your second barrel as an escape from the controversy.

"The Land of Dreams! Pardon me if I suggest you have just come out of it," was the Vicar's remark.

"How can that be?" said the Angel.

"Your wing," said the Vicar, "is bleeding. Before we talk, may I have the pleasure—the melancholy pleasure—of tying it up? I am really most sincerely sorry." The Angel put his hand behind his back and winced.

The Vicar assisted his victim to stand up. The Angel turned gravely and the Vicar, with numberless insignificant panting parentheses, carefully examined the injured wings. (They articulated, he observed with interest, to a kind of second glenoid on the outer and upper edge of the shoulder blade. The left wing had suffered little except the loss of some of the primary wing-quills, and a shot or so in the *ala spuria*, but the humerus bone of the right was evidently smashed.) The Vicar

stanched the bleeding as well as he could and tied up the bone with his pocket handkerchief and the neck wrap his housekeeper made him carry in all weathers.

"I'm afraid you will not be able to fly for some time," said he, feeling the bone.

"I don't like this new sensation," said the Angel.

"The Pain when I feel your bone?"

"The *what*?" said the Angel.

"The Pain."

"'Pain'—you call it. No, I certainly don't like the Pain. Do you have much of this Pain in the Land of Dreams?"

"A very fair share," said the Vicar. "Is it new to you?"

"Quite," said the Angel. "I don't like it."

"How curious!" said the Vicar, and bit at the end of a strip of linen to tie a knot. "I think this bandaging must serve for the present," he said. "I've studied ambulance work before, but never the bandaging up of wing wounds. Is your Pain any better?"

"It glows now instead of flashing," said the Angel.

"I am afraid you will find it glow for some time," said the Vicar, still intent on the wound.

The Angel gave a shrug of the wing and turned round to look at the Vicar again. He had been trying to keep an eye on the Vicar over his shoulder during all their interview. He looked at him from top to toe with raised eyebrows and a growing smile on his beautiful soft-featured face. "It seems so odd," he said with a sweet little laugh, "to be talking to a Man!"

"Do you know," said the Vicar, "now that I come to think of it, it is equally odd to me that I should be talking to an Angel. I am a somewhat matter-of-fact person. A Vicar has to be. Angels I have always regarded as—artistic conceptions——"

"Exactly what we think of men."

"But surely you have seen so many men——"

"Never before today. In pictures and books, times enough of course. But I have seen several since the sunrise, solid real men, besides a horse or so—those Unicorn things you know, without horns—and quite a number of those grotesque knobby things called 'cows.' I was naturally a little frightened at so many mythical monsters, and came to hide here until it was dark. I suppose it will be dark again presently like it was at first. *Phew!* This Pain of yours is poor fun. I hope I shall wake up directly."

"I don't understand quite," said the Vicar, knitting his brows and tapping his forehead with his flat hand. "Mythical monster!" The worst thing he had been called for years hitherto was a 'mediaeval anachronism' (by an advocate of Disestablishment). "Do I understand that you consider me as—as something in a dream?"

"Of course," said the Angel smiling.

"And this world about me, these rugged trees and spreading fronds——"

"Is all so *very* dream like," said the Angel. "Just exactly what one dreams of—or artists imagine."

"You have artists then among the Angels?"

"All kinds of artists, Angels with wonderful imaginations, who invent men and cows and eagles and a thousand impossible creatures."

"Impossible creatures!" said the Vicar.

"Impossible creatures," said the Angel. "Myths."

"But I'm real!" said the Vicar. "I assure you I'm real."

The Angel shrugged his wings and winced and smiled. "I can always tell when I am dreaming," he said.

"*You*—dreaming," said the Vicar. He looked round him.

"*You* dreaming!" he repeated. His mind worked diffusely.

He held out his hand with all his fingers moving. "I have it!" he said. "I begin to see." A really brilliant idea was dawning upon his mind. He had not studied mathematics at Cambridge for nothing, after all. "Tell me please. Some animals of *your* world ... of the Real World, real animals you know."

"Real animals!" said the Angel smiling. "Why—there's Griffins and Dragons—and Jabberwocks—and Cherubim—and Sphinxes—and the Hippogriff—and Mermaids—and Satyrs—and....."

"Thank you," said the Vicar as the Angel appeared to be warming to his work; "thank you. That is *quite* enough. I begin to understand."

He paused for a moment; his face pursed up. "Yes I begin to see it."

"See what?" asked the Angel.

"The Griffins and Satyrs and so forth. It's as clear...."

"I don't see them," said the Angel.

"No, the whole point is they are not to be seen in this world. But our men with imaginations have told us all about them, you know. And even I at times.... there are places in this village where you must simply take what they set before you, or give offence—I, I say, have seen in my dreams Jabberwocks, Bogle brutes, Mandrakes. ... From

95

our point of view, you know, they are Dream Creatures. . . ."

"Dream Creatures!" said the Angel. "How singular! This is a very curious dream. A kind of topsy-turvy one. You call men real and angels a myth. It almost makes one think that in some odd way there must be two worlds as it were. . . ."

"At least Two," said the Vicar.

"Lying somewhere close together, and yet scarcely suspecting. . . ."

"As near as page to page of a book."

"Penetrating each other, living each its own life. This is really a delicious dream!"

"And never dreaming of each other."

"Except when people go a dreaming!"

"Yes," said the Angel thoughtfully. "It must be something of the sort. And that reminds me. Sometimes when I have been dropping asleep, or drowsing under the noon-tide sun, I have seen strange corrugated faces just like yours, going by me, and trees with green leaves upon them, and such queer uneven ground as this. . . . It must be so. I have fallen into another world."

"Sometimes," began the Vicar, "at bedtime, when I have been just on the edge of consciousness, I have seen faces as beautiful as yours, and the strange dazzling vistas of a wonderful scene, that flowed past me, winged shapes soaring over it, and wonderful—sometimes terrible—forms going to and fro. I have even heard sweet music too in my ears. . . . It may be that as we withdraw our attention from the world of sense, the pressing world about us, as we pass into the twilight of repose, other worlds. . . . Just as we see the stars, those other worlds in space, when the glare of day recedes. . . . And the artistic dreamers who see such things most clearly. . . ."

They looked at one another.

"And in some incomprehensible manner I have fallen into this world of yours out of my own!" said the Angel, "into the world of my dreams, grown real."

He looked about him. "Into the world of my dreams."

"It is confusing," said the Vicar. "It almost makes one think there may be (ahem) Four Dimensions after all. In which case, of course," he went on hurriedly—for he loved geometrical speculations and took a certain pride in his knowledge of them—"there may be any number of three dimensional universes packed side by side, and all dimly dreaming of one another. There may be world upon world, universe upon universe. It's perfectly possible. There's nothing so incredible as

the absolutely possible. But I wonder how you came to fall out of your world into mine. . . ."

"Dear me!" said the Angel; "There's deer and a stag! Just as they draw them on the coats of arms. How grotesque it all seems! Can I really be awake?"

He rubbed his knuckles into his eyes.

The half-dozen of dappled deer came in Indian file obliquely through the trees and halted, watching. "It's no dream—I am really a solid concrete Angel, in Dream Land," said the Angel. He laughed. The Vicar stood surveying him. The Reverend gentleman was pulling his mouth askew after a habit he had, and slowly stroking his chin. He was asking himself whether he too was not in the Land of Dreams.

<p style="text-align:center">★★★★★★</p>

Now in the land of the Angels, so the Vicar learnt in the course of many conversations, there is neither pain nor trouble nor death, marrying nor giving in marriage, birth nor forgetting. Only at times new things begin. It is a land without hill or dale, a wonderfully level land, glittering with strange buildings, with incessant sunlight or full moon, and with incessant breezes blowing through the Æolian traceries of the trees. It is Wonderland, with glittering seas hanging in the sky, across which strange fleets go sailing, none know whither. There the flowers glow in Heaven and the stars shine about one's feet and the breath of life is a delight.

The land goes on for ever—there is no solar system nor interstellar space such as there is in our universe—and the air goes upward past the sun into the uttermost abyss of their sky. And there is nothing but Beauty there—all the beauty in our art is but feeble rendering of faint glimpses of that wonderful world, and our composers, our original composers, are those who hear, however faintly, the dust of melody that drives before its winds. And the Angels, and wonderful monsters of bronze and marble and living fire, go to and fro therein.

It is a land of Law—for whatever is, is under the law—but its laws all, in some strange way, differ from ours. Their geometry is different because their space has a curve in it so that all their planes are cylinders; and their law of Gravitation is not according to the law of inverse squares, and there are four-and-twenty primary colours instead of only three. Most of the fantastic things of our science are commonplaces there, and all our earthly science would seem to them the maddest dreaming. There are no flowers upon their plants, for instance, but jets of coloured fire. That, of course, will seem mere nonsense to you

<p style="text-align:center">97</p>

because you do not understand Most of what the Angel told the Vicar, indeed the Vicar could not realise, because his own experiences, being only of this world of matter, warred against his understanding. It was too strange to imagine.

What had jolted these twin universes together so that the Angel had fallen suddenly into Sidderford, neither the Angel nor the Vicar could tell. Nor for the matter of that could the author of this story. The author is concerned with the facts of the case, and has neither the desire nor the confidence to explain them. Explanations are the fallacy of a scientific age. And the cardinal fact of the case is this, that out in Siddermorton Park, with the glory of some wonderful world where there is neither sorrow nor sighing, still clinging to him, on the 4th of August 1895, stood an Angel, bright and beautiful, talking to the Vicar of Siddermorton about the plurality of worlds. The author will swear to the Angel, if need be; and there he draws the line.

<center>★★★★★★</center>

"I have," said the Angel, "a most unusual feeling—*here*. Have had since sunrise. I don't remember ever having any feeling—*here* before."

"Not pain, I hope," said the Vicar.

"Oh no! It is quite different from that—a kind of vacuous feeling."

"The atmospheric pressure, perhaps, is a little different," the Vicar began, feeling his chin.

"And do you know, I have also the most curious sensations in my mouth—almost as if—it's so absurd!—as if I wanted to stuff things into it."

"Bless me!" said the Vicar. "Of course! You're hungry!"

"Hungry!" said the Angel. "What's that?"

"Don't you eat?"

"Eat! The word's quite new to me."

"Put food into your mouth, you know. One has to here. You will soon learn. If you don't, you get thin and miserable, and suffer a great deal—*pain*, you know—and finally you die."

"Die!" said the Angel. "That's another strange word!"

"It's not strange here. It means leaving off, you know," said the Vicar.

"We never leave off," said the Angel.

"You don't know what may happen to you in this world," said the Vicar, thinking him over. "Possibly if you are feeling hungry, and can feel pain and have your wings broken, you may even have to die before you get out of it again. At any rate you had better try eating.

<center>98</center>

For my own part—ahem!—there are many more disagreeable things."

"I suppose I *had* better Eat," said the Angel. "If it's not too difficult. I don't like this 'Pain' of yours, and I don't like this 'Hungry.' If your 'Die' is anything like it, I would prefer to Eat. What a very odd world this is!"

"To Die," said the Vicar, "is generally considered worse than either pain or hunger. . . . It depends."

"You must explain all that to me later," said the Angel. "Unless I wake up. At present, please show me how to eat. If you will. I feel a kind of urgency. . . ."

"Pardon me," said the Vicar, and offered an elbow. "If I may have the pleasure of entertaining you. My house lies yonder—not a couple of miles from here."

"*Your* House!" said the Angel a little puzzled; but he took the Vicar's arm affectionately, and the two, conversing as they went, waded slowly through the luxuriant bracken, sun mottled under the trees, and on over the stile in the park palings, and so across the bee-swarming heather for a mile or more, down the hillside, home.

You would have been charmed at the couple could you have seen them. The Angel, slight of figure, scarcely five feet high, and with a beautiful, almost effeminate face, such as an Italian old Master might have painted. (Indeed, there is one in the National Gallery—*Tobias and the Angel*, by some artist unknown—not at all unlike him so far as face and spirit go.) He was robed simply in a purple-wrought saffron blouse, bare kneed and bare-footed, with his wings (broken now, and a leaden grey) folded behind him.

The Vicar was a short, rather stout figure, rubicund, red-haired, clean-shaven, and with bright ruddy brown eyes. He wore a piebald straw hat with a black ribbon, a very neat white tie, and a fine gold watch-chain. He was so greatly interested in his companion that it only occurred to him when he was in sight of the Vicarage that he had left his gun lying just where he had dropped it amongst the bracken.

He was rejoiced to hear that the pain of the bandaged wing fell rapidly in intensity.

Chapter 5

Parenthesis on Angels

Let us be plain. The Angel of this story is the Angel of Art, not the Angel that one must be irreverent to touch—neither the Angel of religious feeling nor the Angel of popular belief. The last we all

know. She is alone among the angelic hosts in being distinctly femi-nine: she wears a robe of immaculate, unmitigated white with sleeves, is fair, with long golden tresses, and has eyes of the blue of Heaven. Just a pure woman she is, pure maiden or pure matron, in her *robe de nuit*, and with wings attached to her shoulder blades. Her callings are domestic and sympathetic, she watches over a cradle or assists a sister soul heavenward. Often, she bears a palm leaf, but one would not be surprised if one met her carrying a warming-pan softly to some poor chilly sinner. She it was who came down in a bevy to Marguerite in prison, in the amended last scene in *Faust* at the Lyceum, and the interesting and improving little children that are to die young, have visions of such angels in the novels of Mrs Henry Wood.

This white womanliness with her indescribable charm of laven-der-like holiness, her aroma of clean, methodical lives, is, it would seem after all, a purely Teutonic invention. Latin thought knows her not; the old masters have none of her. She is of a piece with that gentle innocent ladylike school of art whereof the greatest triumph is "a lump in one's throat," and where wit and passion, scorn and pomp, have no place.

The white angel was made in Germany, in the land of blonde women and the domestic sentiments. She comes to us cool and wor-shipful, pure and tranquil, as silently soothing as the breadth and calm-ness of the starlit sky, which also is so unspeakably dear to the Teutonic soul. . . . We do her reverence. And to the angels of the Hebrews, those spirits of power and mystery, to Raphael, Zadkiel, and Michael, of whom only Watts has caught the shadow, of whom only Blake has seen the splendour, to them too, do we do reverence.

But this Angel the Vicar shot is, we say, no such angel at all, but the Angel of Italian art, polychromatic and gay. He comes from the land of beautiful dreams and not from any holier place. At best he is a pop-ish creature. Bear patiently, therefore, with his scattered remiges, and be not hasty with your charge of irreverence before the story is read.

CHAPTER 6

At the Vicarage

The Curate's wife and her two daughters and Mrs Jehoram were still playing at tennis on the lawn behind the Vicar's study, playing keenly and talking in gasps about paper patterns for blouses. But the Vicar forgot and came in that way.

They saw the Vicar's hat above the rhododendrons, and a bare curly

head beside him. "I must ask him about Susan Wiggin," said the Curate's wife. She was about to serve, and stood with a racket in one hand and a ball between the fingers of the other. "*He* really ought to have gone to see her—being the Vicar. Not George. I——*Ah!*"

For the two figures suddenly turned the corner and were visible. The Vicar, arm in arm with——

You see, it came on the Curate's wife suddenly. The Angel's face being towards her she saw nothing of the wings. Only a face of unearthly beauty in a halo of chestnut hair, and a graceful figure clothed in a saffron garment that barely reached the knees. The thought of those knees flashed upon the Vicar at once. He too was horror-struck. So were the two girls and Mrs Jehoram. All horror-struck. The Angel stared in astonishment at the horror-struck group. You see, he had never seen anyone horror-struck before.

"Mis—ter Hilyer!" said the Curate's wife. "This is *too* much!" She stood speechless for a moment. "*Oh!*"

She swept round upon the rigid girls. "Come!" The Vicar opened and shut his voiceless mouth. The world hummed and spun about him. There was a whirling of zephyr skirts, four impassioned faces sweeping towards the open door of the passage that ran through the vicarage. He felt his position went with them.

"Mrs Mendham," said the Vicar, stepping forward. "Mrs Mendham. You don't understand——"

"*Oh!*" they all said again.

One, two, three, four skirts vanished in the doorway. The Vicar staggered half way across the lawn and stopped, aghast. "This comes," he heard the Curate's wife say, out of the depth of the passage, "of having an unmarried vicar——." The umbrella stand wobbled. The front door of the vicarage slammed like a minute gun. There was silence for a space.

"I might have thought," he said. "She is always so hasty."

He put his hand to his chin—a habit with him. Then turned his face to his companion. The Angel was evidently well bred. He was holding up Mrs Jehoram's sunshade—she had left it on one of the cane chairs—and examining it with extraordinary interest. He opened it. "What a curious little mechanism!" he said. "What can it be for?"

The Vicar did not answer. The angelic costume certainly was—the Vicar knew it was a case for a French phrase—but he could scarcely remember it. He so rarely used French. It was not *de trop*, he knew. Anything but *de trop*. The Angel was *de trop*, but certainly not his cos-

tume. Ah! *Sans culotte!*

The Vicar examined his visitor critically—for the first time. "He *will* be difficult to explain," he said to himself softly.

The Angel stuck the sunshade into the turf and went to smell the sweet briar. The sunshine fell upon his brown hair and gave it almost the appearance of a halo. He pricked his finger. "Odd!" he said. "Pain again."

"Yes," said the Vicar, thinking aloud. "He's very beautiful and curious as he is. I should like him best so. But I am afraid I must."

He approached the Angel with a nervous cough.

<p style="text-align:center">******</p>

"Those," said the Vicar, "were ladies."

"How grotesque," said the Angel, smiling and smelling the sweet briar. "And such quaint shapes!"

"Possibly," said the Vicar. "Did you, *ahem*, notice how they behaved?"

"They went away. Seemed, indeed, to run away. Frightened? I, of course, was frightened at things without wings. I hope—— they were not frightened at my wings?"

"At your appearance generally," said the Vicar, glancing involuntarily at the pink feet.

"Dear me! It never occurred to me. I suppose I seemed as odd to them as you did to me." He glanced down. "And my feet. *You* have hoofs like a hippogriff."

"Boots," corrected the Vicar.

"Boots, you call them! But anyhow, I am sorry I alarmed——"

"You see," said the Vicar, stroking his chin, "our ladies, *ahem*, have peculiar views—rather inartistic views—about, *ahem*, clothing. Dressed as you are, I am afraid, I am really afraid that—beautiful as your costume certainly is—you will find yourself somewhat, *ahem*, somewhat isolated in society. We have a little proverb, 'When in Rome, *ahem*, one must do as the Romans do.' I can assure you that, assuming you are desirous to, *ahem*, associate with us—during your involuntary stay——"

The Angel retreated a step or so as the Vicar came nearer and nearer in his attempt to be diplomatic and confidential. The beautiful face grew perplexed. "I don't quite understand. Why do you keep making these noises in your throat? Is it Die or Eat, or any of those. . . ."

"As your host," interrupted the Vicar, and stopped.

"As my host," said the Angel.

"*Would* you object, pending more permanent arrangements, to in-

<p style="text-align:center">102</p>

vest yourself, *ahem*, in a suit, an entirely new suit I may say, like this I have on?"

"Oh!" said the Angel. He retreated so as to take in the Vicar from top to toe. "Wear clothes like yours!" he said. He was puzzled but amused. His eyes grew round and bright, his mouth puckered at the corners.

"Delightful!" he said, clapping his hands together. "What a mad, quaint dream this is! Where are they?" He caught at the neck of the saffron robe.

"Indoors!" said the Vicar. "This way. We will change—indoors!"

<p align="center">★★★★★★</p>

So, the Angel was invested in a pair of nether garments of the Vicar's, a shirt, ripped down the back (to accommodate the wings), socks, shoes—the Vicar's dress shoes—collar, tie, and light overcoat. But putting on the latter was painful, and reminded the Vicar that the bandaging was temporary. "I will ring for tea at once, and send Grummet down for Crump," said the Vicar. "And dinner shall be earlier." While the Vicar shouted his orders on the landing rails, the Angel surveyed himself in the cheval glass with immense delight. If he was a stranger to pain, he was evidently no stranger—thanks perhaps to dreaming—to the pleasure of incongruity.

They had tea in the drawing-room. The Angel sat on the music stool (music stool because of his wings). At first, he wanted to lie on the hearthrug. He looked much less radiant in the Vicar's clothes, than he had done upon the moor when dressed in saffron. His face shone still, the colour of his hair and cheeks was strangely bright, and there was a superhuman light in his eyes, but his wings under the overcoat gave him the appearance of a hunchback. The garments, indeed, made quite a terrestrial thing of him, the trousers were puckered transversely, and the shoes a size or so too large.

He was charmingly affable and quite ignorant of the most elementary facts of civilization. Eating came without much difficulty, and the Vicar had an entertaining time teaching him how to take tea. "What a mess it is! What a dear grotesque ugly world you live in!" said the Angel. "Fancy stuffing things into your mouth! We use our mouths just to talk and sing with. Our world, you know, is almost incurably beautiful. We get so very little ugliness, that I find all this. . . . delightful."

Mrs Hinijer, the Vicar's housekeeper, looked at the Angel suspiciously when she brought in the tea. She thought him rather a "queer customer." What she would have thought had she seen him in saffron

no one can tell.

The Angel shuffled about the room with his cup of tea in one hand, and the bread and butter in the other, and examined the Vicar's furniture. Outside the French windows, the lawn with its array of dahlias and sunflowers glowed in the warm sunlight, and Mrs Jehoram's sunshade stood thereon like a triangle of fire. He thought the Vicar's portrait over the mantel very curious indeed, could not understand what it was there for. "You have yourself round," he said, *apropos* of the portrait, "Why want yourself flat?" and he was vastly amused at the glass fire screen. He found the oak chairs odd—"You're not square, are you?" he said, when the Vicar explained their use. "*We* never double ourselves up. We lie about on the asphodel when we want to rest."

"The chair," said the Vicar, "to tell you the truth, has always puzzled *me*. It dates, I think, from the days when the floors were cold and very dirty. I suppose we have kept up the habit. It's become a kind of instinct with us to sit on chairs. Anyhow, if I went to see one of my parishioners, and suddenly spread myself out on the floor—the natural way of it—I don't know what she would do. It would be all over the parish in no time. Yet it seems the natural method of reposing, to recline. The Greeks and Romans——"

"What is this?" said the Angel abruptly.

"That's a stuffed kingfisher. I killed it."

"Killed it!"

"Shot it," said the Vicar, "with a gun."

"Shot! As you did me?"

"I didn't kill you, you see. Fortunately."

"Is killing making like that?"

"In a way."

"Dear me! And you wanted to make me like that—wanted to put glass eyes in me and string me up in a glass case full of ugly green and brown stuff?"

"You see," began the Vicar, "I scarcely understood——"

"Is that 'die'?" asked the Angel suddenly.

"That is dead; it died."

"Poor little thing. I must eat a lot. But you say you killed it. *Why?*"

"You see," said the Vicar, "I take an interest in birds, and I (*ahem*) collect them. I wanted the specimen——"

The Angel stared at him for a moment with puzzled eyes. "A beautiful bird like that!" he said with a shiver. "Because the fancy took you. You wanted the specimen!"

He thought for a minute. "Do you often kill?" he asked the Vicar.

CHAPTER 7

The Man of Science

Then Doctor Crump arrived. Grummet had met him not a hundred yards from the vicarage gate. He was a large, rather heavy-looking man, with a clean-shaven face and a double chin. He was dressed in a grey morning coat (he always affected grey), with a checkered black and white tie. "What's the trouble?" he said, entering and staring without a shadow of surprise at the Angel's radiant face.

"This—*ahem*—gentleman," said the Vicar, "or—*ah*—Angel"—the Angel bowed—"is suffering from a gunshot wound."

"Gunshot wound!" said Doctor Crump. "In July! May I look at it, Mr—Angel, I think you said?"

"He will probably be able to assuage your pain," said the Vicar. "Let me assist you to remove your coat?"

The Angel turned obediently.

"Spinal curvature?" muttered Doctor Crump quite audibly, walking round behind the Angel. "No! abnormal growth. Hullo! This is odd!" He clutched the left wing. "Curious," he said. "Reduplication of the anterior limb—*bifid coracoid*. Possible, of course, but I've never seen it before." The angel winced under his hands. "Humerus. Radius and Ulna. All there. Congenital, of course. Humerus broken. Curious integumentary simulation of feathers. Dear me. Almost avian. Probably of considerable interest in comparative anatomy. I never did!—— How did this gunshot happen, Mr Angel?"

The Vicar was amazed at the Doctor's matter-of-fact manner.

"Our friend," said the Angel, moving his head at the Vicar.

"Unhappily it is my doing," said the Vicar, stepping forward, explanatory. "I mistook the gentleman—the Angel (*ahem*)—for a large bird——"

"Mistook him for a large bird! What next? Your eyes want seeing to," said Doctor Crump. "I've told you so before." He went on patting and feeling, keeping time with a series of grunts and inarticulate mutterings. . . . "But this is really a very good bit of amateur bandaging," said he. "I think I shall leave it. Curious malformation this is! Don't you find it inconvenient, Mr Angel?"

He suddenly walked round so as to look in the Angel's face.

The Angel thought he referred to the wound. "It is rather," he said.

"If it wasn't for the bones, I should say paint with iodine night and

105

morning. Nothing like iodine. You could paint your face flat with it. But the osseous outgrowth, the bones, you know, complicate things. I could saw them off, of course. It's not a thing one should have done in a hurry——"

"Do you mean my wings?" said the Angel in alarm.

"Wings!" said the Doctor. "Eigh? Call 'em wings! Yes—what else should I mean?"

"Saw them off!" said the Angel.

"Don't you think so? It's of course your affair. I am only advising——"

"Saw them off! What a funny creature you are!" said the Angel, beginning to laugh.

"As you will," said the Doctor. He detested people who laughed. "The things are curious," he said, turning to the Vicar. "If inconvenient"—to the Angel. "I never heard of such complete reduplication before—at least among animals. In plants it's common enough. Were you the only one in your family?" He did not wait for a reply. "Partial cases of the fission of limbs are not at all uncommon, of course, Vicar—six-fingered children, calves with six feet, and cats with double toes, you know. May I assist you?" he said, turning to the Angel who was struggling with the coat. "But such a complete reduplication, and so avian, too! It would be much less remarkable if it was simply another pair of arms."

The coat was got on and he and the Angel stared at one another.

"Really," said the Doctor, "one begins to understand how that beautiful myth of the angels arose. You look a little hectic, Mr Angel—feverish. Excessive brilliance is almost worse as a symptom than excessive pallor. Curious your name should be Angel. I must send you a cooling draught, if you should feel thirsty in the night. . . . "

He made a memorandum on his shirt cuff. The Angel watched him thoughtfully, with the dawn of a smile in his eyes.

"One minute, Crump," said the Vicar, taking the Doctor's arm and leading him towards the door.

The Angel's smile grew brighter. He looked down at his black-clad legs. "He positively thinks I am a man!" said the Angel. "What he makes of the wings beats me altogether. What a queer creature he must be! This is really a most extraordinary Dream!"

★★★★★★

"That *is* an Angel," whispered the Vicar. "You don't understand."

"*What?*" said the Doctor in a quick, sharp voice. His eyebrows

went up and he smiled.

"But the wings?"

"Quite natural, quite if a little abnormal."

"Are you sure they are natural?"

"My dear fellow, everything that is, is natural. There is nothing un-natural in the world. If I thought there was, I should give up practice and go into *Le Grand Chartreuse*. There are abnormal phenomena, of course. And——"

"But the way I came upon him," said the Vicar.

"Yes, tell me where you picked him up," said the Doctor. He sat down on the hall table.

The Vicar began rather hesitatingly—he was not very good at story telling—with the rumours of a strange great bird. He told the story in clumsy sentences—for, knowing the Bishop as he did, with that awful example always before him he dreaded getting his pulpit style into his daily conversation—and at every third sentence or so, the Doctor made a downward movement of his head—the corners of his mouth tucked away, so to speak—as though he ticked off the phases of the story and so far found it just as it ought to be. "Self-hypnotism," he murmured once.

"I beg your pardon?" said the Vicar.

"Nothing," said the Doctor. "Nothing, I assure you. Go on. This is extremely interesting."

The Vicar told him he went out with his gun.

"*After* lunch, I think you said?" interrupted the Doctor.

"Immediately after," said the Vicar.

"You should not do such things, you know. But go on, please."

He came to the glimpse of the Angel from the gate.

"In the full glare," said the Doctor, in parenthesis. "It was seventy-nine in the shade."

When the Vicar had finished, the Doctor pressed his lips together tighter than ever, smiled faintly, and looked significantly into the Vicar's eyes.

"You don't . . ." began the Vicar, falteringly.

The Doctor shook his head. "Forgive me," he said, putting his hand on the Vicar's arm.

"You go out," he said, "on a hot lunch and on a hot afternoon. Probably over eighty. Your mind, what there is of it, is whirling with avian expectations. I say, 'what there is of it,' because most of your nervous energy is down there, digesting your dinner. A man who has

been lying in the bracken stands up before you and you blaze away. Over he goes—and as it happens—as it happens—he has reduplicate fore-limbs, one pair being not unlike wings. It's a coincidence certainly. And as for his iridescent colours and so forth———. Have you never had patches of colour swim before your eyes before, on a brilliant sunlight day?. . . Are you sure they were confined to the wings? Think."

"But he says he *is* an Angel!" said the Vicar, staring out of his little round eyes, his plump hands in his pockets.

"*Ah!*" said the Doctor with his eye on the Vicar. "I expected as much." He paused.

"But don't you think. . ." began the Vicar.

"That man," said the Doctor in a low, earnest voice, "is a mattoid."

"A what?" said the Vicar.

"A mattoid. An abnormal man. Did you notice the effeminate delicacy of his face? His tendency to quite unmeaning laughter? His neglected hair? Then consider his singular dress. . ."

The Vicar's hand went up to his chin.

"Marks of mental weakness," said the Doctor. "Many of this type of degenerate show this same disposition to assume some vast mysterious credentials. One will call himself the Prince of Wales, another the Archangel Gabriel, another the Deity even. Ibsen thinks he is a Great Teacher, and Maeterlink a new Shakespeare. I've just been reading all about it—in Nordau. No doubt his odd deformity gave him an idea. . ."

"But really," began the Vicar.

"No doubt he's slipped away from confinement."

"I do not altogether accept. . ."

"You will. If not, there's the police, and failing that, advertisement; but, of course, his people may want to hush it up. It's a sad thing in a family. . ."

"He seems so altogether. . ."

"Probably you'll hear from his friends in a day or so," said the Doctor, feeling for his watch. "He can't live far from here, I should think. He seems harmless enough. I must come along and see that wing again tomorrow." He slid off the hall table and stood up.

"Those old wives' tales still have their hold on you," he said, patting the Vicar on the shoulder. "But an angel, you know—Ha, ha!"

"I certainly *did* think. . ." said the Vicar dubiously.

"Weigh the evidence," said the Doctor, still fumbling at his watch. "Weigh the evidence with our instruments of precision. What does it leave you? Splashes of colour, spots of fancy—*muscae volantes*."

"And yet," said the Vicar, "I could almost swear to the glory on his wings. . ."

"Think it over," said the Doctor (watch out); "hot afternoon—brilliant sunshine—boiling down on your head. . . . But really, I *must* be going. It is a quarter to five. I'll see your—angel (ha, ha!) tomorrow again, if no one has been to fetch him in the meanwhile. Your bandaging was really very good. I flatter *myself* on that score. Our ambulance classes *were* a success you see. . . Good afternoon."

CHAPTER 8

The Curate

The Vicar opened the door half mechanically to let out Crump, and saw Mendham, his curate, coming up the pathway by the hedge of purple vetch and meadowsweet. At that his hand went up to his chin and his eyes grew perplexed. Suppose he *was* deceived. The Doctor passed the Curate with a sweep of his hand from his hat brim. Crump was an extraordinarily clever fellow, the Vicar thought, and knew far more of anyone's brain than one did oneself. The Vicar felt that so acutely. It made the coming explanation difficult. Suppose he were to go back into the drawing-room, and find just a tramp asleep on the hearthrug.

Mendham was a cadaverous man with a magnificent beard. He looked, indeed, as though he had run to beard as a mustard plant does to seed. But when he spoke you found he had a voice as well.

"My wife came home in a dreadful state," he brayed out at long range.

"Come in," said the Vicar; "come in. Most remarkable occurrence. Please come in. Come into the study. I'm really dreadfully sorry. But when I explain. . ."

"And apologise, I hope," brayed the Curate.

"And apologise. No, not that way. This way. The study."

"Now what *was* that woman?" said the Curate, turning on the Vicar as the latter closed the study door.

"What woman?"

"Pah!"

"But really!"

"The painted creature in light attire—disgustingly light attire, to speak freely—with whom you were promenading the garden."

"My dear Mendham—that was an Angel!"

"A very pretty Angel?"

"The world is getting so matter-of-fact," said the Vicar.

"The world," roared the Curate, "grows blacker every day. But to find a man in your position, shamelessly, openly. . ."

"*Bother!*" said the Vicar aside. He rarely swore. "Look here, Mendham, you really misunderstand. I can assure you. . ."

"Very well," said the Curate. "Explain!" He stood with his lank legs apart, his arms folded, scowling at his Vicar over his big beard.

(Explanations, I repeat, I have always considered the peculiar fallacy of this scientific age.)

The Vicar looked about him helplessly. The world had all gone dull and dead. Had he been dreaming all the afternoon? Was there really an angel in the drawing-room? Or was he the sport of a complicated hallucination?

"Well?" said Mendham, at the end of a minute.

The Vicar's hand fluttered about his chin. "It's such a round-about story," he said.

"No doubt it will be," said Mendham harshly.

The Vicar restrained a movement of impatience.

"I went out to look for a strange bird this afternoon. . .Do you believe in angels, Mendham, real angels?"

"I'm not here to discuss theology. I am the husband of an insulted woman."

"But I tell you it's not a figure of speech; this *is* an angel, a real angel with wings. He's in the next room now. You do misunderstand me, so. . . ."

"Really, Hilyer—"

"It is true I tell you, Mendham. I swear it is true." The Vicar's voice grew impassioned. "What sin I have done that I should entertain and clothe angelic visitants, I don't know. I only know that—inconvenient as it undoubtedly will be—I have an angel now in the drawing-room, wearing my new suit and finishing his tea. And he's stopping with me, indefinitely, at my invitation. No doubt it was rash of me. But I can't turn him out, you know, because Mrs Mendham——I may be a weakling, but I am still a gentleman."

"Really, Hilyer—"

"I can assure you it is true." There was a note of hysterical desperation in the Vicar's voice. "I fired at him, taking him for a flamingo, and hit him in the wing."

"I thought this was a case for the Bishop. I find it is a case for the Lunacy Commissioners."

110

"Come and see him, Mendham!"

"But there *are* no angels."

"We teach the people differently," said the Vicar.

"Not as material bodies," said the Curate.

"Anyhow, come and see him."

"I don't want to see your hallucinations," began the Curate.

"I can't explain anything unless you come and see him," said the Vicar. "A man who's more like an angel than anything else in heaven or earth. You simply must see if you wish to understand."

"I don't wish to understand," said the Curate. "I don't wish to lend myself to any imposture. Surely, Hilyer, if this is not an imposition, you can tell me yourself....Flamingo, indeed!"

<p style="text-align:center">★★★★★★</p>

The Angel had finished his tea and was standing looking pensively out of the window. He thought the old church down the valley lit by the light of the setting sun was very beautiful, but he could not understand the serried ranks of tombstones that lay up the hillside beyond. He turned as Mendham and the Vicar came in.

Now Mendham could bully his Vicar cheerfully enough, just as he could bully his congregation; but he was not the sort of man to bully a stranger. He looked at the Angel, and the "strange woman" theory was disposed of. The Angel's beauty was too clearly the beauty of the youth.

"Mr Hilyer tells me," Mendham began, in an almost apologetic tone, "that you—ah—it's so curious—claim to be an Angel."

"*Are* an Angel," said the Vicar.

The Angel bowed.

"Naturally," said Mendham, "we are curious."

"Very," said the Angel. "The blackness and the shape."

"I beg your pardon?" said Mendham.

"The blackness and the flaps," repeated the Angel; "and no wings."

"Precisely," said Mendham, who was altogether at a loss. "We are, of course, curious to know something of how you came into the village in such a peculiar costume."

The Angel looked at the Vicar. The Vicar touched his chin.

"You see," began the Vicar.

"Let *him* explain," said Mendham; "I beg."

"I wanted to suggest," began the Vicar.

"And I don't want you to suggest."

"*Bother!*" said the Vicar.

The Angel looked from one to the other. "Such rugose expressions flit across your faces!" he said.

"You see, Mr—Mr—I don't know your name," said Mendham, with a certain diminution of suavity. "The case stands thus: My wife—four ladies, I might say—are playing lawn tennis, when you suddenly rush out on them, sir; you rush out on them from among the rhododendra in a very defective costume. You and Mr Hilyer."

"But I—" said the Vicar.

"I know. It was this gentleman's costume was defective. Naturally—it is my place in fact—to demand an explanation." His voice was growing in volume. "And I *must* demand an explanation."

The Angel smiled faintly at his note of anger and his sudden attitude of determination—arms tightly folded.

"I am rather new to the world," the Angel began.

"Nineteen at least," said Mendham. "Old enough to know better. That's a poor excuse."

"May I ask one question first?" said the Angel.

"Well?"

"Do you think I am a Man—like yourself? As the chequered man did."

"If you are not a man—"

"One other question. Have you *never* heard of an Angel?"

"I warn you not to try that story upon me," said Mendham, now back at his familiar *crescendo*.

The Vicar interrupted: "But Mendham—he has wings!"

"*Please* let me talk to him," said Mendham.

"You are so quaint," said the Angel; "you interrupt everything I have to say."

"But what *have* you to say?" said Mendham.

"That I really *am* an Angel. . ."

"Pshaw!"

"There you go!"

"But tell me, honestly, how you came to be in the shrubbery of Siddermorton Vicarage—in the state in which you were. And in the Vicar's company. Cannot you abandon this ridiculous story of yours? . . ."

The Angel shrugged his wings. "What is the matter with this man?" he said to the Vicar.

"My dear Mendham," said the Vicar, "a few words from me. . ."

"Surely my question is straightforward enough!"

"But you won't tell me the answer you want, and it's no good my

telling you any other."

"*Pshaw!*" said the Curate again. And then turning suddenly on the Vicar, "Where does he come from?"

The Vicar was in a dreadful state of doubt by this time.

"He *says* he is an Angel!" said the Vicar. "Why don't you listen to him?"

"No angel would alarm four ladies. . ."

"Is *that* what it is all about?" said the Angel.

"Enough cause too, I should think!" said the Curate.

"But I really did not know," said the Angel.

"This is altogether too much!"

"I am sincerely sorry I alarmed these ladies."

"You ought to be. But I see I shall get nothing out of you two." Mendham went towards the door. "I am convinced there is something discreditable at the bottom of this business. Or why not tell a simple straightforward story? I will confess you puzzle me. Why, in this en-lightened age, you should tell this fantastic, this far-fetched story of an Angel, altogether beats me. What good *can* it do? . . ."

"But stop and look at his wings!" said the Vicar. "I can assure you he has wings!"

Mendham had his fingers on the door-handle. "I have seen quite enough," he said. "It may be this is simply a foolish attempt at a hoax, Hilyer."

"But Mendham!" said the Vicar.

The Curate halted in the doorway and looked at the Vicar over his shoulder. The accumulating judgment of months found vent. "I can-not understand, Hilyer, why you are in the Church. For the life of me I cannot. The air is full of Social Movements, of Economic change, the Woman Movement, Rational Dress, The Reunion of Christendom, Socialism, Individualism—all the great and moving Questions of the Hour! Surely, we who follow the Great Reformer. . .And here you are stuffing birds, and startling ladies with your callous disregard. . ."

"But Mendham," began the Vicar.

The Curate would not hear him. "You shame the Apostles with your levity.... But this is only a preliminary enquiry," he said, with a threatening note in his sonorous voice, and so vanished abruptly (with a violent slam) from the room.

★★★★★★

"Are *all* men so odd as this?" said the Angel.

"I'm in such a difficult position," said the Vicar. "You see," he said,

113

and stopped, searching his chin for an idea.

"I'm beginning to see," said the Angel.

"They won't believe it."

"I see that."

"They will think I tell lies."

"And?"

"That will be extremely painful to me."

"Painful! . . . Pain," said the Angel. "I hope not."

The Vicar shook his head. The good report of the village had been the breath of his life, so far. "You see," he said, "it would look so much more plausible if you said you were just a man."

"But I'm not," said the Angel.

"No, you're not," said the Vicar. "So that's no good."

"Nobody here, you know, has ever seen an Angel, or heard of one—except in church. If you had made your *debut* in the chancel—on Sunday—it might have been different. But that's too late now. . . (*Bother!*) Nobody, absolutely nobody, will believe in you."

"I hope I am not inconveniencing you?"

"Not at all," said the Vicar; "not at all. Only——. Naturally it may be inconvenient if you tell a too incredible story. If I might suggest (*ahem*)——."

"Well?"

"You see, people in the world, being men themselves, will almost certainly regard you as a man. If you say you are not, they will simply say you do not tell the truth. Only exceptional people appreciate the exceptional. When in Rome one must—well, respect Roman prejudices a little—talk Latin. You will find it better——"

"You propose I should feign to become a man?"

"You have my meaning at once."

The Angel stared at the Vicar's hollyhocks and thought.

"Possibly, after all," he said slowly, "I *shall* become a man. I may have been too hasty in saying I was not. You say there are no angels in this world. Who am I to set myself up against your experience? A mere thing of a day—so far as this world goes. If you say there are no angels—clearly, I must be something else. I eat—angels do not eat. I *may* be a man already."

"A convenient view, at any rate," said the Vicar.

"If it is convenient to you——"

"It is. And then to account for your presence here."

"*If,*" said the Vicar, after a hesitating moment of reflection, "if, for

instance, you had been an ordinary man with a weakness for wading, and you had gone wading in the Sidder, and your clothes had been stolen, for instance, and I had come upon you in that position of inconvenience; the explanation I shall have to make to Mrs Mendham——would be shorn at least of the supernatural element. There is such a feeling against the supernatural element nowadays—even in the pulpit. You would hardly believe——"

"It's a pity that was not the case," said the Angel.

"Of course," said the Vicar. "It is a great pity that was not the case. But at any rate you will oblige me if you do not obtrude your angelic nature. You will oblige everyone, in fact. There is a settled opinion that angels do not do this kind of thing. And nothing is more painful—as I can testify—than a decaying settled opinion. . .Settled opinions are mental teeth in more ways than one. For my own part,"—the Vicar's hand passed over his eyes for a moment—"I cannot but believe you are an angel. . . Surely I can believe my own eyes."

"We always do ours," said the Angel.

"And so, do we, within limits."

Then the clock upon the mantel chimed seven, and almost simultaneously Mrs Hinijer announced dinner.

CHAPTER 9
After Dinner

The Angel and the Vicar sat at dinner. The Vicar, with his napkin tucked in at his neck, watched the Angel struggling with his soup. "You will soon get into the way of it," said the Vicar. The knife and fork business was done awkwardly but with effect. The Angel looked furtively at Delia, the little waiting maid. When presently they sat cracking nuts—which the Angel found congenial enough—and the girl had gone, the Angel asked: "Was that a lady, too?"

"Well," said the Vicar (*crack*). "No—she is not a lady. She is a servant."

"Yes," said the Angel; "she *had* rather a nicer shape."

"You mustn't tell Mrs Mendham that," said the Vicar, covertly satisfied.

"She didn't stick out so much at the shoulders and hips, and there was more of her in between. And the colour of her robes was not discordant—simply neutral. And her face——"

"Mrs Mendham and her daughters had been playing tennis," said the Vicar, feeling he ought not to listen to detraction even of his mor-

tal enemy. "Do you like these things—these nuts?"

"Very much," said the Angel. *Crack.*

"You see," said the Vicar (*Chum, chum, chum*). "For my own part I entirely believe you are an angel."

"Yes!" said the Angel.

"I shot you—I saw you flutter. It's beyond dispute. In my own mind. I admit it's curious and against my preconceptions, but—practically—I'm assured, perfectly assured in fact, that I saw what I certainly did see. But after the behaviour of these people. (*Crack*). I really don't see how we are to persuade people. Nowadays people are so very particular about evidence. So that I think there is a great deal to be said for the attitude you assume. Temporarily at least I think it would be best of you to do as you propose to do, and behave as a man as far as possible. Of course, there is no knowing how or when you may go back. After what has happened (*Gluck, gluck, gluck*—as the Vicar refills his glass)—after what has happened I should not be surprised to see the side of the room fall away, and the hosts of heaven appear to take you away again—take us both away even. You have so far enlarged my imagination. All these years I have been forgetting Wonderland. But still———. It will certainly be wiser to break the thing gently to them."

"This life of yours," said the Angel. "I'm still in the dark about it. How do you begin?"

"Dear me!" said the Vicar. "Fancy having to explain that! We begin existence here, you know, as babies, silly pink helpless things wrapped in white, with goggling eyes, that yelp dismally at the Font. Then these babies grow larger and become even beautiful—when their faces are washed. And they continue to grow to a certain size. They become children, boys and girls, youths and maidens (*Crack*), young men and young women. That is the finest time in life according to many—certainly the most beautiful. Full of great hopes and dreams, vague emotions and unexpected dangers."

"*That* was a maiden?" said the Angel, indicating the door through which Delia had disappeared.

"Yes," said the Vicar, "that was a maiden." And paused thoughtfully.

"And then?"

"Then," said the Vicar, "the glamour fades and life begins in earnest. The young men and young women pair off—most of them. They come to me shy and bashful, in smart ugly dresses, and I marry them. And then little pink babies come to them, and some of the youths and maidens that were, grow fat and vulgar, and some grow thin and

116

shrewish, and their pretty complexions go, and they get a queer delusion of superiority over the younger people, and all the delight and glory goes out of their lives. So, they call the delight and glory of the younger ones, Illusion. And then they begin to drop to pieces."

"Drop to pieces!" said the Angel. "How grotesque!"

"Their hair comes off and gets dull coloured or ashen grey," said the Vicar. "*I*, for instance." He bowed his head forward to show a circular shining patch the size of a florin. "And their teeth come out. Their faces collapse and become as wrinkled and dry as a shrivelled apple. 'Corrugated' you called mine. They care more and more for what they have to eat and to drink, and less and less for any of the other delights of life. Their limbs get loose in the joints, and their hearts slack, or little pieces from their lungs come coughing up. Pain. . . ."

"Ah!" said the Angel.

"Pain comes into their lives more and more. And then they go. They do not like to go, but they have to—out of this world, very reluctantly, clutching its pain at last in their eagerness to stop. . ."

"Where do they go?"

"Once I thought I knew. But now I am older I know I do not know. We have a Legend—perhaps it is not a legend. One may be a churchman and disbelieve. Stokes says there is nothing in it. . ." The Vicar shook his head at the bananas.

"And you?" said the Angel. "Were you a little pink baby?"

"A little while ago I was a little pink baby."

"Were you robed then as you are now?"

"Oh no! Dear me! What a queer idea! Had long white clothes, I suppose, like the rest of them."

"And then you were a little boy?"

"A little boy."

"And then a glorious youth?"

"I was not a very glorious youth, I am afraid. I was sickly, and too poor to be radiant, and with a timid heart. I studied hard and pored over the dying thoughts of men long dead. So, I lost the glory, and no maiden came to me, and the dullness of life began too soon."

"And you have your little pink babies?"

"None," said the Vicar with a scarce perceptible pause. "Yet all the same, as you see, I am beginning to drop to pieces. Presently my back will droop like a wilting flower-stalk. And then, in a few thousand days more I shall be done with, and I shall go out of this world of mine. . . Whither I do not know."

117

"And you have to eat like this every day?"

"Eat, and get clothes and keep this roof above me. There are some very disagreeable things in this world called Cold and Rain. And the other people here—how and why is too long a story—have made me a kind of chorus to their lives. They bring their little pink babies to me and I have to say a name and some other things over each new pink baby. And when the children have grown to be youths and maidens, they come again and are confirmed. You will understand that better later. Then before they may join in couples and have pink babies of their own, they must come again and hear me read out of a book. They would be outcast, and no other maiden would speak to the maiden who had a little pink baby without I had read over her for twenty minutes out of my book.

"It's a necessary thing, as you will see. Odd as it may seem to you. And afterwards when they are falling to pieces, I try and persuade them of a strange world in which I scarcely believe myself, where life is altogether different from what they have had—or desire. And in the end, I bury them, and read out of my book to those who will presently follow into the unknown land. I stand at the beginning, and at the zenith, and at the setting of their lives. And on every seventh day, I who am a man myself, I who see no further than they do, talk to them of the Life to Come—the life of which we know nothing. If such a life there be. And slowly I drop to pieces amidst my prophesying."

"What a strange life!" said the Angel.

"Yes," said the Vicar. "What a strange life! But the thing that makes it strange to me is new. I had taken it as a matter of course until you came into my life."

"This life of ours is so insistent," said the Vicar. "It, and its petty needs, its temporary pleasures (*Crack*) swathe our souls about. While I am preaching to these people of mine of another life, some are ministering to one appetite and eating sweets, others—the old men—are slumbering, the youths glance at the maidens, the grown men protrude white waistcoats and gold chains, pomp and vanity on a substratum of carnal substance, their wives flaunt garish bonnets at one another. And I go on droning away of the things unseen and unrealised—'Eye hath not seen,' I read, 'nor ear heard, nor hath it entered into the imagination of man to conceive,' and I look up to catch an adult male immortal admiring the fit of a pair of three and sixpenny gloves. It is damping year after year. When I was ailing in my youth, I felt almost the assurance of vision that beneath this temporary phantasm world

was the real world—the enduring world of the Life Everlasting. But now——"

He glanced at his chubby white hand, fingering the stem of his glass. "I have put on flesh since then," he said. (*Pause*).

"I have changed and developed very much. The battle of the Flesh and Spirit does not trouble me as it did. Every day I feel less confidence in my beliefs, and more in God. I live, I am afraid, a quiescent life, duties fairly done, a little ornithology and a little chess, a trifle of mathematical trifling. My times are in His hands——"

The Vicar sighed and became pensive. The Angel watched him, and the Angel's eyes were troubled with the puzzle of him. "*Gluck, gluck, gluck*," went the decanter as the Vicar refilled his glass.

★★★★★★

So, the Angel dined and talked to the Vicar, and presently the night came and he was overtaken by yawning.

"Yah——oh!" said the Angel suddenly. "Dear me! A higher power seemed suddenly to stretch my mouth open and a great breath of air went rushing down my throat."

"You yawned," said the Vicar. "Do you never yawn in the angelic country?"

"Never," said the Angel.

"And yet you are immortal!——I suppose you want to go to bed."

"Bed!" said the Angel. "Where's that?"

So, the Vicar explained darkness to him and the art of going to bed. (The Angels, it seems sleep only in order to dream, and dream, like primitive man, with their foreheads on their knees. And they sleep among the white poppy meadows in the heat of the day.) The Angel found the bedroom arrangements quaint enough.

"Why is everything raised up on big wooden legs?" he said. "You have the floor, and then you put everything you have upon a wooden quadruped. Why do you do it?" The Vicar explained with philosophical vagueness. The Angel burnt his finger in the candle-flame—and displayed an absolute ignorance of the elementary principles of combustion. He was merely charmed when a line of fire ran up the curtains. The Vicar had to deliver a lecture on fire so soon as the flame was extinguished. He had all kinds of explanations to make—even the soap needed explaining. It was an hour or more before the Angel was safely tucked in for the night.

"He's very beautiful," said the Vicar, descending the staircase, quite tired out; "and he's a real angel no doubt. But I am afraid he will be

119

a dreadful anxiety, all the same, before he gets into our earthly way with things."

He seemed quite worried. He helped himself to an extra glass of sherry before he put away the wine in the cellaret.

<center>★★★★★</center>

The Curate stood in front of the looking-glass and solemnly divested himself of his collar.

"I never heard a more fantastic story," said Mrs Mendham from the basket chair. "The man must be mad. Are you sure——."

"Perfectly, my dear. I've told you every word, every incident——."

"*Well!*" said Mrs Mendham, and spread her hands. "There's no sense in it."

"Precisely, my dear."

"The Vicar," said Mrs Mendham, "must be mad."

"This hunchback is certainly one of the strangest creatures I've seen for a long time. Foreign looking, with a big bright coloured face and long brown hair. . . It can't have been cut for months!" The Curate put his studs carefully upon the shelf of the dressing-table. "And a kind of staring look about his eyes, and a simpering smile. Quite a silly looking person. Effeminate."

"But who *can* he be?" said Mrs Mendham.

"I can't imagine, my dear. Nor where he came from. He might be a chorister or something of that sort."

"But *why* should he be about the shrubbery. . . in that dreadful costume?"

"I don't know. The Vicar gave me no explanation. He simply said, 'Mendham, this is an Angel.'"

"I wonder if he drinks. . . They may have been bathing near the spring, of course," reflected Mrs Mendham. "But I noticed no other clothes on his arm."

The Curate sat down on his bed and unlaced his boots.

"It's a perfect mystery to me, my dear." (*Flick, flick* of laces.) "Hallucination is the only charitable——"

"You are sure, George, that it was *not* a woman."

"Perfectly," said the Curate.

"I know what men are, of course."

"It was a young man of nineteen or twenty," said the Curate.

"I can't understand it," said Mrs Mendham. "You say the creature is staying at the Vicarage?"

"Hilyer is simply mad," said the Curate. He got up and went pad-

<center>120</center>

ding round the room to the door to put out his boots. "To judge by his manner, you would really think he believed this cripple was an Angel." ("Are your shoes out, dear?")

("They're just by the wardrobe"), said Mrs Mendham. "He always was a little queer, you know. There was always something childish about him. . . An Angel!"

The Curate came and stood by the fire, fumbling with his braces. Mrs Mendham liked a fire even in the summer. "He shirks all the serious problems in life and is always trifling with some new foolishness," said the Curate. "Angel indeed!" He laughed suddenly. "Hilyer *must* be mad," he said.

Mrs Mendham laughed too. "Even that doesn't explain the hunchback," she said.

"The hunchback must be mad too," said the Curate.

"It's the only way of explaining it in a sensible way," said Mrs Mendham. [*Pause.*]

"Angel or no angel," said Mrs Mendham, "I know what is due to me. Even supposing the man thought he *was* in the company of an angel, that is no reason why he should not behave like a gentleman."

"That is perfectly true."

"You will write to the Bishop, of course?"

Mendham coughed. "No, I shan't write to the Bishop," said Mendham. "I think it seems a little disloyal. . . And he took no notice of the last, you know."

"But surely——"

"I shall write to Austin. In confidence. He will be sure to tell the Bishop, you know. And you must remember, my dear——"

"That Hilyer can dismiss you, you were going to say. My dear, the man's much too weak! *I* should have a word to say about that. And besides, you do all his work for him. Practically, we manage the parish from end to end. I do not know what would become of the poor if it was not for me. They'd have free quarters in the Vicarage tomorrow. There is that Goody Ansell——"

"I know, my dear," said the Curate, turning away and proceeding with his undressing. "You were telling me about her only this afternoon."

★★★★★★

And thus, in the little bedroom over the gable we reach a first resting place in this story. And as we have been hard at it, getting our story spread out before you, it may be perhaps well to recapitulate a little.

Looking back, you will see that much has been done; we began with a blaze of light "not uniform but broken all over by curving flashes like the waving of swords," and the sound of a mighty harping, and the advent of an Angel with polychromatic wings.

Swiftly, dexterously, as the reader must admit, wings have been clipped, halo handled off, the glory clapped into coat and trousers, and the Angel made for all practical purposes a man, under a suspicion of being either a lunatic or an impostor. You have heard too, or at least been able to judge, what the Vicar and the Doctor and the Curate's wife thought of the strange arrival. And further remarkable opinions are to follow.

The afterglow of the summer sunset in the north-west darkens into night and the Angel sleeps, dreaming himself back in the wonderful world where it is always light, and everyone is happy, where fire does not burn and ice does not chill; where rivulets of starlight go streaming through the amaranthine meadows, out to the seas of Peace. He dreams, and it seems to him that once more his wings glow with a thousand colours and flash through the crystal air of the world from which he has come.

So, he dreams. But the Vicar lies awake, too perplexed for dreaming. Chiefly he is troubled by the possibilities of Mrs Mendham; but the evening's talk has opened strange vistas in his mind, and he is stimulated by a sense as of something seen darkly by the indistinct vision of a hitherto unsuspected wonderland lying about his world. For twenty years now he has held his village living and lived his daily life, protected by his familiar creed, by the clamour of the details of life, from any mystical dreaming. But now interweaving with the familiar bother of his persecuting neighbour, is an altogether unfamiliar sense of strange new things.

There was something ominous in the feeling. Once, indeed, it rose above all other considerations, and in a kind of terror he blundered out of bed, bruised his shins very convincingly, found the matches at last, and lit a candle to assure himself of the reality of his own customary world again. But on the whole the more tangible trouble was the Mendham avalanche. Her tongue seemed to be hanging above him like the sword of Damocles. What might she not say of this business, before her indignant imagination came to rest?

And while the successful captor of the Strange Bird was sleeping thus uneasily, Gully of Sidderton was carefully unloading his gun after a wearisome blank day, and Sandy Bright was on his knees in prayer,

with the window carefully fastened. Annie Durgan was sleeping hard with her mouth open, and Amory's mother was dreaming of washing, and both of them had long since exhausted the topics of the Sound and the Glare. Lumpy Durgan was sitting up in his bed, now crooning the fragment of a tune and now listening intently for a sound he had heard once and longed to hear again.

As for the solicitor's clerk at Iping Hanger, he was trying to write poetry about a confectioner's girl at Portburdock, and the Strange Bird was quite out of his head. But the ploughman who had seen it on the confines of Siddermorton Park had a black eye. That had been one of the more tangible consequences of a little argument about birds' legs in the "Ship." It is worthy of this passing mention, since it is probably the only known instance of an Angel causing anything of the kind.

CHAPTER 10

Morning

The Vicar going to call the Angel, found him dressed and leaning out of his window. It was a glorious morning, still dewy, and the rising sunlight slanting round the corner of the house, struck warm and yellow upon the hillside. The birds were astir in the hedges and shrubbery. Up the hillside—for it was late in August—a plough drove slowly. The Angel's chin rested upon his hands and he did not turn as the Vicar came up to him.

"How's the wing?" said the Vicar.

"I'd forgotten it," said the Angel. "Is that yonder a man?"

The Vicar looked. "That's a ploughman."

"Why does he go to and fro like that? Does it amuse him?"

"He's ploughing. That's his work."

"Work! Why does he do it? It seems a monotonous thing to do."

"It is," admitted the Vicar. "But he has to do it to get a living, you know. To get food to eat and all that kind of thing."

"How curious!" said the Angel. "Do all men have to do that? Do you?"

"Oh, no. He does it for me; does my share."

"Why?" asked the Angel.

"Oh! in return for things I do for him, you know. We go in for division of labour in this world. Exchange is no robbery."

"I see," said the Angel, with his eyes still on the ploughman's heavy movements.

"What do you do for him?"

"That seems an easy question to you," said the Vicar, "but really!—it's difficult. Our social arrangements are rather complicated. It's impossible to explain these things all at once, before breakfast. Don't you feel hungry?"

"I think I do," said the Angel slowly, still at the window; and then abruptly, "Somehow I can't help thinking that ploughing must be far from enjoyable."

"Possibly," said the Vicar, "very possibly. But breakfast is ready. Won't you come down?"

The Angel left the window reluctantly.

"Our society," explained the Vicar on the staircase, "is a complicated organisation."

"Yes?"

"And it is so arranged that some do one thing and some another."

"And that lean, bent old man trudges after that heavy blade of iron pulled by a couple of horses while we go down to eat?"

"Yes. You will find it is perfectly just. Ah! mushrooms and poached eggs! It's the Social System. Pray be seated. Possibly it strikes you as unfair?"

"I'm puzzled," said the Angel.

"The drink I'm sending you is called coffee," said the Vicar. "I daresay you are. When I was a young man I was puzzled in the same way. But afterwards comes a broader view of things. (These black things are called mushrooms; they look beautiful.) Other Considerations. All men are brothers, of course, but some are younger brothers, so to speak. There is work that requires culture and refinement, and work in which culture and refinement would be an impediment. And the rights of property must not be forgotten. One must render unto Caesar. . . Do you know, instead of explaining this matter now (this is yours), I think I will lend you a little book to read (*chum, chum, chum*—these mushrooms are well up to their appearance), which sets the whole thing out very clearly."

CHAPTER 11

The Violin

After breakfast the Vicar went into the little room next his study to find a book on Political Economy for the Angel to read. For the Angel's social ignorances were clearly beyond any verbal explanations. The door stood ajar.

"What is that?" said the Angel, following him. "A violin!" He took it down.

"You play?" said the Vicar.

The Angel had the bow in his hand, and by way of answer drove it across the strings. The quality of the note made the Vicar turn suddenly.

The Angel's hand tightened on the instrument. The bow flew back and flickered, and an air the Vicar had never heard before danced in his ears. The Angel shifted the fiddle under his dainty chin and went on playing, and as he played his eyes grew bright and his lips smiled. At first, he looked at the Vicar, then his expression became abstracted. He seemed no longer to look at the Vicar, but through him, at something beyond, something in his memory or his imagination, something infinitely remote, undreamt of hitherto. . .

The Vicar tried to follow the music. The air reminded him of a flame, it rushed up, shone, flickered and danced, passed and reappeared. No!—it did not reappear! Another air—like it and unlike it, shot up after it, wavered, vanished. Then another, the same and not the same. It reminded him of the flaring tongues that palpitate and change above a newly lit fire. There are two airs—or *motifs*, which is it?—thought the Vicar. He knew remarkably little of musical technique. They go dancing up, one pursuing the other, out of the fire of the incantation, pursuing, fluctuating, turning, up into the sky. There below was the fire burning, a flame without fuel upon a level space, and there two flirting butterflies of sound, dancing away from it, up, one over another, swift, abrupt, uncertain.

"Flirting butterflies were they!" What was the Vicar thinking of? Where was he? In the little room next to his study, of course! And the Angel standing in front of him smiling into his face, playing the violin, and looking through him as though he was only a window———. That *motif* again, a yellow flare, spread fanlike by a gust, and now one, then with a swift eddying upward flight the other, the two things of fire and light pursuing one another again up into that clear immensity.

The study and the realities of life suddenly faded out of the Vicar's eyes, grew thinner and thinner like a mist that dissolves into air, and he and the Angel stood together on a pinnacle of wrought music, about which glittering melodies circled, and vanished, and reappeared. He was in the land of Beauty, and once more the glory of heaven was upon the Angel's face, and the glowing delights of colour pulsated in his wings. Himself the Vicar could not see.

But I cannot tell you of the vision of that great and spacious land, of its incredible openness, and height, and nobility. For there is no space there like ours, no time as we know it; one must needs speak by bungling metaphors and own in bitterness after all that one has failed. And it was only a vision. The wonderful creatures flying through the aether saw them not as they stood there, flew through them as one might pass through a whisp of mist. The Vicar lost all sense of duration, all sense of necessity——

"Ah!" said the Angel, suddenly putting down the fiddle.

The Vicar had forgotten the book on Political Economy, had forgotten everything until the Angel had done. For a minute he sat quite still. Then he woke up with a start. He was sitting on the old ironbound chest.

"Really," he said slowly, "you are very clever."

He looked about him in a puzzled way. "I had a kind of vision while you were playing. I seemed to see——. What did I see? It has gone."

He stood up with a dazzled expression upon his face. "I shall never play the violin again," he said. "I wish you would take it to your room—and keep it——. And play to me again. I did not know anything of music until I heard you play. I do not feel as though I had ever heard any music before."

He stared at the Angel, then about him at the room. "I have never felt anything of this kind with music before," he said. He shook his head. "I shall never play again."

CHAPTER 12

The Angel Explores the Village

Very unwisely, as I think, the Vicar allowed the Angel to go down into the village by himself, to enlarge his ideas of humanity. Unwisely, because how was he to imagine the reception the Angel would receive? Not thoughtlessly, I am afraid. He had always carried himself with decorum in the village, and the idea of a slow procession through the little street with all the inevitable curious remarks, explanations, pointings, was too much for him. The Angel might do the strangest things, the village was certain to think them. Peering faces. "Who's *he* got now?" Besides, was it not his duty to prepare his sermon in good time? The Angel, duly directed, went down cheerfully by himself—still innocent of most of the peculiarities of the human as distinguished from the angelic turn of mind.

The Angel walked slowly, his white hands folded behind his hunched back, his sweet face looking this way and that. He peered curiously into the eyes of the people he met. A little child picking a bunch of vetch and honeysuckle looked in his face, and forthwith came and put them in his hand. It was about the only kindness he had from a human being (saving only the Vicar and one other). He heard Mother Gustick scolding that granddaughter of hers as he passed the door. "You *Brazen* Faggit—you!" said Mother Gustick. "You Trumpery Baggage!"

The Angel stopped, startled at the strange sounds of Mother Gustick's voice. "Put yer best clo'es on, and yer feather in yer 'at, and off you goes to meet en, fal lal, and me at 'ome slaving for ye. 'Tis a Fancy Lady you'll be wantin' to be, my gal, a walkin' Touch and Go, with yer idleness and finery———"

The voice ceased abruptly, and a great peace came upon the battered air. "Most grotesque and strange!" said the Angel, still surveying this wonderful box of discords. "Walking Touch and Go!" He did not know that Mrs Gustick had suddenly become aware of his existence, and was scrutinising his appearance through the window-blind. Abruptly the door flew open, and she stared out into the Angel's face. A strange apparition, grey and dusty hair, and the dirty pink dress unhooked to show the stringy throat, a discoloured gargoyle, presently to begin spouting incomprehensible abuse.

"Now, then, Mister," began Mrs Gustick. "Have ye nothin' better to do than listen at people's doors for what you can pick up?"

The Angel stared at her in astonishment.

"D'year!" said Mrs Gustick, evidently very angry indeed. "Listenin'."

"Have you any objection to my hearing. . ."

"Object to my hearing! Course I have! Whad yer think? You aint such a Ninny. . ."

"But if ye didn't want me to hear, why did you cry out so loud? I thought. . ."

"*You thought!* Softie—that's what *you* are! You silly girt staring Gaby, what don't know any better than to come holding yer girt mouth wide open for all that you can catch holt on? And then off up there to tell! You great Fat-Faced, Tale-Bearin' Silly-Billy! I'd be ashamed to come poking and peering round quiet people's houses. . ."

The Angel was surprised to find that some inexplicable quality in her voice excited the most disagreeable sensations in him and a strong

127

desire to withdraw. But, resisting this, he stood listening politely (as the custom is in the Angelic Land, so long as anyone is speaking). The entire eruption was beyond his comprehension. He could not perceive any reason for the sudden projection of this vituperative head, out of infinity, so to speak. And questions without a break for an answer were outside his experience altogether.

Mrs Gustick proceeded with her characteristic fluency, assured him he was no gentleman, enquired if he called himself one, remarked that every tramp did as much nowadays, compared him to a Stuck Pig, marvelled at his impudence, asked him if he wasn't ashamed of himself standing there, enquired if he was rooted to the ground, was curious to be told what he meant by it, wanted to know whether he robbed a scarecrow for his clothes, suggested that an abnormal vanity prompted his behaviour, enquired if his mother knew he was out, and finally remarking, "I got somethin'll move you, my gentleman," disappeared with a ferocious slamming of the door.

The interval struck the Angel as singularly peaceful. His whirling mind had time to analyse his sensations. He ceased bowing and smiling, and stood merely astonished.

"This is a curious painful feeling," said the Angel. "Almost worse than Hungry, and quite different. When one is hungry one wants to eat. I suppose she was a woman. Here one wants to get away. I suppose I might just as well go."

He turned slowly and went down the road meditating. He heard the cottage door re-open, and turning his head, saw through intervening scarlet runners Mrs Gustick with a steaming saucepan full of boiling cabbage water in her hand.

"'Tis well you went, Mister Stolen Breeches," came the voice of Mrs Gustick floating down through the vermilion blossoms. "Don't you come peeping and prying round this yer cottage again or I'll learn ye manners, I will!"

The Angel stood in a state of considerable perplexity. He had no desire to come within earshot of the cottage again—ever. He did not understand the precise import of the black pot, but his general impression was entirely disagreeable. There was no explaining it.

"I *mean* it!" said Mrs Gustick, *crescendo*. "Drat it!—I *mean* it."

The Angel turned and went on, a dazzled look in his eyes.

"She was very grotesque!" said the Angel. "*Very*. Much more than the little man in black. And she means it.—— But what she means I don't know!. . ." He became silent. "I suppose they all mean some-

thing," he said, presently, still perplexed.

Then the Angel came in sight of the forge, where Sandy Bright's brother was shoeing a horse for the carter from Upmorton. Two hobbledehoys were standing by the forge staring in a bovine way at the proceedings. As the Angel approached these two and then the carter turned slowly through an angle of thirty degrees and watched his approach, staring quietly and steadily at him. The expression on their faces was one of abstract interest.

The Angel became self-conscious for the first time in his life. He drew nearer, trying to maintain an amiable expression on his face, an expression that beat in vain against their granitic stare. His hands were behind him. He smiled pleasantly, looking curiously at the (to him) incomprehensible employment of the smith. But the battery of eyes seemed to angle for his regard. Trying to meet the three pairs at once, the Angel lost his alertness and stumbled over a stone. One of the yokels gave a sarcastic cough, and was immediately covered with confusion at the Angel's enquiring gaze, nudging his companion with his elbow to cover his disorder. None spoke, and the Angel did not speak.

So soon as the Angel had passed, one of the three hummed this tune in an aggressive tone.

Then all three of them laughed. One tried to sing something and found his throat contained phlegm. The Angel proceeded on his way.

"Who's e then?" said the second hobbledehoy.

"*Ping, ping, ping,*" went the blacksmith's hammer.

"Spose he's one of these here foweners," said the carter from Upmorton. "Daamned silly fool he do look to be sure."

"Tas the way with them foweners," said the first hobbledehoy sagely.

"Got something very like the 'ump," said the carter from Upmorton. "Daa-a-amned if 'E ent."

Then the silence healed again, and they resumed their quiet expressionless consideration of the Angel's retreating figure.

"Very like the 'ump et is," said the carter after an enormous pause.

The Angel went on through the village, finding it all wonderful

enough. "They begin, and just a little while and then they end," he said to himself in a puzzled voice. "But what are they doing meanwhile?" Once he heard some invisible mouth chant inaudible words to the tune the man at the forge had hummed.

"That's the poor creature the Vicar shot with that great gun of his," said Sarah Glue (of 1, Church Cottages) peering over the blind.

"He looks Frenchified," said Susan Hopper, peering through the interstices of that convenient veil on curiosity.

"He has sweet eyes," said Sarah Glue, who had met them for a moment.

The Angel sauntered on. The postman passed him and touched his hat to him; further down was a dog asleep in the sun. He went on and saw Mendham, who nodded distantly and hurried past. (The Curate did not care to be seen talking to an angel in the village, until more was known about him). There came from one of the houses the sound of a child screaming in a passion, that brought a puzzled look to the angelic face. Then the Angel reached the bridge below the last of the houses, and stood leaning over the parapet watching the glittering little cascade from the mill.

"They begin, and just a little while, and then they end," said the weir from the mill. The water raced under the bridge, green and dark, and streaked with foam.

Beyond the mill rose the square tower of the church, with the churchyard behind it, a spray of tombstones and wooden headboards splashed up the hillside. A half dozen of beech trees framed the picture.

Then the Angel heard a shuffling of feet and the gride of wheels behind him, and turning his head saw a man dressed in dirty brown rags and a felt hat grey with dust, who was standing with a slight swaying motion and fixedly regarding the Angelic back. Beyond him was another almost equally dirty, pushing a knife grinder's barrow over the bridge.

"Mornin'," said the first person smiling weakly. "Goomorn'." He arrested an escaping hiccough.

The Angel stared at him. He had never seen a really fatuous smile before. "Who are you?" said the Angel.

The fatuous smile faded. "No your business whoaaam. Wishergoomorn."

"Carm on:" said the man with the grindstone, passing on his way.

"Wishergoomorn," said the dirty man, in a tone of extreme aggravation. "Carncher Answerme?"

"Carm *on* you fool!" said the man with the grindstone—receding.

"I don't understand," said the Angel.

"Donunderstan'. Sim'l enough. Wishergoomorn'. Willyanswerme? Wontchr? gemwishergem goomorn. Cusom answer goomorn. No gem. Haverteachyer."

The Angel was puzzled. The drunken man stood swaying for a moment, then he made an unsteady snatch at his hat and threw it down at the Angel's feet. "Ver well," he said, as one who decides great issues.

"*Carm* on!" said the voice of the man with the grindstone—stopping perhaps twenty yards off.

"You *wan* fight, you ——" the Angel failed to catch the word. "I'll show yer, not answer gem's goomorn."

He began to struggle with his jacket. "Think I'm drun," he said, "I show yer." The man with the grindstone sat down on the shaft to watch. "Carm on," he said. The jacket was intricate, and the drunken man began to struggle about the road, in his attempts to extricate himself, breathing threatenings and slaughter. Slowly the Angel began to suspect, remotely enough, that these demonstrations were hostile. "Mur wun know yer when I done wi' yer," said the drunken man, coat almost over his head.

At last the garment lay on the ground, and through the frequent interstices of his reminiscences of a waistcoat, the drunken tinker displayed a fine hairy and muscular body to the Angel's observant eyes. He squared up in masterly fashion.

"Take the paint off yer," he remarked, advancing and receding, fists up and elbows out.

"Carm on," floated down the road.

The Angel's attention was concentrated on two huge hairy black fists, that swayed and advanced and retreated. "Come on d'yer say? I'll show yer," said the gentleman in rags, and then with extraordinary ferocity; "My crikey! I'll show yer."

Suddenly he lurched forward, and with a newborn instinct and raising a defensive arm as he did so, the Angel stepped aside to avoid him. The fist missed the Angelic shoulder by a hairsbreadth, and the tinker collapsed in a heap with his face against the parapet of the bridge. The Angel hesitated over the writhing dusty heap of blasphemy for a moment, and then turned towards the man's companion up the road. "Lemmeget up," said the man on the bridge: "Lemmeget up, you swine. I'll show yer."

A strange disgust, a quivering repulsion came upon the Angel. He

walked slowly away from the drunkard towards the man with the grindstone.

"What does it all mean?" said the Angel. "I don't understand it."

"Dam fool! . . . say's it's 'is silver weddin'," answered the man with the grindstone, evidently much annoyed; and then, in a tone of growing impatience, he called down the road once more; "Carm on!"

"Silver wedding!" said the Angel. "What is a silver wedding?"

"Jest is rot," said the man on the barrow. "But 'E's always 'avin' some 'scuse like that. Fair sickenin it is. Lars week it wus 'is bloomin' birthday, and *then* 'e 'ad'nt 'ardly got sober orf a comlimentary drunk to my noo barrer. (*Carm* on, you fool.)"

"But I don't understand," said the Angel. "Why does he sway about so? Why does he keep on trying to pick up his hat like that—and missing it?"

"*Why!*" said the tinker. "Well this *is* a blasted innocent country! *Why!* Because 'E's blind! Wot else? (Carm on—*Dam* yer). Because 'E's just as full as 'E can 'old. That's *why!*"

The Angel noticing the tone of the second tinker's voice, judged it wiser not to question him further. But he stood by the grindstone and continued to watch the mysterious evolutions on the bridge.

"Carm on! I shall 'ave to go and pick up that ''at I suppose . . .'E's always at it. I ne'er 'ad such a blooming pard before. *Always* at it, 'e is."

The man with the barrow meditated. "Taint as if 'e was a gentleman and 'adnt no livin' to get. An' 'e's such a reckless fool when 'e gets a bit on. Goes offerin out everyone 'e meets. (*There* you go!) I'm blessed if 'e didn't offer out a 'ole bloomin' Salvation Army. No judgment in it. (Oh! *Carm* on! *Carm* on!). 'Ave to go and pick this bloomin' 'at up now I s'pose. 'E don't care, *wot* trouble 'e gives."

The Angel watched the second tinker walk back, and, with affectionate blasphemy, assist the first to his hat and his coat. Then he turned, absolutely mystified, towards the village again.

<p style="text-align:center">★★★★★★</p>

After that incident the Angel walked along past the mill and round behind the church, to examine the tombstones.

"This seems to be the place where they put the broken pieces," said the Angel—reading the inscriptions. "Curious word—relict! Resurgam! Then they are not done with quite. What a huge pile it requires to keep her down. . . .It is spirited of her."

"Hawkins?" said the Angel softly . . . "*Hawkins?* The name is strange to me . . . He did not die then . . . It is plain enough,—Joined the An-

<p style="text-align:center">132</p>

gelic Hosts, May 17, 1863. He must have felt as much out of place as I do down here. But I wonder why they put that little pot thing on the top of this monument. Curious! There are several others about—little stone pots with a rag of stiff stone drapery over them."

Just then the boys came pouring out of the National School, and first one and then several stopped agape at the Angel's crooked black figure among the white tombs. "Ent 'e gart a baak on en!" remarked one critic.

"'E's got 'air like a girl!" said another.

The Angel turned towards them. He was struck by the queer little heads sticking up over the lichenous wall. He smiled faintly at their staring faces, and then turned to marvel at the iron railings that enclosed the Fitz-Jarvis tomb. "A queer air of uncertainty," he said. "Slabs, piles of stone, these railings . . . Are they afraid? . . . Do these Dead ever try and get up again? There's an air of repression—fortification——"

"Get yer 'air cut, Get yer 'air cut," sang three little boys together.

"Curious these Human Beings are!" said the Angel. "That man yesterday wanted to cut off my wings, now these little creatures want me to cut off my hair! And the man on the bridge offered to take the 'paint' off me. They will leave nothing of me soon."

"Where did you get that 'at?" sang another little boy. "Where did you get them clo'es?"

"They ask questions that they evidently do not want answered," said the Angel. "I can tell from the tone." He looked thoughtfully at the little boys. "I don't understand the methods of Human intercourse. These are probably friendly advances, a kind of ritual. But I don't know the responses. I think I will go back to the little fat man in black, with the gold chain across his stomach, and ask him to explain. It is difficult."

He turned towards the lych gate. "Oh!" said one of the little boys, in a shrill falsetto, and threw a beech-nut husk. It came bounding across the churchyard path. The Angel stopped in surprise.

This made all the little boys laugh. A second imitating the first, said "Oh!" and hit the Angel. His astonishment was really delicious. They all began crying "Oh!" and throwing beechnut husks. One hit the Angel's hand, another stung him smartly by the ear. The Angel made ungainly movements towards them. He spluttered some expostulation and made for the roadway. The little boys were amazed and shocked at his discomfiture and cowardice. Such sawney behaviour could not

be encouraged. The pelting grew vigorously. You may perhaps be able to imagine those vivid moments, daring small boys running in close and delivering shots, milder small boys rushing round behind with flying discharges. Milton Screever's mongrel dog was roused to yelping ecstasy at the sight, and danced (full of wild imaginings) nearer and nearer to the angelic legs.

"Hi, hi!" said a vigorous voice. "I never did! Where's Mr Jarvis? Manners, manners! you young rascals."

The youngsters scattered right and left, some over the wall into the playground, some down the street.

"Frightful pest these boys are getting!" said Crump, coming up. "I'm sorry they have been annoying you."

The Angel seemed quite upset. "I don't understand," he said. "These Human ways . . ."

"Yes, of course. Unusual to you. How's your excrescence?"

"My what?" said the Angel.

"Bifid limb, you know. How is it? Now you're down this way, come in. Come in and let me have a look at it again. You young roughs! And meanwhile these little louts of ours will be getting off home. They're all alike in these villages. *Can't* understand anything abnormal. See an odd-looking stranger. Chuck a stone. No imagination beyond the parish . . . (I'll give you physic if I catch you annoying strangers again.) . . . I suppose it's what one might expect . . . Come along this way."

So, the Angel, horribly perplexed still, was hurried into the surgery to have his wound re-dressed.

CHAPTER 13

Lady Hammergallow's View

In Siddermorton Park is Siddermorton House, where old Lady Hammergallow lives, chiefly upon Burgundy and the little scandals of the village, a dear old lady with a ropy neck, a ruddled countenance and spasmodic gusts of odd temper, whose three remedies for all human trouble among her dependents are, a bottle of gin, a pair of charity blankets, or a new crown piece. The House is a mile-and-a-half out of Siddermorton. Almost all the village is hers, saving a fringe to the south which belongs to Sir John Gotch, and she rules it with an autocratic rule, refreshing in these days of divided government. She orders and forbids marriages, drives objectionable people out of the village by the simple expedient of raising their rent, dismisses labourers, obliges heretics to go to church, and made Susan Dangett, who

wanted to call her little girl 'Euphemia,' have the infant christened 'Mary-Anne.' She is a sturdy Broad Protestant and disapproves of the Vicar's going bald like a tonsure. She is on the Village Council, which obsequiously trudges up the hill and over the moor to her, and (as she is a trifle deaf) speaks all its speeches into her speaking trumpet instead of a rostrum. She takes no interest now in politics, but until last year she was an active enemy of "that Gladstone." She has parlour maids instead of footmen to do her waiting, because of Hockley, the American stockbroker, and his four Titans in plush.

She exercises what is almost a fascination upon the village. If in the bar-parlour of the Cat and Cornucopia you swear by God no one would be shocked, but if you swore by Lady Hammergallow they would probably be shocked enough to turn you out of the room. When she drives through Siddermorton she always calls upon Bessy Flump, the post-mistress, to hear all that has happened, and then upon Miss Finch, the dressmaker, to check back Bessy Flump. Sometimes she calls upon the Vicar, sometimes upon Mrs Mendham whom she snubs, and even sometimes on Crump. Her sparkling pair of greys almost ran over the Angel as he was walking down to the village.

"So *that's* the genius!" said Lady Hammergallow, and turned and looked at him through the gilt glasses on a stick that she always carried in her shrivelled and shaky hand. "Lunatic indeed! The poor creature has rather a pretty face. I'm sorry I've missed him."

But she went on to the vicarage nevertheless, and demanded news of it all. The conflicting accounts of Miss Flump, Miss Finch, Mrs Mendham, Crump, and Mrs Jehoram had puzzled her immensely. The Vicar, hard pressed, did all he could to say into her speaking trumpet what had really happened. He toned down the wings and the saffron robe. But he felt the case was hopeless. He spoke of his *protégé* as "Mr" Angel. He addressed pathetic asides to the kingfisher. The old lady noticed his confusion. Her queer old head went jerking backwards and forwards, now the speaking trumpet in his face when he had nothing to say, then the shrunken eyes peering at him, oblivious of the explanation that was coming from his lips. A great many Ohs! and Ahs! She caught some fragments certainly.

"You have asked him to stop with you—indefinitely?" said Lady Hammergallow with a Great Idea taking shape rapidly in her mind.

"I did—perhaps inadvertently—make such—"

"And you don't know where he comes from?"

"Not at all."

"Nor who his father is, I suppose?" said Lady Hammergallow mysteriously.

"No," said the Vicar.

"*Now!*" said Lady Hammergallow archly, and keeping her glasses to her eye, she suddenly dug at his ribs with her trumpet.

"My *dear* Lady Hammergallow!"

"I thought so. Don't think *I* would blame you, Mr Hilyer." She gave a corrupt laugh that she delighted in. "The world is the world, and men are men. And the poor boy's a cripple, eh? A kind of judgment. In mourning, I noticed. It reminds me of the *Scarlet Letter*. The mother's dead, I suppose. It's just as well. Really—I'm not a *narrow* woman—I *respect* you for having him. Really I do."

"But, *Lady* Hammergallow!"

"Don't spoil everything by denying it. It is so very, very plain, to a woman of the world. That Mrs Mendham! She amuses me with her suspicions. Such odd ideas! In a Curate's wife. But I hope it didn't happen when you were in orders."

"Lady Hammergallow, I protest. Upon my word."

"Mr Hilyer, I protest. I *know*. Not anything you can say will alter my opinion one jot. Don't try. I never suspected you were nearly such an interesting man."

"But this suspicion is unendurable!"

"We will help him together, Mr Hilyer. You may rely upon me. It is most romantic." She beamed benevolence.

"But, Lady Hammergallow, I *must* speak!"

She gripped her ear-trumpet resolutely, and held it before her and shook her head.

"He has quite a genius for music, Vicar, so I hear?"

"I can assure you most solemnly—"

"I thought so. And being a cripple—"

"You are under a most cruel—"

"I thought that if his gift is really what that Jehoram woman says."

"An unjustifiable suspicion that ever a man—"

("I don't think much of her judgment, of course.")

"Consider my position. Have I gained *no* character?"

"It might be possible to do something for him as a performer."

"Have I—(*Bother! It's no good!*)"

"And so, dear Vicar, I propose to give him an opportunity of showing us what he can do. I have been thinking it all over as I drove here. On Tuesday next, I will invite just a few people of taste, and he shall

bring his violin. Eigh? And if that goes well, I will see if I can get some introductions and really *push* him."

"But *Lady*, Lady Hammergallow."

"Not another word!" said Lady Hammergallow, still resolutely holding her speaking trumpet before her and clutching her eyeglasses. "I really must not leave those horses. Cutler is so annoyed if I keep them too long. He finds waiting tedious, poor man, unless there is a public-house near." She made for the door.

"*Damn!*" said the Vicar, under his breath. He had never used the word since he had taken orders. It shows you how an Angel's visit may disorganize a man.

He stood under the verandah watching the carriage drive away. The world seemed coming to pieces about him. Had he lived a virtuous celibate life for thirty odd years in vain? The things of which these people thought him capable! He stood and stared at the green cornfield opposite, and down at the straggling village. It seemed real enough. And yet for the first time in his life there was a queer doubt of its reality. He rubbed his chin, then turned and went slowly upstairs to his dressing-room, and sat for a long time staring at a garment of some yellow texture. "Know his father!" he said. "And he is immortal, and was fluttering about his heaven when my ancestors were marsupials.I wish he was there now."

He got up and began to feel the robe.

"I wonder how they get such things," said the Vicar. Then he went and stared out of the window. "I suppose everything is wonderful, even the rising and setting of the sun. I suppose there is no adamantine ground for any belief. But one gets into a regular way of taking things. This disturbs it. I seem to be waking up to the Invisible. It is the strangest of uncertainties. I have not felt so stirred and unsettled since my adolescence."

Chapter 14

Further Adventures of the Angel in the Village

"That's all right," said Crump when the bandaging was replaced. "It's a trick of memory, no doubt, but these excrescences of yours don't seem nearly so large as they did yesterday. I suppose they struck me rather forcibly. Stop and have lunch with me now you're down here. Midday meal, you know. The youngsters will be swallowed up by school again in the afternoon."

"I never saw anything heal so well in my life," he said, as they

walked into the dining-room. "Your blood and flesh must be as clean and free from bacteria as they make 'em. Whatever stuff there is in your head," he added *sotto voce*.

At lunch he watched the Angel narrowly, and talked to draw him out.

"Journey tire you yesterday?" he said suddenly.

"Journey!" said the Angel. "Oh! my wings felt a little stiff."

("Not to be had,") said Crump to himself. ("Suppose I must enter into it.")

"So, you flew all the way, eigh? No conveyance?"

"There wasn't any way," explained the Angel, taking mustard. "I was flying up a symphony with some Griffins and Fiery Cherubim, and suddenly everything went dark and I was in this world of yours."

"Dear me!" said Crump. "And that's why you haven't any luggage." He drew his serviette across his mouth, and a smile flickered in his eyes.

"I suppose you know this world of ours pretty well? Watching us over the adamantine walls and all that kind of thing. Eigh?"

"Not very well. We dream of it sometimes. In the moonlight, when the Nightmares have fanned us to sleep with their wings."

"Ah, yes—of course," said Crump. "Very poetical way of putting it. Won't you take some Burgundy? It's just beside you."

"There's a persuasion in this world, you know, that Angels' Visits are by no means infrequent. Perhaps some of your—friends have travelled? They are supposed to come down to deserving persons in prisons, and do refined Nautches and that kind of thing. Faust business, you know."

"I've never heard of anything of the kind," said the Angel.

"Only the other day a lady whose baby was my patient for the time being—indigestion—assured me that certain facial contortions the little creature made indicated that it was Dreaming of Angels. In the novels of Mrs Henry Wood that is spoken of as an infallible symptom of an early departure. I suppose you can't throw any light on that obscure pathological manifestation?"

"I don't understand it at all," said the Angel, puzzled, and not clearly apprehending the Doctor's drift.

("Getting huffy,") said Crump to himself. ("Sees I'm poking fun at him.") "There's one thing I'm curious about. Do the new arrivals complain much about their medical attendants? I've always fancied there must be a good deal of hydropathic talk just at first. I was look-

ing at that picture in the Academy only this June."

"New Arrivals!" said the Angel. "I really don't follow you."

The Doctor stared. "Don't they come?"

"Come!" said the Angel. "Who?"

"The people who die here."

"After they've gone to pieces here?"

"That's the general belief, you know."

"People, like the woman who screamed out of the door, and the black-faced man and his volutations and the horrible little things that threw husks!—certainly not. *I* never saw such creatures before I fell into this world."

"Oh! but come!" said the Doctor. "You'll tell me next your official robes are not white and that you can't play the harp."

"There's no such thing as white in the Angelic Land," said the Angel. "It's that queer blank colour you get by mixing up all the others."

"Why, my dear Sir!" said the doctor, suddenly altering his tone, "you positively know nothing about the Land you come from. White's the very essence of it."

The Angel stared at him. Was the man jesting? He looked perfectly serious.

"Look here," said Crump, and getting up, he went to the sideboard on which a copy of the *Parish Magazine* was lying. He brought it round to the Angel and opened it at the coloured supplement. "Here's some *real* angels," he said. "You see it's not simply the wings make the Angel. White you see, with a curly whisp of robe, sailing up into the sky with their wings furled. Those are angels on the best authority. Hydroxyl kind of hair. One has a bit of a harp, you see, and the other is helping this wingless lady—kind of larval Angel, you know—upward."

"Oh! but really!" said the Angel, "those are not angels at all."

"But they *are*," said Crump, putting the magazine back on the sideboard and resuming his seat with an air of intense satisfaction. "I can assure you I have the *best* authority."

"I can assure you."

Crump tucked in the corners of his mouth and shook his head from side to side even as he had done to the Vicar. "No good," he said, "can't alter our ideas just because an irresponsible visitor."

"If these are angels," said the Angel, "then I have never been in the Angelic Land."

"Precisely," said Crump, ineffably self-satisfied; "that was just what I was getting at."

The Angel stared at him for a minute round-eyed, and then was seized for the second time by the human disorder of laughter.

"Ha, ha, ha!" said Crump, joining in. "I *thought* you were not quite so mad as you seemed. Ha, ha, ha!"

And for the rest of the lunch they were both very merry, for entirely different reasons, and Crump insisted upon treating the Angel as a "dorg" of the highest degree.

After the Angel had left Crump's house, he went up the hill again towards the Vicarage. But—possibly moved by the desire to avoid Mrs Gustick—he turned aside at the stile and made a detour by the Lark's Field and Bradley's Farm.

He came upon the Respectable Tramp slumbering peacefully among the wild-flowers. He stopped to look, struck by the celestial tranquillity of that individual's face. And even as he did so the Respectable Tramp awoke with a start and sat up. He was a pallid creature, dressed in rusty black, with a broken-spirited crush hat cocked over one eye. "Good afternoon," he said affably. "How are you?"

"Very well, thank you," said the Angel, who had mastered the phrase.

The Respectable Tramp eyed the Angel critically. "Padding the Hoof, matey?" he said. "Like me."

The Angel was puzzled by him. "Why," asked the Angel, "do you sleep like this instead of sleeping up in the air on a Bed?"

"Well I'm blowed!" said the Respectable Tramp. "Why don't I sleep in a bed? Well, it's like this. Sandringham's got the painters in, there's the drains up in Windsor Castle, and I 'aven't no other 'ouse to go to. You 'aven't the price of a 'arf pint in your pocket, 'ave yer?"

"I have nothing in my pocket," said the Angel.

"Is this here village called Siddermorton?" said the Tramp, rising creakily to his feet and pointing to the clustering roofs down the hill.

"Yes," said the Angel, "they call it Siddermorton."

"I know it, I know it," said the Tramp. "And a very pretty little village it is too." He stretched and yawned, and stood regarding the place. "'Ouses," he said reflectively; "Projuce"—waving his hand at the cornfields and orchards. "Looks cosy, don't it?"

"It has a quaint beauty of its own," said the Angel.

"It *'as* a quaint beauty of its own—yes. Lord! I'd like to sack the blooming place. I was born there."

"Dear me," said the Angel.

"Yes, I was born there. Ever heard of a pithed frog?"

"Pithed frog," said the Angel. "No!"

"It's a thing these here vivisectionists do. They takes a frog and they cuts out his brains and they shoves a bit of pith in the place of 'em. That's a pithed frog. Well—that there village is full of pithed human beings."

The Angel took it quite seriously. "Is that so?" he said.

"That's so—you take my word for it. Every one of them 'as 'ad their brains cut out and chunks of rotten touchwood put in the place of it. And you see that little red place there?"

"That's called the national school," said the Angel.

"Yes—that's where they piths 'em," said the Tramp, quite in love with his conceit.

"Really! That's very interesting."

"It stands to reason," said the Tramp. "If they 'ad brains they'd 'ave ideas, and if they 'ad ideas they'd think for themselves. And you can go through that village from end to end and never meet anybody do-ing as much. Pithed human beings they are. I know that village. I was born there, and I might be there now, a toilin' for my betters, if I 'adnt struck against the pithin'."

"Is it a painful operation?" asked the Angel.

"In parts. Though it aint the heads gets hurt. And it lasts a long time. They take 'em young into that school, and they says to them, 'come in 'ere and we'll improve your minds,' they says, and in the little kiddies go as good as gold. And they begins shovin' it into them. Bit by bit and 'ard and dry, shovin' out the nice juicy brains. Dates and lists and things. Out they comes, no brains in their 'eads, and wound up nice and tight, ready to touch their 'ats to anyone who looks at them. Why! One touched 'is 'at to me yesterday. And they runs about spry and does all the dirty work, and feels thankful they're allowed to live. They take a positive pride in 'ard work for its own sake. Arter they bin pithed. See that chap ploughin'?"

"Yes," said the Angel; "is *he* pithed?"

"Rather. Else he'd be paddin' the hoof this pleasant weather—like me and the blessed Apostles."

"I begin to understand," said the Angel, rather dubiously.

"I knew you would," said the Philosophical Tramp. "I thought you was the right sort. But speaking serious, aint it ridiculous?—centu-ries and centuries of civilization, and look at that poor swine there, sweatin' 'isself empty and trudging up that 'ill-side. 'E's English, 'e is.

141

'E belongs to the top race in creation, 'e does. 'E's one of the rulers of Indjer. It's enough to make a negro laugh. The flag that's braved a thousand years the battle an' the breeze—that's *'is* flag. There never was a country was as great and glorious as this. Never. And that's wot it makes of us. I'll tell you a little story about them parts as you seems to be a bit of a stranger. There's a chap called Gotch, Sir John Gotch they calls 'im, and when *'e* was a young gent from Oxford, I was a little chap of eight and my sister was a girl of seventeen. Their servant she was. But Lord! everybody's ''eard that story—it's common enough, of ''im or the likes of''im."

"I haven't," said the Angel.

"All that's pretty and lively of the gals they chucks into the gutters, and all the men with a pennorth of spunk or adventure, all who won't drink what the Curate's wife sends 'em instead of beer, and touch their hats promiscous, and leave the rabbits and birds alone for their betters, gets drove out of the villages as rough characters. Patriotism! Talk about improvin' the race! Wot's left aint fit to look a negro in the face, a Chinaman 'ud be ashamed of 'em"

"But I don't understand," said the Angel. "I don't follow you."

At that the Philosophic Tramp became more explicit, and told the Angel the simple story of Sir John Gotch and the kitchen-maid. It's scarcely necessary to repeat it. You may understand that it left the Angel puzzled. It was full of words he did not understand, for the only vehicle of emotion the Tramp possessed was blasphemy. Yet, though their tongues differed so, he could still convey to the Angel some of his own (probably unfounded) persuasion of the injustice and cruelty of life, and of the utter detestableness of Sir John Gotch.

The last the Angel saw of him was his dusty black back receding down the lane towards Iping Hanger. A pheasant appeared by the roadside, and the Philosophical Tramp immediately caught up a stone and sent the bird clucking with a viciously accurate shot. Then he disappeared round the corner.

CHAPTER 15

Mrs Jehoram's Breadth of View

"I heard someone playing the fiddle in the Vicarage, as I came by," said Mrs Jehoram, taking her cup of tea from Mrs Mendham.

"The Vicar plays," said Mrs Mendham. "I have spoken to George about it, but it's no good. I do not think a Vicar should be allowed to do such things. It's so foreign. But there, *he*."

"I know, dear," said Mrs Jehoram. "But I heard the Vicar once at the schoolroom. I don't think this *was* the Vicar. It was quite clever, some of it, quite smart, you know. And new. I was telling dear Lady Hammergallow this morning. I fancy—"

"The lunatic! Very likely. These half-witted people.....My dear, I don't think I shall ever forget that dreadful encounter. Yesterday."

"Nor I."

"My poor girls! They are too shocked to say a word about it. I was telling dear Lady Ham——"

"Quite proper of them. It was *dreadful*, dear. For them."

"And now, dear, I want you to tell me frankly—Do you really believe that creature was a man?"

"You should have heard the violin."

"I still more than half suspect, Jessie ——" Mrs Mendham leant forward as if to whisper.

Mrs Jehoram helped herself to cake. "I'm sure no woman could play the violin quite like I heard it played this morning."

"Of course, if you say so that settles the matter," said Mrs Mendham. Mrs Jehoram was the autocratic authority in Siddermorton upon all questions of art, music and *belles-lettres*. Her late husband had been a minor poet. Then Mrs Mendham added a judicial "Still—"

"Do you know," said Mrs Jehoram, "I'm half inclined to believe the dear Vicar's story."

"How *good* of you, Jessie," said Mrs Mendham.

"But really, I don't think he *could* have had any one in the Vicarage before that afternoon. I feel sure we should have heard of it. I don't see how a strange cat could come within four miles of Siddermorton without the report coming round to us. The people here gossip so....."

"I always distrust the Vicar," said Mrs Mendham. "I know him."

"Yes. But the story is plausible. If this Mr Angel were someone very clever and eccentric—"

"He would have to be *very* eccentric to dress as he did. There are degrees and limits, dear."

"But kilts," said Mrs Jehoram.

"Are all very well in the Highlands. . . ."

Mrs Jehoram's eyes had rested upon a black speck creeping slowly across a patch of yellowish-green up the hill.

"There he goes," said Mrs Jehoram, rising, "across the cornfield. I'm sure that's him. I can see the hump. Unless it's a man with a sack. Bless me, Minnie! here's an opera glass. How convenient for peeping

at the Vicarage! Yes, it's the man. He is a man. With *such* a sweet face."

Very unselfishly she allowed her hostess to share the opera glass. For a minute there was a rustling silence.

"His dress," said Mrs Mendham, "is *quite* respectable now."

"Quite," said Mrs Jehoram.

Pause.

"He looks cross!"

"And his coat is dusty."

"He walks steadily enough," said Mrs Mendham, "or one might think. This hot weather."

Another pause.

"You see, dear," said Mrs Jehoram, putting down the lorgnette. "What I was going to say was, that possibly he might be a genius in disguise."

"If you can call next door to nothing a disguise."

"No doubt it was eccentric. But I've seen children in little blouses, not at all unlike him. So many clever people *are* peculiar in their dress and manners. A genius may steal a horse where a bank-clerk may not look over the hedge. Very possibly he's quite well known and laughing at our Arcadian simplicity. And really it wasn't so improper as some of these New Women bicycling costumes. I saw one in one of the Il-lustrated Papers only a few days ago—the *New Budget* I think—quite tights, you know, dear. No—I cling to the genius theory. Especially after the playing. I'm sure the creature is original. Perhaps very amus-ing. In fact, I intend to ask the Vicar to introduce me."

"My dear!" cried Mrs Mendham.

"I'm resolute," said Mrs Jehoram.

"I'm afraid you're rash," said Mrs Mendham. "Geniuses and people of that kind are all very well in London. But here—at the Vicarage."

"We are going to educate the folks. I love originality. At any rate I mean to see him."

"Take care you don't see too much of him," said Mrs Mendham. "I've heard the fashion is quite changing. I understand that some of the very best people have decided that genius is not to be encouraged any more. These recent scandals."

"Only in literature, I can assure you, dear. In music."

"Nothing you can say, my dear," said Mrs Mendham, going off at a tangent, "will convince me that that person's costume was not ex-tremely suggestive and improper."

CHAPTER 16

A Trivial Incident

The Angel came thoughtfully by the hedge across the field towards the Vicarage. The rays of the setting sun shone on his shoulders, and touched the Vicarage with gold, and blazed like fire in all the windows. By the gate, bathed in the sunlight, stood little Delia, the waiting maid. She stood watching him under her hand. It suddenly came into the Angel's mind that she, at least, was beautiful, and not only beautiful but alive and warm.

She opened the gate for him and stood aside. She was sorry for him, for her elder sister was a cripple. He bowed to her, as he would have done to any woman, and for just one moment looked into her face. She looked back at him and something leapt within her.

The Angel made an irresolute movement. "Your eyes are very beautiful," he said quietly, with a remote wonder in his voice.

"Oh, sir!" she said, starting back. The Angel's expression changed to perplexity. He went on up the pathway between the Vicar's flower-beds, and she stood with the gate held open in her hand, staring after him. Just under the rose-twined verandah he turned and looked at her.

She still stared at him for a moment, and then with a queer gesture turned round with her back to him, shutting the gate as she did so, and seemed to be looking down the valley towards the church tower.

CHAPTER 17

The Warp and the Woof of Things

At the dinner table the Angel told the Vicar the more striking of his day's adventures.

"The strange thing," said the Angel, "is the readiness of you Human Beings—the zest, with which you inflict pain. Those boys pelting me this morning——"

"Seemed to enjoy it," said the Vicar. "I know."

"Yet they don't like pain," said the Angel.

"No," said the Vicar; "*they* don't like it."

"Then," said the Angel, "I saw some beautiful plants rising with a spike of leaves, two this way and two that, and when I caressed one it caused the most uncomfortable——"

"Stinging nettle!" said the Vicar.

"At any rate a new sort of pain. And another plant with a head like a coronet, and richly decorated leaves, spiked and jagged——"

"A thistle, possibly."

"And in your garden, the beautiful, sweet-smelling plant——"

"The sweet briar," said the Vicar. "I remember."

"And that pink flower that sprang out of the box——"

"Out of the box?" said the Vicar.

"Last night," said the Angel, "that went climbing up the curtains—— Flame!"

"Oh!—the matches and the candles! Yes," said the Vicar.

"Then the animals. A dog today behaved most disagreeably——. And these boys, and the way in which people speak——. Everyone seems anxious—willing at any rate—to give this Pain. Everyone seems busy giving pain——"

"Or avoiding it," said the Vicar, pushing his dinner away before him. "Yes—of course. It's fighting everywhere. The whole living world is a battlefield—the whole world. We are driven by Pain. Here. How it lies on the surface! This Angel sees it in a day!"

"But why does everyone—everything—want to give pain?" asked the Angel.

"It is not so in the Angelic Land?" said the Vicar.

"No," said the Angel. "Why is it so here?"

The Vicar wiped his lips with his napkin slowly. "It *is* so," he said. "Pain," said he still more slowly, "is the warp and the woof of this life. Do you know," he said, after a pause, "it is almost impossible for me to imagine.....a world without pain.....And yet, as you played this morning——

"But this world is different. It is the very reverse of an Angelic world. Indeed, a number of people—excellent religious people—have been so impressed by the universality of pain that they think, after death, things will be even worse for a great many of us. It seems to me an excessive view. But it's a deep question. Almost beyond one's power of discussion——"

And incontinently the Vicar plumped into an impromptu dissertation upon "Necessity," how things were so because they were so, how one *had* to do this and that. "Even our food," said the Vicar.

"What?" said the Angel.

"Is not obtained without inflicting Pain," said the Vicar.

The Angel's face went so white that the Vicar checked himself suddenly. Or he was just on the very verge of a concise explanation of the antecedents of a leg of lamb. There was a pause.

"By-the-bye," said the Angel, suddenly. "Have you been pithed?

146

Like the common people."

The Angel's Debut

When Lady Hammergallow made up her mind, things happened as she resolved. And though the Vicar made a spasmodic protest, she carried out her purpose and got audience, Angel, and violin together, at Siddermorton House before the week was out. "A genius the Vicar has discovered," she said; so, with eminent foresight putting any possibility of blame for a failure on the Vicar's shoulders. "The dear Vicar tells me," she would say, and proceed to marvellous anecdotes of the Angel's cleverness with his instrument. But she was quite in love with her idea—she had always had a secret desire to play the patroness to obscure talent. Hitherto it had not turned out to be talent when it came to the test.

"It would be such a good thing for him," she said. "His hair is long already, and with that high colour he would be beautiful, simply beautiful on a platform. The Vicar's clothes fitting him so badly makes him look quite like a fashionable pianist already. And the scandal of his birth—not told, of course, but whispered—would be—quite an Inducement——when he gets to London, that is."

The Vicar had the most horrible sensations as the day approached. He spent hours trying to explain the situation to the Angel, other hours trying to imagine what people would think, still worse hours trying to anticipate the Angel's behaviour. Hitherto the Angel had always played for his own satisfaction. The Vicar would startle him every now and then by rushing upon him with some new point of etiquette that had just occurred to him.

As for instance: "It's very important where you put your hat, you know. Don't put it on a chair, whatever you do. Hold it until you get your tea, you know, and then—let me see—then put it down somewhere, you know." The journey to Siddermorton House was accomplished without misadventure, but at the moment of introduction the Vicar had a spasm of horrible misgivings. He had forgotten to explain introductions. The Angel's *naïve* amusement was evident, but nothing very terrible happened.

"Rummy looking greaser," said Mr Rathbone Slater, who devoted considerable attention to costume. "Wants grooming. No manners. Grinned when he saw me shaking hands. Did it *chic* enough, I thought."

One trivial misadventure occurred. When Lady Hammergallow welcomed the Angel, she looked at him through her glasses. The apparent size of her eyes startled him. His surprise and his quick attempt to peer over the brims was only too evident. But the Vicar had warned him of the ear trumpet.

The Angel's incapacity to sit on anything but a music stool appeared to excite some interest among the ladies, but led to no remarks. They regarded it perhaps as the affectation of a budding professional. He was remiss with the teacups and scattered the crumbs of his cake abroad. (You must remember he was quite an amateur at eating.) He crossed his legs. He fumbled over the hat business after vainly trying to catch the Vicar's eye. The eldest Miss Papaver tried to talk to him about continental watering places and cigarettes, and formed a low opinion of his intelligence.

The Angel was surprised by the production of an easel and several books of music, and a little unnerved at first by the sight of Lady Hammergallow sitting with her head on one side, watching him with those magnified eyes through her gilt glasses.

Mrs Jehoram came up to him before he began to play and asked him the name of the charming piece, he was playing the other afternoon. The Angel said it had no name, and Mrs Jehoram thought music ought never to have any names and wanted to know who it was by, and when the Angel told her he played it out of his head, she said he must be quite a genius and looked open (and indisputably fascinating) admiration at him. The Curate from Iping Hanger (who was professionally a Kelt and who played the piano and talked colour and music with an air of racial superiority) watched him jealously.

The Vicar, who was presently captured and set down next to Lady Hammergallow, kept an anxious eye ever Angelward while she told him particulars of the incomes made by violinists—particulars which, for the most part, she invented as she went along. She had been a little ruffled by the incident of the glasses, but had decided that it came within the limits of permissible originality.

So, figure to yourself the Green Saloon at Siddermorton Park; an Angel thinly disguised in clerical vestments and with a violin in his hands, standing by the grand piano, and a respectable gathering of quiet nice people, nicely dressed, grouped about the room. Anticipatory gabble—one hears scattered fragments of conversation.

"He is *incog*."; said the very eldest Miss Papaver to Mrs Pirbright. "Isn't it quaint and delicious. Jessica Jehoram says she saw him at Vi-

enna, but she can't remember the name. The Vicar knows all about him, but he is so close———"

"How hot and uncomfortable the dear Vicar is looking," said Mrs Pirbright. "I've noticed it before when he sits next to Lady Hammergallow. She simply will *not* respect his cloth. She goes on———"

"His tie is all askew," said the very eldest Miss Papaver, "and his hair! It really hardly looks as though he had brushed it all day."

"Seems a foreign sort of chap. Affected. All very well in a drawing-room," said George Harringay, sitting apart with the younger Miss Pirbright. "But for my part give me a masculine man and a feminine woman. What do you think?"

"Oh!—I think so too," said the younger Miss Pirbright.

"Guineas and guineas," said Lady Hammergallow. "I've heard that some of them keep quite stylish establishments. You would scarcely credit it———"

"I love music, Mr Angel, I adore it. It stirs something in me. I can scarcely describe it," said Mrs Jehoram. "Who is it says that delicious antithesis: Life without music is brutality; music without life is——— Dear me! perhaps you remember? Music without life———it's Ruskin I think?"

"I'm sorry that I do not," said the Angel. "I have read very few books."

"How charming of you!" said Mrs Jehoram. "I wish I didn't. I sympathise with you profoundly. I would do the same, only we poor women———I suppose it's originality we lack——— And down here one is driven to the most desperate proceedings———"

"He's certainly very *pretty*. But the ultimate test of a man is his strength," said George Harringay. "What do you think?"

"Oh!—I think so too," said the younger Miss Pirbright.

"It's the effeminate man who makes the masculine woman. When the glory of a man is his hair, what's a woman to do? And when men go running about with beautiful hectic dabs———"

"Oh George! You are so dreadfully satirical today," said the younger Miss Pirbright. "I'm *sure* it isn't paint."

"I'm really not his guardian, my dear Lady Hammergallow. Of course, it's very kind indeed of you to take such an interest———"

"Are you really going to improvise?" said Mrs Jehoram in a state of cooing delight.

"*SSsh!*" said the curate from Iping Hanger.

Then the Angel began to play, looking straight before him as he

did so, thinking of the wonderful things of the Angelic Land, and yet insensibly letting the sadness he was beginning to feel, steal over the fantasia he was playing. When he forgot his company, the music was strange and sweet; when the sense of his surroundings floated into his mind the music grew capricious and grotesque. But so great was the hold of the Angelic music upon the Vicar that his anxieties fell from him at once, so soon as the Angel began to play.

Mrs Jehoram sat and looked rapt and sympathetic as hard as she could (though the music was puzzling at times) and tried to catch the Angel's eye. He really had a wonderfully mobile face, and the tenderest shades of expression! And Mrs Jehoram was a judge. George Harringay looked bored, until the younger Miss Pirbright, who adored him, put out her mousy little shoe to touch his manly boot, and then he turned his face to catch the feminine delicacy of her *coquettish* eye, and was comforted. The very eldest Miss Papaver and Mrs Pirbright sat quite still and looked churchy for nearly four minutes.

Then said the eldest Miss Papaver in a whisper, "I always enjoy violin music so much."

And Mrs Pirbright answered, "We get so little *nice* music down here."

And Miss Papaver said, "He plays *very* nicely."

And Mrs Pirbright, "Such a Delicate Touch!"

And Miss Papaver, "Does Willie keep up his lessons?" and so to a whispered conversation.

The Curate from Iping Hanger sat (he felt) in full view of the company. He had one hand curled round his ear, and his eyes hard and staring fixedly at the pedestal of the Hammergallow Sèvres vase. He supplied, by the movements of his mouth, a kind of critical guide to any of the company who were disposed to avail themselves of it. It was a generous way he had. His aspect was severely judicial, tempered by starts of evident disapproval and guarded appreciation.

The Vicar leaned back in his chair and stared at the Angel's face, and was presently rapt away in a wonderful dream. Lady Hammergallow, with quick jerky movements of the head and a low but insistent rustling, surveyed and tried to judge of the effect of the Angelic playing. Mr Rathbone-Slater stared very solemnly into his hat and looked very miserable, and Mrs Rathbone-Slater made mental memoranda of Mrs Jehoram's sleeves. And the air about them all was heavy with exquisite music—for all that had ears to hear.

"Scarcely affected enough," whispered Lady Hammergallow

hoarsely, suddenly poking the Vicar in the ribs.

The Vicar came out of Dreamland suddenly. "Eigh?" shouted the Vicar, startled, coming up with a jump.

"Sssh!" said the Curate from Iping Hanger, and everyone looked shocked at the brutal insensibility of Hilyer.

"So unusual of the Vicar," said the very eldest Miss Papaver, "to do things like that!"

The Angel went on playing.

The Curate from Iping Hanger began making mesmeric movements with his index finger, and as the thing proceeded Mr Rathbone-Slater got amazingly limp. He solemnly turned his hat round and altered his view. The Vicar lapsed from an uneasy discomfort into dreamland again. Lady Hammergallow rustled a great deal, and presently found a way of making her chair creak. And at last the thing came to an end. Lady Hammergallow exclaimed "De—licious!" though she had never heard a note, and began clapping her hands. At that everyone clapped except Mr Rathbone-Slater, who rapped his hat brim instead. The Curate from Iping Hanger clapped with a judicial air.

"So, I said (*clap, clap, clap*), if you cannot cook the food my way (*clap, clap, clap*) you must *go*," said Mrs Pirbright, clapping vigorously. "(This music is a delightful treat.)"

"(It is. I always *revel* in music,)" said the very eldest Miss Papaver. "And did she improve after that?"

"Not a bit of it," said Mrs Pirbright.

The Vicar woke up again and stared round the saloon. Did other people see these visions, or were they confined to him alone? Surely, they must all see.....and have a wonderful command of their feelings. It was incredible that such music should not affect them.

"He's a trifle *gauche*," said Lady Hammergallow, jumping upon the Vicar's attention. "He neither bows nor smiles. He must cultivate oddities like that. Every successful executant is more or less *gauche*."

"Did you really make that up yourself?" said Mrs Jehoram, sparkling her eyes at him, "as you went along. Really, it is *wonderful*! Nothing less than wonderful."

"A little amateurish," said the Curate from Iping Hanger to Mr Rathbone-Slater. "A great gift, undoubtedly, but a certain lack of sustained training. There were one or two little things.....I would like to talk to him."

"His trousers look like concertinas," said Mr Rathbone-Slater. "He ought to be told *that*. It's scarcely decent."

151

"Can you do Imitations, Mr Angel?" said Lady Hammergallow.

"Oh *do*, do some Imitations!" said Mrs Jehoram. "I adore Imitations."

"It was a fantastic thing," said the Curate of Iping Hanger to the Vicar of Siddermorton, waving his long indisputably musical hands as he spoke; "a little involved, to my mind. I have heard it before somewhere—I forget where. He has genius undoubtedly, but occasionally he is—loose. There is a certain deadly precision wanting. There are years of discipline yet."

"I *don't* admire these complicated pieces of music," said George Harringay. "I have simple tastes, I'm afraid. There seems to me no *tune* in it. There's nothing I like so much as simple music. Tune, simplicity is the need of the age, in my opinion. We are so over subtle. Everything is far-fetched. Home grown thoughts and 'Home, Sweet Home' for me. What do you think?"

"Oh! I think so—*quite*," said the younger Miss Pirbright.

"Well, Amy, chattering to George as usual?" said Mrs Pirbright, across the room.

"As usual, Ma!" said the younger Miss Pirbright, glancing round with a bright smile at Miss Papaver, and turning again so as not to lose the next utterance from George.

"I wonder if you and Mr Angel could manage a duet?" said Lady Hammergallow to the Curate from Iping Hanger, who was looking preternaturally gloomy.

"I'm sure I should be delighted," said the Curate from Iping Hanger, brightening up.

"Duets!" said the Angel; "the two of us. Then he can play. I understood—the Vicar told me—"

"Mr Wilmerdings is an accomplished pianist," interrupted the Vicar.

"But the Imitations?" said Mrs Jehoram, who detested Wilmerdings.

"Imitations!" said the Angel.

"A pig squeaking, a cock crowing, you know," said Mr Rathbone-Slater, and added lower, "Best fun you can get out of a fiddle—*my* opinion."

"I really don't understand," said the Angel. "A pig crowing!"

"You don't like Imitations," said Mrs Jehoram. "Nor do I—really. I accept the snub. I think they degrade....."

"Perhaps afterwards Mr Angel will relent," said Lady Hammergallow, when Mrs Pirbright had explained the matter to her. She could

scarcely credit her ear-trumpet. When she asked for Imitations, she was accustomed to get Imitations.

Mr Wilmerdings had seated himself at the piano, and had turned to a familiar pile of music in the recess. "What do you think of that Barcarole thing of Spohr's?" he said over his shoulder. "I suppose you know it?"

The Angel looked bewildered.

He opened the folio before the Angel.

"What an odd kind of book!" said the Angel. "What do all those crazy dots mean?" (At that the Vicar's blood ran cold.)

"What dots?" said the Curate.

"There!" said the Angel with incriminating finger.

"Oh *come!*" said the Curate.

There was one of those swift, short silences that mean so much in a social gathering.

Then the eldest Miss Papaver turned upon the Vicar. "Does not Mr Angel play from ordinary.....Music—from the ordinary notation?"

"I have never heard," said the Vicar, getting red now after the first shock of horror. "I have really never seen....."

The Angel felt the situation was strained, though what was straining it he could not understand. He became aware of a doubtful, an unfriendly look upon the faces that regarded him. "Impossible!" he heard Mrs Pirbright say; "after that *beautiful* music." The eldest Miss Papaver went to Lady Hammergallow at once, and began to explain into her ear-trumpet that Mr Angel did not wish to play with Mr Wilmerdings, and alleged an ignorance of written music.

"He cannot play from notes!" said Lady Hammergallow in a voice of measured horror. "Non—sense!"

"Notes!" said the Angel perplexed. "Are these notes?"

"It's carrying the joke too far—simply because he doesn't want to play with Wilmerdings," said Mr Rathbone-Slater to George Harringay.

There was an expectant pause. The Angel perceived he had to be ashamed of himself. He was ashamed of himself.

"Then," said Lady Hammergallow, throwing her head back and speaking with deliberate indignation, as she rustled forward, "if you cannot play with Mr Wilmerdings, I am afraid I cannot ask you to play again." She made it sound like an ultimatum. Her glasses in her hand quivered violently with indignation. The Angel was now human enough to appreciate the fact that he was crushed.

"What is it?" said little Lucy Rustchuck in the further bay.

"He's refused to play with old Wilmerdings," said Tommy Rathbone-Slater. "What a lark! The old girl's purple. She thinks heaps of that ass, Wilmerdings."

"Perhaps, Mr Wilmerdings, you will favour us with that delicious Polonaise of Chopin's," said Lady Hammergallow. Everybody else was hushed. The indignation of Lady Hammergallow inspired much the same silence as a coming earthquake or an eclipse. Mr Wilmerdings perceived he would be doing a real social service to begin at once, and (be it entered to his credit now that his account draws near its settlement) he did.

"If a man pretend to practise an art," said George Harringay, "he ought at least to have the conscience to study the elements of it. What do you."

"Oh! I think so too," said the younger Miss Pirbright.

The Vicar felt that the heavens had fallen. He sat crumpled up in his chair, a shattered man. Lady Hammergallow sat down next to him without appearing to see him. She was breathing heavily, but her face was terribly calm. Everyone sat down. Was the Angel grossly ignorant or only grossly impertinent? The Angel was vaguely aware of some frightful offence, aware that in some mysterious way he had ceased to be the centre of the gathering. He saw reproachful despair in the Vicar's eye. He drifted slowly towards the window in the recess and sat down on the little octagonal Moorish stool by the side of Mrs Jehoram. And under the circumstances he appreciated at more than its proper value Mrs Jehoram's kindly smile. He put down the violin in the window seat.

<p style="text-align:center">★★★★★★</p>

Mrs Jehoram and the Angel (apart)—Mr Wilmerdings playing.

"I have so longed for a quiet word with you," said Mrs Jehoram in a low tone. "To tell you how delightful I found your playing."

"I am glad it pleased you," said the Angel.

"Pleased is scarcely the word," said Mrs Jehoram. "I was moved—profoundly. These others did not understand.I was glad you did not play with him."

The Angel looked at the mechanism called Wilmerdings, and felt glad too. (The Angelic conception of duets is a kind of conversation upon violins.) But he said nothing.

"I worship music," said Mrs Jehoram. "I know nothing about it technically, but there is something in it—a longing, a wish."

The Angel stared at her face. She met his eyes.

"You understand," she said. "I see you understand." He was certainly a very nice boy, sentimentally precocious perhaps, and with deliciously liquid eyes.

There was an interval of Chopin (Op. 40) played with immense precision.

Mrs Jehoram had a sweet face still, in shadow, with the light falling round her golden hair, and a curious theory flashed across the Angel's mind. The perceptible powder only supported his view of something infinitely bright and lovable caught, tarnished, coarsened, coated over.

"Do you," said the Angel in a low tone. "Are you.separated from.*your* world?"

"As you are?" whispered Mrs Jehoram.

"This is so—cold," said the Angel. "So harsh!" He meant the whole world.

"I feel it too," said Mrs Jehoram, referring to Siddermorton Home.

"There are those who cannot live without sympathy," she said after a sympathetic pause. "And times when one feels alone in the world. Fighting a battle against it all. Laughing, flirting, hiding the pain of it. . . ."

"And hoping," said the Angel with a wonderful glance.—"Yes."

Mrs Jehoram (who was an epicure of flirtations) felt the Angel was more than redeeming the promise of his appearance. (Indisputably he worshipped her.) "Do *you* look for sympathy?" she said. "Or have you found it?"

"I think," said the Angel, very softly, leaning forward, "I think I have found it."

Interval of Chopin Op. 40. The very eldest Miss Papaver and Mrs Pirbright whispering. Lady Hammergallow (glasses up) looking down the saloon with an unfriendly expression at the Angel. Mrs Jehoram and the Angel exchanging deep and significant glances.

"Her name," said the Angel (Mrs Jehoram made a movement) "is Delia. She is."

"Delia!" said Mrs Jehoram sharply, slowly realising a terrible misunderstanding. "A fanciful name.Why!No! Not that little housemaid at the Vicarage—?."

The Polonaise terminated with a flourish. The Angel was quite surprised at the change in Mrs Jehoram's expression.

"*I never* did!" said Mrs Jehoram recovering. "To make me your confidant in an intrigue with a servant. Really Mr Angel it's possible to be too original."

Then suddenly their colloquy was interrupted.

★★★★★★

This section is (so far as my memory goes) the shortest in the book.

But the enormity of the offence necessitates the separation of this section from all other sections.

The Vicar, you must understand, had done his best to inculcate the recognised differentiae of a gentleman. "Never allow a lady to carry anything," said the Vicar. "Say, 'permit me' and relieve her." "Always stand until every lady is seated." "Always rise and open a door for a lady." and so forth. (All men who have elder sisters know that code.)

And the Angel (who had failed to relieve Lady Hammergallow of her teacup) danced forward with astonishing dexterity (leaving Mrs Jehoram in the window seat) and with an elegant "permit me" rescued the tea-tray from Lady Hammergallow's pretty parlour-maid and vanished officiously in front of her. The Vicar rose to his feet with an inarticulate cry.

★★★★★★

"He's drunk!" said Mr Rathbone-Slater, breaking a terrific silence. "That's the matter with *him*."

Mrs Jehoram laughed hysterically.

The Vicar stood up, motionless, staring. "Oh! I *forgot* to explain servants to him!" said the Vicar to himself in a swift outbreak of re-morse. "I thought he *did* understand servants."

"Really, Mr Hilyer!" said Lady Hammergallow, evidently exercis-ing enormous self-control and speaking in panting spasms. "Really, Mr Hilyer!—Your genius is *too* terrible. I must, I really *must*, ask you to take him home."

So, to the dialogue in the corridor of alarmed maid-servant and well-meaning (but shockingly *gauche*) Angel—appears the Vicar, his botryoidal little face crimson, gaunt despair in his eyes, and his necktie under his left ear.

"Come," he said—struggling with emotion "Come away.I. . . . I am disgraced for ever."

And the Angel stared for a second at him and obeyed—meekly, perceiving himself in the presence of unknown but evidently terrible forces.

And so, began and ended the Angel's social career.

In the informal indignation meeting that followed, Lady Hammer-gallow took the (informal) chair. "I feel humiliated," she said. "The

Vicar assured me he was an exquisite player. I never imagined."

"He was drunk," said Mr Rathbone-Slater. "You could tell it from the way he fumbled with his tea."

"Such a *fiasco!*" said Mrs Mergle.

"The Vicar assured me," said Lady Hammergallow. "'The man I have staying with me is a musical genius,' he said. His very words."

"His ears must be burning anyhow," said Tommy Rathbone-Slater.

"I was trying to keep him Quiet," said Mrs Jehoram. "By humouring him. And do you know the things he said to me—there!"

"The thing he played," said Mr Wilmerdings,"—I must confess I did not like to charge him to his face. But really! It was merely *drifting.*"

"Just fooling with a fiddle, eigh?" said George Harringay. "Well I thought it was beyond me. So much of your fine music is—"

"Oh, *George!*" said the younger Miss Pirbright.

"The Vicar was a bit on too—to judge by his tie," said Mr Rathbone-Slater. "It's a dashed rummy go. Did you notice how he fussed after the genius?"

"One has to be so very careful," said the very eldest Miss Papaver.

"He told me he is in love with the Vicar's housemaid!" said Mrs Jehoram. "I almost laughed in his face."

"The Vicar ought *never* to have brought him here," said Mrs Rathbone-Slater with decision.

CHAPTER 19

The Trouble of the Barbed Wire

So, ingloriously, ended the Angel's first and last appearance in Society. Vicar and Angel returned to the Vicarage; crestfallen black figures in the bright sunlight, going dejectedly. The Angel, deeply pained that the Vicar was pained. The Vicar, dishevelled and desperate, intercalating spasmodic remorse and apprehension with broken explanations of the Theory of Etiquette. "They do *not* understand," said the Vicar over and over again. "They will all be so very much aggrieved. I do not know what to say to them. It is all so confused, so perplexing." And at the gate of the Vicarage, at the very spot where Delia had first seemed beautiful, stood Horrocks the village constable, awaiting them. He held coiled up about his hand certain short lengths of barbed wire.

"Good evening, Horrocks," said the Vicar as the constable held the gate open.

"Evenin', Sir," said Horrocks, and added in a kind of mysterious

undertone, "*Could* I speak to you a minute, Sir?"

"Certainly," said the Vicar. The Angel walked on thoughtfully to the house, and meeting Delia in the hall stopped her and cross-examined her at length over differences between Servants and Ladies.

"You'll excuse my taking the liberty, Sir," said Horrocks, "but there's trouble brewin' for that crippled gent you got stayin' here."

"Bless me!" said the Vicar. "You don't say so!"

"Sir John Gotch, Sir. He's very angry indeed, Sir. His language, Sir——. But I felt bound to tell you, Sir. He's certain set on taking out a summons on account of that there barbed wire. Certain set, Sir, he is."

"Sir John Gotch!" said the Vicar. "Wire! I don't understand."

"He asked me to find out who did it. Course I've had to do my duty, Sir. Naturally a disagreeable one."

"Barbed wire! Duty! I don't understand you, Horrocks."

"I'm afraid, Sir, there's no denying the evidence. I've made careful enquiries, Sir." And forthwith the constable began telling the Vicar of a new and terrible outrage committed by the Angelic visitor.

But we need not follow that explanation in detail—or the subsequent confession. (For my own part I think there is nothing more tedious than dialogue). It gave the Vicar a new view of the Angelic character, a vignette of the Angelic indignation. A shady lane, sunmottled, sweet hedges full of honeysuckle and vetch on either side, and a little girl gathering flowers, forgetful of the barbed wire which, all along the Sidderford Road, fenced in the dignity of Sir John Gotch from "bounders" and the detested "million." Then suddenly a gashed hand, a bitter outcry, and the Angel sympathetic, comforting, inquisitive. Explanations sob-set, and then—altogether novel phenomenon in the Angelic career—*passion.*

A furious onslaught upon the barbed wire of Sir John Gotch, barbed wire recklessly handled, slashed, bent and broken. Yet the Angel acted without personal malice—saw in the thing only an ugly and vicious plant that trailed insidiously among its fellows. Finally, the Angel's explanations gave the Vicar a picture of the Angel alone amidst his destruction, trembling and amazed at the sudden force, not himself, that had sprung up within him, and set him striking and cutting. Amazed, too, at the crimson blood that trickled down his fingers.

"It is still more horrible," said the Angel when the Vicar explained the artificial nature of the thing. "If I had seen the man who put this silly-cruel stuff there to hurt little children, I know I should have tried

158

to inflict pain upon him. I have never felt like this before. I am indeed becoming tainted and coloured altogether by the wickedness of this world."

"To think, too, that you men should be so foolish as to uphold the laws that let a man do such spiteful things. Yes—I know; you will say it has to be so. For some remoter reason. That is a thing that only makes me angrier. Why cannot an act rest on its own merits? As it does in the Angelic Land."

That was the incident the history of which the Vicar now gradually learnt, getting the bare outline from Horrocks, the colour and emotion subsequently from the Angel. The thing had happened the day before the musical festival at Siddermorton House.

"Have you told Sir John who did it?" asked the Vicar. "And are you sure?"

"Quite sure, Sir. There can be no doubting it was your gentleman, Sir. I've not told Sir John yet, Sir. But I shall have to tell Sir John this evening. Meaning no offence to you, Sir, as I hopes you'll see. It's my duty, Sir. Besides which—"

"Of course," said the Vicar, hastily. "Certainly, it's your duty. And what will Sir John do?"

"He's dreadful set against the person who did it—destroying property like that—and sort of slapping his arrangements in the face."

Pause. Horrocks made a movement. The Vicar, tie almost at the back of his neck now, a most unusual thing for him, stared blankly at his toes.

"I thought I'd tell you, Sir," said Horrocks.

"Yes," said the Vicar. "Thanks, Horrocks, thanks!" He scratched the back of his head. "You might perhaps. I think it's the best way. . . . Quite sure Mr Angel did it?"

"Sherlock 'Omes, Sir, couldn't be cocksurer."

"Then I'd better give you a little note to the Squire."

★★★★★★

The Vicar's table-talk at dinner that night, after the Angel had stated his case, was full of grim explanations, prisons, madness.

"It's too late to tell the truth about you now," said the Vicar. "Besides, that's impossible. I really do not know what to say. We must face our circumstances, I suppose. I am so undecided—so torn. It's the two worlds. If your Angelic world were only a dream, or if *this* world were only a dream—or if I could believe either or both dreams, it would be all right with me. But here is a real Angel and a real summons—how

to reconcile them I do not know. I must talk to Gotch.But he won't understand. Nobody will understand."

"I am putting you to terrible inconvenience, I am afraid. My appalling unworldliness—"

"It's not you," said the Vicar. "It's not you. I perceive you have brought something strange and beautiful into my life. It's not you. It's myself. If I had more faith either way. If I could believe entirely in this world, and call you an Abnormal Phenomenon, as Crump does. But no. Terrestrial Angelic, Angelic Terrestrial.See-Saw."

"Still, Gotch is certain to be disagreeable, *most* disagreeable. He always is. It puts me into his hands. He is a bad moral influence, I know. Drinking. Gambling. Worse. Still, one must render unto Caesar the things that are Caesar's. And he is against Disestablishment."

Then the Vicar would revert to the social collapse of the afternoon. "You are so very fundamental, you know," he said—several times.

The Angel went to his own room puzzled but very depressed. Every day the world had frowned darker upon him and his angelic ways. He could see how the trouble affected the Vicar, yet he could not imagine how he could avert it. It was all so strange and unreasonable. Twice again, too, he had been pelted out of the village.

He found the violin lying on his bed where he had laid it before dinner. And taking it up he began to play to comfort himself. But now he played no delicious vision of the Angelic Land. The iron of the world was entering into his soul. For a week now he had known pain and rejection, suspicion and hatred; a strange new spirit of revolt was growing up in his heart. He played a melody, still sweet and tender as those of the Angelic Land, but charged with a new note, the note of human sorrow and effort, now swelling into something like defiance, dying now into a plaintive sadness. He played softly, playing to himself to comfort himself, but the Vicar heard, and all his finite bothers were swallowed up in a hazy melancholy, a melancholy that was quite remote from sorrow. And besides the Vicar, the Angel had another hearer of whom neither Angel nor Vicar was thinking.

Chapter 20
Delia

She was only four or five yards away from the Angel in the westward gable. The diamond-paned window of her little white room was open. She knelt on her box of japanned tin, and rested her chin on her hands, her elbows on the window-sill. The young moon hung over

160

the pine trees, and its light, cool and colourless, lay softly upon the silent-sleeping world. Its light fell upon her white face, and discovered new depths in her dreaming eyes. Her soft lips fell apart and showed the little white teeth.

Delia was thinking, vaguely, wonderfully, as girls will think. It was feeling rather than thinking; clouds of beautiful translucent emotion drove across the clear sky of her mind, taking shape that changed and vanished. She had all that wonderful emotional tenderness, that subtle exquisite desire for self-sacrifice, which exists so inexplicably in a girl's heart, exists it seems only to be presently trampled underfoot by the grim and gross humours of daily life, to be ploughed in again roughly and remorselessly, as the farmer ploughs in the clover that has sprung up in the soil. She had been looking out at the tranquillity of the moonlight long before the Angel began to play—waiting; then suddenly the quiet, motionless beauty of silver and shadow was suffused with tender music.

She did not move, but her lips closed and her eyes grew even softer. She had been thinking before of the strange glory that had suddenly flashed out about the stooping hunchback when he spoke to her in the sunset; of that and of a dozen other glances, chance turns, even once the touching of her hand. That afternoon he had spoken to her, asking strange questions. Now the music seemed to bring his very face before her, his look of half curious solicitude, peering into her face, into her eyes, into her and through her, deep down into her soul.

He seemed now to be speaking directly to her, telling her of his solitude and trouble. Oh! that regret, that longing! For he was in trouble. And how could a servant-girl help him, this soft-spoken gentleman who carried himself so kindly, who played so sweetly. The music was so sweet and keen, it came so near to the thought of her heart, that presently one hand tightened on the other, and the tears came streaming down her face.

As Crump would tell you, people do not do that kind of thing unless there is something wrong with the nervous system. But then, from the scientific point of view, being in love is a pathological condition.

★★★★★★

I am painfully aware of the objectionable nature of my story here. I have even thought of wilfully perverting the truth to propitiate the Lady Reader. But I could not. The story has been too much for me. I do the thing with my eyes open. Delia must remain what she really was—a servant girl. I know that to give a mere servant girl, or at

least an English servant girl, the refined feelings of a human being, to present her as speaking with anything but an intolerable confusion of aspirates, places me outside the pale of respectable writers. Association with servants, even in thought, is dangerous in these days. I can only plead (pleading vainly, I know), that Delia was a very exceptional servant girl. Possibly, if one enquired, it might be found that her parentage was upper middle-class—that she was made of the finer upper middle-class clay.

And (this perhaps may avail me better) I will promise that in some future work I will redress the balance, and the patient reader shall have the recognised article, enormous feet and hands, systematic aspiration of vowels and elimination of aspirates, no figure (only middle-class girls have figures—the thing is beyond a servant-girl's means), a fringe (by agreement), and a cheerful readiness to dispose of her self-respect for half-a-crown. That is the accepted English servant, the typical English woman (when stripped of money and accomplishments) as she appears in the works of contemporary writers. But Delia somehow was different. I can only regret the circumstance—it was altogether beyond my control.

<div align="center">

CHAPTER 21

Doctor Crump Acts

</div>

Early the next morning the Angel went down through the village, and climbing the fence, waded through the waist-high reeds that fringe the Sidder. He was going to Bandram Bay to take a nearer view of the sea, which one could just see on a clear day from the higher parts of Siddermorton Park. And suddenly he came upon Crump sitting on a log and smoking. (Crump always smoked exactly two ounces per week—and he always smoked it in the open air.)

"Hullo!" said Crump, in his healthiest tone. "How's the wing?"

"Very well," said the Angel. "The pain's gone."

"I suppose you know you are trespassing?"

"Trespassing!" said the Angel.

"I suppose you don't know what that means," said Crump.

"I don't," said the Angel.

"I must congratulate you. I don't know how long you will last, but you are keeping it up remarkably well. I thought at first you were a mattoid, but you're so amazingly consistent. Your attitude of entire ignorance of the elementary facts of Life is really a very amusing pose. You make slips of course, but very few. But surely we two understand

one another."

He smiled at the Angel. "You would beat Sherlock Holmes. I wonder who you really are."

The Angel smiled back, with eyebrows raised and hands extended. "It's impossible for you to know who I am. Your eyes are blind, your ears deaf, your soul dark, to all that is wonderful about me. It's no good my telling that I fell into your world."

The Doctor waved his pipe. "Not that, please. I don't want to pry if you have your reasons for keeping quiet. Only I would like you to think of Hilyer's mental health. He really believes this story."

The Angel shrugged his dwindling wings.

"You did not know him before this affair. He's changed tremendously. He used to be neat and comfortable. For the last fortnight he's been hazy, with a far-away look in his eyes. He preached last Sunday without his cuff links, and something wrong with his tie, and he took for his text, 'Eye hath not seen nor ear heard.' He really believes all this nonsense about the Angel-land. The man is verging on monomania!"

"You *will* see things from your own standpoint," said the Angel.

"Everyone must. At any rate, I think it jolly regrettable to see this poor old fellow hypnotised, as you certainly have hypnotized him. I don't know where you come from nor who you are, but I warn you I'm not going to see the old boy made a fool of much longer."

"But he's not being made a fool of. He's simply beginning to dream of a world outside his knowledge——"

"It won't do," said Crump. "I'm not one of the dupe class. You are either of two things—a lunatic at large (which I don't believe), or a knave. Nothing else is possible. I think I know a little of this world, whatever I do of yours. Very well. If you don't leave Hilyer alone I shall communicate with the police, and either clap you into a prison, if you go back on your story, or into a madhouse if you don't. It's stretching a point, but I swear I'd certify you insane tomorrow to get you out of the village. It's not only the Vicar. As you know. I hope that's plain. Now what have you to say?"

With an affectation of great calm, the Doctor took out his penknife and began to dig the blade into his pipe bowl. His pipe had gone out during this last speech.

For a moment neither spoke. The Angel looked about him with a face that grew pale. The Doctor extracted a plug of tobacco from his pipe and flung it away, shut his penknife and put it in his waistcoat pocket. He had not meant to speak quite so emphatically, but speech

163

always warmed him.

"Prison," said the Angel. "Madhouse! Let me see." Then he remembered the Vicar's explanation. "Not that!" he said. He approached Crump with eyes dilated and hands outstretched.

"I knew *you* would know what those things meant—at any rate. Sit down," said Crump, indicating the tree trunk beside him by a movement of the head.

The Angel, shivering, sat down on the tree trunk and stared at the Doctor.

Crump was getting out his pouch. "You are a strange man," said the Angel. "Your beliefs are like—a steel trap."

"They are," said Crump—flattered.

"But I tell you—I assure you the thing is so—I know nothing, or at least remember nothing of anything I knew of this world before I found myself in the darkness of night on the moorland above Sidderford."

"Where did you learn the language then?"

"I don't know. Only I tell you—But I haven't an atom of the sort of proof that would convince you."

"And you really," said Crump, suddenly coming round upon him and looking into his eyes; "You really believe you were eternally in a kind of glorious heaven before then?"

"I do," said the Angel.

"Pshaw!" said Crump, and lit his pipe. He sat smoking, elbow on knee, for some time, and the Angel sat and watched him. Then his face grew less troubled.

"It is just possible," he said to himself rather than to the Angel, and began another piece of silence.

"You see;" he said, when that was finished. "There is such a thing as double personality. . . . A man sometimes forgets who he is and thinks he is someone else. Leaves home, friends, and everything, and leads a double life. There was a case in *Nature* only a month or so ago. The man was sometimes English and right-handed, and sometimes Welsh and left-handed. When he was English, he knew no Welsh, when he was Welsh, he knew no English.H'm."

He turned suddenly on the Angel and said "Home!" He fancied he might revive in the Angel some latent memory of his lost youth. He went on "Dadda, Pappa, Daddy, Mammy, Pappy, Father, Dad, Governor, Old Boy, Mother, dear Mother, Ma, Mumsy.No good? What are you laughing at?"

"Nothing," said the Angel. "You surprised me a little—that is all. A week ago, I should have been puzzled by that vocabulary."

For a minute Crump rebuked the Angel silently out of the corner of his eye.

"You have such an ingenuous face. You almost force me to believe you. You are certainly not an ordinary lunatic. Your mind—except for your isolation from the past—seems balanced enough. I wish Nordau or Lombroso or some of these *Saltpetriere* men could have a look at you. Down here one gets no practice worth speaking about in mental cases. There's one idiot—and he's just a damned idiot of an idiot—; all the rest are thoroughly sane people."

"Possibly that accounts for their behaviour," said the Angel thoughtfully.

"But to consider your general position here," said Crump, ignoring his comment, "I really regard you as a bad influence here. These fancies are contagious. It is not simply the Vicar. There is a man named Shine has caught the fad, and he has been in the drink for a week, off and on, and offering to fight anyone who says you are not an Angel. Then a man over at Sidderford is, I hear, affected with a kind of religious mania on the same tack. These things spread. There ought to be a quarantine in mischievous ideas. And I have heard another story....."

"But what can I do?" said the Angel. "Suppose I am (quite unintentionally) doing mischief......"

"You can leave the village," said Crump.

"Then I shall only go into another village."

"That's not my affair," said Crump. "Go where you like. Only go. Leave these three people, the Vicar, Shine, the little servant girl, whose heads are all spinning with galaxies of Angels....."

"But," said the Angel. "Face your world! I tell you I can't. And leave Delia! I don't understand.....I do not know how to set about getting Work and Food and Shelter. And I am growing afraid of human beings....."

"Fancies, fancies," said Crump, watching him, "mania."

"It's no good my persisting in worrying you," he said suddenly, "but certainly the situation is impossible as it stands." He stood up with a jerk.

"Good-morning, Mr—Angel," he said, "the long and the short of it is—I say it as the medical adviser of this parish—you are an unhealthy influence. We can't have you. You must go."

He turned, and went striding through the grass towards the road-

way, leaving the Angel sitting disconsolately on the tree trunk. "An unhealthy influence," said the Angel slowly, staring blankly in front of him, and trying to realise what it meant.

CHAPTER 22
Sir John Gotch Acts

Sir John Gotch was a little man with scrubby hair, a small, thin nose sticking out of a face crackled with wrinkles, tight brown gaiters, and a riding whip. "I've come, you see," he said, as Mrs Hinijer closed the door.

"Thank you," said the Vicar, "I'm obliged to you. I'm really obliged to you."

"Glad to be of any service to you," said Sir John Gotch. (Angular attitude.)

"This business," said the Vicar, "this unfortunate business of the barbed wire—is really, you know, a most unfortunate business."

Sir John Gotch became decidedly more angular in his attitude. "It is," he said.

"This Mr Angel being my guest—"

"No reason why he should cut my wire," said Sir John Gotch, briefly.

"None whatever."

"May I ask *who* this Mr Angel is?" asked Sir John Gotch with the abruptness of long premeditation.

The Vicar's fingers jumped to his chin. What *was* the good of talking to a man like Sir John Gotch about Angels?

"To tell you the exact truth," said the Vicar, "there is a little secret—"

"Lady Hammergallow told me as much."

The Vicar's face suddenly became bright red.

"Do you know," said Sir John, with scarcely a pause, "he's been going about this village preaching Socialism?"

"Good heavens!" said the Vicar, "*No!*"

"He has. He has been buttonholing every yokel he came across, and asking them why they had to work, while we—I and you, you know—did nothing. He has been saying we ought to educate every man up to your level and mine—out of the rates, I suppose, as usual. He has been suggesting that we—I and you, you know—keep these people down—pith 'em."

"*Dear* me!" said the Vicar, "I had no idea."

166

"He has done this wire-cutting as a demonstration, I tell you, as a Socialistic demonstration. If we don't come down on him pretty sharply, I tell you, we shall have the palings down in Flinders Lane next, and the next thing will be ricks afire, and every damned (I beg your pardon, Vicar. I know I'm too fond of that word), every blessed pheasant's egg in the parish smashed. I know these—"

"A Socialist," said the Vicar, quite put out, "I had *no* idea."

"You see why I am inclined to push matters against our gentleman though he *is* your guest. It seems to me he has been taking advantage of your paternal—"

"Oh, *not* paternal!" said the Vicar. "Really—"

"(I beg your pardon, Vicar—it was a slip.) Of your kindness, to go mischief-making everywhere, setting class against class, and the poor man against his bread and butter."

The Vicar's fingers were at his chin again.

"So, there's one of two things," said Sir John Gotch. "Either that guest of yours leaves the parish, or—I take proceedings. That's final."

The Vicar's mouth was all askew.

"That's the position," said Sir John, jumping to his feet, "if it were not for you, I should take proceedings at once. As it is—am I to take proceedings or no?"

"You see," said the Vicar in horrible perplexity.

"Well?"

"Arrangements have to be made."

"He's a mischief-making idler.I know the breed. But I'll give you a week——"

"Thank you," said the Vicar. "I understand your position. I perceive the situation is getting intolerable."

"Sorry to give you this bother, of course," said Sir John.

"A week," said the Vicar.

"A week," said Sir John, leaving.

<p style="text-align:center">★★★★★★</p>

The Vicar returned, after accompanying Gotch out, and for a long time he remained sitting before the desk in his study, plunged in thought. "A week!" he said, after an immense silence. "Here is an Angel, a glorious Angel, who has quickened my soul to beauty and delight, who has opened my eyes to Wonderland, and something more than Wonderland.and I have promised to get rid of him in a week! What are we men made of?How *can* I tell him?"

He began to walk up and down the room, then he went into the

dining-room, and stood staring blankly out at the cornfield. The table was already laid for lunch. Presently he turned, still dreaming, and almost mechanically helped himself to a glass of sherry.

CHAPTER 23

The Sea Cliff

The Angel lay upon the summit of the cliff above Bandram Bay, and stared out at the glittering sea. Sheer from under his elbows fell the cliff, five hundred and seven feet of it down to the datum line, and the sea-birds eddied and soared below him. The upper part of the cliff was a greenish chalky rock, the lower two-thirds a warm red, marbled with gypsum bands, and from half-a-dozen places spurted jets of water, to fall in long cascades down its face. The swell frothed white on the flinty beach, and the water beyond where the shadows of an outstanding rock lay, was green and purple in a thousand tints and marked with streaks and flakes of foam. The air was full of sunlight and the tinkling of the little waterfalls and the slow soughing of the seas below. Now and then a butterfly flickered over the face of the cliff, and a multitude of sea birds perched and flew hither and thither.

The Angel lay with his crippled, shrivelled wings humped upon his back, watching the gulls and jackdaws and rooks, circling in the sunlight, soaring, eddying, sweeping down to the water or upward into the dazzling blue of the sky.

Long the Angel lay there and watched them going to and fro on outspread wings. He watched, and as he watched them, he remembered with infinite longing the rivers of starlight and the sweetness of the land from which he came. And a gull came gliding overhead, swiftly and easily, with its broad wings spreading white and fair against the blue. And suddenly a shadow came into the Angel's eyes, the sunlight left them, he thought of his own crippled pinions, and put his face upon his arm and wept.

A woman who was walking along the footpath across the Cliff Field saw only a twisted hunchback dressed in the Vicar of Siddermorton's cast-off clothes, sprawling foolishly at the edge of the cliff and with his forehead on his arm. She looked at him and looked again. "The silly creature has gone to sleep," she said, and though she had a heavy basket to carry, came towards him with an idea of waking him up. But as she drew near, she saw his shoulders heave and heard the sound of his sobbing.

She stood still a minute, and her features twitched into a kind of

grin. Then treading softly, she turned and went back towards the pathway. "'Tis so hard to think of anything to say," she said. "Poor afflicted soul!"

Presently the Angel ceased sobbing, and stared with a tear-stained face at the beach below him.

"This world," he said, "wraps me round and swallows me up. My wings grow shrivelled and useless. Soon I shall be nothing more than a crippled man, and I shall age, and bow myself to pain, and die.I am miserable. And I am alone."

Then he rested his chin on his hands upon the edge of the cliff, and began to think of Delia's face with the light in her eyes. The Angel felt a curious desire to go to her and tell her of his withered wings. To place his arms about her and weep for the land he had lost. "Delia!" he said to himself very softly. And presently a cloud drove in front of the sun.

CHAPTER 24

Mrs Hinijer Acts

Mrs Hinijer surprised the Vicar by tapping at his study door after tea. "Begging your pardon, Sir," said Mrs Hinijer. "But might I make so bold as to speak to you for a moment?"

"Certainly, Mrs Hinijer," said the Vicar, little dreaming of the blow that was coming. He held a letter in his hand, a very strange and disagreeable letter from his bishop, a letter that irritated and distressed him, criticising in the strongest language the guests he chose to entertain in his own house. Only a popular bishop living in a democratic age, a bishop who was still half a pedagogue, could have written such a letter.

Mrs Hinijer coughed behind her hand and struggled with some respiratory disorganisation. The Vicar felt apprehensive. Usually in their interviews he was the most disconcerted. Invariably so when the interview ended.

"Well?" he said.

"May I make so bold, sir, as to arst when Mr Angel is a-going?" (Cough.)

The Vicar started. "To ask when Mr Angel is going?" he repeated slowly to gain time. "*Another!*"

"I'm sorry, sir. But I've been used to waitin' on gentlefolks, sir; and you'd hardly imagine how it feels quite to wait on such as 'im."

"Such as.'*im*! Do I understand you, Mrs Hinijer, that you don't

169

like Mr Angel?"

"You see, sir, before I came to you, sir, I was at Lord Dundoller's seventeen years, and you, sir—if you will excuse me—are a perfect gentleman yourself, sir—though in the Church. And then."

"Dear, dear!" said the Vicar. "And don't you regard Mr Angel as a gentleman?"

"I'm sorry to 'ave to say it, sir."

"But what.? Dear me! Surely!"

"I'm sorry to 'ave to say it, sir. But when a party goes turning vegetarian suddenly and putting out all the cooking, and hasn't no proper luggage of his own, and borry's shirts and socks from his 'ost, and don't know no better than to try his knife at peas (as I seed my very self), and goes talking in odd corners to the housemaids, and folds up his napkin after meals, and eats with his fingers at minced veal, and plays the fiddle in the middle of the night keeping everybody awake, and stares and grins at his elders a-getting upstairs, and generally misconducts himself with things that I can scarcely tell you all, one can't help thinking, sir. Thought is free, sir, and one can't help coming to one's own conclusions.

"Besides which, there is talk all over the village about him—what with one thing and another. I know a gentleman when I sees a gentleman, and I know a gentleman when I don't see a gentleman, and me, and Susan, and George, we've talked it over, being the upper servants, so to speak, and experienced, and leaving out that girl Delia, who I only hope won't come to any harm through him, and depend upon it, sir, that Mr Angel ain't what you think he is, sir, and the sooner he leaves this house the better."

Mrs Hinijer ceased abruptly and stood panting but stern, and with her eyes grimly fixed on the Vicar's face.

"*Really*, Mrs Hinijer!" said the Vicar, and then, "Oh *Lord!*"

"What *have* I done?" said the Vicar, suddenly starting up and appealing to the inexorable fates. "What *have* I done?"

"There's no knowing," said Mrs Hinijer. "Though a deal of talk in the village."

"*Bother!*" said the Vicar, going and staring out of the window. Then he turned. "Look here, Mrs Hinijer! Mr Angel will be leaving this house in the course of a week. Is that enough?"

"Quite," said Mrs Hinijer. "And I feel sure, sir."

The Vicar's eyes fell with unwonted eloquence upon the door.

170

The Angel in Trouble

"The fact is," said the Vicar, "this is no world for Angels."

The blinds had not been drawn, and the twilight outer world under an overcast sky seemed unspeakably grey and cold. The Angel sat at table in dejected silence. His inevitable departure had been proclaimed. Since his presence hurt people and made the Vicar wretched, he acquiesced in the justice of the decision, but what would happen to him after his plunge he could not imagine. Something very disagreeable certainly.

"There is the violin," said the Vicar. "Only after our experience——

"I must get you clothes—a general outfit.—— Dear me! you don't understand railway travelling! And coinage! Taking lodgings! Eating-houses!—— I must come up at least and see you settled. Get work for you. But an Angel in London! Working for his living! That grey cold wilderness of people! What *wil* become of you?—— If I had one friend in the world I could trust to believe me!

"I ought not to be sending you away——"

"Do not trouble overmuch for me, my friend," said the Angel. "At least this life of yours ends. And there are things in it. There is something in this life of yours——Your care for me! I thought there was nothing beautiful at all in life——"

"And I have betrayed you!" said the Vicar, with a sudden wave of remorse. "Why did I not face them all—say, 'This is the best of life'? What do these everyday things matter?"

He stopped suddenly. "What *do* they matter?" he said.

"I have only come into your life to trouble it," said the Angel.

"Don't say that," said the Vicar. "You have come into my life to awaken me. I have been dreaming—dreaming. Dreaming this was necessary and that. Dreaming that this narrow prison was the world. And the dream still hangs about me and troubles me. That is all. Even your departure——. Am I not dreaming that you must go?"

When he was in bed that night the mystical aspect of the case came still more forcibly before the Vicar. He lay awake and had the most horrible visions of his sweet and delicate visitor drifting through this unsympathetic world and happening upon the cruellest misadventures. His guest *was* an Angel assuredly. He tried to go over the whole story of the past eight days again. He thought of the hot afternoon,

the shot fired out of sheer surprise, the fluttering iridescent wings, the beautiful saffron-robed figure upon the ground. How wonderful that had seemed to him!

Then his mind turned to the things he had heard of the other world, to the dreams the violin had conjured up, to the vague, fluctuating, wonderful cities of the Angelic Land. He tried to recall the forms of the buildings, the shapes of the fruits upon the trees, the aspect of the winged shapes that traversed its ways. They grew from a memory into a present reality, grew every moment just a little more vivid and his troubles a little less immediate; and so, softly and quietly, the Vicar slipped out of his troubles and perplexities into the Land of Dreams.

<p style="text-align:center">★★★★★★</p>

Delia sat with her window open, hoping to hear the Angel play. But that night there was to be no playing. The sky was overcast, yet not so thickly but that the moon was visible. High up a broken cloud-lace drove across the sky, and now the moon was a hazy patch of light, and now it was darkened, and now rode clear and bright and sharply outlined against the blue gulf of night. And presently she heard the door into the garden opening, and a figure came out under the drifting pallor of the moonlight.

It was the Angel. But he wore once more the saffron robe in the place of his formless overcoat. In the uncertain light this garment had only a colourless shimmer, and his wings behind him seemed a leaden grey. He began taking short runs, flapping his wings and leaping, going to and fro amidst the drifting patches of light and the shadows of the trees. Delia watched him in amazement. He gave a despondent cry, leaping higher. His shrivelled wings flashed and fell. A thicker patch in the cloud-film made everything obscure. He seemed to spring five or six feet from the ground and fall clumsily. She saw him in the dimness crouching on the ground and then she heard him sobbing.

"He's hurt!" said Delia, pressing her lips together hard and staring. "I ought to help him."

She hesitated, then stood up and flitted swiftly towards the door, went slipping quietly downstairs and out into the moonlight. The Angel still lay upon the lawn, and sobbed for utter wretchedness.

"Oh! what is the matter?" said Delia, stooping over him and touching his head timidly.

The Angel ceased sobbing, sat up abruptly, and stared at her. He saw her face, moonlit, and soft with pity. "What is the matter?" she

172

whispered. "Are you hurt?"

The Angel stared about him, and his eyes came to rest on her face. "Delia!" he whispered.

"Are you hurt?" said Delia.

"My wings," said the Angel. "I cannot use my wings."

Delia did not understand, but she realised that it was something very dreadful.

"It is dark, it is cold," whispered the Angel; "I cannot use my wings."

It hurt her unaccountably to see the tears on his face. She did not know what to do.

"Pity me, Delia," said the Angel, suddenly extending his arms towards her; "pity me."

Impulsively she knelt down and took his face between her hands. "I do not know," she said; "but I am sorry. I am sorry for you, with all my heart."

The Angel said not a word. He was looking at her little face in the bright moonlight, with an expression of uncomprehending wonder in his eyes. "This strange world!" he said.

She suddenly withdrew her hands. A cloud drove over the moon. "What can I do to help you?" she whispered. "I would do anything to help you."

He still held her at arm's length, perplexity replacing misery in his face. "This strange world!" he repeated.

Both whispered, she kneeling, he sitting, in the fluctuating moonlight and darkness of the lawn.

<p style="text-align:center">******</p>

"Delia!" said Mrs Hinijer, suddenly projecting from her window; "Delia, is that you?"

They both looked up at her in consternation.

"Come in at once, Delia," said Mrs Hinijer. "If that Mr Angel was a gentleman (which he isn't), he'd feel ashamed of hisself. And you an orphan too!"

Chapter 26
The Last Day of the Visit

On the morning of the next day the Angel, after he had breakfasted, went out towards the moor, and Mrs Hinijer had an interview with the Vicar. What happened need not concern us now. The Vicar was visibly disconcerted. "He *must* go," he said; "certainly he must go," and straightway he forgot the particular accusation in the general

trouble. He spent the morning in hazy meditation, interspersed by a spasmodic study of Skiff and Waterlow's price list, and the catalogue of the Medical, Scholastic, and Clerical Stores. A schedule grew slowly on a sheet of paper that lay on the desk before him. He cut out a self-measurement form from the tailoring department of the Stores and pinned it to the study curtains. This was the kind of document he was making:

1 Black Melton Frock Coat, patts? £3, 10s.
? Trousers. 2 pairs or one.
1 Cheviot Tweed Suit (write for patterns. Self-meas.?)

The Vicar spent some time studying a pleasing array of model gentlemen. They were all very nice-looking, but he found it hard to imagine the Angel so transfigured. For, although six days had passed, the Angel remained without any suit of his own. The Vicar had vacillated between a project of driving the Angel into Portbroddock and getting him measured for a suit, and his absolute horror of the insinuating manners of the tailor he employed. He knew that tailor would demand an exhaustive explanation. Besides which, one never knew when the Angel might leave. So, the six days had passed, and the Angel had grown steadily in the wisdom of this world and shrouded his brightness still in the ample retirement of the Vicar's newest clothes.

1 Soft Felt Hat, No. G. 7 (say), 8s 6d.
1 Silk Hat, 14s 6d. Hatbox?

("I suppose he ought to have a silk hat," said the Vicar; "it's the correct thing up there. Shape No. 3 seems best suited to his style. But it's dreadful to think of him all alone in that great city. Everyone will misunderstand him, and he will misunderstand everybody. However, I suppose it *must* be. Where was I?)"

1 Toothbrush. 1 Brush and Comb. Razor?
½ doz. Shirts (? measure his neck), 6s ea.
Socks? Pants?
2 suits Pyjamas. Price? Say 15s.
1 doz. Collars ('The Life Guardsman'), 8s.
Braces. Oxon Patent Versatile, 1s 11½d."
("But how will he get them on?" said the Vicar.)
1 Rubber Stamp, T. Angel, and Marking Ink in box complete, 9d.
("Those washerwomen are certain to steal all his things.")
1 Single-bladed Penknife with Corkscrew, say 1s 6d.

174

"N.B.—Don't forget Cuff Links, Collar Stud, &c. (The Vicar loved "&c.", it gave things such a precise and business-like air.) *"1 Leather Portmanteau (had better see these).*

And so forth—meanderingly. It kept the Vicar busy until lunch time, though his heart ached.

The Angel did not return to lunch. This was not so very remarkable—once before he had missed the midday meal. Yet, considering how short was the time they would have together now, he might perhaps have come back. Doubtless he had excellent reasons, though, for his absence. The Vicar made an indifferent lunch. In the afternoon he rested in his usual manner, and did a little more to the list of requirements. He did not begin to feel nervous about the Angel till tea-time. He waited, perhaps, half an hour before he took tea. "Odd," said the Vicar, feeling still more lonely as he drank his tea.

As the time for dinner crept on and no Angel appeared the Vicar's imagination began to trouble him. "He will come in to dinner, surely," said the Vicar, caressing his chin, and beginning to fret about the house upon inconsiderable errands, as his habit was when anything occurred to break his routine. The sun set, a gorgeous spectacle, amidst tumbled masses of purple cloud. The gold and red faded into twilight; the evening star gathered her robe of light together from out the brightness of the sky in the West. Breaking the silence of evening that crept over the outer world, a corncrake began his whirring chant. The Vicar's face grew troubled; twice he went and stared at the darkening hillside, and then fretted back to the house again. Mrs Hinijer served dinner. "Your dinner's ready," she announced for the second time, with a reproachful intonation. "Yes, yes," said the Vicar, fussing off upstairs.

He came down and went into his study and lit his reading lamp, a patent affair with an incandescent wick, dropping the match into his waste-paper basket without stopping to see if it was extinguished. Then he fretted into the dining-room and began a desultory attack on the cooling dinner.

(Dear Reader, the time is almost ripe to say farewell to this little Vicar of ours.)

Sir John Gotch (still smarting over the business of the barbed wire) was riding along one of the grassy ways through the preserves by the Sidder, when he saw, strolling slowly through the trees beyond the undergrowth, the one particular human being he did not want to see.

"I'm damned," said Sir John Gotch, with immense emphasis; "if this isn't altogether too much."

He raised himself in the stirrups. "Hi!" he shouted. "You there!"

The Angel turned smiling.

"Get out of this wood!" said Sir John Gotch.

"*Why?*" said the Angel.

"I'm ———," said Sir John Gotch, meditating some cataclysmal expletive. But he could think of nothing more than "damned." "Get out of this wood," he said.

The Angel's smile vanished. "Why should I get out of this wood?" he said, and stood still.

Neither spoke for a full half minute perhaps, and then Sir John Gotch dropped out of his saddle and stood by the horse.

(Now you must remember—lest the Angelic Hosts be discredited hereby—that this Angel had been breathing the poisonous air of this Struggle for Existence of ours for more than a week. It was not only his wings and the brightness of his face that suffered. He had eaten and slept and learnt the lesson of pain—had travelled so far on the road to humanity. All the length of his Visit he had been meeting more and more of the harshness and conflict of this world, and losing touch with the glorious altitudes of his own.)

"You won't go, eigh!" said Gotch, and began to lead his horse through the bushes towards the Angel. The Angel stood, all his muscles tight and his nerves quivering, watching his antagonist approach.

"Get out of this wood," said Gotch, stopping three yards away, his face white with rage, his bridle in one hand and his riding whip in the other.

Strange floods of emotion were running through the Angel. "Who are you," he said, in a low quivering voice; "who am I—that you should order me out of this place? What has the World done that men like you."

"You're the fool who cut my barbed wire," said Gotch, threatening, "If you want to know!"

"*Your* barbed wire," said the Angel. "Was that your barbed wire? Are you the man who put down that barbed wire? What right have you."

"Don't you go talking Socialist rot," said Gotch in short gasps. "This wood's mine, and I've a right to protect it how I can. I know your kind of muck. Talking rot and stirring up discontent. And if you don't get out of it jolly sharp."

"*Well!*" said the Angel, a brimming reservoir of unaccountable energy.

"Get out of this damned wood!" said Gotch, flashing into the bully out of sheer alarm at the light in the Angel's face.

He made one step towards him, with the whip raised, and then something happened that neither he nor the Angel properly understood. The Angel seemed to leap into the air, a pair of grey wings flashed out at the Squire, he saw a face bearing down upon him, full of the wild beauty of passionate anger. His riding whip was torn out of his hand. His horse reared behind him, pulled him over, gained his bridle and fled.

The whip cut across his face as he fell back, stung across his face again as he sat on the ground. He saw the Angel, radiant with anger, in the act to strike again. Gotch flung up his hands, pitched himself forward to save his eyes, and rolled on the ground under the pitiless fury of the blows that rained down upon him.

"You brute," cried the Angel, striking wherever he saw flesh to feel. "You bestial thing of pride and lies! You who have overshadowed the souls of other men. You shallow fool with your horses and dogs! To lift your face against any living thing! Learn! Learn! Learn!"

Gotch began screaming for help. Twice he tried to clamber to his feet, got to his knees, and went headlong again under the ferocious anger of the Angel. Presently he made a strange noise in his throat, and ceased even to writhe under his punishment.

Then suddenly the Angel awakened from his wrath, and found himself standing, panting and trembling, one foot on a motionless figure, under the green stillness of the sunlit woods.

He stared about him, then down at his feet where, among the tangled dead leaves, the hair was matted with blood. The whip dropped from his hands, the hot colour fled from his face. "*Pain!*" he said. "Why does he lie so still?"

He took his foot off Gotch's shoulder, bent down towards the prostrate figure, stood listening, knelt—shook him. "Awake!" said the Angel. Then still more softly, "*Awake!*"

He remained listening some minutes or more, stood up sharply, and looked round him at the silent trees. A feeling of profound horror descended upon him, wrapped him round about. With an abrupt gesture he turned. "What has happened to me?" he said, in an awe-stricken whisper.

He started back from the motionless figure. "*Dead!*" he said sud-

denly, and turning, panic stricken, fled headlong through the wood.

<center>******</center>

It was some minutes after the footsteps of the Angel had died away in the distance that Gotch raised himself on his hand. "By Jove!" he said. "Crump's right."

"Cut at the head, too!"

He put his hand to his face and felt the two weals running across it, hot and fat. "I'll think twice before I lift my hand against a lunatic again," said Sir John Gotch.

"He may be a person of weak intellect, but I'm damned if he hasn't a pretty strong arm. *Phew!* He's cut a bit clean off the top of my ear with that infernal lash."

"That infernal horse will go galloping to the house in the approved dramatic style. Little Madam'll be scared out of her wits. And II shall have to explain how it all happened. While she vivisects me with questions.

"I'm a jolly good mind to have spring guns and man-traps put in this preserve. Confound the Law!"

<center>******</center>

But the Angel, thinking that Gotch was dead, went wandering off in a passion of remorse and fear through the brakes and copses along the Sidder. You can scarcely imagine how appalled he was at this last and overwhelming proof of his encroaching humanity. All the darkness, passion and pain of life seemed closing in upon him, inexorably, becoming part of him, chaining him to all that a week ago he had found strange and pitiful in men.

"Truly, this is no world for an Angel!" said the Angel. "It is a World of War, a World of Pain, a World of Death. Anger comes upon one ... I who knew not pain and anger, stand here with blood stains on my hands. I have fallen. To come into this world is to fall. One must hunger and thirst and be tormented with a thousand desires. One must fight for foothold, be angry and strike——"

He lifted up his hands to Heaven, the ultimate bitterness of helpless remorse in his face, and then flung them down with a gesture of despair. The prison walls of this narrow passionate life seemed creeping in upon him, certainly and steadily, to crush him presently altogether. He felt what all we poor mortals have to feel sooner or later—the pitiless force of the Things that Must Be, not only without us but (where the real trouble lies) within, all the inevitable tormenting of one's high resolves, those inevitable seasons when the better self

<center>178</center>

is forgotten. But with us it is a gentle descent, made by imperceptible degrees over a long space of years; with him it was the horrible discovery of one short week. He felt he was being crippled, caked over, blinded, stupefied in the wrappings of this life, he felt as a man might feel who has taken some horrible poison, and feels destruction spreading within him.

He took no account of hunger or fatigue or the flight of time.

On and on he went, avoiding houses and roads, turning away from the sight and sound of a human being in a wordless desperate argument with Fate. His thoughts did not flow but stood banked back in inarticulate remonstrance against his degradation. Chance directed his footsteps homeward and, at last, after nightfall, he found himself faint and weary and wretched, stumbling along over the moor at the back of Siddermorton. He heard the rats run and squeal in the heather, and once a noiseless big bird came out of the darkness, passed, and vanished again. And he saw without noticing it a dull red glow in the sky before him.

<p style="text-align:center">******</p>

But when he came over the brow of the moor, a vivid light sprang up before him and refused to be ignored. He came on down the hill and speedily saw more distinctly what the glare was. It came from darting and trembling tongues of fire, golden and red, that shot from the windows and a hole in the roof of the Vicarage. A cluster of black heads, all the village in fact, except the fire-brigade—who were down at Aylmer's Cottage trying to find the key of the machine-house— came out in silhouette against the blaze. There was a roaring sound, and a humming of voices, and presently a furious outcry. There was a shouting of "No! No!"—"Come back!" and an inarticulate roar.

He began to run towards the burning house. He stumbled and almost fell, but he ran on. He found black figures running about him. The flaring fire blew gustily this way and that, and he smelt the smell of burning.

"She went in," said one voice, "she went in."

"The mad girl!" said another.

"Stand back! Stand back!" cried others.

He found himself thrusting through an excited, swaying crowd, all staring at the flames, and with the red reflection in their eyes.

"Stand back!" said a labourer, clutching him.

"What is it?" said the Angel. "What does this mean?"

"There's a girl in the house, and she can't get out!"

179

"Went in after a fiddle," said another.

"'Tas hopeless," he heard someone else say.

"I was standing near her. I heerd her. Says she: 'I *can* get his fiddle.' I heerd her—Just like that! 'I *can* get his fiddle.'"

For a moment the Angel stood staring. Then in a flash he saw it all, saw this grim little world of battle and cruelty, transfigured in a splendour that outshone the Angelic Land, suffused suddenly and insupportably glorious with the wonderful light of Love and Self-Sacrifice. He gave a strange cry, and before anyone could stop him, was running towards the burning building. There were cries of "The Hunchback! The Fowener!"

The Vicar, whose scalded hand was being tied up, turned his head, and he and Crump saw the Angel, a black outline against the intense, red glare of the doorway. It was the sensation of the tenth of a second, yet both men could not have remembered that transitory attitude more vividly had it been a picture they had studied for hours together. Then the Angel was hidden by something massive (no one knew what) that fell, incandescent, across the doorway.

<p style="text-align:center">★★★★★★</p>

There was a cry of "Delia" and no more. But suddenly the flames spurted out in a blinding glare that shot upward to an immense height, a blinding brilliance broken by a thousand flickering gleams like the waving of swords. And a gust of sparks, flashing in a thousand colours, whirled up and vanished. Just then, and for a moment by some strange accident, a rush of music, like the swell of an organ, wove into the roaring of the flames.

The whole village standing in black knots heard the sound, except Gaffer Siddons who is deaf—strange and beautiful it was, and then gone again. Lumpy Durgan, the idiot boy from Sidderford, said it began and ended like the opening and shutting of a door.

But little Hetty Penzance had a pretty fancy of two figures with wings, that flashed up and vanished among the flames.

(And after that it was she began to pine for the things she saw in her dreams, and was abstracted and strange. It grieved her mother sorely at the time. She grew fragile, as though she was fading out of the world, and her eyes had a strange, far-away look. She talked of angels and rainbow colours and golden wings, and was for ever singing an unmeaning fragment of an air that nobody knew. Until Crump took her in hand and cured her with fattening dietary, syrup of hypophosphites and cod liver oil.)

The Epilogue

And there the story of the Wonderful Visit ends. The Epilogue is in the mouth of Mrs Mendham. There stand two little white crosses in the Siddermorton churchyard, near together, where the brambles come clambering over the stone wall. One is inscribed Thomas Angel and the other Delia Hardy, and the dates of the deaths are the same. Really there is nothing beneath them but the ashes of the Vicar's stuffed ostrich. (You will remember the Vicar had his ornithological side.) I noticed them when Mrs Mendham was showing me the new De la Beche monument. (Mendham has been Vicar since Hilyer died.) "The granite came from somewhere in Scotland," said Mrs Mendham, "and cost ever so much—I forget how much—but a wonderful lot! It's quite the talk of the village."

"Mother," said Cissie Mendham, "you are stepping on a grave."

"Dear me!" said Mrs Mendham, "How heedless of me! And the cripple's grave too. But really you've no idea how much this monument cost them."

"These two people, by the bye," said Mrs Mendham, "were killed when the old Vicarage was burnt. It's rather a strange story. He was a curious person, a hunchbacked fiddler, who came from nobody knows where, and imposed upon the late Vicar to a frightful extent. He played in a pretentious way by ear, and we found out afterwards that he did not know a note of music—not a note. He was exposed before quite a lot of people. Among other things, he seems to have been 'carrying on,' as people say, with one of the servants, a sly little drab.But Mendham had better tell you all about it. The man was half-witted and curiously deformed. It's strange the fancies girls have."

She looked sharply at Cissie, and Cissie blushed to the eyes.

"She was left in the house and he rushed into the flames in an attempt to save her. Quite romantic—isn't it? He was rather clever with the fiddle in his uneducated way.

"All the poor Vicar's stuffed skins were burned at the same time. It was almost all he cared for. He never really got over the blow. He came to stop with us—for there wasn't another house available in the village. But he never seemed happy. He seemed all shaken. I never saw a man so changed. I tried to stir him up, but it was no good—no good at all.

"He had the queerest delusions about angels and that kind of thing. It made him odd company at times. He would say he heard music, and

181

stare quite stupidly at nothing for hours together. He got quite careless about his dress.He died within a twelvemonth of the fire."

The Island of Doctor Moreau

Contents

Introduction

On February the First 1887, the *Lady Vain* was lost by collision with a derelict when about the latitude 1° S. and longitude 107° W.

On January the Fifth, 1888—that is eleven months and four days after—my uncle, Edward Prendick, a private gentleman, who certainly went aboard the *Lady Vain* at Callao, and who had been considered drowned, was picked up in latitude 5° 3' S. and longitude 101° W. in a small open boat of which the name was illegible, but which is supposed to have belonged to the missing schooner *Ipecacuanha*. He gave such a strange account of himself that he was supposed demented. Subsequently he alleged that his mind was a blank from the moment of his escape from the *Lady Vain*. His case was discussed among psychologists at the time as a curious instance of the lapse of memory consequent upon physical and mental stress. The following narrative was found among his papers by the undersigned, his nephew and heir, but unaccompanied by any definite request for publication.

The only island known to exist in the region in which my uncle was picked up is Noble's Isle, a small volcanic islet and uninhabited. It was visited in 1891 by *H. M. S. Scorpion*. A party of sailors then landed, but found nothing living thereon except certain curious white moths, some hogs and rabbits, and some rather peculiar rats. So that this narrative is without confirmation in its most essential particular. With that understood, there seems no harm in putting this strange story before the public in accordance, as I believe, with my uncle's intentions. There is at least this much in its behalf: my uncle passed out of human knowledge about latitude 5° S. and longitude 105° E., and reappeared in the same part of the ocean after a space of eleven months.

In some way he must have lived during the interval. And it seems that a schooner called the *Ipecacuanha* with a drunken captain, John Davies, did start from Africa with a puma and certain other animals aboard in January, 1887, that the vessel was well known at several ports in the South Pacific, and that it finally disappeared from those seas (with a considerable amount of copra aboard), sailing to its unknown

fate from Bayna in December, 1887, a date that tallies entirely with my uncle's story.

Charles Edward Prendick.

(THE STORY WRITTEN BY EDWARD PRENDICK.)

CHAPTER 1
In the Dingey of the "Lady Vain"

I do not propose to add anything to what has already been written concerning the loss of the *Lady Vain*. As everyone knows, she collided with a derelict when ten days out from Callao. The longboat, with seven of the crew, was picked up eighteen days after by H. M. gunboat *Myrtle*, and the story of their terrible privations has become quite as well known as the far more horrible *Medusa* case. But I have to add to the published story of the *Lady Vain* another, possibly as horrible and far stranger. It has hitherto been supposed that the four men who were in the dingey perished, but this is incorrect. I have the best of evidence for this assertion: I was one of the four men.

But in the first place I must state that there never were four men in the dingey—the number was three. Constans, who was "seen by the captain to jump into the gig," (*Daily News*, March 17, 1887), luckily for us and unluckily for himself did not reach us. He came down out of the tangle of ropes under the stays of the smashed bowsprit, some small rope caught his heel as he let go, and he hung for a moment head downward, and then fell and struck a block or spar floating in the water. We pulled towards him, but he never came up.

I say luckily for us he did not reach us, and I might almost say luckily for himself; for we had only a small beaker of water and some soddened ship's biscuits with us, so sudden had been the alarm, so unprepared the ship for any disaster. We thought the people on the launch would be better provisioned (though it seems they were not), and we tried to hail them. They could not have heard us, and the next morning when the drizzle cleared—which was not until past midday—we could see nothing of them. We could not stand up to look about us, because of the pitching of the boat. The two other men who had escaped so far with me were a man named Helmar, a passenger like myself, and a seaman whose name I don't know—a short sturdy man, with a stammer.

We drifted famishing, and, after our water had come to an end, tormented by an intolerable thirst, for eight days altogether. After the

second day the sea subsided slowly to a glassy calm. It is quite impossible for the ordinary reader to imagine those eight days. He has not, luckily for himself, anything in his memory to imagine with. After the first day we said little to one another, and lay in our places in the boat and stared at the horizon, or watched, with eyes that grew larger and more haggard every day, the misery and weakness gaining upon our companions. The sun became pitiless. The water ended on the fourth day, and we were already thinking strange things and saying them with our eyes; but it was, I think, the sixth before Helmar gave voice to the thing we had all been thinking. I remember our voices were dry and thin, so that we bent towards one another and spared our words. I stood out against it with all my might, was rather for scuttling the boat and perishing together among the sharks that followed us; but when Helmar said that if his proposal was accepted, we should have drink, the sailor came round to him.

I would not draw lots however, and in the night the sailor whispered to Helmar again and again, and I sat in the bows with my clasp-knife in my hand, though I doubt if I had the stuff in me to fight; and in the morning I agreed to Helmar's proposal, and we handed halfpence to find the odd man. The lot fell upon the sailor; but he was the strongest of us and would not abide by it, and attacked Helmar with his hands. They grappled together and almost stood up. I crawled along the boat to them, intending to help Helmar by grasping the sailor's leg; but the sailor stumbled with the swaying of the boat, and the two fell upon the gunwale and rolled overboard together. They sank like stones. I remember laughing at that, and wondering why I laughed. The laugh caught me suddenly like a thing from without.

I lay across one of the thwarts for I know not how long, thinking that if I had the strength, I would drink sea-water and madden myself to die quickly. And even as I lay there I saw, with no more interest than if it had been a picture, a sail come up towards me over the sky-line. My mind must have been wandering, and yet I remember all that happened, quite distinctly. I remember how my head swayed with the seas, and the horizon with the sail above it danced up and down; but I also remember as distinctly that I had a persuasion that I was dead, and that I thought what a jest it was that they should come too late by such a little to catch me in my body.

For an endless period, as it seemed to me, I lay with my head on the thwart watching the schooner (she was a little ship, schooner-rigged fore and aft) come up out of the sea. She kept tacking to and

fro in a widening compass, for she was sailing dead into the wind. It never entered my head to attempt to attract attention, and I do not remember anything distinctly after the sight of her side until I found myself in a little cabin aft. There's a dim half-memory of being lifted up to the gangway, and of a big round countenance covered with freckles and surrounded with red hair staring at me over the bulwarks. I also had a disconnected impression of a dark face, with extraordinary eyes, close to mine; but that I thought was a nightmare, until I met it again. I fancy I recollect some stuff being poured in between my teeth; and that is all.

<div align="center">CHAPTER 2</div>

The Man Who was Going Nowhere

The cabin in which I found myself was small and rather untidy. A youngish man with flaxen hair, a bristly straw-coloured moustache, and a dropping nether lip, was sitting and holding my wrist. For a minute we stared at each other without speaking. He had watery grey eyes, oddly void of expression. Then just overhead came a sound like an iron bedstead being knocked about, and the low angry growling of some large animal. At the same time the man spoke. He repeated his question—"How do you feel now?"

I think I said I felt all right. I could not recollect how I had got there. He must have seen the question in my face, for my voice was inaccessible to me.

"You were picked up in a boat, starving. The name on the boat was the *Lady Vain*, and there were spots of blood on the gunwale."

At the same time my eye caught my hand, so thin that it looked like a dirty skin-purse full of loose bones, and all the business of the boat came back to me.

"Have some of this," said he, and gave me a dose of some scarlet stuff, iced.

It tasted like blood, and made me feel stronger.

"You were in luck," said he, "to get picked up by a ship with a medical man aboard." He spoke with a slobbering articulation, with the ghost of a lisp.

"What ship is this?" I said slowly, hoarse from my long silence.

"It's a little trader from Arica and Callao. I never asked where she came from in the beginning—out of the land of born fools, I guess. I'm a passenger myself, from Arica. The silly ass who owns her—he's captain too, named Davies—he's lost his certificate, or something. You

know the kind of man—calls the thing the *Ipecacuanha*, of all silly, infernal names; though when there's much of a sea without any wind, she certainly acts according."

(Then the noise overhead began again, a snarling growl and the voice of a human being together. Then another voice, telling some "Heaven-forsaken idiot" to desist.)

"You were nearly dead," said my interlocutor. "It was a very near thing, indeed. But I've put some stuff into you now. Notice your arm's sore? Injections. You've been insensible for nearly thirty hours."

I thought slowly. (I was distracted now by the yelping of a number of dogs.) "Am I eligible for solid food?" I asked.

"Thanks to me," he said. "Even now the mutton is boiling."

"Yes," I said with assurance; "I could eat some mutton."

"But," said he with a momentary hesitation, "you know I'm dying to hear of how you came to be alone in that boat. *Damn that howling!*" I thought I detected a certain suspicion in his eyes.

He suddenly left the cabin, and I heard him in violent controversy with someone, who seemed to me to talk gibberish in response to him. The matter sounded as though it ended in blows, but in that I thought my ears were mistaken. Then he shouted at the dogs, and returned to the cabin.

"Well?" said he in the doorway. "You were just beginning to tell me."

I told him my name, Edward Prendick, and how I had taken to Natural History as a relief from the dullness of my comfortable independence.

He seemed interested in this. "I've done some science myself. I did my Biology at University College—getting out the ovary of the earthworm and the radula of the snail, and all that. Lord! It's ten years ago. But go on! go on! tell me about the boat."

He was evidently satisfied with the frankness of my story, which I told in concise sentences enough, for I felt horribly weak; and when it was finished, he reverted at once to the topic of Natural History and his own biological studies. He began to question me closely about Tottenham Court Road and Gower Street. "Is Caplatzi still flourishing? What a shop that was!" He had evidently been a very ordinary medical student, and drifted incontinently to the topic of the music halls. He told me some anecdotes.

"Left it all," he said, "ten years ago. How jolly it all used to be! But I made a young ass of myself—played myself out before I was twenty-

one. I daresay it's all different now. But I must look up that ass of a cook, and see what he's done to your mutton."

The growling overhead was renewed, so suddenly and with so much savage anger that it startled me. "What's that?" I called after him, but the door had closed. He came back again with the boiled mutton, and I was so excited by the appetising smell of it that I forgot the noise of the beast that had troubled me.

After a day of alternate sleep and feeding I was so far recovered as to be able to get from my bunk to the scuttle, and see the green seas trying to keep pace with us. I judged the schooner was running before the wind. Montgomery—that was the name of the flaxen-haired man—came in again as I stood there, and I asked him for some clothes. He lent me some duck things of his own, for those I had worn in the boat had been thrown overboard. They were rather loose for me, for he was large and long in his limbs. He told me casually that the captain was three-parts drunk in his own cabin. As I assumed the clothes, I began asking him some questions about the destination of the ship. He said the ship was bound to Hawaii, but that it had to land him first.

"Where?" said I.

"It's an island, where I live. So far as I know, it hasn't got a name."

He stared at me with his nether lip dropping, and looked so wilfully stupid of a sudden that it came into my head that he desired to avoid my questions. I had the discretion to ask no more.

Chapter 3
The Strange Face.

We left the cabin and found a man at the companion obstructing our way. He was standing on the ladder with his back to us, peering over the combing of the hatchway. He was, I could see, a misshapen man, short, broad, and clumsy, with a crooked back, a hairy neck, and a head sunk between his shoulders. He was dressed in dark-blue serge, and had peculiarly thick, coarse, black hair. I heard the unseen dogs growl furiously, and forthwith he ducked back—coming into contact with the hand I put out to fend him off from myself. He turned with animal swiftness.

In some indefinable way the black face thus flashed upon me shocked me profoundly. It was a singularly deformed one. The facial part projected, forming something dimly suggestive of a muzzle, and the huge half-open mouth showed as big white teeth as I had ever

seen in a human mouth. His eyes were blood-shot at the edges, with scarcely a rim of white round the hazel pupils. There was a curious glow of excitement in his face.

"Confound you!" said Montgomery. "Why the devil don't you get out of the way?"

The black-faced man started aside without a word. I went on up the companion, staring at him instinctively as I did so. Montgomery stayed at the foot for a moment. "You have no business here, you know," he said in a deliberate tone. "Your place is forward."

The black-faced man cowered. "They—won't have me forward." He spoke slowly, with a queer, hoarse quality in his voice.

"Won't have you forward!" said Montgomery, in a menacing voice. "But I tell you to go!" He was on the brink of saying something further, then looked up at me suddenly and followed me up the ladder.

I had paused half way through the hatchway, looking back, still astonished beyond measure at the grotesque ugliness of this black-faced creature. I had never beheld such a repulsive and extraordinary face before, and yet—if the contradiction is credible—I experienced at the same time an odd feeling that in some way I *had* already encountered exactly the features and gestures that now amazed me. Afterwards it occurred to me that probably I had seen him as I was lifted aboard; and yet that scarcely satisfied my suspicion of a previous acquaintance. Yet how one could have set eyes on so singular a face and yet have forgotten the precise occasion, passed my imagination.

Montgomery's movement to follow me released my attention, and I turned and looked about me at the flush deck of the little schooner. I was already half prepared by the sounds I had heard for what I saw. Certainly, I never beheld a deck so dirty. It was littered with scraps of carrot, shreds of green stuff, and indescribable filth. Fastened by chains to the mainmast were a number of grisly staghounds, who now began leaping and barking at me, and by the mizzen a huge puma was cramped in a little iron cage far too small even to give it turning room. Farther under the starboard bulwark were some big hutches containing a number of rabbits, and a solitary llama was squeezed in a mere box of a cage forward. The dogs were muzzled by leather straps. The only human being on deck was a gaunt and silent sailor at the wheel.

The patched and dirty spankers were tense before the wind, and up aloft the little ship seemed carrying every sail she had. The sky was clear, the sun midway down the western sky; long waves, capped by the breeze with froth, were running with us. We went past the steers-

man to the taffrail, and saw the water come foaming under the stern and the bubbles go dancing and vanishing in her wake. I turned and surveyed the unsavoury length of the ship.

"Is this an ocean menagerie?" said I.

"Looks like it," said Montgomery.

"What are these beasts for? Merchandise, curios? Does the captain think he is going to sell them somewhere in the South Seas?"

"It looks like it, doesn't it?" said Montgomery, and turned towards the wake again.

Suddenly we heard a yelp and a volley of furious blasphemy from the companion hatchway, and the deformed man with the black face came up hurriedly. He was immediately followed by a heavy red-haired man in a white cap. At the sight of the former the staghounds, who had all tired of barking at me by this time, became furiously excited, howling and leaping against their chains. The black hesitated before them, and this gave the red-haired man time to come up with him and deliver a tremendous blow between the shoulder-blades. The poor devil went down like a felled ox, and rolled in the dirt among the furiously excited dogs. It was lucky for him that they were muzzled. The red-haired man gave a yawp of exultation and stood staggering, and as it seemed to me in serious danger of either going backwards down the companion hatchway or forwards upon his victim.

So soon as the second man had appeared, Montgomery had started forward. "Steady on there!" he cried, in a tone of remonstrance. A couple of sailors appeared on the forecastle. The black-faced man, howling in a singular voice rolled about under the feet of the dogs. No one attempted to help him. The brutes did their best to worry him, butting their muzzles at him. There was a quick dance of their lithe grey-figured bodies over the clumsy, prostrate figure. The sailors forward shouted, as though it was admirable sport. Montgomery gave an angry exclamation, and went striding down the deck, and I followed him. The black-faced man scrambled up and staggered forward, going and leaning over the bulwark by the main shrouds, where he remained, panting and glaring over his shoulder at the dogs. The red-haired man laughed a satisfied laugh.

"Look here, Captain," said Montgomery, with his lisp a little accentuated, gripping the elbows of the red-haired man, "this won't do!"

I stood behind Montgomery. The captain came half round, and regarded him with the dull and solemn eyes of a drunken man. "Wha' won't do?" he said, and added, after looking sleepily into Montgom-

ery's face for a minute, "Blasted Sawbones!"

With a sudden movement he shook his arms free, and after two ineffectual attempts stuck his freckled fists into his side pockets.

"That man's a passenger," said Montgomery. "I'd advise you to keep your hands off him."

"Go to hell!" said the captain, loudly. He suddenly turned and staggered towards the side. "Do what I like on my own ship," he said.

I think Montgomery might have left him then, seeing the brute was drunk; but he only turned a shade paler, and followed the captain to the bulwarks.

"Look you here, Captain," he said; "that man of mine is not to be ill-treated. He has been hazed ever since he came aboard."

For a minute, alcoholic fumes kept the captain speechless. "Blasted Sawbones!" was all he considered necessary.

I could see that Montgomery had one of those slow, pertinacious tempers that will warm day after day to a white heat, and never again cool to forgiveness; and I saw too that this quarrel had been some time growing. "The man's drunk," said I, perhaps officiously; "you'll do no good."

Montgomery gave an ugly twist to his dropping lip. "He's always drunk. Do you think that excuses his assaulting his passengers?"

"My ship," began the captain, waving his hand unsteadily towards the cages, "was a clean ship. Look at it now!" It was certainly anything but clean. "Crew," continued the captain, "clean, respectable crew."

"You agreed to take the beasts."

"I wish I'd never set eyes on your infernal island. What the devil— want beasts for on an island like that? Then, that man of yours—understood he was a man. He's a lunatic; and he hadn't no business aft. Do you think the whole damned ship belongs to you?"

"Your sailors began to haze the poor devil as soon as he came aboard."

"That's just what he is—he's a devil! an ugly devil! My men can't stand him. I can't stand him. None of us can't stand him. Nor you either!"

Montgomery turned away. "You leave that man alone, anyhow," he said, nodding his head as he spoke.

But the captain meant to quarrel now. He raised his voice. "If he comes this end of the ship again, I'll cut his insides out, I tell you. Cut out his blasted insides! Who are you, to tell me what I'm to do? I tell you I'm captain of this ship—captain and owner. I'm the law here, I

tell you—the law and the prophets. I bargained to take a man and his attendant to and from Arica, and bring back some animals. I never bargained to carry a mad devil and a silly Sawbones, a—"

Well, never mind what he called Montgomery. I saw the latter take a step forward, and interposed. "He's drunk," said I. The captain began some abuse even fouler than the last. "Shut up!" I said, turning on him sharply, for I had seen danger in Montgomery's white face. With that I brought the downpour on myself.

However, I was glad to avert what was uncommonly near a scuffle, even at the price of the captain's drunken ill-will. I do not think I have ever heard quite so much vile language come in a continuous stream from any man's lips before, though I have frequented eccentric company enough. I found some of it hard to endure, though I am a mild-tempered man; but, certainly, when I told the captain to "shut up" I had forgotten that I was merely a bit of human flotsam, cut off from my resources and with my fare unpaid; a mere casual dependant on the bounty, or speculative enterprise, of the ship. He reminded me of it with considerable vigour; but at any rate I prevented a fight.

Chapter 4
At the Schooner's Rail

That night land was sighted after sundown, and the schooner hove to. Montgomery intimated that was his destination. It was too far to see any details; it seemed to me then, simply a low-lying patch of dim blue in the uncertain blue-grey sea. An almost vertical streak of smoke went up from it into the sky. The captain was not on deck when it was sighted. After he had vented his wrath on me, he had staggered below, and I understand he went to sleep on the floor of his own cabin. The mate practically assumed the command. He was the gaunt, taciturn individual we had seen at the wheel.

Apparently, he was in an evil temper with Montgomery. He took not the slightest notice of either of us. We dined with him in a sulky silence, after a few ineffectual efforts on my part to talk. It struck me too that the men regarded my companion and his animals in a singularly unfriendly manner. I found Montgomery very reticent about his purpose with these creatures, and about his destination; and though I was sensible of a growing curiosity as to both, I did not press him.

We remained talking on the quarter deck until the sky was thick with stars. Except for an occasional sound in the yellow-lit forecastle and a movement of the animals now and then, the night was very

still. The puma lay crouched together, watching us with shining eyes, a black heap in the corner of its cage. Montgomery produced some cigars. He talked to me of London in a tone of half-painful reminiscence, asking all kinds of questions about changes that had taken place. He spoke like a man who had loved his life there, and had been suddenly and irrevocably cut off from it. I gossiped as well as I could of this and that. All the time the strangeness of him was shaping itself in my mind; and as I talked, I peered at his odd, pallid face in the dim light of the binnacle lantern behind me. Then I looked out at the darkling sea, where in the dimness his little island was hidden.

This man, it seemed to me, had come out of Immensity merely to save my life. Tomorrow he would drop over the side, and vanish again out of my existence. Even had it been under commonplace circumstances, it would have made me a trifle thoughtful; but in the first place was the singularity of an educated man living on this unknown little island, and coupled with that the extraordinary nature of his luggage. I found myself repeating the captain's question. What did he want with the beasts? Why, too, had he pretended they were not his when I had remarked about them at first? Then, again, in his personal attendant there was a bizarre quality which had impressed me profoundly. These circumstances threw a haze of mystery round the man. They laid hold of my imagination, and hampered my tongue.

Towards midnight our talk of London died away, and we stood side by side leaning over the bulwarks and staring dreamily over the silent, starlit sea, each pursuing his own thoughts. It was the atmosphere for sentiment, and I began upon my gratitude.

"If I may say it," said I, after a time, "you have saved my life."

"Chance," he answered. "Just chance."

"I prefer to make my thanks to the accessible agent."

"Thank no one. You had the need, and I had the knowledge; and I injected and fed you much as I might have collected a specimen. I was bored and wanted something to do. If I'd been jaded that day, or hadn't liked your face, well—it's a curious question where you would have been now!"

This damped my mood a little. "At any rate," I began.

"It's a chance, I tell you," he interrupted, "as everything is in a man's life. Only the asses won't see it! Why am I here now, an outcast from civilisation, instead of being a happy man enjoying all the pleasures of London? Simply because eleven years ago—I lost my head for ten minutes on a foggy night."

He stopped. "Yes?" said I.

"That's all."

We relapsed into silence. Presently he laughed. "There's something in this starlight that loosens one's tongue. I'm an ass, and yet somehow I would like to tell you."

"Whatever you tell me, you may rely upon my keeping to myself—if that's it."

He was on the point of beginning, and then shook his head, doubtfully.

"Don't," said I. "It is all the same to me. After all, it is better to keep your secret. There's nothing gained but a little relief if I respect your confidence. If I don't—well?"

He grunted undecidedly. I felt I had him at a disadvantage, had caught him in the mood of indiscretion; and to tell the truth I was not curious to learn what might have driven a young medical student out of London. I have an imagination. I shrugged my shoulders and turned away. Over the taffrail leant a silent black figure, watching the stars. It was Montgomery's strange attendant. It looked over its shoulder quickly with my movement, then looked away again.

It may seem a little thing to you, perhaps, but it came like a sudden blow to me. The only light near us was a lantern at the wheel. The creature's face was turned for one brief instant out of the dimness of the stern towards this illumination, and I saw that the eyes that glanced at me shone with a pale-green light. I did not know then that a reddish luminosity, at least, is not uncommon in human eyes. The thing came to me as stark inhumanity. That black figure with its eyes of fire struck down through all my adult thoughts and feelings, and for a moment the forgotten horrors of childhood came back to my mind. Then the effect passed as it had come. An uncouth black figure of a man, a figure of no particular import, hung over the taffrail against the starlight, and I found Montgomery was speaking to me.

"I'm thinking of turning in, then," said he, "if you've had enough of this."

I answered him incongruously. We went below, and he wished me goodnight at the door of my cabin.

That night I had some very unpleasant dreams. The waning moon rose late. Its light struck a ghostly white beam across my cabin, and made an ominous shape on the planking by my bunk. Then the staghounds woke, and began howling and baying; so that I dreamt fitfully, and scarcely slept until the approach of dawn.

CHAPTER 5
The Man Who Had Nowhere to Go

In the early morning (it was the second morning after my recovery, and I believe the fourth after I was picked up), I awoke through an avenue of tumultuous dreams—dreams of guns and howling mobs—and became sensible of a hoarse shouting above me. I rubbed my eyes and lay listening to the noise, doubtful for a little while of my whereabouts. Then came a sudden pattering of bare feet, the sound of heavy objects being thrown about, a violent creaking and the rattling of chains. I heard the swish of the water as the ship was suddenly brought round, and a foamy yellow-green wave flew across the little round window and left it streaming. I jumped into my clothes and went on deck.

As I came up the ladder I saw against the flushed sky—for the sun was just rising—the broad back and red hair of the captain, and over his shoulder the puma spinning from a tackle rigged on to the mizzen spanker-boom.

The poor brute seemed horribly scared, and crouched in the bottom of its little cage.

"Overboard with 'em!" bawled the captain. "Overboard with 'em! We'll have a clean ship soon of the whole bilin' of 'em."

He stood in my way, so that I had perforce to tap his shoulder to come on deck. He came round with a start, and staggered back a few paces to stare at me. It needed no expert eye to tell that the man was still drunk.

"Hullo!" said he, stupidly; and then with a light coming into his eyes, "Why, it's Mister—Mister?"

"Prendick," said I.

"Prendick be damned!" said he. "Shut-up—that's your name. Mister Shut-up."

It was no good answering the brute; but I certainly did not expect his next move. He held out his hand to the gangway by which Montgomery stood talking to a massive grey-haired man in dirty-blue flannels, who had apparently just come aboard.

"That way, Mister Blasted Shut-up! that way!" roared the captain.

Montgomery and his companion turned as he spoke.

"What do you mean?" I said.

"That way, Mister Blasted Shut-up—that's what I mean! Overboard, Mister Shut-up—and sharp! We're cleaning the ship out—

cleaning the whole blessed ship out; and overboard you go!"

I stared at him dumfounded. Then it occurred to me that it was exactly the thing I wanted. The lost prospect of a journey as sole passenger with this quarrelsome sot was not one to mourn over. I turned towards Montgomery.

"Can't have you," said Montgomery's companion, concisely.

"You can't have me!" said I, aghast. He had the squarest and most resolute face I ever set eyes upon.

"Look here," I began, turning to the captain.

"Overboard!" said the captain. "This ship aint for beasts and cannibals and worse than beasts, any more. Overboard you go, Mister Shut-up. If they can't have you, you goes overboard. But, anyhow, you go—with your friends. I've done with this blessed island for evermore, amen! I've had enough of it."

"But, Montgomery," I appealed.

He distorted his lower lip, and nodded his head hopelessly at the grey-haired man beside him, to indicate his powerlessness to help me.

"I'll see to *you*, presently," said the captain.

Then began a curious three-cornered altercation. Alternately I appealed to one and another of the three men—first to the grey-haired man to let me land, and then to the drunken captain to keep me aboard. I even bawled entreaties to the sailors. Montgomery said never a word, only shook his head. "You're going overboard, I tell you," was the captain's refrain. "Law be damned! I'm king here." At last I must confess my voice suddenly broke in the middle of a vigorous threat. I felt a gust of hysterical petulance, and went aft and stared dismally at nothing.

Meanwhile the sailors progressed rapidly with the task of unshipping the packages and caged animals. A large launch, with two standing lugs, lay under the lee of the schooner; and into this the strange assortment of goods were swung. I did not then see the hands from the island that were receiving the packages, for the hull of the launch was hidden from me by the side of the schooner. Neither Montgomery nor his companion took the slightest notice of me, but busied themselves in assisting and directing the four or five sailors who were unloading the goods. The captain went forward interfering rather than assisting.

I was alternately despairful and desperate. Once or twice as I stood waiting there for things to accomplish themselves, I could not resist an impulse to laugh at my miserable quandary. I felt all the wretcheder

for the lack of a breakfast. Hunger and a lack of blood-corpuscles take all the manhood from a man. I perceived pretty clearly that I had not the stamina either to resist what the captain chose to do to expel me, or to force myself upon Montgomery and his companion. So, I waited passively upon fate; and the work of transferring Montgomery's possessions to the launch went on as if I did not exist.

Presently that work was finished, and then came a struggle. I was hauled, resisting weakly enough, to the gangway. Even then I noticed the oddness of the brown faces of the men who were with Montgomery in the launch; but the launch was now fully laden, and was shoved off hastily. A broadening gap of green water appeared under me, and I pushed back with all my strength to avoid falling headlong. The hands in the launch shouted derisively, and I heard Montgomery curse at them; and then the captain, the mate, and one of the seamen helping him, ran me aft towards the stern.

The dingey of the *Lady Vain* had been towing behind; it was half full of water, had no oars, and was quite unvictualled. I refused to go aboard her, and flung myself full length on the deck. In the end, they swung me into her by a rope (for they had no stern ladder), and then they cut me adrift. I drifted slowly from the schooner. In a kind of stupor, I watched all hands take to the rigging, and slowly but surely, she came round to the wind; the sails fluttered, and then bellied out as the wind came into them. I stared at her weather-beaten side heeling steeply towards me; and then she passed out of my range of view.

I did not turn my head to follow her. At first, I could scarcely believe what had happened. I crouched in the bottom of the dingey, stunned, and staring blankly at the vacant, oily sea. Then I realised that I was in that little hell of mine again, now half swamped; and looking back over the gunwale, I saw the schooner standing away from me, with the red-haired captain mocking at me over the taffrail, and turning towards the island saw the launch growing smaller as she approached the beach.

Abruptly the cruelty of this desertion became clear to me. I had no means of reaching the land unless I should chance to drift there. I was still weak, you must remember, from my exposure in the boat; I was empty and very faint, or I should have had more heart. But as it was, I suddenly began to sob and weep, as I had never done since I was a little child. The tears ran down my face. In a passion of despair, I struck with my fists at the water in the bottom of the boat, and kicked savagely at the gunwale. I prayed aloud for God to let me die.

The Evil-Looking Boatmen

But the islanders, seeing that I was really adrift, took pity on me. I drifted very slowly to the eastward, approaching the island slantingly; and presently I saw, with hysterical relief, the launch come round and return towards me. She was heavily laden, and I could make out as she drew nearer Montgomery's white-haired, broad-shouldered companion sitting cramped up with the dogs and several packing-cases in the stern sheets. This individual stared fixedly at me without moving or speaking. The black-faced cripple was glaring at me as fixedly in the bows near the puma. There were three other men besides—three strange brutish-looking fellows, at whom the staghounds were snarling savagely. Montgomery, who was steering, brought the boat by me, and rising, caught and fastened my painter to the tiller to tow me, for there was no room aboard.

I had recovered from my hysterical phase by this time and answered his hail, as he approached, bravely enough. I told him the dingey was nearly swamped, and he reached me a piggin. I was jerked back as the rope tightened between the boats. For some time, I was busy baling.

It was not until I had got the water under (for the water in the dingey had been shipped; the boat was perfectly sound) that I had leisure to look at the people in the launch again.

The white-haired man I found was still regarding me steadfastly, but with an expression, as I now fancied, of some perplexity. When my eyes met his, he looked down at the staghound that sat between his knees. He was a powerfully-built man, as I have said, with a fine forehead and rather heavy features; but his eyes had that odd drooping of the skin above the lids which often comes with advancing years, and the fall of his heavy mouth at the corners gave him an expression of pugnacious resolution. He talked to Montgomery in a tone too low for me to hear.

From him my eyes travelled to his three men; and a strange crew they were. I saw only their faces, yet there was something in their faces—I knew not what—that gave me a queer spasm of disgust. I looked steadily at them, and the impression did not pass, though I failed to see what had occasioned it. They seemed to me then to be brown men; but their limbs were oddly swathed in some thin, dirty, white stuff down even to the fingers and feet: I have never seen men so wrapped up before, and women so only in the East. They wore turbans too, and

202

thereunder peered out their elfin faces at me—faces with protruding lower-jaws and bright eyes. They had lank black hair, almost like horsehair, and seemed as they sat to exceed in stature any race of men I have seen. The white-haired man, who I knew was a good six feet in height, sat a head below any one of the three. I found afterwards that really none were taller than myself; but their bodies were abnormally long, and the thigh-part of the leg short and curiously twisted.

At any rate, they were an amazingly ugly gang, and over the heads of them under the forward lug peered the black face of the man whose eyes were luminous in the dark. As I stared at them, they met my gaze; and then first one and then another turned away from my direct stare, and looked at me in an odd, furtive manner. It occurred to me that I was perhaps annoying them, and I turned my attention to the island we were approaching.

It was low, and covered with thick vegetation—chiefly a kind of palm, that was new to me. From one point a thin white thread of vapour rose slantingly to an immense height, and then frayed out like a down feather. We were now within the embrace of a broad bay flanked on either hand by a low promontory. The beach was of dull-grey sand, and sloped steeply up to a ridge, perhaps sixty or seventy feet above the sea-level, and irregularly set with trees and undergrowth. Half way up was a square enclosure of some greyish stone, which I found subsequently was built partly of coral and partly of pumiceous lava. Two thatched roofs peeped from within this enclosure.

A man stood awaiting us at the water's edge. I fancied while we were still far off that I saw some other and very grotesque-looking creatures scuttle into the bushes upon the slope; but I saw nothing of these as we drew nearer. This man was of a moderate size, and with a black negroid face. He had a large, almost lipless, mouth, extraordinary lank arms, long thin feet, and bow-legs, and stood with his heavy face thrust forward staring at us. He was dressed like Montgomery and his white-haired companion, in jacket and trousers of blue serge. As we came still nearer, this individual began to run to and fro on the beach, making the most grotesque movements.

At a word of command from Montgomery, the four men in the launch sprang up, and with singularly awkward gestures struck the lugs. Montgomery steered us round and into a narrow little dock excavated in the beach. Then the man on the beach hastened towards us. This dock, as I call it, was really a mere ditch just long enough at this phase of the tide to take the longboat. I heard the bows ground

in the sand, staved the dingey off the rudder of the big boat with my piggin, and freeing the painter, landed. The three muffled men, with the clumsiest movements, scrambled out upon the sand, and forthwith set to landing the cargo, assisted by the man on the beach. I was struck especially by the curious movements of the legs of the three swathed and bandaged boatmen—not stiff they were, but distorted in some odd way, almost as if they were jointed in the wrong place.

The dogs were still snarling, and strained at their chains after these men, as the white-haired man landed with them. The three big fellows spoke to one another in odd guttural tones, and the man who had waited for us on the beach began chattering to them excitedly—a foreign language, as I fancied—as they laid hands on some bales piled near the stern. Somewhere I had heard such a voice before, and I could not think where. The white-haired man stood, holding in a tumult of six dogs, and bawling orders over their din. Montgomery, having unshipped the rudder, landed likewise, and all set to work at unloading. I was too faint, what with my long fast and the sun beating down on my bare head, to offer any assistance.

Presently the white-haired man seemed to recollect my presence, and came up to me.

"You look," said he, "as though you had scarcely breakfasted." His little eyes were a brilliant black under his heavy brows. "I must apologise for that. Now you are our guest, we must make you comfortable—though you are uninvited, you know." He looked keenly into my face. "Montgomery says you are an educated man, Mr. Prendick; says you know something of science. May I ask what that signifies?"

I told him I had spent some years at the Royal College of Science, and had done some researches in biology under Huxley. He raised his eyebrows slightly at that.

"That alters the case a little, Mr. Prendick," he said, with a trifle more respect in his manner. "As it happens, we are biologists here. This is a biological station—of a sort." His eye rested on the men in white who were busily hauling the puma, on rollers, towards the walled yard. "I and Montgomery, at least," he added. Then, "When you will be able to get away, I can't say. We're off the track to anywhere. We see a ship once in a twelve-month or so."

He left me abruptly, and went up the beach past this group, and I think entered the enclosure. The other two men were with Montgomery, erecting a pile of smaller packages on a low-wheeled truck. The llama was still on the launch with the rabbit hutches; the stag-

hounds were still lashed to the thwarts. The pile of things completed, all three men laid hold of the truck and began shoving the ton-weight or so upon it after the puma. Presently Montgomery left them, and coming back to me held out his hand.

"I'm glad," said he, "for my own part. That captain was a silly ass. He'd have made things lively for you."

"It was you," said I, "that saved me again."

"That depends. You'll find this island an infernally rum place, I promise you. I'd watch my goings carefully, if I were you. *He*—" He hesitated, and seemed to alter his mind about what was on his lips. "I wish you'd help me with these rabbits," he said.

His procedure with the rabbits was singular. I waded in with him, and helped him lug one of the hutches ashore. No sooner was that done than he opened the door of it, and tilting the thing on one end turned its living contents out on the ground. They fell in a struggling heap one on the top of the other. He clapped his hands, and forthwith they went off with that hopping run of theirs, fifteen or twenty of them I should think, up the beach.

"Increase and multiply, my friends," said Montgomery. "Replenish the island. Hitherto we've had a certain lack of meat here."

As I watched them disappearing, the white-haired man returned with a brandy-flask and some biscuits. "Something to go on with, Prendick," said he, in a far more familiar tone than before. I made no ado, but set to work on the biscuits at once, while the white-haired man helped Montgomery to release about a score more of the rabbits. Three big hutches, however, went up to the house with the puma. The brandy I did not touch, for I have been an abstainer from my birth.

CHAPTER 7

The Locked Door

The reader will perhaps understand that at first everything was so strange about me, and my position was the outcome of such unexpected adventures, that I had no discernment of the relative strangeness of this or that thing. I followed the llama up the beach, and was overtaken by Montgomery, who asked me not to enter the stone enclosure. I noticed then that the puma in its cage and the pile of packages had been placed outside the entrance to this quadrangle.

I turned and saw that the launch had now been unloaded, run out again, and was being beached, and the white-haired man was walking towards us. He addressed Montgomery.

"And now comes the problem of this uninvited guest. What are we to do with him?"

"He knows something of science," said Montgomery.

"I'm itching to get to work again—with this new stuff," said the white-haired man, nodding towards the enclosure. His eyes grew brighter.

"I daresay you are," said Montgomery, in anything but a cordial tone.

"We can't send him over there, and we can't spare the time to build him a new shanty; and we certainly can't take him into our confidence just yet."

"I'm in your hands," said I. I had no idea of what he meant by "over there."

"I've been thinking of the same things," Montgomery answered. "There's my room with the outer door—"

"That's it," said the elder man, promptly, looking at Montgomery; and all three of us went towards the enclosure. "I'm sorry to make a mystery, Mr. Prendick; but you'll remember you're uninvited. Our little establishment here contains a secret or so, is a kind of Blue-Beard's chamber, in fact. Nothing very dreadful, really, to a sane man; but just now, as we don't know you—"

"Decidedly," said I, "I should be a fool to take offence at any want of confidence."

He twisted his heavy mouth into a faint smile—he was one of those saturnine people who smile with the corners of the mouth down—and bowed his acknowledgment of my complaisance. The main entrance to the enclosure was passed; it was a heavy wooden gate, framed in iron and locked, with the cargo of the launch piled outside it, and at the corner we came to a small doorway I had not previously observed. The white-haired man produced a bundle of keys from the pocket of his greasy blue jacket, opened this door, and entered. His keys, and the elaborate locking-up of the place even while it was still under his eye, struck me as peculiar.

I followed him, and found myself in a small apartment, plainly but not uncomfortably furnished and with its inner door, which was slightly ajar, opening into a paved courtyard. This inner door Montgomery at once closed. A hammock was slung across the darker corner of the room, and a small unglazed window defended by an iron bar looked out towards the sea.

This the white-haired man told me was to be my apartment; and

the inner door, which "for fear of accidents," he said, he would lock on the other side, was my limit inward. He called my attention to a convenient deck-chair before the window, and to an array of old books, chiefly, I found, surgical works and editions of the Latin and Greek classics (languages I cannot read with any comfort), on a shelf near the hammock. He left the room by the outer door, as if to avoid opening the inner one again.

"We usually have our meals in here," said Montgomery, and then, as if in doubt, went out after the other. "Moreau!" I heard him call, and for the moment I do not think I noticed. Then as I handled the books on the shelf it came up in consciousness: Where had I heard the name of Moreau before? I sat down before the window, took out the biscuits that still remained to me, and ate them with an excellent appetite. Moreau!

Through the window I saw one of those unaccountable men in white, lugging a packing-case along the beach. Presently the window-frame hid him. Then I heard a key inserted and turned in the lock behind me. After a little while I heard through the locked door the noise of the staghounds, that had now been brought up from the beach. They were not barking, but sniffing and growling in a curious fashion. I could hear the rapid patter of their feet, and Montgomery's voice soothing them.

I was very much impressed by the elaborate secrecy of these two men regarding the contents of the place, and for some time I was thinking of that and of the unaccountable familiarity of the name of Moreau; but so odd is the human memory that I could not then recall that well-known name in its proper connection. From that my thoughts went to the indefinable queerness of the deformed man on the beach. I never saw such a gait, such odd motions as he pulled at the box. I recalled that none of these men had spoken to me, though most of them I had found looking at me at one time or another in a peculiarly furtive manner, quite unlike the frank stare of your unsophisticated savage. Indeed, they had all seemed remarkably taciturn, and when they did speak, endowed with very uncanny voices. What was wrong with them? Then I recalled the eyes of Montgomery's ungainly attendant.

Just as I was thinking of him, he came in. He was now dressed in white, and carried a little tray with some coffee and boiled vegetables thereon. I could hardly repress a shuddering recoil as he came, bending amiably, and placed the tray before me on the table. Then aston-

ishment paralysed me. Under his stringy black locks, I saw his ear; it jumped upon me suddenly close to my face. The man had pointed ears, covered with a fine brown fur!

"Your breakfast, sair," he said.

I stared at his face without attempting to answer him. He turned and went towards the door, regarding me oddly over his shoulder. I followed him out with my eyes; and as I did so, by some odd trick of unconscious cerebration, there came surging into my head the phrase, "The Moreau Hollows"—was it? "The Moreau—" Ah! It sent my memory back ten years. "The Moreau Horrors!" The phrase drifted loose in my mind for a moment, and then I saw it in red lettering on a little buff-coloured pamphlet, to read which made one shiver and creep. Then I remembered distinctly all about it. That long-forgotten pamphlet came back with startling vividness to my mind. I had been a mere lad then, and Moreau was, I suppose, about fifty—a prominent and masterful physiologist, well-known in scientific circles for his extraordinary imagination and his brutal directness in discussion.

Was this the same Moreau? He had published some very astonishing facts in connection with the transfusion of blood, and in addition was known to be doing valuable work on morbid growths. Then suddenly his career was closed. He had to leave England. A journalist obtained access to his laboratory in the capacity of laboratory-assistant, with the deliberate intention of making sensational exposures; and by the help of a shocking accident (if it was an accident), his gruesome pamphlet became notorious. On the day of its publication a wretched dog, flayed and otherwise mutilated, escaped from Moreau's house. It was in the silly season, and a prominent editor, a cousin of the temporary laboratory-assistant, appealed to the conscience of the nation.

It was not the first time that conscience has turned against the methods of research. The doctor was simply howled out of the country. It may be that he deserved to be; but I still think that the tepid support of his fellow-investigators and his desertion by the great body of scientific workers was a shameful thing. Yet some of his experiments, by the journalist's account, were wantonly cruel. He might perhaps have purchased his social peace by abandoning his investigations; but he apparently preferred the latter, as most men would who have once fallen under the overmastering spell of research. He was unmarried, and had indeed nothing but his own interest to consider.

I felt convinced that this must be the same man. Everything pointed to it. It dawned upon me to what end the puma and the oth-

er animals—which had now been brought with other luggage into the enclosure behind the house—were destined; and a curious faint odour, the halitus of something familiar, an odour that had been in the background of my consciousness hitherto, suddenly came forward into the forefront of my thoughts. It was the antiseptic odour of the dissecting-room. I heard the puma growling through the wall, and one of the dogs yelped as though it had been struck.

Yet surely, and especially to another scientific man, there was nothing so horrible in vivisection as to account for this secrecy; and by some odd leap in my thoughts the pointed ears and luminous eyes of Montgomery's attendant came back again before me with the sharpest definition. I stared before me out at the green sea, frothing under a freshening breeze, and let these and other strange memories of the last few days chase one another through my mind.

What could it all mean? A locked enclosure on a lonely island, a notorious vivisector, and these crippled and distorted men?

Chapter 8
The Crying of the Puma

Montgomery interrupted my tangle of mystification and suspicion about one o'clock, and his grotesque attendant followed him with a tray bearing bread, some herbs and other eatables, a flask of whiskey, a jug of water, and three glasses and knives. I glanced askance at this strange creature, and found him watching me with his queer, restless eyes. Montgomery said he would lunch with me, but that Moreau was too preoccupied with some work to come.

"Moreau!" said I. "I know that name."

"The devil you do!" said he. "What an ass I was to mention it to you! I might have thought. Anyhow, it will give you an inkling of our—mysteries. Whiskey?"

"No, thanks; I'm an abstainer."

"I wish I'd been. But it's no use locking the door after the steed is stolen. It was that infernal stuff which led to my coming here—that, and a foggy night. I thought myself in luck at the time, when Moreau offered to get me off. It's queer—"

"Montgomery," said I, suddenly, as the outer door closed, "why has your man pointed ears?"

"Damn!" he said, over his first mouthful of food. He stared at me for a moment, and then repeated, "Pointed ears?"

"Little points to them," said I, as calmly as possible, with a catch in

my breath; "and a fine black fur at the edges?"

He helped himself to whiskey and water with great deliberation. "I was under the impression—that his hair covered his ears."

"I saw them as he stooped by me to put that coffee you sent to me on the table. And his eyes shine in the dark."

By this time Montgomery had recovered from the surprise of my question. "I always thought," he said deliberately, with a certain accentuation of his flavouring of lisp, "that there *was* something the matter with his ears, from the way he covered them. What were they like?"

I was persuaded from his manner that this ignorance was a pretence. Still, I could hardly tell the man that I thought him a liar. "Pointed," I said; "rather small and furry—distinctly furry. But the whole man is one of the strangest beings I ever set eyes on."

A sharp, hoarse cry of animal pain came from the enclosure behind us. Its depth and volume testified to the puma. I saw Montgomery wince.

"Yes?" he said.

"Where did you pick up the creature?"

"San Francisco. He's an ugly brute, I admit. Half-witted, you know. Can't remember where he came from. But I'm used to him, you know. We both are. How does he strike you?"

"He's unnatural," I said. "There's something about him—don't think me fanciful, but it gives me a nasty little sensation, a tightening of my muscles, when he comes near me. It's a touch—of the diabolical, in fact."

Montgomery had stopped eating while I told him this. "Rum!" he said. "I can't see it." He resumed his meal. "I had no idea of it," he said, and masticated. "The crew of the schooner must have felt it the same. Made a dead set at the poor devil. You saw the captain?"

Suddenly the puma howled again, this time more painfully. Montgomery swore under his breath. I had half a mind to attack him about the men on the beach. Then the poor brute within gave vent to a series of short, sharp cries.

"Your men on the beach," said I; "what race are they?"

"Excellent fellows, aren't they?" said he, absentmindedly, knitting his brows as the animal yelled out sharply.

I said no more. There was another outcry worse than the former. He looked at me with his dull grey eyes, and then took some more whiskey. He tried to draw me into a discussion about alcohol, professing to have saved my life with it. He seemed anxious to lay stress on

the fact that I owed my life to him. I answered him distractedly.

Presently our meal came to an end; the misshapen monster with the pointed ears cleared the remains away, and Montgomery left me alone in the room again. All the time he had been in a state of ill-concealed irritation at the noise of the vivisected puma. He had spoken of his odd want of nerve, and left me to the obvious application.

I found myself that the cries were singularly irritating, and they grew in depth and intensity as the afternoon wore on. They were painful at first, but their constant resurgence at last altogether upset my balance. I flung aside a crib of Horace I had been reading, and began to clench my fists, to bite my lips, and to pace the room. Presently I got to stopping my ears with my fingers.

The emotional appeal of those yells grew upon me steadily, grew at last to such an exquisite expression of suffering that I could stand it in that confined room no longer. I stepped out of the door into the slumberous heat of the late afternoon, and walking past the main entrance—locked again, I noticed—turned the corner of the wall.

The crying sounded even louder out of doors. It was as if all the pain in the world had found a voice. Yet had I known such pain was in the next room, and had it been dumb, I believe—I have thought since—I could have stood it well enough. It is when suffering finds a voice and sets our nerves quivering that this pity comes troubling us. But in spite of the brilliant sunlight and the green fans of the trees waving in the soothing sea-breeze, the world was a confusion, blurred with drifting black and red phantasms, until I was out of earshot of the house in the chequered wall.

Chapter 9

The Thing in the Forest

I strode through the undergrowth that clothed the ridge behind the house, scarcely heeding whither I went; passed on through the shadow of a thick cluster of straight-stemmed trees beyond it, and so presently found myself some way on the other side of the ridge, and descending towards a streamlet that ran through a narrow valley. I paused and listened. The distance I had come, or the intervening masses of thicket, deadened any sound that might be coming from the enclosure. The air was still. Then with a rustle a rabbit emerged, and went scampering up the slope before me. I hesitated, and sat down in the edge of the shade.

The place was a pleasant one. The rivulet was hidden by the luxu-

riant vegetation of the banks save at one point, where I caught a triangular patch of its glittering water. On the farther side I saw through a bluish haze a tangle of trees and creepers, and above these again the luminous blue of the sky. Here and there a splash of white or crimson marked the blooming of some trailing epiphyte. I let my eyes wander over this scene for a while, and then began to turn over in my mind again the strange peculiarities of Montgomery's man. But it was too hot to think elaborately, and presently I fell into a tranquil state midway between dozing and waking.

From this I was aroused, after I know not how long, by a rustling amidst the greenery on the other side of the stream. For a moment I could see nothing but the waving summits of the ferns and reeds. Then suddenly upon the bank of the stream appeared something—at first, I could not distinguish what it was. It bowed its round head to the water, and began to drink. Then I saw it was a man, going on all-fours like a beast. He was clothed in bluish cloth, and was of a copper-coloured hue, with black hair. It seemed that grotesque ugliness was an invariable character of these islanders. I could hear the suck of the water at his lips as he drank.

I leant forward to see him better, and a piece of lava, detached by my hand, went pattering down the slope. He looked up guiltily, and his eyes met mine. Forthwith he scrambled to his feet, and stood wiping his clumsy hand across his mouth and regarding me. His legs were scarcely half the length of his body. So, staring one another out of countenance, we remained for perhaps the space of a minute. Then, stopping to look back once or twice, he slunk off among the bushes to the right of me, and I heard the swish of the fronds grow faint in the distance and die away. Long after he had disappeared, I remained sitting up staring in the direction of his retreat. My drowsy tranquillity had gone.

I was startled by a noise behind me, and turning suddenly saw the flapping white tail of a rabbit vanishing up the slope. I jumped to my feet. The apparition of this grotesque, half-bestial creature had suddenly populated the stillness of the afternoon for me. I looked around me rather nervously, and regretted that I was unarmed. Then I thought that the man I had just seen had been clothed in bluish cloth, had not been naked as a savage would have been; and I tried to persuade myself from that fact that he was after all probably a peaceful character, that the dull ferocity of his countenance belied him.

Yet I was greatly disturbed at the apparition. I walked to the left

along the slope, turning my head about and peering this way and that among the straight stems of the trees. Why should a man go on all-fours and drink with his lips? Presently I heard an animal wailing again, and taking it to be the puma, I turned about and walked in a direction diametrically opposite to the sound. This led me down to the stream, across which I stepped and pushed my way up through the undergrowth beyond.

I was startled by a great patch of vivid scarlet on the ground, and going up to it found it to be a peculiar fungus, branched and corrugated like a foliaceous lichen, but deliquescing into slime at the touch; and then in the shadow of some luxuriant ferns I came upon an unpleasant thing,—the dead body of a rabbit covered with shining flies, but still warm and with the head torn off. I stopped aghast at the sight of the scattered blood. Here at least was one visitor to the island disposed of! There were no traces of other violence about it. It looked as though it had been suddenly snatched up and killed; and as I stared at the little furry body came the difficulty of how the thing had been done.

The vague dread that had been in my mind since I had seen the inhuman face of the man at the stream grew distincter as I stood there. I began to realise the hardihood of my expedition among these unknown people. The thicket about me became altered to my imagination. Every shadow became something more than a shadow—became an ambush; every rustle became a threat. Invisible things seemed watching me. I resolved to go back to the enclosure on the beach. I suddenly turned away and thrust myself violently, possibly even frantically, through the bushes, anxious to get a clear space about me again.

I stopped just in time to prevent myself emerging upon an open space. It was a kind of glade in the forest, made by a fall; seedlings were already starting up to struggle for the vacant space; and beyond, the dense growth of stems and twining vines and splashes of fungus and flowers closed in again. Before me, squatting together upon the fungoid ruins of a huge fallen tree and still unaware of my approach, were three grotesque human figures. One was evidently a female; the other two were men. They were naked, save for swathings of scarlet cloth about the middle; and their skins were of a dull pinkish-drab colour, such as I had seen in no savages before. They had fat, heavy, chinless faces, retreating foreheads, and a scant bristly hair upon their heads. I never saw such bestial-looking creatures.

They were talking, or at least one of the men was talking to the

other two, and all three had been too closely interested to heed the rustling of my approach. They swayed their heads and shoulders from side to side. The speaker's words came thick and sloppy, and though I could hear them distinctly I could not distinguish what he said. He seemed to me to be reciting some complicated gibberish. Presently his articulation became shriller, and spreading his hands he rose to his feet. At that the others began to gibber in unison, also rising to their feet, spreading their hands and swaying their bodies in rhythm with their chant.

I noticed then the abnormal shortness of their legs, and their lank, clumsy feet. All three began slowly to circle round, raising and stamping their feet and waving their arms; a kind of tune crept into their rhythmic recitation, and a refrain—"*Aloola*," or "*Balloola*," it sounded like. Their eyes began to sparkle, and their ugly faces to brighten, with an expression of strange pleasure. Saliva dripped from their lipless mouths.

Suddenly, as I watched their grotesque and unaccountable gestures, I perceived clearly for the first time what it was that had offended me, what had given me the two inconsistent and conflicting impressions of utter strangeness and yet of the strangest familiarity. The three creatures engaged in this mysterious rite were human in shape, and yet human beings with the strangest air about them of some familiar animal. Each of these creatures, despite its human form, its rag of clothing, and the rough humanity of its bodily form, had woven into it—into its movements, into the expression of its countenance, into its whole presence—some now irresistible suggestion of a hog, a swinish taint, the unmistakable mark of the beast.

I stood overcome by this amazing realisation and then the most horrible questionings came rushing into my mind. They began leaping in the air, first one and then the other, whooping and grunting. Then one slipped, and for a moment was on all-fours—to recover, indeed, forthwith. But that transitory gleam of the true animalism of these monsters was enough.

I turned as noiselessly as possible, and becoming every now and then rigid with the fear of being discovered, as a branch cracked or a leaf rustled, I pushed back into the bushes. It was long before I grew bolder, and dared to move freely. My only idea for the moment was to get away from these foul beings, and I scarcely noticed that I had emerged upon a faint pathway amidst the trees. Then suddenly traversing a little glade, I saw with an unpleasant start two clumsy legs among

the trees, walking with noiseless footsteps parallel with my course, and perhaps thirty yards away from me. The head and upper part of the body were hidden by a tangle of creeper. I stopped abruptly, hoping the creature did not see me. The feet stopped as I did.

So nervous was I that I controlled an impulse to headlong flight with the utmost difficulty. Then looking hard, I distinguished through the interlacing network the head and body of the brute I had seen drinking. He moved his head. There was an emerald flash in his eyes as he glanced at me from the shadow of the trees, a half-luminous colour that vanished as he turned his head again. He was motionless for a moment, and then with a noiseless tread began running through the green confusion. In another moment he had vanished behind some bushes. I could not see him, but I felt that he had stopped and was watching me again.

What on earth was he—man or beast? What did he want with me? I had no weapon, not even a stick. Flight would be madness. At any rate the Thing, whatever it was, lacked the courage to attack me. Setting my teeth hard, I walked straight towards him. I was anxious not to show the fear that seemed chilling my backbone. I pushed through a tangle of tall white-flowered bushes, and saw him twenty paces beyond, looking over his shoulder at me and hesitating. I advanced a step or two, looking steadfastly into his eyes.

"Who are you?" said I.

He tried to meet my gaze. "No!" he said suddenly, and turning went bounding away from me through the undergrowth. Then he turned and stared at me again. His eyes shone brightly out of the dusk under the trees.

My heart was in my mouth; but I felt my only chance was bluff, and walked steadily towards him. He turned again, and vanished into the dusk. Once more I thought I caught the glint of his eyes, and that was all.

For the first time I realised how the lateness of the hour might affect me. The sun had set some minutes since, the swift dusk of the tropics was already fading out of the eastern sky, and a pioneer moth fluttered silently by my head. Unless I would spend the night among the unknown dangers of the mysterious forest, I must hasten back to the enclosure. The thought of a return to that pain-haunted refuge was extremely disagreeable, but still more so was the idea of being overtaken in the open by darkness and all that darkness might conceal. I gave one more look into the blue shadows that had swallowed up

this odd creature, and then retraced my way down the slope towards the stream, going as I judged in the direction from which I had come.

I walked eagerly, my mind confused with many things, and presently found myself in a level place among scattered trees. The colourless clearness that comes after the sunset flush was darkling; the blue sky above grew momentarily deeper, and the little stars one by one pierced the attenuated light; the interspaces of the trees, the gaps in the further vegetation, that had been hazy blue in the daylight, grew black and mysterious. I pushed on. The colour vanished from the world. The tree-tops rose against the luminous blue sky in inky silhouette, and all below that outline melted into one formless blackness.

Presently the trees grew thinner, and the shrubby undergrowth more abundant. Then there was a desolate space covered with a white sand, and then another expanse of tangled bushes. I did not remember crossing the sand-opening before. I began to be tormented by a faint rustling upon my right hand. I thought at first it was fancy, for whenever I stopped there was silence, save for the evening breeze in the tree-tops. Then when I turned to hurry on again there was an echo to my footsteps.

I turned away from the thickets, keeping to the more open ground, and endeavouring by sudden turns now and then to surprise something in the act of creeping upon me. I saw nothing, and nevertheless my sense of another presence grew steadily. I increased my pace, and after some time came to a slight ridge, crossed it, and turned sharply, regarding it steadfastly from the further side. It came out black and clear-cut against the darkling sky; and presently a shapeless lump heaved up momentarily against the sky-line and vanished again. I felt assured now that my tawny-faced antagonist was stalking me once more; and coupled with that was another unpleasant realisation, that I had lost my way.

For a time, I hurried on hopelessly perplexed, and pursued by that stealthy approach. Whatever it was, the Thing either lacked the courage to attack me, or it was waiting to take me at some disadvantage. I kept studiously to the open. At times I would turn and listen; and presently I had half persuaded myself that my pursuer had abandoned the chase, or was a mere creation of my disordered imagination. Then I heard the sound of the sea. I quickened my footsteps almost into a run, and immediately there was a stumble in my rear.

I turned suddenly, and stared at the uncertain trees behind me. One black shadow seemed to leap into another. I listened, rigid, and

heard nothing but the creep of the blood in my ears. I thought that my nerves were unstrung, and that my imagination was tricking me, and turned resolutely towards the sound of the sea again.

In a minute or so the trees grew thinner, and I emerged upon a bare, low headland running out into the sombre water. The night was calm and clear, and the reflection of the growing multitude of the stars shivered in the tranquil heaving of the sea. Some way out, the wash upon an irregular band of reef shone with a pallid light of its own. Westward I saw the zodiacal light mingling with the yellow brilliance of the evening star. The coast fell away from me to the east, and westward it was hidden by the shoulder of the cape. Then I recalled the fact that Moreau's beach lay to the west.

A twig snapped behind me, and there was a rustle. I turned, and stood facing the dark trees. I could see nothing—or else I could see too much. Every dark form in the dimness had its ominous quality, its peculiar suggestion of alert watchfulness. So, I stood for perhaps a minute, and then, with an eye to the trees still, turned westward to cross the headland; and as I moved, one among the lurking shadows moved to follow me.

My heart beat quickly. Presently the broad sweep of a bay to the westward became visible, and I halted again. The noiseless shadow halted a dozen yards from me. A little point of light shone on the further bend of the curve, and the grey sweep of the sandy beach lay faint under the starlight. Perhaps two miles away was that little point of light. To get to the beach I should have to go through the trees where the shadows lurked, and down a bushy slope.

I could see the Thing rather more distinctly now. It was no animal, for it stood erect. At that I opened my mouth to speak, and found a hoarse phlegm choked my voice. I tried again, and shouted, "Who is there?" There was no answer. I advanced a step. The Thing did not move, only gathered itself together. My foot struck a stone. That gave me an idea. Without taking my eyes off the black form before me, I stooped and picked up this lump of rock; but at my motion the Thing turned abruptly as a dog might have done, and slunk obliquely into the further darkness. Then I recalled a schoolboy expedient against big dogs, and twisted the rock into my handkerchief, and gave this a turn round my wrist. I heard a movement further off among the shadows, as if the Thing was in retreat. Then suddenly my tense excitement gave way; I broke into a profuse perspiration and fell a-trembling, with my adversary routed and this weapon in my hand.

It was some time before I could summon resolution to go down through the trees and bushes upon the flank of the headland to the beach. At last I did it at a run; and as I emerged from the thicket upon the sand, I heard some other body come crashing after me. At that I completely lost my head with fear, and began running along the sand. Forthwith there came the swift patter of soft feet in pursuit. I gave a wild cry, and redoubled my pace. Some dim, black things about three or four times the size of rabbits went running or hopping up from the beach towards the bushes as I passed.

So long as I live, I shall remember the terror of that chase. I ran near the water's edge, and heard every now and then the splash of the feet that gained upon me. Far away, hopelessly far, was the yellow light. All the night about us was black and still. Splash, splash, came the pursuing feet, nearer and nearer. I felt my breath going, for I was quite out of training; it whooped as I drew it, and I felt a pain like a knife at my side. I perceived the Thing would come up with me long before I reached the enclosure, and, desperate and sobbing for my breath, I wheeled round upon it and struck at it as it came up to me—struck with all my strength. The stone came out of the sling of the handkerchief as I did so.

As I turned, the Thing, which had been running on all-fours, rose to its feet, and the missile fell fair on its left temple. The skull rang loud, and the animal-man blundered into me, thrust me back with its hands, and went staggering past me to fall headlong upon the sand with its face in the water; and there it lay still.

I could not bring myself to approach that black heap. I left it there, with the water rippling round it, under the still stars, and giving it a wide berth pursued my way towards the yellow glow of the house; and presently, with a positive effect of relief, came the pitiful moaning of the puma, the sound that had originally driven me out to explore this mysterious island. At that, though I was faint and horribly fatigued, I gathered together all my strength, and began running again towards the light. I thought I heard a voice calling me.

Chapter 10

The Crying of the Man

As I drew near the house, I saw that the light shone from the open door of my room; and then I heard coming from out of the darkness at the side of that orange oblong of light, the voice of Montgomery shouting, "Prendick!" I continued running. Presently I heard him

again. I replied by a feeble "Hullo!" and in another moment had staggered up to him.

"Where have you been?" said he, holding me at arm's length, so that the light from the door fell on my face. "We have both been so busy that we forgot you until about half an hour ago." He led me into the room and sat me down in the deck chair. For a while I was blinded by the light. "We did not think you would start to explore this island of ours without telling us," he said; and then, "I was afraid—But—what—Hullo!"

My last remaining strength slipped from me, and my head fell forward on my chest. I think he found a certain satisfaction in giving me brandy.

"For God's sake," said I, "fasten that door."

"You've been meeting some of our curiosities, eh?" said he.

He locked the door and turned to me again. He asked me no questions, but gave me some more brandy and water and pressed me to eat. I was in a state of collapse. He said something vague about his forgetting to warn me, and asked me briefly when I left the house and what I had seen.

I answered him as briefly, in fragmentary sentences. "Tell me what it all means," said I, in a state bordering on hysterics.

"It's nothing so very dreadful," said he. "But I think you have had about enough for one day." The puma suddenly gave a sharp yell of pain. At that he swore under his breath. "I'm damned," said he, "if this place is not as bad as Gower Street, with its cats."

"Montgomery," said I, "what was that thing that came after me? Was it a beast or was it a man?"

"If you don't sleep tonight," he said, "you'll be off your head tomorrow."

I stood up in front of him. "What was that thing that came after me?" I asked.

He looked me squarely in the eyes, and twisted his mouth askew. His eyes, which had seemed animated a minute before, went dull. "From your account," said he, "I'm thinking it was a bogle."

I felt a gust of intense irritation, which passed as quickly as it came. I flung myself into the chair again, and pressed my hands on my forehead. The puma began once more.

Montgomery came round behind me and put his hand on my shoulder. "Look here, Prendick," he said, "I had no business to let you drift out into this silly island of ours. But it's not so bad as you feel,

man. Your nerves are worked to rags. Let me give you something that will make you sleep. *That*—will keep on for hours yet. You must simply get to sleep, or I won't answer for it."

I did not reply. I bowed forward, and covered my face with my hands. Presently he returned with a small measure containing a dark liquid. This he gave me. I took it unresistingly, and he helped me into the hammock.

When I awoke, it was broad day. For a little while I lay flat, staring at the roof above me. The rafters, I observed, were made out of the timbers of a ship. Then I turned my head, and saw a meal prepared for me on the table. I perceived that I was hungry, and prepared to clamber out of the hammock, which, very politely anticipating my intention, twisted round and deposited me upon all-fours on the floor.

I got up and sat down before the food. I had a heavy feeling in my head, and only the vaguest memory at first of the things that had happened over night. The morning breeze blew very pleasantly through the unglazed window, and that and the food contributed to the sense of animal comfort which I experienced. Presently the door behind me—the door inward towards the yard of the enclosure—opened. I turned and saw Montgomery's face.

"All right," said he. "I'm frightfully busy." And he shut the door.

Afterwards I discovered that he forgot to re-lock it. Then I recalled the expression of his face the previous night, and with that the memory of all I had experienced reconstructed itself before me. Even as that fear came back to me came a cry from within; but this time it was not the cry of a puma. I put down the mouthful that hesitated upon my lips, and listened. Silence, save for the whisper of the morning breeze. I began to think my ears had deceived me.

After a long pause I resumed my meal, but with my ears still vigilant. Presently I heard something else, very faint and low. I sat as if frozen in my attitude. Though it was faint and low, it moved me more profoundly than all that I had hitherto heard of the abominations behind the wall. There was no mistake this time in the quality of the dim, broken sounds; no doubt at all of their source. For it was groaning, broken by sobs and gasps of anguish. It was no brute this time; it was a human being in torment!

As I realised this I rose, and in three steps had crossed the room, seized the handle of the door into the yard, and flung it open before me.

"Prendick, man! Stop!" cried Montgomery, intervening.

A startled deerhound yelped and snarled. There was blood, I saw, in the sink—brown, and some scarlet—and I smelt the peculiar smell of carbolic acid. Then through an open doorway beyond, in the dim light of the shadow, I saw something bound painfully upon a framework, scarred, red, and bandaged; and then blotting this out appeared the face of old Moreau, white and terrible. In a moment he had gripped me by the shoulder with a hand that was smeared red, had twisted me off my feet, and flung me headlong back into my own room. He lifted me as though I was a little child. I fell at full length upon the floor, and the door slammed and shut out the passionate intensity of his face. Then I heard the key turn in the lock, and Montgomery's voice in expostulation.

"Ruin the work of a lifetime," I heard Moreau say.

"He does not understand," said Montgomery. and other things that were inaudible.

"I can't spare the time yet," said Moreau.

The rest I did not hear. I picked myself up and stood trembling, my mind a chaos of the most horrible misgivings. Could it be possible, I thought, that such a thing as the vivisection of men was carried on here? The question shot like lightning across a tumultuous sky; and suddenly the clouded horror of my mind condensed into a vivid realisation of my own danger.

CHAPTER 11

The Hunting of the Man

It came before my mind with an unreasonable hope of escape that the outer door of my room was still open to me. I was convinced now, absolutely assured, that Moreau had been vivisecting a human being. All the time since I had heard his name, I had been trying to link in my mind in some way the grotesque animalism of the islanders with his abominations; and now I thought I saw it all. The memory of his work on the transfusion of blood recurred to me. These creatures I had seen were the victims of some hideous experiment. These sickening scoundrels had merely intended to keep me back, to fool me with their display of confidence, and presently to fall upon me with a fate more horrible than death—with torture; and after torture the most hideous degradation it is possible to conceive—to send me off a lost soul, a beast, to the rest of their Comus rout.

I looked round for some weapon. Nothing. Then with an inspiration I turned over the deck chair, put my foot on the side of it, and

tore away the side rail. It happened that a nail came away with the wood, and projecting, gave a touch of danger to an otherwise petty weapon. I heard a step outside, and incontinently flung open the door and found Montgomery within a yard of it. He meant to lock the outer door! I raised this nailed stick of mine and cut at his face; but he sprang back. I hesitated a moment, then turned and fled, round the corner of the house. "Prendick, man!" I heard his astonished cry, "don't be a silly ass, man!"

Another minute, thought I, and he would have had me locked in, and as ready as a hospital rabbit for my fate. He emerged behind the corner, for I heard him shout, "Prendick!" Then he began to run after me, shouting things as he ran. This time running blindly, I went north-eastward in a direction at right angles to my previous expedition. Once, as I went running headlong up the beach, I glanced over my shoulder and saw his attendant with him. I ran furiously up the slope, over it, then turning eastward along a rocky valley fringed on either side with jungle I ran for perhaps a mile altogether, my chest straining, my heart beating in my ears; and then hearing nothing of Montgomery or his man, and feeling upon the verge of exhaustion, I doubled sharply back towards the beach as I judged, and lay down in the shelter of a canebrake. There I remained for a long time, too fearful to move, and indeed too fearful even to plan a course of action. The wild scene about me lay sleeping silently under the sun, and the only sound near me was the thin hum of some small gnats that had discovered me. Presently I became aware of a drowsy breathing sound, the soughing of the sea upon the beach.

After about an hour I heard Montgomery shouting my name, far away to the north. That set me thinking of my plan of action. As I interpreted it then, this island was inhabited only by these two vivisectors and their animalised victims. Some of these no doubt they could press into their service against me if need arose. I knew both Moreau and Montgomery carried revolvers; and, save for a feeble bar of deal spiked with a small nail, the merest mockery of a mace, I was unarmed.

So, I lay still there, until I began to think of food and drink; and at that thought the real hopelessness of my position came home to me. I knew no way of getting anything to eat. I was too ignorant of botany to discover any resort of root or fruit that might lie about me; I had no means of trapping the few rabbits upon the island. It grew blanker the more I turned the prospect over. At last in the desperation of my position, my mind turned to the animal men I had encountered. I tried

222

to find some hope in what I remembered of them. In turn I recalled each one I had seen, and tried to draw some augury of assistance from my memory.

Then suddenly I heard a staghound bay, and at that realised a new danger. I took little time to think, or they would have caught me then, but snatching up my nailed stick, rushed headlong from my hiding-place towards the sound of the sea. I remember a growth of thorny plants, with spines that stabbed like pen-knives. I emerged bleeding and with torn clothes upon the lip of a long creek opening northward. I went straight into the water without a minute's hesitation, wading up the creek, and presently finding myself knee-deep in a little stream. I scrambled out at last on the westward bank, and with my heart beating loudly in my ears, crept into a tangle of ferns to await the issue. I heard the dog (there was only one) draw nearer, and yelp when it came to the thorns. Then I heard no more, and presently began to think I had escaped.

The minutes passed; the silence lengthened out, and at last after an hour of security my courage began to return to me. By this time, I was no longer very much terrified or very miserable. I had, as it were, passed the limit of terror and despair. I felt now that my life was practically lost, and that persuasion made me capable of daring anything. I had even a certain wish to encounter Moreau face to face; and as I had waded into the water, I remembered that if I were too hard pressed at least one path of escape from torment still lay open to me—they could not very well prevent my drowning myself. I had half a mind to drown myself then; but an odd wish to see the whole adventure out, a queer, impersonal, spectacular interest in myself, restrained me.

I stretched my limbs, sore and painful from the pricks of the spiny plants, and stared around me at the trees; and, so suddenly that it seemed to jump out of the green tracery about it, my eyes lit upon a black face watching me. I saw that it was the simian creature who had met the launch upon the beach. He was clinging to the oblique stem of a palm-tree. I gripped my stick, and stood up facing him. He began chattering. "You, you, you," was all I could distinguish at first. Suddenly he dropped from the tree, and in another moment was holding the fronds apart and staring curiously at me.

I did not feel the same repugnance towards this creature which I had experienced in my encounters with the other Beast Men. "You," he said, "in the boat." He was a man, then—at least as much of a man as Montgomery's attendant—for he could talk.

"Yes," I said, "I came in the boat. From the ship."

"Oh!" he said, and his bright, restless eyes travelled over me, to my hands, to the stick I carried, to my feet, to the tattered places in my coat, and the cuts and scratches I had received from the thorns. He seemed puzzled at something. His eyes came back to my hands. He held his own hand out and counted his digits slowly, "One, two, three, four, five—eigh?"

I did not grasp his meaning then; afterwards I was to find that a great proportion of these Beast People had malformed hands, lacking sometimes even three digits. But guessing this was in some way a greeting, I did the same thing by way of reply. He grinned with immense satisfaction. Then his swift roving glance went round again; he made a swift movement—and vanished. The fern fronds he had stood between came swishing together.

I pushed out of the brake after him, and was astonished to find him swinging cheerfully by one lank arm from a rope of creepers that looped down from the foliage overhead. His back was to me.

"Hullo!" said I.

He came down with a twisting jump, and stood facing me.

"I say," said I, "where can I get something to eat?"

"Eat!" he said. "Eat Man's food, now." And his eye went back to the swing of ropes. "At the huts."

"But where are the huts?"

"Oh!"

"I'm new, you know."

At that he swung round, and set off at a quick walk. All his motions were curiously rapid. "Come along," said he.

I went with him to see the adventure out. I guessed the huts were some rough shelter where he and some more of these Beast People lived. I might perhaps find them friendly, find some handle in their minds to take hold of. I did not know how far they had forgotten their human heritage.

My ape-like companion trotted along by my side, with his hands hanging down and his jaw thrust forward. I wondered what memory he might have in him. "How long have you been on this island?" said I.

"How long?" he asked; and after having the question repeated, he held up three fingers.

The creature was little better than an idiot. I tried to make out what he meant by that, and it seems I bored him. After another question or two he suddenly left my side and went leaping at some fruit

that hung from a tree. He pulled down a handful of prickly husks and went on eating the contents. I noted this with satisfaction, for here at least was a hint for feeding. I tried him with some other questions, but his chattering, prompt responses were as often as not quite at cross purposes with my question. Some few were appropriate, others quite parrot-like.

I was so intent upon these peculiarities that I scarcely noticed the path we followed. Presently we came to trees, all charred and brown, and so to a bare place covered with a yellow-white incrustation, across which a drifting smoke, pungent in whiffs to nose and eyes, went drifting. On our right, over a shoulder of bare rock, I saw the level blue of the sea. The path coiled down abruptly into a narrow ravine between two tumbled and knotty masses of blackish scoriae. Into this we plunged.

It was extremely dark, this passage, after the blinding sunlight reflected from the sulphurous ground. Its walls grew steep, and approached each other. Blotches of green and crimson drifted across my eyes. My conductor stopped suddenly. "Home!" said he, and I stood in a floor of a chasm that was at first absolutely dark to me. I heard some strange noises, and thrust the knuckles of my left hand into my eyes. I became aware of a disagreeable odour, like that of a monkey's cage ill-cleaned. Beyond, the rock opened again upon a gradual slope of sunlit greenery, and on either hand the light smote down through narrow ways into the central gloom.

Chapter 12
The Sayers of the Law

Then something cold touched my hand. I started violently, and saw close to me a dim pinkish thing, looking more like a flayed child than anything else in the world. The creature had exactly the mild but repulsive features of a sloth, the same low forehead and slow gestures.

As the first shock of the change of light passed, I saw about me more distinctly. The little sloth-like creature was standing and staring at me. My conductor had vanished. The place was a narrow passage between high walls of lava, a crack in the knotted rock, and on either side interwoven heaps of sea-mat, palm-fans, and reeds leaning against the rock formed rough and impenetrably dark dens. The winding way up the ravine between these was scarcely three yards wide, and was disfigured by lumps of decaying fruit-pulp and other refuse, which accounted for the disagreeable stench of the place.

The little pink sloth-creature was still blinking at me when my Ape-man reappeared at the aperture of the nearest of these dens, and beckoned me in. As he did so a slouching monster wriggled out of one of the places, further up this strange street, and stood up in featureless silhouette against the bright green beyond, staring at me. I hesitated, having half a mind to bolt the way I had come; and then, determined to go through with the adventure, I gripped my nailed stick about the middle and crawled into the little evil-smelling lean-to after my conductor.

It was a semi-circular space, shaped like the half of a bee-hive; and against the rocky wall that formed the inner side of it was a pile of variegated fruits, cocoa-nuts among others. Some rough vessels of lava and wood stood about the floor, and one on a rough stool. There was no fire. In the darkest corner of the hut sat a shapeless mass of darkness that grunted "Hey!" as I came in, and my Ape-man stood in the dim light of the doorway and held out a split cocoa-nut to me as I crawled into the other corner and squatted down. I took it, and began gnawing it, as serenely as possible, in spite of a certain trepidation and the nearly intolerable closeness of the den. The little pink sloth-creature stood in the aperture of the hut, and something else with a drab face and bright eyes came staring over its shoulder.

"Hey!" came out of the lump of mystery opposite. "It is a man."

"It is a man," gabbled my conductor, "a man, a man, a five-man, like me."

"Shut up!" said the voice from the dark, and grunted. I gnawed my cocoa-nut amid an impressive stillness.

I peered hard into the blackness, but could distinguish nothing.

"It is a man," the voice repeated. "He comes to live with us?"

It was a thick voice, with something in it—a kind of whistling overtone—that struck me as peculiar; but the English accent was strangely good.

The Ape-man looked at me as though he expected something. I perceived the pause was interrogative. "He comes to live with you," I said.

"It is a man. He must learn the Law."

I began to distinguish now a deeper blackness in the black, a vague outline of a hunched-up figure. Then I noticed the opening of the place was darkened by two more black heads. My hand tightened on my stick.

The thing in the dark repeated in a louder tone, "Say the words." I

had missed its last remark. "Not to go on all-fours; that is the Law," it repeated in a kind of sing-song.

I was puzzled.

"Say the words," said the Ape-man, repeating, and the figures in the doorway echoed this, with a threat in the tone of their voices.

I realised that I had to repeat this idiotic formula; and then began the insanest ceremony. The voice in the dark began intoning a mad litany, line by line, and I and the rest to repeat it. As they did so, they swayed from side to side in the oddest way, and beat their hands upon their knees; and I followed their example. I could have imagined I was already dead and in another world. That dark hut, these grotesque dim figures, just flecked here and there by a glimmer of light, and all of them swaying in unison and chanting:

Not to go on all-fours; that is the Law. Are we not Men?
Not to suck up Drink; that is the Law. Are we not Men?
Not to eat Fish or Flesh; that is the Law. Are we not Men?
Not to claw the Bark of Trees; that is the Law. Are we not Men?
Not to chase other Men; that is the Law. Are we not Men?

And so, from the prohibition of these acts of folly, on to the prohibition of what I thought then were the maddest, most impossible, and most indecent things one could well imagine. A kind of rhythmic fervour fell on all of us; we gabbled and swayed faster and faster, repeating this amazing Law. Superficially the contagion of these brutes was upon me, but deep down within me the laughter and disgust struggled together. We ran through a long list of prohibitions, and then the chant swung round to a new formula.

His is the House of Pain.
His is the Hand that makes.
His is the Hand that wounds.
His is the Hand that heals.

And so on for another long series, mostly quite incomprehensible gibberish to me about *Him*, whoever he might be. I could have fancied it was a dream, but never before have I heard chanting in a dream.

"*His is the lightning flash,*" we sang. "*His is the deep, salt sea.*"

A horrible fancy came into my head that Moreau, after animalising these men, had infected their dwarfed brains with a kind of deification of himself. However, I was too keenly aware of white teeth and strong claws about me to stop my chanting on that account.

His are the stars in the sky.

At last that song ended. I saw the Ape-man's face shining with perspiration; and my eyes being now accustomed to the darkness, I saw more distinctly the figure in the corner from which the voice came. It was the size of a man, but it seemed covered with a dull grey hair almost like a Skye-terrier. What was it? What were they all? Imagine yourself surrounded by all the most horrible cripples and maniacs it is possible to conceive, and you may understand a little of my feelings with these grotesque caricatures of humanity about me.

"He is a five-man, a five-man, a five-man—like me," said the Ape-man.

I held out my hands. The grey creature in the corner leant forward.

"Not to run on all-fours; that is the Law. Are we not Men?" he said.

He put out a strangely distorted talon and gripped my fingers. The thing was almost like the hoof of a deer produced into claws. I could have yelled with surprise and pain. His face came forward and peered at my nails, came forward into the light of the opening of the hut and I saw with a quivering disgust that it was like the face of neither man nor beast, but a mere shock of grey hair, with three shadowy over-archings to mark the eyes and mouth.

"He has little nails," said this grisly creature in his hairy beard. "It is well."

He threw my hand down, and instinctively I gripped my stick.

"Eat roots and herbs; it is His will," said the Ape-man.

"I am the Sayer of the Law," said the grey figure. "Here come all that be new to learn the Law. I sit in the darkness and say the Law."

"It is even so," said one of the beasts in the doorway.

"Evil are the punishments of those who break the Law. None escape."

"None escape," said the Beast Folk, glancing furtively at one another.

"None, none," said the Ape-man,—"none escape. See! I did a little thing, a wrong thing, once. I jabbered, jabbered, stopped talking. None could understand. I am burnt, branded in the hand. He is great. He is good!"

"None escape," said the grey creature in the corner.

"None escape," said the Beast People, looking askance at one another.

"For every one the want that is bad," said the grey Sayer of the Law.

"What you will want we do not know; we shall know. Some want to follow things that move, to watch and slink and wait and spring; to kill and bite, bite deep and rich, sucking the blood. It is bad. 'Not to chase other Men; that is the Law. Are we not Men? Not to eat Flesh or Fish; that is the Law. Are we not Men?'"

"None escape," said a dappled brute standing in the doorway.

"For every one the want is bad," said the grey Sayer of the Law. "Some want to go tearing with teeth and hands into the roots of things, snuffing into the earth. It is bad."

"None escape," said the men in the door.

"Some go clawing trees; some go scratching at the graves of the dead; some go fighting with foreheads or feet or claws; some bite suddenly, none giving occasion; some love uncleanness."

"None escape," said the Ape-man, scratching his calf.

"None escape," said the little pink sloth-creature.

"Punishment is sharp and sure. Therefore, learn the Law. Say the words."

And incontinently he began again the strange litany of the Law, and again I and all these creatures began singing and swaying. My head reeled with this jabbering and the close stench of the place; but I kept on, trusting to find presently some chance of a new development.

"Not to go on all-fours; that is the Law. Are we not Men?"

We were making such a noise that I noticed nothing of a tumult outside, until someone, who I think was one of the two Swine Men I had seen, thrust his head over the little pink sloth-creature and shouted something excitedly, something that I did not catch. Incontinently those at the opening of the hut vanished; my Ape-man rushed out; the thing that had sat in the dark followed him (I only observed that it was big and clumsy, and covered with silvery hair), and I was left alone. Then before I reached the aperture, I heard the yelp of a staghound.

In another moment I was standing outside the hovel, my chair-rail in my hand, every muscle of me quivering. Before me were the clumsy backs of perhaps a score of these Beast People, their misshapen heads half hidden by their shoulder-blades. They were gesticulating excitedly. Other half-animal faces glared interrogation out of the hovels. Looking in the direction in which they faced, I saw coming through the haze under the trees beyond the end of the passage of dens the dark figure and awful white face of Moreau. He was holding the leaping staghound back, and close behind him came Montgomery revolver in hand.

For a moment I stood horror-struck. I turned and saw the passage behind me blocked by another heavy brute, with a huge grey face and twinkling little eyes, advancing towards me. I looked round and saw to the right of me and a half-dozen yards in front of me a narrow gap in the wall of rock through which a ray of light slanted into the shadows.

"Stop!" cried Moreau as I strode towards this, and then, "Hold him!"

At that, first one face turned towards me and then others. Their bestial minds were happily slow. I dashed my shoulder into a clumsy monster who was turning to see what Moreau meant, and flung him forward into another. I felt his hands fly round, clutching at me and missing me. The little pink sloth-creature dashed at me, and I gashed down its ugly face with the nail in my stick and in another minute was scrambling up a steep side pathway, a kind of sloping chimney, out of the ravine. I heard a howl behind me, and cries of "Catch him!" "Hold him!" and the grey-faced creature appeared behind me and jammed his huge bulk into the cleft. "Go on! go on!" they howled. I clambered up the narrow cleft in the rock and came out upon the sulphur on the westward side of the village of the Beast Men.

That gap was altogether fortunate for me, for the narrow chimney, slanting obliquely upward, must have impeded the nearer pursuers. I ran over the white space and down a steep slope, through a scattered growth of trees, and came to a low-lying stretch of tall reeds, through which I pushed into a dark, thick undergrowth that was black and succulent under foot. As I plunged into the reeds, my foremost pursuers emerged from the gap. I broke my way through this undergrowth for some minutes.

The air behind me and about me was soon full of threatening cries. I heard the tumult of my pursuers in the gap up the slope, then the crashing of the reeds, and every now and then the crackling crash of a branch. Some of the creatures roared like excited beasts of prey. The staghound yelped to the left. I heard Moreau and Montgomery shouting in the same direction. I turned sharply to the right. It seemed to me even then that I heard Montgomery shouting for me to run for my life.

Presently the ground gave rich and oozy under my feet; but I was desperate and went headlong into it, struggled through knee-deep, and so came to a winding path among tall canes. The noise of my pursuers passed away to my left. In one place three strange, pink, hopping animals, about the size of cats, bolted before my footsteps. This pathway

ran up hill, across another open space covered with white incrustation, and plunged into a canebrake again. Then suddenly it turned parallel with the edge of a steep-walled gap, which came without warning, like the ha-ha (surprise sunken fence), of an English park—turned with an unexpected abruptness. I was still running with all my might, and I never saw this drop until I was flying headlong through the air.

I fell on my forearms and head, among thorns, and rose with a torn ear and bleeding face. I had fallen into a precipitous ravine, rocky and thorny, full of a hazy mist which drifted about me in wisps, and with a narrow streamlet from which this mist came meandering down the centre. I was astonished at this thin fog in the full blaze of daylight; but I had no time to stand wondering then. I turned to my right, down-stream, hoping to come to the sea in that direction, and so have my way open to drown myself. It was only later I found that I had dropped my nailed stick in my fall.

Presently the ravine grew narrower for a space, and carelessly I stepped into the stream. I jumped out again pretty quickly, for the water was almost boiling. I noticed too there was a thin sulphurous scum drifting upon its coiling water. Almost immediately came a turn in the ravine, and the indistinct blue horizon. The nearer sea was flashing the sun from a myriad facets. I saw my death before me; but I was hot and panting, with the warm blood oozing out on my face and running pleasantly through my veins. I felt more than a touch of exultation too, at having distanced my pursuers. It was not in me then to go out and drown myself yet. I stared back the way I had come.

I listened. Save for the hum of the gnats and the chirp of some small insects that hopped among the thorns, the air was absolutely still. Then came the yelp of a dog, very faint, and a chattering and gibbering, the snap of a whip, and voices. They grew louder, then fainter again. The noise receded up the stream and faded away. For a while the chase was over; but I knew now how much hope of help for me lay in the Beast People.

CHAPTER 13

A Parley

I turned again and went on down towards the sea. I found the hot stream broadened out to a shallow, weedy sand, in which an abundance of crabs and long-bodied, many-legged creatures started from my footfall. I walked to the very edge of the salt water, and then I felt I was safe. I turned and stared, arms akimbo, at the thick green behind

me, into which the steamy ravine cut like a smoking gash. But, as I say, I was too full of excitement and (a true saying, though those who have never known danger may doubt it) too desperate to die.

Then it came into my head that there was one chance before me yet. While Moreau and Montgomery and their bestial rabble chased me through the island, might I not go round the beach until I came to their enclosure—make a flank march upon them, in fact, and then with a rock lugged out of their loosely-built wall, perhaps, smash in the lock of the smaller door and see what I could find (knife, pistol, or what not) to fight them with when they returned? It was at any rate something to try.

So, I turned to the westward and walked along by the water's edge. The setting sun flashed his blinding heat into my eyes. The slight Pacific tide was running in with a gentle ripple. Presently the shore fell away southward, and the sun came round upon my right hand. Then suddenly, far in front of me, I saw first one and then several figures emerging from the bushes—Moreau, with his grey staghound, then Montgomery, and two others. At that I stopped.

They saw me, and began gesticulating and advancing. I stood watching them approach. The two Beast Men came running forward to cut me off from the undergrowth, inland. Montgomery came, running also, but straight towards me. Moreau followed slower with the dog.

At last I roused myself from my inaction, and turning seaward walked straight into the water. The water was very shallow at first. I was thirty yards out before the waves reached to my waist. Dimly I could see the intertidal creatures darting away from my feet.

"What are you doing, man?" cried Montgomery.

I turned, standing waist deep, and stared at them. Montgomery stood panting at the margin of the water. His face was bright-red with exertion, his long flaxen hair blown about his head, and his dropping nether lip showed his irregular teeth. Moreau was just coming up, his face pale and firm, and the dog at his hand barked at me. Both men had heavy whips. Farther up the beach stared the Beast Men.

"What am I doing? I am going to drown myself," said I.

Montgomery and Moreau looked at each other. "Why?" asked Moreau.

"Because that is better than being tortured by you."

"I told you so," said Montgomery, and Moreau said something in a low tone.

"What makes you think I shall torture you?" asked Moreau.

"What I saw," I said. "And those—yonder."

"Hush!" said Moreau, and held up his hand.

"I will not," said I. "They were men: what are they now? I at least will not be like them."

I looked past my interlocutors. Up the beach were M'ling, Montgomery's attendant, and one of the white-swathed brutes from the boat. Farther up, in the shadow of the trees, I saw my little Ape-man, and behind him some other dim figures.

"Who are these creatures?" said I, pointing to them and raising my voice more and more that it might reach them. "They were men, men like yourselves, whom you have infected with some bestial taint—men whom you have enslaved, and whom you still fear.

"You who listen," I cried, pointing now to Moreau and shouting past him to the Beast Men—"You who listen! Do you not see these men still fear you, go in dread of you? Why, then, do you fear them? You are many—"

"For God's sake," cried Montgomery, "stop that, Prendick!"

"Prendick!" cried Moreau.

They both shouted together, as if to drown my voice; and behind them lowered the staring faces of the Beast Men, wondering, their deformed hands hanging down, their shoulders hunched up. They seemed, as I fancied, to be trying to understand me, to remember, I thought, something of their human past.

I went on shouting, I scarcely remember what—that Moreau and Montgomery could be killed, that they were not to be feared: that was the burden of what I put into the heads of the Beast People. I saw the green-eyed man in the dark rags, who had met me on the evening of my arrival, come out from among the trees, and others followed him, to hear me better. At last for want of breath I paused.

"Listen to me for a moment," said the steady voice of Moreau; "and then say what you will."

"Well?" said I.

He coughed, thought, then shouted: "Latin, Prendick! bad Latin, schoolboy Latin; but try and understand. *Hi non sunt homines; sunt animalia qui nos habemus*—vivisected. A humanising process. I will explain. Come ashore."

I laughed. "A pretty story," said I. "They talk, build houses. They were men. It's likely I'll come ashore."

"The water just beyond where you stand is deep—and full of

sharks."

"That's my way," said I. "Short and sharp. Presently."

"Wait a minute." He took something out of his pocket that flashed back the sun, and dropped the object at his feet. "That's a loaded revolver," said he. "Montgomery here will do the same. Now we are going up the beach until you are satisfied the distance is safe. Then come and take the revolvers."

"Not I! You have a third between you."

"I want you to think over things, Prendick. In the first place, I never asked you to come upon this island. If we vivisected men, we should import men, not beasts. In the next, we had you drugged last night, had we wanted to work you any mischief; and in the next, now your first panic is over and you can think a little, is Montgomery here quite up to the character you give him? We have chased you for your good. Because this island is full of inimical phenomena. Besides, why should we want to shoot you when you have just offered to drown yourself?"

"Why did you set—your people onto me when I was in the hut?"

"We felt sure of catching you, and bringing you out of danger. Afterwards we drew away from the scent, for your good."

I mused. It seemed just possible. Then I remembered something again. "But I saw," said I, "in the enclosure—"

"That was the puma."

"Look here, Prendick," said Montgomery, "you're a silly ass! Come out of the water and take these revolvers, and talk. We can't do anything more than we could do now."

I will confess that then, and indeed always, I distrusted and dreaded Moreau; but Montgomery was a man I felt I understood.

"Go up the beach," said I, after thinking, and added, "holding your hands up."

"Can't do that," said Montgomery, with an explanatory nod over his shoulder. "Undignified."

"Go up to the trees, then," said I, "as you please."

"It's a damned silly ceremony," said Montgomery.

Both turned and faced the six or seven grotesque creatures, who stood there in the sunlight, solid, casting shadows, moving, and yet so incredibly unreal. Montgomery cracked his whip at them, and forthwith they all turned and fled helter-skelter into the trees; and when Montgomery and Moreau were at a distance, I judged sufficient, I waded ashore, and picked up and examined the revolvers. To satisfy

myself against the subtlest trickery, I discharged one at a round lump of lava, and had the satisfaction of seeing the stone pulverised and the beach splashed with lead. Still I hesitated for a moment.

"I'll take the risk," said I, at last; and with a revolver in each hand I walked up the beach towards them.

"That's better," said Moreau, without affectation. "As it is, you have wasted the best part of my day with your confounded imagination." And with a touch of contempt which humiliated me, he and Montgomery turned and went on in silence before me.

The knot of Beast Men, still wondering, stood back among the trees. I passed them as serenely as possible. One started to follow me, but retreated again when Montgomery cracked his whip. The rest stood silent—watching. They may once have been animals; but I never before saw an animal trying to think.

<div align="center">Chapter 14</div>

Doctor Moreau Explains

"And now, Prendick, I will explain," said Doctor Moreau, so soon as we had eaten and drunk. "I must confess that you are the most dictatorial guest I ever entertained. I warn you that this is the last I shall do to oblige you. The next thing you threaten to commit suicide about, I shan't do—even at some personal inconvenience."

He sat in my deckchair; a cigar half consumed in his white, dexterous-looking fingers. The light of the swinging lamp fell on his white hair; he stared through the little window out at the starlight. I sat as far away from him as possible, the table between us and the revolvers to hand. Montgomery was not present. I did not care to be with the two of them in such a little room.

"You admit that the vivisected human being, as you called it, is, after all, only the puma?" said Moreau. He had made me visit that horror in the inner room, to assure myself of its inhumanity.

"It is the puma," I said, "still alive, but so cut and mutilated as I pray, I may never see living flesh again. Of all vile—"

"Never mind that," said Moreau; "at least, spare me those youthful horrors. Montgomery used to be just the same. You admit that it is the puma. Now be quiet, while I reel off my physiological lecture to you."

And forthwith, beginning in the tone of a man supremely bored, but presently warming a little, he explained his work to me. He was very simple and convincing. Now and then there was a touch of sarcasm in his voice. Presently I found myself hot with shame at our

mutual positions.

The creatures I had seen were not men, had never been men. They were animals, humanised animals—triumphs of vivisection.

"You forget all that a skilled vivisector can do with living things," said Moreau. "For my own part, I'm puzzled why the things I have done here have not been done before. Small efforts, of course, have been made—amputation, tongue-cutting, excisions. Of course, you know a squint may be induced or cured by surgery? Then in the case of excisions you have all kinds of secondary changes, pigmentary disturbances, modifications of the passions, alterations in the secretion of fatty tissue. I have no doubt you have heard of these things?"

"Of course," said I. "But these foul creatures of yours—"

"All in good time," said he, waving his hand at me; "I am only beginning. Those are trivial cases of alteration. Surgery can do better things than that. There is building up as well as breaking down and changing. You have heard, perhaps, of a common surgical operation resorted to in cases where the nose has been destroyed: a flap of skin is cut from the forehead, turned down on the nose, and heals in the new position. This is a kind of grafting in a new position of part of an animal upon itself. Grafting of freshly obtained material from another animal is also possible—the case of teeth, for example.

"The grafting of skin and bone is done to facilitate healing: the surgeon places in the middle of the wound pieces of skin snipped from another animal, or fragments of bone from a victim freshly killed. Hunter's cock-spur—possibly you have heard of that—flourished on the bull's neck; and the rhinoceros rats of the Algerian zouaves are also to be thought of,—monsters manufactured by transferring a slip from the tail of an ordinary rat to its snout, and allowing it to heal in that position."

"Monsters manufactured!" said I. "Then you mean to tell me—"

"Yes. These creatures you have seen are animals carven and wrought into new shapes. To that, to the study of the plasticity of living forms, my life has been devoted. I have studied for years, gaining in knowledge as I go. I see you look horrified, and yet I am telling you nothing new. It all lay in the surface of practical anatomy years ago, but no one had the temerity to touch it. It is not simply the outward form of an animal which I can change. The physiology, the chemical rhythm of the creature, may also be made to undergo an enduring modification—of which vaccination and other methods of inoculation with living or dead matter are examples that will, no doubt, be familiar to you.

"A similar operation is the transfusion of blood—with which subject, indeed, I began. These are all familiar cases. Less so, and probably far more extensive, were the operations of those mediaeval practitioners who made dwarfs and beggar-cripples, show-monsters—some vestiges of whose art still remain in the preliminary manipulation of the young mountebank or contortionist.

"Victor Hugo gives an account of them in *L'Homme qui Rit.*— But perhaps my meaning grows plain now. You begin to see that it is a possible thing to transplant tissue from one part of an animal to another, or from one animal to another; to alter its chemical reactions and methods of growth; to modify the articulations of its limbs; and, indeed, to change it in its most intimate structure.

"And yet this extraordinary branch of knowledge has never been sought as an end, and systematically, by modern investigators until I took it up! Some such things have been hit upon in the last resort of surgery; most of the kindred evidence that will recur to your mind has been demonstrated as it were by accident,—by tyrants, by criminals, by the breeders of horses and dogs, by all kinds of untrained clumsy-handed men working for their own immediate ends. I was the first man to take up this question armed with antiseptic surgery, and with a really scientific knowledge of the laws of growth. Yet one would imagine it must have been practised in secret before. Such creatures as the Siamese Twins—And in the vaults of the Inquisition. No doubt their chief aim was artistic torture, but some at least of the inquisitors must have had a touch of scientific curiosity."

"But," said I, "these things—these animals talk!"

He said that was so, and proceeded to point out that the possibility of vivisection does not stop at a mere physical metamorphosis. A pig may be educated. The mental structure is even less determinate than the bodily. In our growing science of hypnotism, we find the promise of a possibility of superseding old inherent instincts by new suggestions, grafting upon or replacing the inherited fixed ideas. Very much indeed of what we call moral education, he said, is such an artificial modification and perversion of instinct; pugnacity is trained into courageous self-sacrifice, and suppressed sexuality into religious emotion.

And the great difference between man and monkey is in the larynx, he continued—in the incapacity to frame delicately different sound-symbols by which thought could be sustained. In this I failed to agree with him, but with a certain incivility he declined to notice my objection. He repeated that the thing was so, and continued his

account of his work.

I asked him why he had taken the human form as a model. There seemed to me then, and there still seems to me now, a strange wickedness for that choice.

He confessed that he had chosen that form by chance. "I might just as well have worked to form sheep into llamas and llamas into sheep. I suppose there is something in the human form that appeals to the artistic turn of mind more powerfully than any animal shape can. But I've not confined myself to man-making. Once or twice—" He was silent, for a minute perhaps. "These years! How they have slipped by! And here I have wasted a day saving your life, and am now wasting an hour explaining myself!"

"But," said I, "I still do not understand. Where is your justification for inflicting all this pain? The only thing that could excuse vivisection to me would be some application—"

"Precisely," said he. "But, you see, I am differently constituted. We are on different platforms. You are a materialist."

"I am *not* a materialist," I began hotly.

"In my view—in my view. For it is just this question of pain that parts us. So long as visible or audible pain turns you sick; so long as your own pains drive you; so long as pain underlies your propositions about sin—so long, I tell you, you are an animal, thinking a little less obscurely what an animal feels. This pain—"

I gave an impatient shrug at such sophistry.

"Oh, but it is such a little thing! A mind truly opened to what science has to teach must see that it is a little thing. It may be that save in this little planet, this speck of cosmic dust, invisible long before the nearest star could be attained—it may be, I say, that nowhere else does this thing called pain occur. But the laws we feel our way towards— Why, even on this earth, even among living things, what pain is there?"

As he spoke, he drew a little penknife from his pocket, opened the smaller blade, and moved his chair so that I could see his thigh. Then, choosing the place deliberately, he drove the blade into his leg and withdrew it.

"No doubt," he said, "you have seen that before. It does not hurt a pin-prick. But what does it show? The capacity for pain is not needed in the muscle, and it is not placed there—is but little needed in the skin, and only here and there over the thigh is a spot capable of feeling pain. Pain is simply our intrinsic medical adviser to warn us and stimulate us. Not all living flesh is painful; nor is all nerve, not even all

238

sensory nerve. There's no taint of pain, real pain, in the sensations of the optic nerve. If you wound the optic nerve, you merely see flashes of light—just as disease of the auditory nerve merely means a humming in our ears. Plants do not feel pain, nor the lower animals; it's possible that such animals as the starfish and crayfish do not feel pain at all. Then with men, the more intelligent they become, the more intelligently they will see after their own welfare, and the less they will need the goad to keep them out of danger. I never yet heard of a useless thing that was not ground out of existence by evolution sooner or later. Did you? And pain gets needless.

"Then I am a religious man, Prendick, as every sane man must be. It may be, I fancy, that I have seen more of the ways of this world's Maker than you—for I have sought his laws, in *my* way, all my life, while you, I understand, have been collecting butterflies. And I tell you, pleasure and pain have nothing to do with heaven or hell. Pleasure and pain—bah! What is your theologian's ecstasy but Mahomet's *houri* in the dark? This store which men and women set on pleasure and pain, Prendick, is the mark of the beast upon them—the mark of the beast from which they came! Pain, pain and pleasure, they are for us only so long as we wriggle in the dust.

"You see, I went on with this research just the way it led me. That is the only way I ever heard of true research going. I asked a question, devised some method of obtaining an answer, and got a fresh question. Was this possible or that possible? You cannot imagine what this means to an investigator, what an intellectual passion grows upon him! You cannot imagine the strange, colourless delight of these intellectual desires! The thing before you is no longer an animal, a fellow-creature, but a problem! Sympathetic pain—all I know of it I remember as a thing I used to suffer from years ago. I wanted—it was the one thing I wanted—to find out the extreme limit of plasticity in a living shape."

"But," said I, "the thing is an abomination—"

"To this day I have never troubled about the ethics of the matter," he continued. "The study of Nature makes a man at last as remorseless as Nature. I have gone on, not heeding anything but the question I was pursuing; and the material has—dripped into the huts yonder. It is nearly eleven years since we came here, I and Montgomery and six Kanakas. I remember the green stillness of the island and the empty ocean about us, as though it was yesterday. The place seemed waiting for me.

"The stores were landed and the house was built. The Kanakas

founded some huts near the ravine. I went to work here upon what I had brought with me. There were some disagreeable things happened at first. I began with a sheep, and killed it after a day and a half by a slip of the scalpel. I took another sheep, and made a thing of pain and fear and left it bound up to heal. It looked quite human to me when I had finished it; but when I went to it I was discontented with it. It remembered me, and was terrified beyond imagination; and it had no more than the wits of a sheep. The more I looked at it the clumsier it seemed, until at last I put the monster out of its misery. These animals without courage, these fear-haunted, pain-driven things, without a spark of pugnacious energy to face torment—they are no good for man-making.

"Then I took a gorilla I had; and upon that, working with infinite care and mastering difficulty after difficulty, I made my first man. All the week, night and day, I moulded him. With him it was chiefly the brain that needed moulding; much had to be added, much changed. I thought him a fair specimen of the negroid type when I had finished him, and he lay bandaged, bound, and motionless before me. It was only when his life was assured that I left him and came into this room again, and found Montgomery much as you are. He had heard some of the cries as the thing grew human—cries like those that disturbed *you* so. I didn't take him completely into my confidence at first. And the Kanakas too, had realised something of it. They were scared out of their wits by the sight of me.

"I got Montgomery over to me—in a way; but I and he had the hardest job to prevent the Kanakas deserting. Finally, they did; and so we lost the yacht. I spent many days educating the brute—altogether I had him for three or four months. I taught him the rudiments of English; gave him ideas of counting; even made the thing read the alphabet. But at that he was slow, though I've met with idiots slower. He began with a clean sheet, mentally; had no memories left in his mind of what he had been. When his scars were quite healed, and he was no longer anything but painful and stiff, and able to converse a little, I took him yonder and introduced him to the Kanakas as an interesting stowaway.

"They were horribly afraid of him at first, somehow—which offended me rather, for I was conceited about him; but his ways seemed so mild, and he was so abject, that after a time they received him and took his education in hand. He was quick to learn, very imitative and adaptive, and built himself a hovel rather better, it seemed to me, than

240

their own shanties. There was one among the boys a bit of a missionary, and he taught the thing to read, or at least to pick out letters, and gave him some rudimentary ideas of morality; but it seems the beast's habits were not all that is desirable.

"I rested from work for some days after this, and was in a mind to write an account of the whole affair to wake up English physiology. Then I came upon the creature squatting up in a tree and gibbering at two of the Kanakas who had been teasing him. I threatened him, told him the inhumanity of such a proceeding, aroused his sense of shame, and came home resolved to do better before I took my work back to England. I have been doing better. But somehow the things drift back again: the stubborn beast-flesh grows day by day back again. But I mean to do better things still. I mean to conquer that. This puma—

"But that's the story. All the Kanaka boys are dead now; one fell overboard of the launch, and one died of a wounded heel that he poisoned in some way with plant-juice. Three went away in the yacht, and I suppose and hope were drowned. The other one—was killed. Well, I have replaced them. Montgomery went on much as you are disposed to do at first, and then—

"What became of the other one?" said I, sharply—"the other Kanaka who was killed?"

"The fact is, after I had made a number of human creatures, I made a Thing—" He hesitated.

"Yes?" said I.

"It was killed."

"I don't understand," said I; "do you mean to say—"

"It killed the Kanaka—yes. It killed several other things that it caught. We chased it for a couple of days. It only got loose by accident—I never meant it to get away. It wasn't finished. It was purely an experiment. It was a limbless thing, with a horrible face, that writhed along the ground in a serpentine fashion. It was immensely strong, and in infuriating pain. It lurked in the woods for some days, until we hunted it; and then it wriggled into the northern part of the island, and we divided the party to close in upon it. Montgomery insisted upon coming with me. The man had a rifle; and when his body was found, one of the barrels was curved into the shape of an S and very nearly bitten through. Montgomery shot the thing. After that I stuck to the ideal of humanity—except for little things."

He became silent. I sat in silence watching his face.

"So, for twenty years altogether—counting nine years in Eng-

land—I have been going on; and there is still something in everything I do that defeats me, makes me dissatisfied, challenges me to further effort. Sometimes I rise above my level, sometimes I fall below it; but always I fall short of the things I dream. The human shape I can get now, almost with ease, so that it is lithe and graceful, or thick and strong; but often there is trouble with the hands and the claws—painful things, that I dare not shape too freely. But it is in the subtle grafting and reshaping one must needs do to the brain that my trouble lies. The intelligence is often oddly low, with unaccountable blank ends, unexpected gaps.

"And least satisfactory of all is something that I cannot touch, somewhere—I cannot determine where—in the seat of the emotions. Cravings, instincts, desires that harm humanity, a strange hidden reservoir to burst forth suddenly and inundate the whole being of the creature with anger, hate, or fear. These creatures of mine seemed strange and uncanny to you so soon as you began to observe them; but to me, just after I make them, they seem to be indisputably human beings. It's afterwards, as I observe them, that the persuasion fades. First one animal trait, then another, creeps to the surface and stares out at me. But I will conquer yet! Each time I dip a living creature into the bath of burning pain, I say, 'This time I will burn out all the animal; this time I will make a rational creature of my own!' After all, what is ten years? Men have been a hundred thousand in the making." He thought darkly. "But I am drawing near the fastness. This puma of mine—" After a silence, "And they revert. As soon as my hand is taken from them the beast begins to creep back, begins to assert itself again." Another long silence.

"Then you take the things you make into those dens?" said I.

"They go. I turn them out when I begin to feel the beast in them, and presently they wander there. They all dread this house and me. There is a kind of travesty of humanity over there. Montgomery knows about it, for he interferes in their affairs. He has trained one or two of them to our service. He's ashamed of it, but I believe he half likes some of those beasts. It's his business, not mine. They only sicken me with a sense of failure. I take no interest in them. I fancy they follow in the lines the Kanaka missionary marked out, and have a kind of mockery of a rational life, poor beasts! There's something they call the Law. Sing hymns about 'all thine.' They build themselves their dens, gather fruit, and pull herbs—marry even. But I can see through it all, see into their very souls, and see there nothing but the souls of beasts,

beasts that perish, anger and the lusts to live and gratify themselves—
Yet they're odd; complex, like everything else alive. There is a kind of
upward striving in them, part vanity, part waste sexual emotion, part
waste curiosity. It only mocks me. I have some hope of this puma. I
have worked hard at her head and brain—

"And now," said he, standing up after a long gap of silence, during
which we had each pursued our own thoughts, "what do you think?
Are you in fear of me still?"

I looked at him, and saw but a white-faced, white-haired man,
with calm eyes. Save for his serenity, the touch almost of beauty that
resulted from his set tranquillity and his magnificent build, he might
have passed muster among a hundred other comfortable old gentle-
men. Then I shivered. By way of answer to his second question, I
handed him a revolver with either hand.

"Keep them," he said, and snatched at a yawn. He stood up, stared
at me for a moment, and smiled. "You have had two eventful days,"
said he. "I should advise some sleep. I'm glad it's all clear. Goodnight."
He thought me over for a moment, then went out by the inner door.

I immediately turned the key in the outer one. I sat down again; sat
for a time in a kind of stagnant mood, so weary, emotionally, mentally,
and physically, that I could not think beyond the point at which he
had left me. The black window stared at me like an eye. At last with
an effort I put out the light and got into the hammock. Very soon I
was asleep.

Chapter 15
Concerning the Beast Folk

I woke early. Moreau's explanation stood before my mind, clear
and definite, from the moment of my awakening. I got out of the
hammock and went to the door to assure myself that the key was
turned. Then I tried the window-bar, and found it firmly fixed. That
these man-like creatures were in truth only bestial monsters, mere
grotesque travesties of men, filled me with a vague uncertainty of their
possibilities which was far worse than any definite fear.

A tapping came at the door, and I heard the glutinous accents of
M'ling speaking. I pocketed one of the revolvers (keeping one hand
upon it), and opened to him.

"Good morning, sair," he said, bringing in, in addition to the cus-
tomary herb-breakfast, an ill-cooked rabbit. Montgomery followed
him. His roving eye caught the position of my arm and he smiled askew.

The puma was resting to heal that day; but Moreau, who was singularly solitary in his habits, did not join us. I talked with Montgomery to clear my ideas of the way in which the Beast Folk lived. In particular, I was urgent to know how these inhuman monsters were kept from falling upon Moreau and Montgomery and from rending one another. He explained to me that the comparative safety of Moreau and himself was due to the limited mental scope of these monsters. In spite of their increased intelligence and the tendency of their animal instincts to reawaken, they had certain fixed ideas implanted by Moreau in their minds, which absolutely bounded their imaginations. They were really hypnotised; had been told that certain things were impossible, and that certain things were not to be done, and these prohibitions were woven into the texture of their minds beyond any possibility of disobedience or dispute.

Certain matters, however, in which old instinct was at war with Moreau's convenience, were in a less stable condition. A series of propositions called the Law (I had already heard them recited) battled in their minds with the deep-seated, ever-rebellious cravings of their animal natures. This Law they were ever repeating, I found, and ever breaking. Both Montgomery and Moreau displayed particular solicitude to keep them ignorant of the taste of blood; they feared the inevitable suggestions of that flavour. Montgomery told me that the Law, especially among the feline Beast People, became oddly weakened about nightfall; that then the animal was at its strongest; that a spirit of adventure sprang up in them at the dusk, when they would dare things they never seemed to dream about by day. To that I owed my stalking by the Leopard-man, on the night of my arrival. But during these earlier days of my stay they broke the Law only furtively and after dark; in the daylight there was a general atmosphere of respect for its multifarious prohibitions.

And here perhaps I may give a few general facts about the island and the Beast People. The island, which was of irregular outline and lay low upon the wide sea, had a total area, I suppose, of seven or eight square miles. (This description corresponds in every respect to Noble's Isle, C.E.P.) It was volcanic in origin, and was now fringed on three sides by coral reefs; some fumaroles to the northward, and a hot spring, were the only vestiges of the forces that had long since originated it. Now and then a faint quiver of earthquake would be sensible, and sometimes the ascent of the spire of smoke would be rendered tumultuous by gusts of steam; but that was all. The population of the island,

Montgomery informed me, now numbered rather more than sixty of these strange creations of Moreau's art, not counting the smaller monstrosities which lived in the undergrowth and were without human form. Altogether he had made nearly a hundred and twenty; but many had died, and others—like the writhing Footless Thing of which he had told me—had come by violent ends. In answer to my question, Montgomery said that they actually bore offspring, but that these generally died. When they lived, Moreau took them and stamped the human form upon them. There was no evidence of the inheritance of their acquired human characteristics. The females were less numerous than the males, and liable to much furtive persecution in spite of the monogamy the Law enjoined.

It would be impossible for me to describe these Beast People in detail; my eye has had no training in details, and unhappily I cannot sketch. Most striking, perhaps, in their general appearance was the disproportion between the legs of these creatures and the length of their bodies; and yet—so relative is our idea of grace—my eye became habituated to their forms, and at last I even fell in with their persuasion that my own long thighs were ungainly. Another point was the forward carriage of the head and the clumsy and inhuman curvature of the spine. Even the Ape-man lacked that inward sinuous curve of the back which makes the human figure so graceful. Most had their shoulders hunched clumsily, and their short forearms hung weakly at their sides. Few of them were conspicuously hairy, at least until the end of my time upon the island.

The next most obvious deformity was in their faces, almost all of which were prognathous, malformed about the ears, with large and protuberant noses, very furry or very bristly hair, and often strangely-coloured or strangely-placed eyes. None could laugh, though the Ape-man had a chattering titter. Beyond these general characters their heads had little in common; each preserved the quality of its particular species: the human mark distorted but did not hide the leopard, the ox, or the sow, or other animal or animals, from which the creature had been moulded. The voices, too, varied exceedingly. The hands were always malformed; and though some surprised me by their unexpected human appearance, almost all were deficient in the number of the digits, clumsy about the finger-nails, and lacking any tactile sensibility.

The two most formidable Animal Men were my Leopard-man and a creature made of hyena and swine. Larger than these were the

three bull-creatures who pulled in the boat. Then came the silvery-hairy-man, who was also the Sayer of the Law, M'ling, and a satyr-like creature of ape and goat. There were three Swine-men and a Swine-woman, a mare-rhinoceros-creature, and several other females whose sources I did not ascertain. There were several wolf-creatures, a bear-bull, and a Saint-Bernard-man. I have already described the Ape-man, and there was a particularly hateful (and evil-smelling) old woman made of vixen and bear, whom I hated from the beginning. She was said to be a passionate votary of the Law. Smaller creatures were certain dappled youths and my little sloth-creature. But enough of this catalogue.

At first, I had a shivering horror of the brutes, felt all too keenly that they were still brutes; but insensibly I became a little habituated to the idea of them, and moreover I was affected by Montgomery's attitude towards them. He had been with them so long that he had come to regard them as almost normal human beings. His London days seemed a glorious, impossible past to him. Only once in a year or so did he go to Arica to deal with Moreau's agent, a trader in animals there. He hardly met the finest type of mankind in that seafaring village of Spanish mongrels. The men aboard-ship, he told me, seemed at first just as strange to him as the Beast Men seemed to me—unnaturally long in the leg, flat in the face, prominent in the forehead, suspicious, dangerous, and cold-hearted. In fact, he did not like men: his heart had warmed to me, he thought, because he had saved my life. I fancied even then that he had a sneaking kindness for some of these metamorphosed brutes, a vicious sympathy with some of their ways, but that he attempted to veil it from me at first.

M'ling, the black-faced man, Montgomery's attendant, the first of the Beast Folk I had encountered, did not live with the others across the island, but in a small kennel at the back of the enclosure. The creature was scarcely so intelligent as the Ape-man, but far more docile, and the most human-looking of all the Beast Folk; and Montgomery had trained it to prepare food, and indeed to discharge all the trivial domestic offices that were required. It was a complex trophy of Moreau's horrible skill—a bear, tainted with dog and ox, and one of the most elaborately made of all his creatures. It treated Montgomery with a strange tenderness and devotion. Sometimes he would notice it, pat it, call it half-mocking, half-jocular names, and so make it caper with extraordinary delight; sometimes he would ill-treat it, especially after he had been at the whiskey, kicking it, beating it, pelting it with

stones or lighted fusees. But whether he treated it well or ill, it loved nothing so much as to be near him.

I say I became habituated to the Beast People, that a thousand things which had seemed unnatural and repulsive speedily became natural and ordinary to me. I suppose everything in existence takes its colour from the average hue of our surroundings. Montgomery and Moreau were too peculiar and individual to keep my general impressions of humanity well defined. I would see one of the clumsy bovine-creatures who worked the launch treading heavily through the undergrowth, and find myself asking, trying hard to recall, how he differed from some really human yokel trudging home from his mechanical labours; or I would meet the Fox-bear woman's vulpine, shifty face, strangely human in its speculative cunning, and even imagine I had met it before in some city byway.

Yet every now and then the beast would flash out upon me beyond doubt or denial. An ugly-looking man, a hunch-backed human savage to all appearance, squatting in the aperture of one of the dens, would stretch his arms and yawn, showing with startling suddenness scissor-edged incisors and sabre-like canines, keen and brilliant as knives. Or in some narrow pathway, glancing with a transitory daring into the eyes of some lithe, white-swathed female figure, I would suddenly see (with a spasmodic revulsion) that she had slit-like pupils, or glancing down note the curving nail with which she held her shapeless wrap about her. It is a curious thing, by the bye, for which I am quite unable to account, that these weird creatures—the females, I mean—had in the earlier days of my stay an instinctive sense of their own repulsive clumsiness, and displayed in consequence a more than human regard for the decency and decorum of extensive costume.

CHAPTER 16

How the Beast Folk Taste Blood

My inexperience as a writer betrays me, and I wander from the thread of my story.

After I had breakfasted with Montgomery, he took me across the island to see the fumarole and the source of the hot spring into whose scalding waters I had blundered on the previous day. Both of us carried whips and loaded revolvers. While going through a leafy jungle on our road thither, we heard a rabbit squealing. We stopped and listened, but we heard no more; and presently we went on our way, and the incident dropped out of our minds. Montgomery called my

attention to certain little pink animals with long hind-legs, that went leaping through the undergrowth. He told me they were creatures made of the offspring of the Beast People, that Moreau had invented. He had fancied they might serve for meat, but a rabbit-like habit of devouring their young had defeated this intention.

I had already encountered some of these creatures—once during my moonlight flight from the Leopard-man, and once during my pursuit by Moreau on the previous day. By chance, one hopping to avoid us leapt into the hole caused by the uprooting of a wind-blown tree; before it could extricate itself, we managed to catch it. It spat like a cat, scratched and kicked vigorously with its hind-legs, and made an attempt to bite; but its teeth were too feeble to inflict more than a painless pinch. It seemed to me rather a pretty little creature; and as Montgomery stated that it never destroyed the turf by burrowing, and was very cleanly in its habits, I should imagine it might prove a convenient substitute for the common rabbit in gentlemen's parks.

We also saw on our way the trunk of a tree barked in long strips and splintered deeply. Montgomery called my attention to this. "Not to claw bark of trees, *that* is the Law," he said. "Much some of them care for it!" It was after this, I think, that we met the Satyr and the Ape-man. The Satyr was a gleam of classical memory on the part of Moreau—his face ovine in expression, like the coarser Hebrew type; his voice a harsh bleat, his nether extremities Satanic. He was gnawing the husk of a pod-like fruit as he passed us. Both of them saluted Montgomery.

"Hail," said they, "to the Other with the Whip!"

"There's a Third with a Whip now," said Montgomery. "So, you'd better mind!"

"Was he not made?" said the Ape-man. "He said—he said he was made."

The Satyr-man looked curiously at me. "The Third with the Whip, he that walks weeping into the sea, has a thin white face."

"He has a thin long whip," said Montgomery.

"Yesterday he bled and wept," said the Satyr. "You never bleed nor weep. The Master does not bleed or weep."

"Ollendorffian beggar!" said Montgomery, "you'll bleed and weep if you don't look out!"

"He has five fingers, he is a five-man like me," said the Ape-man.

"Come along, Prendick," said Montgomery, taking my arm; and I went on with him.

The Satyr and the Ape-man stood watching us and making other remarks to each other.

"He says nothing," said the Satyr. "Men have voices."

"Yesterday he asked me of things to eat," said the Ape-man. "He did not know."

Then they spoke inaudible things, and I heard the Satyr laughing.

It was on our way back that we came upon the dead rabbit. The red body of the wretched little beast was rent to pieces, many of the ribs stripped white, and the backbone indisputably gnawed.

At that Montgomery stopped. "Good God!" said he, stooping down, and picking up some of the crushed vertebrae to examine them more closely. "Good God!" he repeated, "what can this mean?"

"Some carnivore of yours has remembered its old habits," I said after a pause. "This backbone has been bitten through."

He stood staring, with his face white and his lip pulled askew. "I don't like this," he said slowly.

"I saw something of the same kind," said I, "the first day I came here."

"The devil you did! What was it?"

"A rabbit with its head twisted off."

"The day you came here?"

"The day I came here. In the undergrowth at the back of the enclosure, when I went out in the evening. The head was completely wrung off."

He gave a long, low whistle.

"And what is more, I have an idea which of your brutes did the thing. It's only a suspicion, you know. Before I came on the rabbit, I saw one of your monsters drinking in the stream."

"Sucking his drink?"

"Yes."

"'Not to suck your drink; that is the Law.' Much the brutes care for the Law, eh? when Moreau's not about!"

"It was the brute who chased me."

"Of course," said Montgomery; "it's just the way with carnivores. After a kill, they drink. It's the taste of blood, you know—What was the brute like?" he continued. "Would you know him again?" He glanced about us, standing astride over the mess of dead rabbit, his eyes roving among the shadows and screens of greenery, the lurking-places and ambuscades of the forest that bounded us in. "The taste of blood," he said again.

He took out his revolver, examined the cartridges in it and replaced it. Then he began to pull at his dropping lip.

"I think I should know the brute again," I said. "I stunned him. He ought to have a handsome bruise on the forehead of him."

"But then we have to *prove* that he killed the rabbit," said Montgomery. "I wish I'd never brought the things here."

I should have gone on, but he stayed there thinking over the mangled rabbit in a puzzle-headed way. As it was, I went to such a distance that the rabbit's remains were hidden.

"Come on!" I said.

Presently he woke up and came towards me. "You see," he said, almost in a whisper, "they are all supposed to have a fixed idea against eating anything that runs on land. If some brute has by any accident tasted blood—"

We went on some way in silence. "I wonder what can have happened," he said to himself. Then, after a pause again: "I did a foolish thing the other day. That servant of mine—I showed him how to skin and cook a rabbit. It's odd—I saw him licking his hands—It never occurred to me."

Then: "We must put a stop to this. I must tell Moreau."

He could think of nothing else on our homeward journey.

Moreau took the matter even more seriously than Montgomery, and I need scarcely say that I was affected by their evident consternation.

"We must make an example," said Moreau. "I've no doubt in my own mind that the Leopard-man was the sinner. But how can we prove it? I wish, Montgomery, you had kept your taste for meat in hand, and gone without these exciting novelties. We may find ourselves in a mess yet, through it."

"I was a silly ass," said Montgomery. "But the thing's done now; and you said I might have them, you know."

"We must see to the thing at once," said Moreau. "I suppose if anything should turn up, M'ling can take care of himself?"

"I'm not so sure of M'ling," said Montgomery. "I think I ought to know him."

In the afternoon, Moreau, Montgomery, myself, and M'ling went across the island to the huts in the ravine. We three were armed; M'ling carried the little hatchet he used in chopping firewood, and some coils of wire. Moreau had a huge cowherd's horn slung over his shoulder.

"You will see a gathering of the Beast People," said Montgomery.

"It is a pretty sight!"

Moreau said not a word on the way, but the expression of his heavy, white-fringed face was grimly set.

We crossed the ravine down which smoked the stream of hot water, and followed the winding pathway through the canebrakes until we reached a wide area covered over with a thick, powdery yellow substance which I believe was sulphur. Above the shoulder of a weedy bank the sea glittered. We came to a kind of shallow natural amphitheatre, and here the four of us halted. Then Moreau sounded the horn, and broke the sleeping stillness of the tropical afternoon. He must have had strong lungs. The hooting note rose and rose amidst its echoes, to at last an ear-penetrating intensity.

"Ah!" said Moreau, letting the curved instrument fall to his side again.

Immediately there was a crashing through the yellow canes, and a sound of voices from the dense green jungle that marked the morass through which I had run on the previous day. Then at three or four points on the edge of the sulphurous area appeared the grotesque forms of the Beast People hurrying towards us. I could not help a creeping horror, as I perceived first one and then another trot out from the trees or reeds and come shambling along over the hot dust. But Moreau and Montgomery stood calmly enough; and, perforce, I stuck beside them.

First to arrive was the Satyr, strangely unreal for all that he cast a shadow and tossed the dust with his hoofs. After him from the brake came a monstrous lout, a thing of horse and rhinoceros, chewing a straw as it came; then appeared the Swine-woman and two Wolf-women; then the Fox-bear witch, with her red eyes in her peaked red face, and then others—all hurrying eagerly. As they came forward they began to cringe towards Moreau and chant, quite regardless of one another, fragments of the latter half of the litany of the Law—"*His is the Hand that wounds; His is the Hand that heals*," and so forth. As soon as they had approached within a distance of perhaps thirty yards they halted, and bowing on knees and elbows began flinging the white dust upon their heads.

Imagine the scene if you can! We three blue-clad men, with our misshapen black-faced attendant, standing in a wide expanse of sunlit yellow dust under the blazing blue sky, and surrounded by this circle of crouching and gesticulating monstrosities—some almost human save in their subtle expression and gestures, some like cripples,

251

some so strangely distorted as to resemble nothing but the denizens of our wildest dreams; and, beyond, the reedy lines of a canebrake in one direction, a dense tangle of palm-trees on the other, separating us from the ravine with the huts, and to the north the hazy horizon of the Pacific Ocean.

"Sixty-two, sixty-three," counted Moreau. "There are four more."

"I do not see the Leopard-man," said I.

Presently Moreau sounded the great horn again, and at the sound of it all the Beast People writhed and grovelled in the dust. Then, slinking out of the canebrake, stooping near the ground and trying to join the dust-throwing circle behind Moreau's back, came the Leopard-man. The last of the Beast People to arrive was the little Ape-man. The earlier animals, hot and weary with their grovelling, shot vicious glances at him.

"Cease!" said Moreau, in his firm, loud voice; and the Beast People sat back upon their hams and rested from their worshipping.

"Where is the Sayer of the Law?" said Moreau, and the hairy-grey monster bowed his face in the dust.

"Say the words!" said Moreau.

Forthwith all in the kneeling assembly, swaying from side to side and dashing up the sulphur with their hands—first the right hand and a puff of dust, and then the left—began once more to chant their strange litany. When they reached, "*Not to eat Flesh or Fish, that is the Law,*" Moreau held up his lank white hand.

"Stop!" he cried, and there fell absolute silence upon them all.

I think they all knew and dreaded what was coming. I looked round at their strange faces. When I saw their wincing attitudes and the furtive dread in their bright eyes, I wondered that I had ever believed them to be men.

"That Law has been broken!" said Moreau.

"None escape," from the faceless creature with the silvery hair. "None escape," repeated the kneeling circle of Beast People.

"Who is he?" cried Moreau, and looked round at their faces, cracking his whip. I fancied the Hyena-swine looked dejected, so too did the Leopard-man. Moreau stopped, facing this creature, who cringed towards him with the memory and dread of infinite torment.

"Who is he?" repeated Moreau, in a voice of thunder.

"Evil is he who breaks the Law," chanted the Sayer of the Law.

Moreau looked into the eyes of the Leopard-man, and seemed to be dragging the very soul out of the creature.

"Who breaks the Law—" said Moreau, taking his eyes off his victim, and turning towards us (it seemed to me there was a touch of exultation in his voice).

"Goes back to the House of Pain," they all clamoured—"goes back to the House of Pain, O Master!"

"Back to the House of Pain—back to the House of Pain," gabbled the Ape-man, as though the idea was sweet to him.

"Do you hear?" said Moreau, turning back to the criminal, "my friend—Hullo!"

For the Leopard-man, released from Moreau's eye, had risen straight from his knees, and now, with eyes aflame and his huge feline tusks flashing out from under his curling lips, leapt towards his tormentor. I am convinced that only the madness of unendurable fear could have prompted this attack. The whole circle of threescore monsters seemed to rise about us. I drew my revolver. The two figures collided. I saw Moreau reeling back from the Leopard-man's blow. There was a furious yelling and howling all about us. Everyone was moving rapidly. For a moment I thought it was a general revolt.

The furious face of the Leopard-man flashed by mine, with M'ling close in pursuit. I saw the yellow eyes of the Hyena-swine blazing with excitement, his attitude as if he were half resolved to attack me. The Satyr, too, glared at me over the Hyena-swine's hunched shoulders. I heard the crack of Moreau's pistol, and saw the pink flash dart across the tumult. The whole crowd seemed to swing round in the direction of the glint of fire, and I too was swung round by the magnetism of the movement. In another second, I was running, one of a tumultuous shouting crowd, in pursuit of the escaping Leopard-man.

That is all I can tell definitely. I saw the Leopard-man strike Moreau, and then everything spun about me until I was running headlong. M'ling was ahead, close in pursuit of the fugitive. Behind, their tongues already lolling out, ran the Wolf-women in great leaping strides. The Swine folk followed, squealing with excitement, and the two Bull-men in their swathings of white. Then came Moreau in a cluster of the Beast People, his wide-brimmed straw hat blown off, his revolver in hand, and his lank white hair streaming out. The Hyena-swine ran beside me, keeping pace with me and glancing furtively at me out of his feline eyes, and the others came pattering and shouting behind us.

The Leopard-man went bursting his way through the long canes, which sprang back as he passed, and rattled in M'ling's face. We others

in the rear found a trampled path for us when we reached the brake. The chase lay through the brake for perhaps a quarter of a mile, and then plunged into a dense thicket, which retarded our movements exceedingly, though we went through it in a crowd together—fronds flicking into our faces, ropy creepers catching us under the chin or gripping our ankles, thorny plants hooking into and tearing cloth and flesh together.

"He has gone on all-fours through this," panted Moreau, now just ahead of me.

"None escape," said the Wolf-bear, laughing into my face with the exultation of hunting. We burst out again among rocks, and saw the quarry ahead running lightly on all-fours and snarling at us over his shoulder. At that the Wolf Folk howled with delight. The Thing was still clothed, and at a distance its face still seemed human; but the carriage of its four limbs was feline, and the furtive droop of its shoulder was distinctly that of a hunted animal. It leapt over some thorny yellow-flowering bushes, and was hidden. M'ling was halfway across the space.

Most of us now had lost the first speed of the chase, and had fallen into a longer and steadier stride. I saw as we traversed the open that the pursuit was now spreading from a column into a line. The Hyena-swine still ran close to me, watching me as it ran, every now and then puckering its muzzle with a snarling laugh. At the edge of the rocks the Leopard-man, realising that he was making for the projecting cape upon which he had stalked me on the night of my arrival, had doubled in the undergrowth; but Montgomery had seen the manoeuvre, and turned him again. So, panting, tumbling against rocks, torn by brambles, impeded by ferns and reeds, I helped to pursue the Leopard-man who had broken the Law, and the Hyena-swine ran, laughing savagely, by my side. I staggered on, my head reeling and my heart beating against my ribs, tired almost to death, and yet not daring to lose sight of the chase lest I should be left alone with this horrible companion. I staggered on in spite of infinite fatigue and the dense heat of the tropical afternoon.

At last the fury of the hunt slackened. We had pinned the wretched brute into a corner of the island. Moreau, whip in hand, marshalled us all into an irregular line, and we advanced now slowly, shouting to one another as we advanced and tightening the cordon about our victim. He lurked noiseless and invisible in the bushes through which I had run from him during that midnight pursuit.

"Steady!" cried Moreau, "steady!" as the ends of the line crept round the tangle of undergrowth and hemmed the brute in.

"Ware a rush!" came the voice of Montgomery from beyond the thicket.

I was on the slope above the bushes; Montgomery and Moreau beat along the beach beneath. Slowly we pushed in among the fretted network of branches and leaves. The quarry was silent.

"Back to the House of Pain, the House of Pain, the House of Pain!" yelped the voice of the Ape-man, some twenty yards to the right.

When I heard that, I forgave the poor wretch all the fear he had inspired in me. I heard the twigs snap and the boughs swish aside before the heavy tread of the Horse-rhinoceros upon my right. Then suddenly through a polygon of green, in the half-darkness under the luxuriant growth, I saw the creature we were hunting. I halted. He was crouched together into the smallest possible compass, his luminous green eyes turned over his shoulder regarding me.

It may seem a strange contradiction in me—I cannot explain the fact—but now, seeing the creature there in a perfectly animal attitude, with the light gleaming in its eyes and its imperfectly human face distorted with terror, I realised again the fact of its humanity. In another moment other of its pursuers would see it, and it would be overpowered and captured, to experience once more the horrible tortures of the enclosure. Abruptly I slipped out my revolver, aimed between its terror-struck eyes, and fired. As I did so, the Hyena-swine saw the Thing, and flung itself upon it with an eager cry, thrusting thirsty teeth into its neck. All about me the green masses of the thicket were swaying and cracking as the Beast People came rushing together. One face and then another appeared.

"Don't kill it, Prendick!" cried Moreau. "Don't kill it!" and I saw him stooping as he pushed through under the fronds of the big ferns.

In another moment he had beaten off the Hyena-swine with the handle of his whip, and he and Montgomery were keeping away the excited carnivorous Beast People, and particularly M'ling, from the still quivering body. The hairy-grey Thing came sniffing at the corpse under my arm. The other animals, in their animal ardour, jostled me to get a nearer view.

"Confound you, Prendick!" said Moreau. "I wanted him."

"I'm sorry," said I, though I was not. "It was the impulse of the moment." I felt sick with exertion and excitement. Turning, I pushed my

way out of the crowding Beast People and went on alone up the slope towards the higher part of the headland. Under the shouted directions of Moreau, I heard the three white-swathed Bull-men begin dragging the victim down towards the water.

It was easy now for me to be alone. The Beast People manifested a quite human curiosity about the dead body, and followed it in a thick knot, sniffing and growling at it as the Bull-men dragged it down the beach. I went to the headland and watched the bull-men, black against the evening sky as they carried the weighted dead body out to sea; and like a wave across my mind came the realisation of the unspeakable aimlessness of things upon the island. Upon the beach among the rocks beneath me were the Ape-man, the Hyena-swine, and several other of the Beast People, standing about Montgomery and Moreau. They were all still intensely excited, and all overflowing with noisy expressions of their loyalty to the Law; yet I felt an absolute assurance in my own mind that the Hyena-swine was implicated in the rabbit-killing. A strange persuasion came upon me, that, save for the grossness of the line, the grotesqueness of the forms, I had here before me the whole balance of human life in miniature, the whole interplay of instinct, reason, and fate in its simplest form. The Leopard-man had happened to go under: that was all the difference. Poor brute!

Poor brutes! I began to see the viler aspect of Moreau's cruelty. I had not thought before of the pain and trouble that came to these poor victims after they had passed from Moreau's hands. I had shivered only at the days of actual torment in the enclosure. But now that seemed to me the lesser part. Before, they had been beasts, their instincts fitly adapted to their surroundings, and happy as living things may be. Now they stumbled in the shackles of humanity, lived in a fear that never died, fretted by a law they could not understand; their mock-human existence, begun in an agony, was one long internal struggle, one long dread of Moreau—and for what? It was the wantonness of it that stirred me.

Had Moreau had any intelligible object, I could have sympathised at least a little with him. I am not so squeamish about pain as that. I could have forgiven him a little even, had his motive been only hate. But he was so irresponsible, so utterly careless! His curiosity, his mad, aimless investigations, drove him on; and the Things were thrown out to live a year or so, to struggle and blunder and suffer, and at last to die painfully. They were wretched in themselves; the old animal hate moved them to trouble one another; the Law held them back from a

brief hot struggle and a decisive end to their natural animosities.

In those days my fear of the Beast People went the way of my personal fear for Moreau. I fell indeed into a morbid state, deep and enduring, and alien to fear, which has left permanent scars upon my mind. I must confess that I lost faith in the sanity of the world when I saw it suffering the painful disorder of this island. A blind Fate, a vast pitiless mechanism, seemed to cut and shape the fabric of existence and I, Moreau (by his passion for research), Montgomery (by his passion for drink), the Beast People with their instincts and mental restrictions, were torn and crushed, ruthlessly, inevitably, amid the infinite complexity of its incessant wheels. But this condition did not come all at once: I think indeed that I anticipate a little in speaking of it now.

CHAPTER 17

A Catastrophe

Scarcely six weeks passed before I had lost every feeling but dislike and abhorrence for this infamous experiment of Moreau's. My one idea was to get away from these horrible caricatures of my Maker's image, back to the sweet and wholesome intercourse of men. My fellow-creatures, from whom I was thus separated, began to assume idyllic virtue and beauty in my memory. My first friendship with Montgomery did not increase. His long separation from humanity, his secret vice of drunkenness, his evident sympathy with the Beast People, tainted him to me.

Several times I let him go alone among them. I avoided intercourse with them in every possible way. I spent an increasing proportion of my time upon the beach, looking for some liberating sail that never appeared—until one day there fell upon us an appalling disaster, which put an altogether different aspect upon my strange surroundings.

It was about seven or eight weeks after my landing—rather more, I think, though I had not troubled to keep account of the time,—when this catastrophe occurred. It happened in the early morning—I should think about six. I had risen and breakfasted early, having been aroused by the noise of three Beast Men carrying wood into the enclosure.

After breakfast I went to the open gateway of the enclosure, and stood there smoking a cigarette and enjoying the freshness of the early morning. Moreau presently came round the corner of the enclosure and greeted me. He passed by me, and I heard him behind me unlock and enter his laboratory. So indurated was I at that time to the

abomination of the place, that I heard without a touch of emotion the puma victim begin another day of torture. It met its persecutor with a shriek, almost exactly like that of an angry *virago*.

Then suddenly something happened—I do not know what, to this day. I heard a short, sharp cry behind me, a fall, and turning saw an awful face rushing upon me—not human, not animal, but hellish, brown, seamed with red branching scars, red drops starting out upon it, and the lidless eyes ablaze. I threw up my arm to defend myself from the blow that flung me headlong with a broken forearm; and the great monster, swathed in lint and with red-stained bandages fluttering about it, leapt over me and passed. I rolled over and over down the beach, tried to sit up, and collapsed upon my broken arm. Then Moreau appeared, his massive white face all the more terrible for the blood that trickled from his forehead. He carried a revolver in one hand. He scarcely glanced at me, but rushed off at once in pursuit of the puma.

I tried the other arm and sat up. The muffled figure in front ran in great striding leaps along the beach, and Moreau followed her. She turned her head and saw him, then doubling abruptly made for the bushes. She gained upon him at every stride. I saw her plunge into them, and Moreau, running slantingly to intercept her, fired and missed as she disappeared. Then he too vanished in the green confusion. I stared after them, and then the pain in my arm flamed up, and with a groan I staggered to my feet. Montgomery appeared in the doorway, dressed, and with his revolver in his hand.

"Great God, Prendick!" he said, not noticing that I was hurt, "that brute's loose! Tore the fetter out of the wall! Have you seen them?" Then sharply, seeing I gripped my arm, "What's the matter?"

"I was standing in the doorway," said I.

He came forward and took my arm. "Blood on the sleeve," said he, and rolled back the flannel. He pocketed his weapon, felt my arm about painfully, and led me inside. "Your arm is broken," he said, and then, "Tell me exactly how it happened—what happened?"

I told him what I had seen; told him in broken sentences, with gasps of pain between them, and very dexterously and swiftly he bound my arm meanwhile. He slung it from my shoulder, stood back and looked at me.

"You'll do," he said. "And now?"

He thought. Then he went out and locked the gates of the enclosure. He was absent some time.

I was chiefly concerned about my arm. The incident seemed merely one more of many horrible things. I sat down in the deck chair, and I must admit swore heartily at the island. The first dull feeling of injury in my arm had already given way to a burning pain when Montgomery reappeared. His face was rather pale, and he showed more of his lower gums than ever.

"I can neither see nor hear anything of him," he said. "I've been thinking he may want my help." He stared at me with his expressionless eyes. "That was a strong brute," he said. "It simply wrenched its fetter out of the wall." He went to the window, then to the door, and there turned to me. "I shall go after him," he said. "There's another revolver I can leave with you. To tell you the truth, I feel anxious somehow."

He obtained the weapon, and put it ready to my hand on the table; then went out, leaving a restless contagion in the air. I did not sit long after he left, but took the revolver in hand and went to the doorway.

The morning was as still as death. Not a whisper of wind was stirring; the sea was like polished glass, the sky empty, the beach desolate. In my half-excited, half-feverish state, this stillness of things oppressed me. I tried to whistle, and the tune died away. I swore again—the second time that morning. Then I went to the corner of the enclosure and stared inland at the green bush that had swallowed up Moreau and Montgomery. When would they return, and how? Then far away up the beach a little grey Beast Man appeared, ran down to the water's edge and began splashing about.

I strolled back to the doorway, then to the corner again, and so began pacing to and fro like a sentinel upon duty. Once I was arrested by the distant voice of Montgomery bawling, "Coo-ee—Moreau!" My arm became less painful, but very hot. I got feverish and thirsty. My shadow grew shorter. I watched the distant figure until it went away again. Would Moreau and Montgomery never return? Three sea-birds began fighting for some stranded treasure.

Then from far away behind the enclosure I heard a pistol-shot. A long silence, and then came another. Then a yelling cry nearer, and another dismal gap of silence. My unfortunate imagination set to work to torment me. Then suddenly a shot close by. I went to the corner, startled, and saw Montgomery—his face scarlet, his hair disordered, and the knee of his trousers torn. His face expressed profound consternation. Behind him slouched the Beast Man, M'ling, and round M'ling's jaws were some queer dark stains.

"Has he come?" said Montgomery.

"Moreau?" said I. "No."

"My God!" The man was panting, almost sobbing. "Go back in," he said, taking my arm. "They're mad. They're all rushing about mad. What can have happened? I don't know. I'll tell you, when my breath comes. Where's some brandy?"

Montgomery limped before me into the room and sat down in the deck chair. M'ling flung himself down just outside the doorway and began panting like a dog. I got Montgomery some brandy-and-water. He sat staring in front of him at nothing, recovering his breath. After some minutes he began to tell me what had happened.

He had followed their track for some way. It was plain enough at first on account of the crushed and broken bushes, white rags torn from the puma's bandages, and occasional smears of blood on the leaves of the shrubs and undergrowth. He lost the track, however, on the stony ground beyond the stream where I had seen the Beast Man drinking, and went wandering aimlessly westward shouting Moreau's name. Then M'ling had come to him carrying a light hatchet. M'ling had seen nothing of the puma affair; had been felling wood, and heard him calling. They went on shouting together. Two Beast Men came crouching and peering at them through the undergrowth, with gestures and a furtive carriage that alarmed Montgomery by their strangeness. He hailed them, and they fled guiltily. He stopped shouting after that, and after wandering some time farther in an undecided way, determined to visit the huts.

He found the ravine deserted.

Growing more alarmed every minute, he began to retrace his steps. Then it was he encountered the two Swine-men I had seen dancing on the night of my arrival; bloodstained they were about the mouth, and intensely excited. They came crashing through the ferns, and stopped with fierce faces when they saw him. He cracked his whip in some trepidation, and forthwith they rushed at him. Never before had a Beast Man dared to do that. One he shot through the head; M'ling flung himself upon the other, and the two rolled grappling. M'ling got his brute under and with his teeth in its throat, and Montgomery shot that too as it struggled in M'ling's grip.

He had some difficulty in inducing M'ling to come on with him. Thence they had hurried back to me. On the way, M'ling had suddenly rushed into a thicket and driven out an under-sized Ocelot-man, also blood-stained, and lame through a wound in the foot. This brute

260

had run a little way and then turned savagely at bay, and Montgomery—with a certain wantonness, I thought—had shot him.

"What does it all mean?" said I.

He shook his head, and turned once more to the brandy.

CHAPTER 18

The Finding of Moreau

When I saw Montgomery swallow a third dose of brandy, I took it upon myself to interfere. He was already more than half fuddled. I told him that some serious thing must have happened to Moreau by this time, or he would have returned before this, and that it behoved us to ascertain what that catastrophe was. Montgomery raised some feeble objections, and at last agreed. We had some food, and then all three of us started.

It is possibly due to the tension of my mind, at the time, but even now that start into the hot stillness of the tropical afternoon is a singularly vivid impression. M'ling went first, his shoulder hunched, his strange black head moving with quick starts as he peered first on this side of the way and then on that. He was unarmed; his axe he had dropped when he encountered the Swine-man. Teeth were *his* weapons, when it came to fighting. Montgomery followed with stumbling footsteps, his hands in his pockets, his face downcast; he was in a state of muddled sullenness with me on account of the brandy.

My left arm was in a sling (it was lucky it was my left), and I carried my revolver in my right. Soon we traced a narrow path through the wild luxuriance of the island, going north-westward; and presently M'ling stopped, and became rigid with watchfulness. Montgomery almost staggered into him, and then stopped too. Then, listening intently, we heard coming through the trees the sound of voices and footsteps approaching us.

"He is dead," said a deep, vibrating voice.

"He is not dead; he is not dead," jabbered another.

"We saw, we saw," said several voices.

"Hullo!" suddenly shouted Montgomery, "Hullo, there!"

"Confound you!" said I, and gripped my pistol.

There was a silence, then a crashing among the interlacing vegetation, first here, then there, and then half-a-dozen faces appeared—strange faces, lit by a strange light. M'ling made a growling noise in his throat. I recognised the Ape-man: I had indeed already identified his voice, and two of the white-swathed brown-featured creatures I

261

had seen in Montgomery's boat. With these were the two dappled brutes and that grey, horribly crooked creature who said the Law, with grey hair streaming down its cheeks, heavy grey eyebrows, and grey locks pouring off from a central parting upon its sloping forehead,— a heavy, faceless thing, with strange red eyes, looking at us curiously from amidst the green.

For a space no one spoke. Then Montgomery hiccoughed, "Who—said he was dead?"

The Monkey-man looked guiltily at the hairy-grey Thing. "He is dead," said this monster. "They saw."

There was nothing threatening about this detachment, at any rate. They seemed awestricken and puzzled.

"Where is he?" said Montgomery.

"Beyond," and the grey creature pointed.

"Is there a Law now?" asked the Monkey-man. "Is it still to be this and that? Is he dead indeed?"

"Is there a Law?" repeated the man in white. "Is there a Law, thou Other with the Whip?"

"He is dead," said the hairy-grey Thing. And they all stood watching us.

"Prendick," said Montgomery, turning his dull eyes to me. "He's dead, evidently."

I had been standing behind him during this colloquy. I began to see how things lay with them. I suddenly stepped in front of Montgomery and lifted up my voice:—"Children of the Law," I said, "he is *not* dead!" M'ling turned his sharp eyes on me. "He has changed his shape; he has changed his body," I went on. "For a time, you will not see him. He is—there," I pointed upward, "where he can watch you. You cannot see him, but he can see you. Fear the Law!"

I looked at them squarely. They flinched.

"He is great, he is good," said the Ape-man, peering fearfully upward among the dense trees.

"And the other Thing?" I demanded.

"The Thing that bled, and ran screaming and sobbing—that is dead too," said the grey Thing, still regarding me.

"That's well," grunted Montgomery.

"The Other with the Whip—" began the grey Thing.

"Well?" said I.

"Said he was dead."

But Montgomery was still sober enough to understand my motive

in denying Moreau's death. "He is not dead," he said slowly, "not dead at all. No more dead than I am."

"Some," said I, "have broken the Law: they will die. Some have died. Show us now where his old body lies—the body he cast away because he had no more need of it."

"It is this way, Man who walked in the Sea," said the grey Thing.

And with these six creatures guiding us, we went through the tumult of ferns and creepers and tree-stems towards the northwest. Then came a yelling, a crashing among the branches, and a little pink homunculus rushed by us shrieking. Immediately after appeared a monster in headlong pursuit, blood-bedabbled, who was amongst us almost before he could stop his career. The grey Thing leapt aside. M'ling, with a snarl, flew at it, and was struck aside. Montgomery fired and missed, bowed his head, threw up his arm, and turned to run. I fired, and the Thing still came on; fired again, point-blank, into its ugly face. I saw its features vanish in a flash: its face was driven in. Yet it passed me, gripped Montgomery, and holding him, fell headlong beside him and pulled him sprawling upon itself in its death-agony.

I found myself alone with M'ling, the dead brute, and the prostrate man. Montgomery raised himself slowly and stared in a muddled way at the shattered Beast Man beside him. It more than half sobered him. He scrambled to his feet. Then I saw the grey Thing returning cautiously through the trees.

"See," said I, pointing to the dead brute, "is the Law not alive? This came of breaking the Law."

He peered at the body. "He sends the Fire that kills," said he, in his deep voice, repeating part of the Ritual. The others gathered round and stared for a space.

At last we drew near the westward extremity of the island. We came upon the gnawed and mutilated body of the puma, its shoulder-bone smashed by a bullet, and perhaps twenty yards farther found at last what we sought. Moreau lay face downward in a trampled space in a canebrake. One hand was almost severed at the wrist and his silvery hair was dabbled in blood. His head had been battered in by the fetters of the puma. The broken canes beneath him were smeared with blood. His revolver we could not find. Montgomery turned him over.

Resting at intervals, and with the help of the seven Beast People (for he was a heavy man), we carried Moreau back to the enclosure. The night was darkling. Twice we heard unseen creatures howling and shrieking past our little band, and once the little pink sloth-crea-

ture appeared and stared at us, and vanished again. But we were not attacked again. At the gates of the enclosure our company of Beast People left us, M'ling going with the rest. We locked ourselves in, and then took Moreau's mangled body into the yard and laid it upon a pile of brushwood. Then we went into the laboratory and put an end to all we found living there.

Chapter 19
Montgomery's "Bank Holiday"

When this was accomplished, and we had washed and eaten, Montgomery and I went into my little room and seriously discussed our position for the first time. It was then near midnight. He was almost sober, but greatly disturbed in his mind. He had been strangely under the influence of Moreau's personality: I do not think it had ever occurred to him that Moreau could die. This disaster was the sudden collapse of the habits that had become part of his nature in the ten or more monotonous years he had spent on the island. He talked vaguely, answered my questions crookedly, wandered into general questions.

"This silly ass of a world," he said; "what a muddle it all is! I haven't had any life. I wonder when it's going to begin. Sixteen years being bullied by nurses and schoolmasters at their own sweet will; five in London grinding hard at medicine, bad food, shabby lodgings, shabby clothes, shabby vice, a blunder—I didn't know any better—and hustled off to this beastly island. Ten years here! What's it all for, Prendick? Are we bubbles blown by a baby?"

It was hard to deal with such ravings. "The thing we have to think of now," said I, "is how to get away from this island."

"What's the good of getting away? I'm an outcast. Where am *I* to join on? It's all very well for *you*, Prendick. Poor old Moreau! We can't leave him here to have his bones picked. As it is—And besides, what will become of the decent part of the Beast Folk?"

"Well," said I, "that will do tomorrow. I've been thinking we might make the brushwood into a pyre and burn his body—and those other things. Then what will happen with the Beast Folk?"

"*I* don't know. I suppose those that were made of beasts of prey will make silly asses of themselves sooner or later. We can't massacre the lot—can we? I suppose that's what *your* humanity would suggest? But they'll change. They are sure to change."

He talked thus inconclusively until at last I felt my temper going.

"Damnation!" he exclaimed at some petulance of mine; "can't you

see I'm in a worse hole than you are?" And he got up, and went for the brandy. "Drink!" he said returning, "you logic-chopping, chalky-faced saint of an atheist, drink!"

"Not I," said I, and sat grimly watching his face under the yellow paraffine flare, as he drank himself into a garrulous misery.

I have a memory of infinite tedium. He wandered into a maudlin defence of the Beast People and of M'ling. M'ling, he said, was the only thing that had ever really cared for him. And suddenly an idea came to him.

"I'm damned!" said he, staggering to his feet and clutching the brandy bottle.

By some flash of intuition, I knew what it was he intended. "You don't give drink to that beast!" I said, rising and facing him.

"Beast!" said he. "You're the beast. He takes his liquor like a Christian. Come out of the way, Prendick!"

"For God's sake," said I.

"Get—out of the way!" he roared, and suddenly whipped out his revolver.

"Very well," said I, and stood aside, half-minded to fall upon him as he put his hand upon the latch, but deterred by the thought of my useless arm. "You've made a beast of yourself—to the beasts you may go."

He flung the doorway open, and stood half facing me between the yellow lamp-light and the pallid glare of the moon; his eye-sockets were blotches of black under his stubbly eyebrows.

"You're a solemn prig, Prendick, a silly ass! You're always fearing and fancying. We're on the edge of things. I'm bound to cut my throat tomorrow. I'm going to have a damned Bank Holiday tonight." He turned and went out into the moonlight. "M'ling!" he cried; "M'ling, old friend!"

Three dim creatures in the silvery light came along the edge of the wan beach—one a white-wrapped creature, the other two blotches of blackness following it. They halted, staring. Then I saw M'ling's hunched shoulders as he came round the corner of the house.

"Drink!" cried Montgomery, "drink, you brutes! Drink and be men! Damme, I'm the cleverest. Moreau forgot this; this is the last touch. Drink, I tell you!" And waving the bottle in his hand he started off at a kind of quick trot to the westward, M'ling ranging himself between him and the three dim creatures who followed.

I went to the doorway. They were already indistinct in the mist

265

of the moonlight before Montgomery halted. I saw him administer a dose of the raw brandy to M'ling, and saw the five figures melt into one vague patch.

"Sing!" I heard Montgomery shout—"sing all together,'*Confound old Prendick!*'That's right; now again,'*Confound old Prendick!*'"

The black group broke up into five separate figures, and wound slowly away from me along the band of shining beach. Each went howling at his own sweet will, yelping insults at me, or giving whatever other vent this new inspiration of brandy demanded. Presently I heard Montgomery's voice shouting, "Right turn!" and they passed with their shouts and howls into the blackness of the landward trees. Slowly, very slowly, they receded into silence.

The peaceful splendour of the night healed again. The moon was now past the meridian and travelling down the west. It was at its full, and very bright riding through the empty blue sky. The shadow of the wall lay, a yard wide and of inky blackness, at my feet. The eastward sea was a featureless grey, dark and mysterious; and between the sea and the shadow the grey sands (of volcanic glass and crystals) flashed and shone like a beach of diamonds. Behind me the paraffine lamp flared hot and ruddy.

Then I shut the door, locked it, and went into the enclosure where Moreau lay beside his latest victims,—the staghounds and the llama and some other wretched brutes,—with his massive face calm even after his terrible death, and with the hard eyes open, staring at the dead white moon above. I sat down upon the edge of the sink, and with my eyes upon that ghastly pile of silvery light and ominous shadows began to turn over my plans. In the morning I would gather some provisions in the dingey, and after setting fire to the pyre before me, push out into the desolation of the high sea once more. I felt that for Montgomery there was no help; that he was, in truth, half akin to these Beast Folk, unfitted for human kindred.

I do not know how long I sat there scheming. It must have been an hour or so. Then my planning was interrupted by the return of Montgomery to my neighbourhood. I heard a yelling from many throats, a tumult of exultant cries passing down towards the beach, whooping and howling, and excited shrieks that seemed to come to a stop near the water's edge. The riot rose and fell; I heard heavy blows and the splintering smash of wood, but it did not trouble me then. A discordant chanting began.

My thoughts went back to my means of escape. I got up, brought

the lamp, and went into a shed to look at some kegs I had seen there. Then I became interested in the contents of some biscuit-tins, and opened one. I saw something out of the tail of my eye—a red figure—and turned sharply.

Behind me lay the yard, vividly black-and-white in the moonlight, and the pile of wood and faggots on which Moreau and his mutilated victims lay, one over another. They seemed to be gripping one another in one last revengeful grapple. His wounds gaped, black as night, and the blood that had dripped lay in black patches upon the sand. Then I saw, without understanding, the cause of my phantom—a ruddy glow that came and danced and went upon the wall opposite. I misinterpreted this, fancied it was a reflection of my flickering lamp, and turned again to the stores in the shed. I went on rummaging among them, as well as a one-armed man could, finding this convenient thing and that, and putting them aside for tomorrow's launch. My movements were slow, and the time passed quickly. Insensibly the daylight crept upon me.

The chanting died down, giving place to a clamour; then it began again, and suddenly broke into a tumult. I heard cries of, "More! more!" a sound like quarrelling, and a sudden wild shriek. The quality of the sounds changed so greatly that it arrested my attention. I went out into the yard and listened. Then cutting like a knife across the confusion came the crack of a revolver.

I rushed at once through my room to the little doorway. As I did so I heard some of the packing-cases behind me go sliding down and smash together with a clatter of glass on the floor of the shed. But I did not heed these. I flung the door open and looked out.

Up the beach by the boathouse a bonfire was burning, raining up sparks into the indistinctness of the dawn. Around this struggled a mass of black figures. I heard Montgomery call my name. I began to run at once towards this fire, revolver in hand. I saw the pink tongue of Montgomery's pistol lick out once, close to the ground. He was down. I shouted with all my strength and fired into the air. I heard someone cry, "The Master!" The knotted black struggle broke into scattering units, the fire leapt and sank down. The crowd of Beast People fled in sudden panic before me, up the beach. In my excitement I fired at their retreating backs as they disappeared among the bushes. Then I turned to the black heaps upon the ground.

Montgomery lay on his back, with the hairy-grey Beast-man sprawling across his body. The brute was dead, but still gripping Mont-

267

gomery's throat with its curving claws. Nearby lay M'ling on his face and quite still, his neck bitten open and the upper part of the smashed brandy-bottle in his hand. Two other figures lay near the fire—the one motionless, the other groaning fitfully, every now and then raising its head slowly, then dropping it again.

I caught hold of the grey man and pulled him off Montgomery's body; his claws drew down the torn coat reluctantly as I dragged him away. Montgomery was dark in the face and scarcely breathing. I splashed sea-water on his face and pillowed his head on my rolled-up coat. M'ling was dead. The wounded creature by the fire—it was a Wolf-brute with a bearded grey face—lay, I found, with the fore part of its body upon the still glowing timber. The wretched thing was injured so dreadfully that in mercy I blew its brains out at once. The other brute was one of the Bull-men swathed in white. He too was dead. The rest of the Beast People had vanished from the beach.

I went to Montgomery again and knelt beside him, cursing my ignorance of medicine. The fire beside me had sunk down, and only charred beams of timber glowing at the central ends and mixed with a grey ash of brushwood remained. I wondered casually where Montgomery had got his wood. Then I saw that the dawn was upon us. The sky had grown brighter, the setting moon was becoming pale and opaque in the luminous blue of the day. The sky to the eastward was rimmed with red.

Suddenly I heard a thud and a hissing behind me, and, looking round, sprang to my feet with a cry of horror. Against the warm dawn great tumultuous masses of black smoke were boiling up out of the enclosure, and through their stormy darkness shot flickering threads of blood-red flame. Then the thatched roof caught. I saw the curving charge of the flames across the sloping straw. A spurt of fire jetted from the window of my room.

I knew at once what had happened. I remembered the crash I had heard. When I had rushed out to Montgomery's assistance, I had overturned the lamp.

The hopelessness of saving any of the contents of the enclosure stared me in the face. My mind came back to my plan of flight, and turning swiftly I looked to see where the two boats lay upon the beach. They were gone! Two axes lay upon the sands beside me; chips and splinters were scattered broadcast, and the ashes of the bonfire were blackening and smoking under the dawn. Montgomery had burnt the boats to revenge himself upon me and prevent our return

to mankind!

A sudden convulsion of rage shook me. I was almost moved to batter his foolish head in, as he lay there helpless at my feet. Then suddenly his hand moved, so feebly, so pitifully, that my wrath vanished. He groaned, and opened his eyes for a minute. I knelt down beside him and raised his head. He opened his eyes again, staring silently at the dawn, and then they met mine. The lids fell.

"Sorry," he said presently, with an effort. He seemed trying to think. "The last," he murmured, "the last of this silly universe. What a mess—"

I listened. His head fell helplessly to one side. I thought some drink might revive him; but there was neither drink nor vessel in which to bring drink at hand. He seemed suddenly heavier. My heart went cold. I bent down to his face, put my hand through the rent in his blouse. He was dead; and even as he died a line of white heat, the limb of the sun, rose eastward beyond the projection of the bay, splashing its radiance across the sky and turning the dark sea into a weltering tumult of dazzling light. It fell like a glory upon his death-shrunken face.

I let his head fall gently upon the rough pillow I had made for him, and stood up. Before me was the glittering desolation of the sea, the awful solitude upon which I had already suffered so much; behind me the island, hushed under the dawn, its Beast People silent and unseen. The enclosure, with all its provisions and ammunition, burnt noisily, with sudden gusts of flame, a fitful crackling, and now and then a crash. The heavy smoke drove up the beach away from me, rolling low over the distant tree-tops towards the huts in the ravine. Beside me were the charred vestiges of the boats and these five dead bodies.

Then out of the bushes came three Beast People, with hunched shoulders, protruding heads, misshapen hands awkwardly held, and inquisitive, unfriendly eyes and advanced towards me with hesitating gestures.

Chapter 20
Alone with the Beast Folk

I faced these people, facing my fate in them, single-handed now— literally single-handed, for I had a broken arm. In my pocket was a revolver with two empty chambers. Among the chips scattered about the beach lay the two axes that had been used to chop up the boats. The tide was creeping in behind me. There was nothing for it but courage. I looked squarely into the faces of the advancing monsters.

They avoided my eyes, and their quivering nostrils investigated the bodies that lay beyond me on the beach. I took half-a-dozen steps, picked up the bloodstained whip that lay beneath the body of the Wolf-man, and cracked it. They stopped and stared at me.

"Salute!" said I. "Bow down!"

They hesitated. One bent his knees. I repeated my command, with my heart in my mouth, and advanced upon them. One knelt, then the other two.

I turned and walked towards the dead bodies, keeping my face towards the three kneeling Beast Men, very much as an actor passing up the stage faces the audience.

"They broke the Law," said I, putting my foot on the Sayer of the Law. "They have been slain—even the Sayer of the Law; even the Other with the Whip. Great is the Law! Come and see."

"None escape," said one of them, advancing and peering.

"None escape," said I. "Therefore, hear and do as I command." They stood up, looking questioningly at one another.

"Stand there," said I.

I picked up the hatchets and swung them by their heads from the sling of my arm; turned Montgomery over; picked up his revolver still loaded in two chambers, and bending down to rummage, found half-a-dozen cartridges in his pocket.

"Take him," said I, standing up again and pointing with the whip; "take him, and carry him out and cast him into the sea."

They came forward, evidently still afraid of Montgomery, but still more afraid of my cracking red whip-lash; and after some fumbling and hesitation, some whip-cracking and shouting, they lifted him gingerly, carried him down to the beach, and went splashing into the dazzling welter of the sea.

"On!" said I, "on! Carry him far."

They went in up to their armpits and stood regarding me.

"Let go," said I; and the body of Montgomery vanished with a splash. Something seemed to tighten across my chest.

"Good!" said I, with a break in my voice; and they came back, hurrying and fearful, to the margin of the water, leaving long wakes of black in the silver. At the water's edge they stopped, turning and glaring into the sea as though they presently expected Montgomery to arise therefrom and exact vengeance.

"Now these," said I, pointing to the other bodies.

They took care not to approach the place where they had thrown

Montgomery into the water, but instead, carried the four dead Beast People slantingly along the beach for perhaps a hundred yards before they waded out and cast them away.

As I watched them disposing of the mangled remains of M'ling, I heard a light footfall behind me, and turning quickly saw the big Hyena-swine perhaps a dozen yards away. His head was bent down, his bright eyes were fixed upon me, his stumpy hands clenched and held close by his side. He stopped in this crouching attitude when I turned, his eyes a little averted.

For a moment we stood eye to eye. I dropped the whip and snatched at the pistol in my pocket; for I meant to kill this brute, the most formidable of any left now upon the island, at the first excuse. It may seem treacherous, but so I was resolved. I was far more afraid of him than of any other two of the Beast Folk. His continued life was I knew a threat against mine.

I was perhaps a dozen seconds collecting myself. Then cried I, "Salute! Bow down!"

His teeth flashed upon me in a snarl. "Who are *you* that I should—"

Perhaps a little too spasmodically I drew my revolver, aimed quickly and fired. I heard him yelp, saw him run sideways and turn, knew I had missed, and clicked back the cock with my thumb for the next shot. But he was already running headlong, jumping from side to side, and I dared not risk another miss. Every now and then he looked back at me over his shoulder. He went slanting along the beach, and vanished beneath the driving masses of dense smoke that were still pouring out from the burning enclosure. For some time, I stood staring after him. I turned to my three obedient Beast Folk again and signalled them to drop the body they still carried. Then I went back to the place by the fire where the bodies had fallen and kicked the sand until all the brown blood-stains were absorbed and hidden.

I dismissed my three serfs with a wave of the hand, and went up the beach into the thickets. I carried my pistol in my hand, my whip thrust with the hatchets in the sling of my arm. I was anxious to be alone, to think out the position in which I was now placed. A dreadful thing that I was only beginning to realise was, that over all this island there was now no safe place where I could be alone and secure to rest or sleep. I had recovered strength amazingly since my landing, but I was still inclined to be nervous and to break down under any great stress.

I felt that I ought to cross the island and establish myself with

the Beast People, and make myself secure in their confidence. But my heart failed me. I went back to the beach, and turning eastward past the burning enclosure, made for a point where a shallow spit of coral sand ran out towards the reef. Here I could sit down and think, my back to the sea and my face against any surprise. And there I sat, chin on knees, the sun beating down upon my head and unspeakable dread in my mind, plotting how I could live on against the hour of my rescue (if ever rescue came). I tried to review the whole situation as calmly as I could, but it was difficult to clear the thing of emotion.

I began turning over in my mind the reason of Montgomery's despair. "They will change," he said; "they are sure to change." And Moreau, what was it that Moreau had said? "The stubborn beast-flesh grows day by day back again." Then I came round to the Hyena-swine. I felt sure that if I did not kill that brute, he would kill me. The Sayer of the Law was dead: worse luck. They knew now that we of the Whips could be killed even as they themselves were killed. Were they peering at me already out of the green masses of ferns and palms over yonder, watching until I came within their spring? Were they plotting against me? What was the Hyena-swine telling them? My imagination was running away with me into a morass of unsubstantial fears.

My thoughts were disturbed by a crying of sea-birds hurrying towards some black object that had been stranded by the waves on the beach near the enclosure. I knew what that object was, but I had not the heart to go back and drive them off. I began walking along the beach in the opposite direction, designing to come round the eastward corner of the island and so approach the ravine of the huts, without traversing the possible ambuscades of the thickets.

Perhaps half a mile along the beach I became aware of one of my three Beast Folk advancing out of the landward bushes towards me. I was now so nervous with my own imaginings that I immediately drew my revolver. Even the propitiatory gestures of the creature failed to disarm me. He hesitated as he approached.

"Go away!" cried I.

There was something very suggestive of a dog in the cringing attitude of the creature. It retreated a little way, very like a dog being sent home, and stopped, looking at me imploringly with canine brown eyes.

"Go away," said I. "Do not come near me."

"May I not come near you?" it said.

"No; go away," I insisted, and snapped my whip. Then putting my

whip in my teeth, I stooped for a stone, and with that threat drove the creature away.

So in solitude I came round by the ravine of the Beast People, and hiding among the weeds and reeds that separated this crevice from the sea I watched such of them as appeared, trying to judge from their gestures and appearance how the death of Moreau and Montgomery and the destruction of the House of Pain had affected them. I know now the folly of my cowardice. Had I kept my courage up to the level of the dawn, had I not allowed it to ebb away in solitary thought, I might have grasped the vacant sceptre of Moreau and ruled over the Beast People. As it was, I lost the opportunity, and sank to the position of a mere leader among my fellows.

Towards noon certain of them came and squatted basking in the hot sand. The imperious voices of hunger and thirst prevailed over my dread. I came out of the bushes, and, revolver in hand, walked down towards these seated figures. One, a Wolf-woman, turned her head and stared at me, and then the others. None attempted to rise or salute me. I felt too faint and weary to insist, and I let the moment pass.

"I want food," said I, almost apologetically, and drawing near.

"There is food in the huts," said an Ox-boar-man, drowsily, and looking away from me.

I passed them, and went down into the shadow and odours of the almost deserted ravine. In an empty hut I feasted on some specked and half-decayed fruit; and then after I had propped some branches and sticks about the opening, and placed myself with my face towards it and my hand upon my revolver, the exhaustion of the last thirty hours claimed its own, and I fell into a light slumber, hoping that the flimsy barricade I had erected would cause sufficient noise in its removal to save me from surprise.

CHAPTER 21

The Reversion of the Beast Folk

In this way I became one among the Beast People in the Island of Doctor Moreau. When I awoke, it was dark about me. My arm ached in its bandages. I sat up, wondering at first where I might be. I heard coarse voices talking outside. Then I saw that my barricade had gone, and that the opening of the hut stood clear. My revolver was still in my hand.

I heard something breathing, saw something crouched together close beside me. I held my breath, trying to see what it was. It be-

gan to move slowly, interminably. Then something soft and warm and moist passed across my hand. All my muscles contracted. I snatched my hand away. A cry of alarm began and was stifled in my throat. Then I just realised what had happened sufficiently to stay my fingers on the revolver.

"Who is that?" I said in a hoarse whisper, the revolver still pointed.

"I—Master."

"Who are you?"

"They say there is no Master now. But I know, I know. I carried the bodies into the sea, O Walker in the Sea! the bodies of those you slew. I am your slave, Master."

"Are you the one I met on the beach?" I asked.

"The same, Master."

The Thing was evidently faithful enough, for it might have fallen upon me as I slept. "It is well," I said, extending my hand for another licking kiss. I began to realise what its presence meant, and the tide of my courage flowed. "Where are the others?" I asked.

"They are mad; they are fools," said the Dog-man. "Even now they talk together beyond there. They say, 'The Master is dead. The Other with the Whip is dead. That Other who walked in the Sea is as we are. We have no Master, no Whips, no House of Pain, any more. There is an end. We love the Law, and will keep it; but there is no Pain, no Master, no Whips for ever again.' So, they say. But I know, Master, I know."

I felt in the darkness, and patted the Dog-man's head. "It is well," I said again.

"Presently you will slay them all," said the Dog-man.

"Presently," I answered, "I will slay them all—after certain days and certain things have come to pass. Every one of them save those you spare, every one of them shall be slain."

"What the Master wishes to kill, the Master kills," said the Dog-man with a certain satisfaction in his voice.

"And that their sins may grow," I said, "let them live in their folly until their time is ripe. Let them not know that I am the Master."

"The Master's will is sweet," said the Dog-man, with the ready tact of his canine blood.

"But one has sinned," said I. "Him I will kill, whenever I may meet him. When I say to you, 'That is he,' see that you fall upon him. And now I will go to the men and women who are assembled together."

For a moment the opening of the hut was blackened by the exit of the Dog-man. Then I followed and stood up, almost in the exact spot

where I had been when I had heard Moreau and his staghound pursuing me. But now it was night, and all the miasmatic ravine about me was black; and beyond, instead of a green, sunlit slope, I saw a red fire, before which hunched, grotesque figures moved to and fro. Farther were the thick trees, a bank of darkness, fringed above with the black lace of the upper branches. The moon was just riding up on the edge of the ravine, and like a bar across its face drove the spire of vapour that was for ever streaming from the fumaroles of the island.

"Walk by me," said I, nerving myself; and side by side we walked down the narrow way, taking little heed of the dim Things that peered at us out of the huts.

None about the fire attempted to salute me. Most of them disregarded me, ostentatiously. I looked round for the Hyena-swine, but he was not there. Altogether, perhaps twenty of the Beast Folk squatted, staring into the fire or talking to one another.

"He is dead, he is dead! the Master is dead!" said the voice of the Ape-man to the right of me. "The House of Pain—there is no House of Pain!"

"He is not dead," said I, in a loud voice. "Even now he watches us!"

This startled them. Twenty pairs of eyes regarded me.

"The House of Pain is gone," said I. "It will come again. The Master you cannot see; yet even now he listens among you."

"True, true!" said the Dog-man.

They were staggered at my assurance. An animal may be ferocious and cunning enough, but it takes a real man to tell a lie.

"The Man with the Bandaged Arm speaks a strange thing," said one of the Beast Folk.

"I tell you it is so," I said. "The Master and the House of Pain will come again. Woe be to him who breaks the Law!"

They looked curiously at one another. With an affectation of indifference, I began to chop idly at the ground in front of me with my hatchet. They looked, I noticed, at the deep cuts I made in the turf.

Then the Satyr raised a doubt. I answered him. Then one of the dappled things objected, and an animated discussion sprang up round the fire. Every moment I began to feel more convinced of my present security. I talked now without the catching in my breath, due to the intensity of my excitement, that had troubled me at first. In the course of about an hour I had really convinced several of the Beast Folk of the truth of my assertions, and talked most of the others into a dubious state. I kept a sharp eye for my enemy the Hyena-swine, but he

never appeared. Every now and then a suspicious movement would startle me, but my confidence grew rapidly. Then as the moon crept down from the zenith, one by one the listeners began to yawn (showing the oddest teeth in the light of the sinking fire), and first one and then another retired towards the dens in the ravine; and I, dreading the silence and darkness, went with them, knowing I was safer with several of them than with one alone.

In this manner began the longer part of my sojourn upon this Island of Doctor Moreau. But from that night until the end came, there was but one thing happened to tell save a series of innumerable small unpleasant details and the fretting of an incessant uneasiness. So that I prefer to make no chronicle for that gap of time, to tell only one cardinal incident of the ten months I spent as an intimate of these half-humanised brutes. There is much that sticks in my memory that I could write—things that I would cheerfully give my right hand to forget; but they do not help the telling of the story.

In the retrospect it is strange to remember how soon I fell in with these monsters' ways, and gained my confidence again. I had my quarrels with them of course, and could show some of their teeth-marks still; but they soon gained a wholesome respect for my trick of throwing stones and for the bite of my hatchet. And my Saint-Bernard-man's loyalty was of infinite service to me. I found their simple scale of honour was based mainly on the capacity for inflicting trenchant wounds. Indeed, I may say—without vanity, I hope—that I held something like pre-eminence among them. One or two, whom in a rare access of high spirits I had scarred rather badly, bore me a grudge; but it vented itself chiefly behind my back, and at a safe distance from my missiles, in grimaces.

The Hyena-swine avoided me, and I was always on the alert for him. My inseparable Dog-man hated and dreaded him intensely. I really believe that was at the root of the brute's attachment to me. It was soon evident to me that the former monster had tasted blood, and gone the way of the Leopard-man. He formed a lair somewhere in the forest, and became solitary. Once I tried to induce the Beast Folk to hunt him, but I lacked the authority to make them co-operate for one end. Again, and again I tried to approach his den and come upon him unaware; but always he was too acute for me, and saw or winded me and got away. He too made every forest pathway dangerous to me and my ally with his lurking ambuscades. The Dog-man scarcely dared to leave my side.

In the first month or so the Beast Folk, compared with their latter condition, were human enough, and for one or two besides my canine friend I even conceived a friendly tolerance. The little pink sloth-creature displayed an odd affection for me, and took to following me about. The Monkey-man bored me, however; he assumed, on the strength of his five digits, that he was my equal, and was for ever jabbering at me—jabbering the most arrant nonsense. One thing about him entertained me a little: he had a fantastic trick of coining new words. He had an idea, I believe, that to gabble about names that meant nothing was the proper use of speech. He called it "Big Thinks" to distinguish it from "Little Thinks," the sane every-day interests of life.

If ever I made a remark he did not understand, he would praise it very much, ask me to say it again, learn it by heart, and go off repeating it, with a word wrong here or there, to all the milder of the Beast People. He thought nothing of what was plain and comprehensible. I invented some very curious "Big Thinks" for his especial use. I think now that he was the silliest creature I ever met; he had developed in the most wonderful way the distinctive silliness of man without losing one jot of the natural folly of a monkey.

This, I say, was in the earlier weeks of my solitude among these brutes. During that time, they respected the usage established by the Law, and behaved with general decorum. Once I found another rabbit torn to pieces—by the Hyena-swine, I am assured—but that was all. It was about May when I first distinctly perceived a growing difference in their speech and carriage, a growing coarseness of articulation, a growing disinclination to talk. My Monkey-man's jabber multiplied in volume but grew less and less comprehensible, more and more simian.

Some of the others seemed altogether slipping their hold upon speech, though they still understood what I said to them at that time. (Can you imagine language, once clear-cut and exact, softening and guttering, losing shape and import, becoming mere lumps of sound again?) And they walked erect with an increasing difficulty. Though they evidently felt ashamed of themselves, every now and then I would come upon one or another running on toes and finger-tips, and quite unable to recover the vertical attitude. They held things more clumsily; drinking by suction, feeding by gnawing, grew commoner every day. I realised more keenly than ever what Moreau had told me about the "stubborn beast-flesh." They were reverting, and reverting very rapidly.

Some of them—the pioneers in this, I noticed with some surprise,

were all females—began to disregard the injunction of decency, deliberately for the most part. Others even attempted public outrages upon the institution of monogamy. The tradition of the Law was clearly losing its force. I cannot pursue this disagreeable subject.

My Dog-man imperceptibly slipped back to the dog again; day by day he became dumb, quadrupedal, hairy. I scarcely noticed the transition from the companion on my right hand to the lurching dog at my side.

As the carelessness and disorganisation increased from day to day, the lane of dwelling places, at no time very sweet, became so loathsome that I left it, and going across the island made myself a hovel of boughs amid the black ruins of Moreau's enclosure. Some memory of pain, I found, still made that place the safest from the Beast Folk.

It would be impossible to detail every step of the lapsing of these monsters,—to tell how, day by day, the human semblance left them; how they gave up bandagings and wrappings, abandoned at last every stitch of clothing; how the hair began to spread over the exposed limbs; how their foreheads fell away and their faces projected; how the quasi-human intimacy I had permitted myself with some of them in the first month of my loneliness became a shuddering horror to recall.

The change was slow and inevitable. For them and for me it came without any definite shock. I still went among them in safety, because no jolt in the downward glide had released the increasing charge of explosive animalism that ousted the human day by day. But I began to fear that soon now that shock must come. My Saint-Bernard-brute followed me to the enclosure every night, and his vigilance enabled me to sleep at times in something like peace. The little pink sloth-thing became shy and left me, to crawl back to its natural life once more among the tree-branches. We were in just the state of equilibrium that would remain in one of those "Happy Family" cages which animal-tamers exhibit, if the tamer were to leave it for ever.

Of course, these creatures did not decline into such beasts as the reader has seen in zoological gardens—into ordinary bears, wolves, tigers, oxen, swine, and apes. There was still something strange about each; in each Moreau had blended this animal with that. One perhaps was ursine chiefly, another feline chiefly, another bovine chiefly; but each was tainted with other creatures—a kind of generalised animalism appearing through the specific dispositions. And the dwindling shreds of the humanity still startled me every now and then—a momentary recrudescence of speech perhaps, an unexpected dexterity of

the fore-feet, a pitiful attempt to walk erect.

I too must have undergone strange changes. My clothes hung about me as yellow rags, through whose rents showed the tanned skin. My hair grew long, and became matted together. I am told that even now my eyes have a strange brightness, a swift alertness of movement.

At first, I spent the daylight hours on the southward beach watching for a ship, hoping and praying for a ship. I counted on the *Ipecacuanha* returning as the year wore on; but she never came. Five times I saw sails, and thrice smoke; but nothing ever touched the island. I always had a bonfire ready, but no doubt the volcanic reputation of the island was taken to account for that.

It was only about September or October that I began to think of making a raft. By that time my arm had healed, and both my hands were at my service again. At first, I found my helplessness appalling. I had never done any carpentry or such-like work in my life, and I spent day after day in experimental chopping and binding among the trees. I had no ropes, and could hit on nothing wherewith to make ropes; none of the abundant creepers seemed limber or strong enough, and with all my litter of scientific education I could not devise any way of making them so. I spent more than a fortnight grubbing among the black ruins of the enclosure and on the beach where the boats had been burnt, looking for nails and other stray pieces of metal that might prove of service. Now and then some Beast-creature would watch me, and go leaping off when I called to it. There came a season of thunder-storms and heavy rain, which greatly retarded my work; but at last the raft was completed.

I was delighted with it. But with a certain lack of practical sense which has always been my bane, I had made it a mile or more from the sea; and before I had dragged it down to the beach the thing had fallen to pieces. Perhaps it is as well that I was saved from launching it; but at the time my misery at my failure was so acute that for some days I simply moped on the beach, and stared at the water and thought of death.

I did not, however, mean to die, and an incident occurred that warned me unmistakably of the folly of letting the days pass so—for each fresh day was fraught with increasing danger from the Beast People.

I was lying in the shade of the enclosure wall, staring out to sea, when I was startled by something cold touching the skin of my heel, and starting round found the little pink sloth-creature blinking into

my face. He had long since lost speech and active movement, and the lank hair of the little brute grew thicker every day and his stumpy claws more askew. He made a moaning noise when he saw he had attracted my attention, went a little way towards the bushes and looked back at me.

At first I did not understand, but presently it occurred to me that he wished me to follow him; and this I did at last—slowly, for the day was hot. When we reached the trees, he clambered into them, for he could travel better among their swinging creepers than on the ground. And suddenly in a trampled space I came upon a ghastly group. My Saint-Bernard-creature lay on the ground, dead; and near his body crouched the Hyena-swine, gripping the quivering flesh with its misshapen claws, gnawing at it, and snarling with delight. As I approached, the monster lifted its glaring eyes to mine, its lips went trembling back from its red-stained teeth, and it growled menacingly. It was not afraid and not ashamed; the last vestige of the human taint had vanished. I advanced a step farther, stopped, and pulled out my revolver. At last I had him face to face.

The brute made no sign of retreat; but its ears went back, its hair bristled, and its body crouched together. I aimed between the eyes and fired. As I did so, the Thing rose straight at me in a leap, and I was knocked over like a ninepin. It clutched at me with its crippled hand, and struck me in the face. Its spring carried it over me. I fell under the hind part of its body; but luckily, I had hit as I meant, and it had died even as it leapt. I crawled out from under its unclean weight and stood up trembling, staring at its quivering body. That danger at least was over; but this, I knew was only the first of the series of relapses that must come.

I burnt both of the bodies on a pyre of brushwood; but after that I saw that unless I left the island my death was only a question of time. The Beast People by that time had, with one or two exceptions, left the ravine and made themselves lairs according to their taste among the thickets of the island. Few prowled by day, most of them slept, and the island might have seemed deserted to a new-comer; but at night the air was hideous with their calls and howling. I had half a mind to make a massacre of them; to build traps, or fight them with my knife. Had I possessed sufficient cartridges, I should not have hesitated to begin the killing. There could now be scarcely a score left of the dangerous carnivores; the braver of these were already dead. After the death of this poor dog of mine, my last friend, I too adopted to

some extent the practice of slumbering in the daytime in order to be on my guard at night. I rebuilt my den in the walls of the enclosure, with such a narrow opening that anything attempting to enter must necessarily make a considerable noise. The creatures had lost the art of fire too, and recovered their fear of it. I turned once more, almost passionately now, to hammering together stakes and branches to form a raft for my escape.

I found a thousand difficulties. I am an extremely unhandy man (my schooling was over before the days of *Slöjd*); but most of the requirements of a raft I met at last in some clumsy, circuitous way or other, and this time I took care of the strength. The only insurmountable obstacle was that I had no vessel to contain the water I should need if I floated forth upon these untravelled seas. I would have even tried pottery, but the island contained no clay. I used to go moping about the island trying with all my might to solve this one last difficulty. Sometimes I would give way to wild outbursts of rage, and hack and splinter some unlucky tree in my intolerable vexation. But I could think of nothing.

And then came a day, a wonderful day, which I spent in ecstasy. I saw a sail to the southwest, a small sail like that of a little schooner; and forthwith I lit a great pile of brushwood, and stood by it in the heat of it, and the heat of the midday sun, watching. All day I watched that sail, eating or drinking nothing, so that my head reeled; and the Beasts came and glared at me, and seemed to wonder, and went away. It was still distant when night came and swallowed it up; and all night I toiled to keep my blaze bright and high, and the eyes of the Beasts shone out of the darkness, marvelling. In the dawn the sail was nearer, and I saw it was the dirty lug-sail of a small boat. But it sailed strangely. My eyes were weary with watching, and I peered and could not believe them. Two men were in the boat, sitting low down—one by the bows, the other at the rudder. The head was not kept to the wind; it yawed and fell away.

As the day grew brighter, I began waving the last rag of my jacket to them; but they did not notice me, and sat still, facing each other. I went to the lowest point of the low headland, and gesticulated and shouted. There was no response, and the boat kept on her aimless course, making slowly, very slowly, for the bay. Suddenly a great white bird flew up out of the boat, and neither of the men stirred nor noticed it; it circled round, and then came sweeping overhead with its strong wings outspread.

Then I stopped shouting, and sat down on the headland and rested

my chin on my hands and stared. Slowly, slowly, the boat drove past towards the west. I would have swum out to it, but something—a cold, vague fear—kept me back. In the afternoon the tide stranded the boat, and left it a hundred yards or so to the westward of the ruins of the enclosure. The men in it were dead, had been dead so long that they fell to pieces when I tilted the boat on its side and dragged them out. One had a shock of red hair, like the captain of the *Ipecacuanha*, and a dirty white cap lay in the bottom of the boat.

As I stood beside the boat, three of the Beasts came slinking out of the bushes and sniffing towards me. One of my spasms of disgust came upon me. I thrust the little boat down the beach and clambered on board her. Two of the brutes were Wolf-beasts, and came forward with quivering nostrils and glittering eyes; the third was the horrible nondescript of bear and bull. When I saw them approaching those wretched remains, heard them snarling at one another and caught the gleam of their teeth, a frantic horror succeeded my repulsion. I turned my back upon them, struck the lug and began paddling out to sea. I could not bring myself to look behind me.

I lay, however, between the reef and the island that night, and the next morning went round to the stream and filled the empty keg aboard with water. Then, with such patience as I could command, I collected a quantity of fruit, and waylaid and killed two rabbits with my last three cartridges. While I was doing this, I left the boat moored to an inward projection of the reef, for fear of the Beast People.

CHAPTER 22

The Man Alone

In the evening I started, and drove out to sea before a gentle wind from the southwest, slowly, steadily; and the island grew smaller and smaller, and the lank spire of smoke dwindled to a finer and finer line against the hot sunset. The ocean rose up around me, hiding that low, dark patch from my eyes. The daylight, the trailing glory of the sun, went streaming out of the sky, was drawn aside like some luminous curtain, and at last I looked into the blue gulf of immensity which the sunshine hides, and saw the floating hosts of the stars. The sea was silent, the sky was silent. I was alone with the night and silence.

So, I drifted for three days, eating and drinking sparingly, and meditating upon all that had happened to me—not desiring very greatly then to see men again. One unclean rag was about me, my hair a black tangle: no doubt my discoverers thought me a madman.

It is strange, but I felt no desire to return to mankind. I was only glad to be quit of the foulness of the Beast People. And on the third day I was picked up by a brig from Apia to San Francisco. Neither the captain nor the mate would believe my story, judging that solitude and danger had made me mad; and fearing their opinion might be that of others, I refrained from telling my adventure further, and professed to recall nothing that had happened to me between the loss of the *Lady Vain* and the time when I was picked up again,—the space of a year.

I had to act with the utmost circumspection to save myself from the suspicion of insanity. My memory of the Law, of the two dead sailors, of the ambuscades of the darkness, of the body in the cane-brake, haunted me; and, unnatural as it seems, with my return to man-kind came, instead of that confidence and sympathy I had expected, a strange enhancement of the uncertainty and dread I had experienced during my stay upon the island. No one would believe me; I was al-most as queer to men as I had been to the Beast People. I may have caught something of the natural wildness of my companions. They say that terror is a disease, and anyhow I can witness that for several years now a restless fear has dwelt in my mind—such a restless fear as a half-tamed lion cub may feel.

My trouble took the strangest form. I could not persuade myself that the men and women I met were not also another Beast People, animals, half wrought into the outward image of human souls, and that they would presently begin to revert—to show first this bestial mark and then that. But I have confided my case to a strangely able man—a man who had known Moreau, and seemed half to credit my story; a mental specialist—and he has helped me mightily, though I do not expect that the terror of that island will ever altogether leave me. At most times it lies far in the back of my mind, a mere distant cloud, a memory, and a faint distrust; but there are times when the little cloud spreads until it obscures the whole sky. Then I look about me at my fellow-men; and I go in fear. I see faces, keen and bright; others dull or dangerous; others, unsteady, insincere—none that have the calm authority of a reasonable soul.

I feel as though the animal was surging up through them; that presently the degradation of the Islanders will be played over again on a larger scale. I know this is an illusion; that these seeming men and women about me are indeed men and women—men and women for ever, perfectly reasonable creatures, full of human desires and tender solicitude, emancipated from instinct and the slaves of no fantastic

Law—beings altogether different from the Beast Folk. Yet I shrink from them, from their curious glances, their inquiries and assistance, and long to be away from them and alone. For that reason, I live near the broad free downland, and can escape thither when this shadow is over my soul; and very sweet is the empty downland then, under the wind-swept sky.

When I lived in London the horror was well-nigh insupportable. I could not get away from men: their voices came through windows; locked doors were flimsy safeguards. I would go out into the streets to fight with my delusion, and prowling women would mew after me; furtive, craving men glance jealously at me; weary, pale workers go coughing by me with tired eyes and eager paces, like wounded deer dripping blood; old people, bent and dull, pass murmuring to themselves; and, all unheeding, a ragged tail of gibing children. Then I would turn aside into some chapel—and even there, such was my disturbance, it seemed that the preacher gibbered "Big Thinks," even as the Ape-man had done; or into some library, and there the intent faces over the books seemed but patient creatures waiting for prey.

Particularly nauseous were the blank, expressionless faces of people in trains and omnibuses; they seemed no more my fellow-creatures than dead bodies would be, so that I did not dare to travel unless I was assured of being alone. And even it seemed that I too was not a reasonable creature, but only an animal tormented with some strange disorder in its brain which sent it to wander alone, like a sheep stricken with gid.

This is a mood, however, that comes to me now, I thank God, more rarely. I have withdrawn myself from the confusion of cities and multitudes, and spend my days surrounded by wise books—bright windows in this life of ours, lit by the shining souls of men. I see few strangers, and have but a small household. My days I devote to reading and to experiments in chemistry, and I spend many of the clear nights in the study of astronomy. There is—though I do not know how there is or why there is—a sense of infinite peace and protection in the glittering hosts of heaven. There it must be, I think, in the vast and eternal laws of matter, and not in the daily cares and sins and troubles of men, that whatever is more than animal within us must find its solace and its hope. I hope, or I could not live.

And so, in hope and solitude, my story ends.

Edward Prendick.

LEONAUR

ALSO FROM LEONAUR
AVAILABLE IN SOFTCOVER OR HARDCOVER WITH DUST JACKET

MR MUKERJI'S GHOSTS *by S. Mukerji*—Supernatural tales from the British Raj period by India's Ghost story collector.

KIPLINGS GHOSTS *by Rudyard Kipling*—Twelve stories of Ghosts, Hauntings, Curses, Werewolves & Magic.

THE COLLECTED SUPERNATURAL AND WEIRD FICTION OF WASHINGTON IRVING: VOLUME 1 *by Washington Irving*—Including one novel 'A History of New York', and nine short stories of the Strange and Unusual.

THE COLLECTED SUPERNATURAL AND WEIRD FICTION OF WASHINGTON IRVING: VOLUME 2 *by Washington Irving*—Including three novelettes 'The Legend of the Sleepy Hollow', 'Dolph Heyliger', 'The Adventure of the Black Fisherman' and thirty-two short stories of the Strange and Unusual.

THE COLLECTED SUPERNATURAL AND WEIRD FICTION OF JOHN KENDRICK BANGS: VOLUME 1 *by John Kendrick Bangs*—Including one novel 'Toppleton's Client or A Spirit in Exile', and ten short stories of the Strange and Unusual.

THE COLLECTED SUPERNATURAL AND WEIRD FICTION OF JOHN KENDRICK BANGS: VOLUME 2 *by John Kendrick Bangs*—Including four novellas 'A House-Boat on the Styx', 'The Pursuit of the House-Boat', 'The Enchanted Typewriter' and 'Mr. Munchausen' of the Strange and Unusual.

THE COLLECTED SUPERNATURAL AND WEIRD FICTION OF JOHN KENDRICK BANGS: VOLUME 3 *by John Kendrick Bangs*—Including twor novellas 'Olympian Nights', 'Roger Camerden: A Strange Story', and ten short stories of the Strange and Unusual.

THE COLLECTED SUPERNATURAL AND WEIRD FICTION OF MARY SHELLEY: VOLUME 1 *by Mary Shelley*—Including one novel 'Frankenstein or the Modern Prometheus', and fourteen short stories of the Strange and Unusual.

THE COLLECTED SUPERNATURAL AND WEIRD FICTION OF MARY SHELLEY: VOLUME 2 *by Mary Shelley*—Including one novel 'The Last Man', and three short stories of the Strange and Unusual.

THE COLLECTED SUPERNATURAL AND WEIRD FICTION OF AMELIA B. EDWARDS *by Amelia B. Edwards*—Contains two novelettes 'Monsieur Maurice', and 'The Discovery of the Treasure Isles', one ballad 'A Legend of Boisguilbert'and seventeen short stories to cill the blood.

ALSO FROM LEONAUR

AVAILABLE IN SOFTCOVER OR HARDCOVER WITH DUST JACKET

THE COMPLETE FOUR JUST MEN: VOLUME 2 *by Edgar Wallace*—*The Law of the Four Just Men & The Three Just Men*—disillusioned with a world where the wicked and the abusers of power perpetually go unpunished, the Just Men set about to rectify matters according to their own standards, and retribution is dispensed on swift and deadly wings.

THE COMPLETE RAFFLES: 1 *by E. W. Hornung*—*The Amateur Cracksman & The Black Mask*—By turns urbane gentleman about town and accomplished cricketer, life is just too ordinary for Raffles and that sets him on a series of adventures that have long been treasured as a real antidote to the 'white knights' who are the usual heroes of the crime fiction of this period.

THE COMPLETE RAFFLES: 2 *by E. W. Hornung*—*A Thief in the Night & Mr Justice Raffles*—By turns urbane gentleman about town and accomplished cricketer, life is just too ordinary for Raffles and that sets him on a series of adventures that have long been treasured as a real antidote to the 'white knights' who are the usual heroes of the crime fiction of this period.

THE COLLECTED SUPERNATURAL AND WEIRD FICTION OF WILKIE COLLINS: VOLUME 1 *by Wilkie Collins*—Contains one novel 'The Haunted Hotel', one novella 'Mad Monkton', three novelettes 'Mr Percy and the Prophet', 'The Biter Bit' and 'The Dead Alive' and eight short stories to chill the blood.

THE COLLECTED SUPERNATURAL AND WEIRD FICTION OF WILKIE COLLINS: VOLUME 2 *by Wilkie Collins*—Contains one novel 'The Two Destinies', three novellas 'The Frozen deep', 'Sister Rose' and 'The Yellow Mask' and two short stories to chill the blood.

THE COLLECTED SUPERNATURAL AND WEIRD FICTION OF WILKIE COLLINS: VOLUME 3 *by Wilkie Collins*—Contains one novel 'Dead Secret,' two novelettes 'Mrs Zant and the Ghost' and 'The Nun's Story of Gabriel's Marriage' and five short stories to chill the blood.

FUNNY BONES *selected by Dorothy Scarborough*—An Anthology of Humorous Ghost Stories.

MONTEZUMA'S CASTLE AND OTHER WEIRD TALES *by Charles B. Cory*—Cory has written a superb collection of eighteen ghostly and weird stories to chill and thrill the avid enthusiast of supernatural fiction.

SUPERNATURAL BUCHAN *by John Buchan*—Stories of Ancient Spirits, Uncanny Places & Strange Creatures.

AVAILABLE ONLINE AT **www.leonaur.com**
AND FROM ALL GOOD BOOK STORES
07/09